PRAISE FOR ORACLE OF IX CHEL

Another beautiful book from Rosita Arvigo. I was transported to the time of the ancient Maya. I love her vivid descriptions and characters, which come alive on the page.

Tracey Ullman

The Oracle of Ix Chel is a tour de force of narrative, history, and insight into a culture and cosmology. Set in the Mayan city of Chichen during pre-Columbian times, it tells the story of a gifted woman committed to her lineage and its sacred path. Rosita Arvigo's intimate knowledge of ancient Mayan practices infuses every page. As soon as I finished, I was ready for the next installment.

Hope Edelman
Author, *Motherless Daughters* and *The Possibility of Everything*

Rosita Arvigo expertly weaves a tale of life in a post-Toltec Mayan landscape—part fiction, part deep intuitive knowing from Rosita, but mostly a refreshing 'her'-story that brings alive these particular peoples during their time. Both immensely entertaining and deeply inspiring, *The Oracle of Ix Chel* will leave readers waiting impatiently for Book 2.

Pam Montgomery
Author, *Partner Earth: A Spiritual Ecology*

A wonderfully engaging journey through magic, myth and time. Through this beautiful tale, in her very special voice, Rosita Arvigo brings us to a place that once was. Arvigo's remarkable descriptions of rainforest plants and shamanic ritual adds a beautiful richness to the page-turning plot. Her fascinating story is written from the heart and will delight the reader as well as convey wisdom of the ancients.

Michael J. Balick, Ph.D.
Ethnobotanist, The New York Botanical Garden

From the first paragraph, it grabbed my attention and held it. I didn't want to put it down. A wonderfully captivating book filled with alive, complex characters.

Rosemary Gladstar
Author, *Planting the Future: Saving Our Medicinal Herbs*

THE ORACLE OF
IX CHEL

ROSITA ARVIGO

Story Bridge Books
Tucson, Arizona
2015

Story Bridge Books 2015
Tucson, Arizona, USA
www.storybridgebooks.com

To my husband, Greg Shropshire,
for his loving inspiration and endless support,
and for being my Jaguar Shield.

Map of Jade Skirt's World

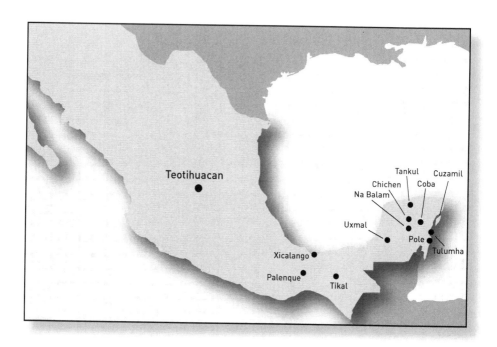

Table of Contents

Introduction

The *Oracle of Ix Chel* takes place in the Mesoamerican late Classic era, which spanned 600-900 AD. Scholars and historians consider it to have been the high point of Maya civilization, with the nobility enjoying unprecedented advancements in mathematics, astronomy, architecture, art, sculpture and writing. For reasons still a mystery to pre-Colombian scholars, this flourishing intellectual and artistic culture ended abruptly sometime between 860-960 AD, a time referred to as the "Maya Collapse." The ancient Maya nobles, who built the cities, wrote glyphic books, studied the paths of the stars and created splendid works of art and sculpture, abandoned their ceremonial centers and as a result their cities and culture atrophied.

As a person who has lived in Central America for 45 years, I know that the Maya people, the *macehual* (natives), are still here and have been since before the Maya Collapse. I have made their culture and traditional healing knowledge my life's study. In 1970, with a small group of commune friends from Black Bear Ranch in Northern California, I immigrated to Tlacotepec, Guerrero—a remote Nahuatl village in Mexico's Sierra Madre Mountains. Here, in a village of six houses, I lived as the natives did. I learned to speak Spanish, cook over an open hearth fire, maintain a dirt floor and make tortillas. On a cold, wintry night I even witnessed the birth of a baby, who was born by torchlight. In 1976, I moved to Belize, where my daughter, Crystal Ray Arvigo, was born in a thatch hut at the edge of a tropical fruit orchard. In Mexico and Belize I found my life's passion: preservation of medicinal plants and traditional healing knowledge for the good of all humankind. When my husband and I founded the Rainforest Medicine Trail, we had to come up with a name for our homestead in Cayo District. We called it Ix Chel Farm after the Maya goddess of medicine, weaving, the moon, all bodies of water, fertility and childbirth.

The first time I heard the name Ix Chel I was in the Belize rainforest with my mentor, Don Elijio Panti, the great Maya shaman of Belize. "It is good fortune to hunt for medicine with a woman companion because Ix Chel, the goddess of medicine, shows her healing plants more readily," he said with great reverence. Since that hot and steamy day in the jungle, I have searched for images, myths, stories and every possible detail of this American goddess who has come to be a powerful presence in my life. In this book, she is the spiritual mother of my heroine, Jade Skirt, the Oracle of Ix Chel, much as I feel she is my spiritual mother.

When the Story Takes Place

Jade Skirt's story is set in 700 AD, in present-day Chichen Itzá, which lies in northern Yucatán, Mexico. The history of this Maya city is still debated by historians. Any attempt to sort out history from myth begets more questions than it answers. *The Oracle of Ix Chel* is an act of imagination about what might have happened to those Ancient Ones. I play with the idea that human sacrifice was actually a foreign idea introduced to Jade Skirt's society by outsiders who worshiped different gods. There are ethnohistorians who believe the Maya's own priesthood used human sacrifice to appease their gods much earlier than this, but since this is an act of fiction and not history I've taken many liberties with "facts."

Most historians do agree that some time during the Classic Period, the original settlers of Chichen were overrun by a federation of Chontal-speaking Maya groups, which are lumped together as the Putun. These warrior-traders from Tabasco, Mexico, gained dominance in the region through military and commercial incursions during the tenth century. Historians say the Itzá Putun gave their name to Chichen, which became Chichen Itzá. They believe the Putun gained control of seacoast trade around the Yucatán Peninsula, which made them quite wealthy. Paintings on the wall of The Temple of the Jaguars at Chichen Itzá lead scholars to believe that the Putun were extremely powerful.

In *The Oracle of Ix Chel*, the growing popularity of human sacrifice in Chichen is linked to the influence of Putun refugees who moved to Chichen after their homes in Teotihuacan were destroyed by invaders some time during the seventh century. There is evidence that some Maya refugees left that ceremonial center, which is located near modern-day Mexico City, and moved back to the Yucatán. In my fictional version of history, the Putun introduced the Maya of Chichen to the Mexican War God Tezcatlipoca, a bloodthirsty god who demanded mass sacrifice, royal blood-letting to sanctify lineage rule, and the repulsive practice of skinning sacrificial victims and using the skins to make ceremonial costumes for the War God's priests. The tension between the peaceful, biophilic beliefs of followers of Ix Chel and the bloody, necrophilic beliefs of followers of Tezcatlipoca is the heart of my story.

Where the Story Takes Place

The Oracle of Ix Chel is set in my made-up version of the ancient Maya city of Chichen, based on the location of modern-day Chichen Itzá, during a time when the settlement was ruled by a fictitious group of Maya called the Puuc (after the Puuc Hills of western Yucatán). Chichen means "mouth of the well." Chichen Itzá is a dry, parched land with no rivers or lakes, but it has two great wells and many magnificent caves, which surely made it a holy site. Indeed, historians say the Great Well was considered sacred to the Rain God, Chac, and caves in the area were considered sacred to the Mother Goddess, Ix Chel. The so-called Well of Sacrifice was believed to be the entrance to the sacred Under-world. To ensure abundant rainfall, the Itzá tossed pubescent girls into the well to become brides of Chac.

Modern-day Chichen Itzá was probably known as *Uuc abnal* or "seven great rulers" (sometimes translated as "seven great bushes"). It's a reference to the Itzá government, which was made up of seven nobles rather than a single king or queen. Today's Chichen Itzá is famous for the structure known as "El Castillo," a large, four-stairway pyramid supporting a flat-topped temple. Archaeologists discovered the ruins of an earlier temple inside it, where they unearthed two remarkable artifacts: the famous *chacmool*, which is a seated figure looking to the side and holding a stone bowl in his lap; and a red-painted jaguar throne with inlaid jade. The two finds sparked my fantasies about the ancient city. What must it have been like to live in that culture and time, with such advanced artistry and architecture, and a rich belief system?

Jade Skirt's husband's family belongs to the Cocom lineage of nobles. Scholars say the Cocom served as lords and rulers until the Spanish conquest of the Americas. Jade Skirt comes from the Chel lineage, which held positions as rulers. The Chel of my tale are the women rulers of Cuzamil Island—seers, psychics, midwives and teachers. Modern-day Cozumel Island was known as

Cuzamil— "place of swallows," a reference to the flocks of swallows that return to the island every year to roost and nest.

Lying just off the eastern coast of Yucatán, Cuzamil was once a well-traveled pilgrimage site for women to worship Ix Chel, the Maya goddess of fertility, the moon, the earth, weaving and all bodies of water. The Goddess Ix Chel was revered as First Mother, the Creatrix, the Seer and Knower who, together with her consort, Itzámna, the First Father, created the entire world—people, animals, plants, bodies of water and mountains. A Franciscan monk named Diego de Landa, infamous for his cruelty during the Spanish conquest, wrote: "They held Cozumel and the well at Chichen Itzá in as great veneration as we have in our pilgrimages to Jerusalem and Rome; they visited them to offer gifts, especially at Cozumel, as we do at our holy places; and when they did not visit they sent offerings."

Reading this passage, I imagined that Maya women would have made two pilgrimages in their lifetimes to Cuzamil: the first at menarche so they could ask the goddess for fertility; and the second at menopause to give thanks for fertility. I imagined what it must have been like for women and girls during that time. For centuries there would have been a constant stream of women from far and near flooding the island sanctuary to visit Ix Chel's many temples. They would have made the journey to give birth, receive healing, solicit advice from the oracle or attend the famous *calmecac*, the women's mystery school where priestesses taught astronomy, astrology, writing, midwifery, and scrying with crystals. It sounded wonderful to me. The Cuzamil of my invention is a women-only sanctuary of the Goddess Ix Chel.

Cuzamil had a settlement of traders and merchants on the far north side of the island. They carried on a lucrative trade in salt and honey and held a monopoly on the sea mollusks that yielded purple and blue dyes. The taxes they paid to the Chel rulers generated enormous wealth for the women of Cuzamil. It was not hard to imagine how tempting a target they would have been to adversaries and plotters, especially the rapacious Putun.

I have taken literary license to juxtapose some historical events of the eighth and ninth centuries to suit the needs of my story. *The Oracle of Ix Chel* is not meant to present a chronological Maya history, but I have tried to stay true to what we know and can guess about the daily life, religion and role of women healers during that time.

Rosita Arvigo, DN
Cayo District, Belize

Cast of Characters

The Family of Jade Skirt
Jade Skirt – the Oracle of Ix Chel, noble of the Chel lineage
Water Lily – Jade Skirt's only daughter
Nine Macaw – Jade Skirt's granddaughter; heir to the Rainbow Throne of Cuzamil
Blood Gatherer –Jade Skirt's brother; High Priest of the Rain God, Chac
Red Earth – Jade Skirt's granddaughter
Jaguar Paw – Jade Skirt's grandson; Nine Macaw's twin brother
Tree Orchid – orphaned cousin adopted by Water Lily
Moon Eagle – Jade Skirt's deceased husband; noble of the Cocom linage
Jaguar Shield – Moon Eagle's brother; a military commander
Heart of Water – Jade Skirt's sister; Queen of Cuzamil
Nine Wind – mother of Jade Skirt, Heart of Water and Blood Gatherer
Spear Thrower – son of Jade Skirt

Characters in Chichen
Blue Monkey – a noble of the Cocom lineage and Jade Skirt's nemesis
Blue Quetzal – one of seven nobles who rule Chichen
Flesh Flower – oldest female member of the Cocom clan
Iguana Wind – Moon Eagle's captured warrior-slave
Nahoch Pop – market magistrate
Seven Lizard – oldest male member of the Cocom clan
Sky House – one of the seven leaders of Chichen
Smoke Shell – the Holder; keeper of the cacao in the Temple of Ix Chel
Smoking Frog – son of Jaguar Shield
Smoking Mirror – one of seven nobles who rule Chichen
Snake Woman – one of seven nobles who rule Chichen
Sun Shield – one of seven nobles who rule Chichen
Thirteen Rabbit – Blue Monkey's granddaughter
Three Cloud – friend of Jade Skirt, market seller
Turtle Star – Jade Skirt's apprentice in the Temple of Ix Chel

Characters on the Journey
Cloud Deer – soldier
Eagle Rain – soldier
Earth Star – elderly uncle of Jade Skirt
Great Skull Pech Tzib – magistrate of Na Balam
Sky House Chel – soldier in palace of Na Balam
Sting Ray – hermit dwarf
White Dog Muluc Chel – Jade Skirt's relative in Na Balam
World Bridge – elderly aunt of Jade Skirt

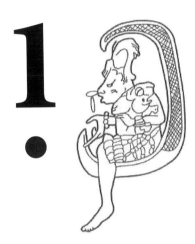

Chichen, Tzimentan Province, in the land of the Maya, 600 AD

In the chilly air before dawn I sit alone on a hill and wait for the Sun God to return from his nocturnal journey into *mitnal*, the Underworld. For a long moment it seems as if the Lord of the Night's dark purple shadows will never break, and then all at once they yield to the sudden burst of pink light. Father Kin returns! We will live another day. Below me, the people of Chichen offer staccato drum beats and someone blows the deep note of a conch shell in gratitude.

I'm grateful, too, because each passing day moves me closer to my true home. I don't mean death—not yet, anyway. I mean the Island of Women, Cuzamil, the place where I was born and where I soon hope to return.

As the Lord of the Night passes his burden to the Lord of the Day, the Moon Goddess, Ix Chel, silently slips into the west to hide from the Sun, her jealous consort. Riding a black jaguar, my Goddess dips back into the Underworld, throwing back a glance at her old rival. This daily ritual comforts me. Another day dawns and the Great Ones are following their predictable patterns. No matter what schemes men and women plot and whisper, day follows night and night follows day.

The morning air is cold and the damp seeps into my old bones, but I linger for another few minutes on this hilltop perch. The truth is I'm procrastinating. This day will be a busy one for me because tonight we celebrate the ceremony of the full moon. And I do love this view of the nine mud-and-wattle houses below, where the people of the Cocom lineage live. I'm like a bird up here. I can see through gaps in the thatch roofs where warm lights of morning hearth fires glow. Rich aromas of corn tamales, chocolate brews and turkey stews ride the air on thin wisps of smoke. Down there are three generations of my dead husband's lineage. His brothers, sisters, cousins, aunts and uncles share the open courtyard, the central fire pit and a deep, generous well. Family vegetable gardens are tucked to the sides and behind each family's compound. It's a good life. The Cocom are prosperous (thanks in part to me). These people are my family by marriage, but since I have lived here for many years and delivered the children who are just now rubbing sleep from their eyes, and doctored the men and women who are sharpening tools and grinding corn for the new day, I claim them as my people, too. Nevertheless, because of who I am I have always been set apart from them; these days, even more so.

My eyes are drawn to the house where I once lived as Moon Eagle's wife. Now my daughter, Water Lily, her two daughters and the adopted orphan girl live in our old dwelling. I moved into the Temple of Ix Chel after Moon Eagle's murder. I sigh unhappily thinking about my only daughter. I'm guessing there will be only a thin stew in the pot today, as usual.

My daughter is a drunk. Three corn harvests ago, her husband publicly divorced her. It was a scandal in Chichen. I was distressed, but not surprised. No one could blame the man. He and Water Lily had counseled with one of the magistrates for months, but in spite of her many promises Water Lily would not put down the gourd. She still won't, even after the scandal and shame. Since her husband left, Water Lily's vice knows no boundaries. I visit as often as I can to see how the children are getting on and to try to talk sense to her. Water Lily gives me a defiant look every time she turns to her pot of fermented *bal-che* bark and honey. Those reeking brews use all the sacks of corn that are meant for tamales to feed her and the children. I supplement with whatever I can spare, but it's hard on the children.

My feelings for my child dance wildly between love, pity and anger. I once had high hopes for Water Lily. I had hoped she would take my place as Chichen's Oracle and High Priestess of Ix Chel, Moon Goddess. But it was not to be. The sad fact is that she was born without the gifts that run strong in our female line, and I'm sure her own disappointment has something to do with her drinking problem. We were all disappointed, but life must go on. Moon Eagle and I loved her and encouraged her, and we made her a very good marriage. She had a good husband, two daughters and a son who are all healthy, fine children. But she is squandering all her good fortune. It is a constant struggle for me—my anger at Water Lily, my fear for her children, the shame I feel in public, my own lingering sense of guilt. What kind of mother raises a daughter who acts this way? I know what the gossips say.

I'm suddenly aware that I'm gripping my necklace, and I force my hand away. I always fidget with it when I'm upset. It's made from a single, rare bead of shiny, black obsidian, which is set in the center of a round piece of green jade and surrounded by sparkling quartz crystals. I love this necklace. I've worn it since Water Lily was a small girl. The obsidian was a gift from Moon Eagle. He had just returned from a military campaign in the southern lowlands and I was so relieved to see him home, safe. I still remember how happy I'd felt when he grasped both my hands in his and tucked the stone in my palm. He'd whispered, "My love, this stone is the only thing that comes near to capturing the brilliance of your black eyes."

I sigh a little, remembering how it felt to be held in his steady gaze. Missing him is like an ache in an old wound; it never goes away.

The jade in my necklace was also a gift from my husband. He brought it back from another journey, and we both worked on the brilliantly green stone, turning it into two beaded necklaces. One was for me and the other we gave to Water Lily, so we would always be spiritually connected. It works too well. Whenever she is ill or in serious trouble, the jade beads vibrate in my hands. At other times I can feel her craving and her weakness. It makes me despair in the depths of my heart.

Water Lily. Soon she will be a mother-in-law. In only three moons, her oldest daughter, Red Earth, will marry. Red Earth is a sweet child, and like her mother she did not inherit any of the gifts of our female line. She will be happy in her marriage, I'm sure. She already knows how to keep house, weave and prepare the tamales. She's had to run the household since her mother is often too drunk or passed out to do any of the tasks a mother ought to do.

I have been worrying constantly since the marriage was announced about what Water Lily will do during the celebration. There is a law against drunkenness outside of public ceremonies, and Water Lily is sure to break it during the wedding feast, which is not considered a public ceremony. What a terrible example she sets for her daughters and son. I would leave for Cuzamil before the wedding, but I am too afraid of leaving Water Lily on her own. Also, I must wait for my second granddaughter, Nine Macaw, to complete her initiation as a woman before I can take her with me to the Island of Women to begin her training. If she had not gotten sick last year and missed the ritual, we would be in Cuzamil already. Twenty seven more days until her initiation. I'm counting the minutes.

An eagle rides the wind above me and I wish I could fly away from my worries. Chichen used to be a place of peace for me, but not anymore. Water Lily is only one of the burdens on my heart. Right beside the Cocom compound is one of the four white roads, *sacbes*, which lead from the four directions into the heart of Chichen and the plaza where Ix Chel's temple squats like a big, stone womb. My Goddess's temple is the heart of Chichen, but in the past few years, the temple of Chac, the Rain God, has become more and more central to Chichen, and its priests more and more powerful. I honor Chac, of course, but I don't honor those priests who have taken up despicable practices brought by followers of the Putun War God Tezcatlipoca. Who would have thought the civilized people of Chichen would throw their virgin girls into the well to feed the God? It's a barbaric practice, yet the people allow it! They call it the New Order.

My mother named me Jade Skirt after the beaded jade skirt worn by the Goddess. I was dedicated to Ix Chel before I was even in my mother's womb. I was married to Moon Eagle, a man of Chichen, so that I could come and serve the Goddess in her temple in this city. Long have the people of Chichen honored Ix Chel, who is the Creator, Healer and Giver of Life. I have been held in esteem here as Oracle and High Priestess of Ix Chel, and as midwife and healer. But of late, the things that Ix Chel stands for—life and healing—are subsumed by the foreigners' practice of worshipping the Gods through human sacrifice, what they call the "Flowery Death."

I had no animosity toward my husband's people until popularity began to grow for this New Order. My dearest Moon Eagle died the Flowery Death under the New Order in our enemy's land. He was a military doctor who accompanied the warriors into battles. They were fighting the Putun when my husband was captured. He was murdered on the altar of their War God. Because Moon Eagle was a nobleman, the Putun cremated the remains of my husband's headless, heartless corpse with full honors.

I will never forget that dark and cloudy day when the black-robed Putun priest arrived at my door carrying a bundle wrapped in white cotton. In his filthy, tattooed hands he held what remained of my beloved Moon Eagle.

"Good wife, your husband was honored to die the Flowery Death and he now dwells in paradise," he had the audacity to tell me. "When the Gods will it, he will live again as a noble and a healer."

That man genuinely believed I would be grateful my Moon Eagle was brutally murdered. Hah! I wish I had spit on him!

Sacrifice under the New Order came to Chichen only ten *tuns* ago. Traders and priests of Tenochitlan poured into Chichen after a fire destroyed their city. They brought yellow metal and green jade to trade for our salt, feathers and shells. Somehow, their War God, Tezcatlipoca, stayed in Chichen even after the Tenochitlan men departed for other lands. Captured warriors, virgin girls, slaves, orphans and even infants are the favorite choices for sacrifice by the War God's priests. The War God seems to have an insatiable appetite for warm blood and still-beating human hearts torn from the chests of innocents.

In a short time, the priests of our Gods took up the practice. Now Chac's priests tell the people that the Rain God requires human sacrifices. In my opinion, it is an abomination of our culture, but my opinion is not shared by many these days. Chichen warriors once fought battles for trade, tribute and lands, but under the New Order they wage battles to capture sacrificial victims.

The people believe that those who are sacrificed are blessed in their deaths, but in dreams I have seen their souls wandering the Netherworld. Their howling cries; the gaping holes where their hearts were torn out; their clutching hands—these visions haunt my sleep. For months and months I mourned and worried myself sick about Moon Eagle. Was his soul lost and alone in the cold mist of the Underworld? Mercifully, one day I was gifted by my Goddess with a lucid dream. I saw Moon Eagle's father take him by the hand and lead him into a dugout canoe. It was paddled by a hooded crocodile. A dog, brown and white in color, swam beside the canoe until the boat reached the far shore. As he stepped out of the canoe, Moon Eagle turned his face toward me and I saw from his expression that when his feet touched the ground he was at peace. Only then could I begin to heal from my grief.

Even I, Oracle and High Priestess of Ix Chel, was afraid of the blood priests and their lust for death. But after my husband's murder I realized just how dangerous the priests have become. We're living under a reign of terror. The priests are feared and obeyed. The people won't risk contradicting the priests because they're afraid the priests will retaliate by choosing them to be Chac's next sacrifice. I often wonder how it happened that the peaceful folk of Chichen allowed the priests to take over our lives. When first the black-robed priests of

Tenochitlan taught the people that Tezcatlipoca must be fed human hearts and rivers of blood or the sun would not rise up from the Underworld, I really expected the people of Chichen to run them out of the city. But Chichen happened to be suffering through a long drought. Crops withered and died. Wells ran dry and water in the Great *Cenote* turned into a muddy swamp for the first time in living memory. The people were facing starvation and they were desperate for rain. The priests of the War God said that Chac was hungry for blood; that Chac was too weak to bring life-giving rain.

I wish there was a way to blot out the memory of that first sacrifice. The priest eagerly tore the slave's chest open and lifted the flowing heart to the sun. From the assembled crowd in the plaza below there was a collective murmur of shock and grief. The next day, one hundred and four slaves were lined up on the temple stairs awaiting their Flowery Death. Within a few days, as the calendar priests had already predicted it would, the rains came. Since then, the gentle ways of Ix Chel have taken second place to the cruel ways of the New Order. The temple steps run with rivers of blood. After generations of throwing precious stones and other valuable objects into Chac's Great Well, we now throw maidens to their deaths.

Our Gods don't need human deaths! But few in Chichen are bold enough to speak against the priests. Those frightened faces of heavily drugged "brides of Chac" are etched into everyone's minds. The people are so afraid that they or their loved ones will be named as Chac's next sacrifice that they treat the priests like gods. It turns my stomach to witness this perversion of faith. The priests of the Flowery Deaths, once ordained, never bathe again. They take pride in their matted, blood-soaked hair and filthy robes. It says much about the decay of Chichen society that these men are respected and revered by our leaders and the people.

They ripped his heart out, my poor Moon Eagle. I used to lay my ear against his chest and listen to the steady patter of that beautiful heart. I often wonder if it was that same vile priest who brought me the ashes who was the one to rip Moon Eagle's heart from his chest while it still beat.

Not long after Moon Eagle's death, Ix Chel came to me in a dream. Standing on a white-capped wave, She looked sad and distressed. She turned to me where I sat on the shore of Cuzamil.

"Do not bring me the blood of those whom I have created," She told me. "I am the Supreme Giver of Life, Mother of all creation. I do not require your beating hearts for my sustenance, for I am fed by the stars and my own Sun."

That was all the confirmation I needed. I spoke against the Flowery Death and the New Order in the name of Ix Chel, the Creator. The other priestesses of Ix Chel stood with me. We counseled with the Seven Leaders against the so-called Flowery Death and reminded them about the sanctity of life, which is a gift from the Goddess. Of the Seven Leaders, three are noblewomen and they stood with us against sacrifice. With their support we were able to hold back the obsidian knives for a time. But over the years we lost ground. All the leaders support it now.

My apprentice, Turtle Star, reminds me that we are in an unfavorable *ka-tun*— a period of twenty *tuns*. She counsels me not to make waves, but it's my duty to bring the word of the Goddess to our people and our leaders. Many of the men of Chichen who used to honor Ix Chel now support the New Order. Fewer and fewer seem willing to listen to Ix Chel's priestesses—"mere women"—even though we speak with the Goddess's voice.

And here is another great sadness for me: my own younger brother, Blood Gatherer, is a High Priest of Chac and the most powerful priest in Chichen. There is no love lost between us in this battle for the spiritual heart of Chichen, but I remember the boy he was and I can't help feeling sad that he turned to the ways of the War God. He was raised to know Ix Chel. How could he forsake his Goddess for the bloodthirsty usurper?

There is no peace for me in these days of blood and politics. All the women in our family, including Water Lily and her two daughters, were born on Cuzamil Island. We are Chel, a lineage of healers, oracles and midwives. I remember as a young girl hearing my grandmother, Queen of Cuzamil, speak as she stood on the steps of the temple of Ix Chel on the Island of Women.

"The people of our land have taken a wrong turn," she warned. "Women and children will need refuge and a safe harbor once the evil War God and his blood-thirsty priests take over. Many storms of life befall women and there are few to protect those who need it the most. From this day, I declare that only women and children will live on our sacred island."

What would she think if she knew that her own grandson, now known as Blood Gatherer, would become one of the priests she warned against? In time, my grandmother expelled all men from Cuzamil. Our men serve the people as temple priests, military doctors, snake doctors and guardians of the forest where we grow our medicinal plants and trees, but they do not reside on the island with the women. My grandmother renounced the War God and refused to allow human sacrifice on the island she ruled. Behind a natural barrier of hostile mangrove swamps, sea-faring traders are allowed on the northern shores only, which are plagued by mosquitoes as large as small birds, venomous snakes, deadly scorpions and poisonwood trees. In other words, it's not a hospitable place, so not many men care to settle there. But our share of trade goods from all over the Known World has made the island coffers unbelievably wealthy.

Nine Macaw is a Chel woman, and she is destined to serve Ix Chel when she learns to read the stars and use the healing plants. She will learn to be a midwife and eventually train other midwives. She has also inherited my gifts for dreams and visions. That means Nine Macaw will receive her training in the sacred mysteries. And someday, Nine Macaw will take my sister's place as ruler of Cuzamil and Oracle of the Goddess. My sister, Heart of Water, always preferred women lovers and has no children of her own.

Fond memories of the blue sea, the sandy shore and of my long-awaited re-union with Heart of Water comfort me. Here, I came up to this hill to compose my mind and find some peace, and I've spent most of the morning contemplating the New Order like a tongue worrying a broken tooth. I must stop wasting this precious leisure time! I focus on clusters of traders and craftsmen making their way along the southern *sacbe* to the great central plaza, where they will work in noble households or trade in the marketplace, which is one of the largest and wealthiest in the Known World. Members of the royal Mai family, rulers of Chichen for generations, live in sumptuous palaces beside the great plaza overlooking the temple of Chac and the great Observatory. Despite the troubling changes in the last ten *tuns*, my adopted home is still outwardly lovely. I admire the fertile plain spread out below me. Chichen rests on wide, flat land surrounded by a few low hills, like the one I'm sitting on. As nobles of privilege, the Cocom people have a compound only a short distance from the ceremonial center of the city. Other noble lineages also have compounds close to the center. Further out are the neighborhoods of lesser nobles, and beyond those are the homes of traders, craftsmen and farmers. At the borders of Chichen, edging up to the forest, are the rough hovels for servants and slaves. Although it's not my true home, Chichen is a fine city with a long history and a proud people. Out past the residential areas are lush, green fields of corn, beans, pumpkins, pineapples and our fruit orchards of avocado, *sapote* and plums. I close my eyes and listen to the familiar sounds of Chichen at dawn. Cocks and birds and dogs and babies sing their morning songs. The early-morning sounds of domestic activity gather and swell like a wave.

I miss the sea, the blue and white waves riding on salty ocean breezes. I feel a familiar ache in my chest, the old feeling of homesickness. Cuzamil!

Can I not just sit here in peace and enjoy the moment? Apparently not!

I was born on an island and I always think of home as a place tucked comfortably in the arms of the sea like a baby held by its mother. Even sitting here on this hill, many days' walk from the sea, if I concentrate I can feel the Goddess's heartbeat rising up from the blue ocean. It doesn't matter where I am; Ix Chel's presence pulses through my body.

Soon, soon, soon, my heart.

The sun is strong in the sky. I can't put off the tasks of the day any longer. I brush the dust off the back of my mantle and walk down the hill toward the bustling central courtyard of the Cocom. A haughty, knee-high male turkey struts and preens near the well. From deep within his crimson-and-blue pimpled throat he bellows a sharp, high caw. A naked toddler runs up behind the bird to grab one of its dropped tail feathers. I'm too far away to intervene, but just before the arrogant bird can turn and peck at the child, his father scoops him up. He lifts the giggling baby into the air and smothers his round face with noisy kisses. The wife runs over to gather up her chubby boy. I know these cousins of my husband's. The father is on his way to supervise slaves who must clear weeds from the Cocom corn field today. He has to shift his *sisal* shoulder bag to the side as he hands over the child. One by one, Cocom men and older boys, dressed in white loincloths and hemp sandals, join him at the well. They circle around to fill their water gourds and talk amiably. Under an avocado tree several other men sit on the ground and sharpen their stone tools. The sounds of their banter, teasing and stone scraping is a morning melody that has not changed for generations. The thought comforts me. I must be getting old to take such pleasure in things that don't change.

I exchange morning greetings with women who call out to me from doorways and windows. The scene is so utterly familiar that I could close my eyes and still know everything that is going on around me. Inside the stone-and-thatch houses, women are grinding wet corn meal for tamales. Daughters are poking at the hearth fires with charred sticks. Sons are balancing clay pots of water on their shoulders. A gang of little girls toss corn kernels from brown gourds to the turkey families getting underfoot in the courtyard. Hairless, pot-bellied dogs roam inside their fenced pens on short, stubby legs, waiting to be fed. They are being fattened for the stew pots.

Here in Chichen, women wear embroidered, knee-length cotton skirts held in place around their waists by woven belts. The embroidery of deer and turkeys on their skirts indicate their villages, while the embroidery on their belts—snakes and marigold flowers—announce their profession and lineage. Mine identifies me as herbalist and healer of the noble Chel lineage. Women in the courtyard who are not yet grandmothers are bare breasted. Older women of the third age, including me, cover our black-and-purple tattooed torsos with a plain, sand-colored square of cotton. Our tattoos record the important events of our lives, including marriage, childbirth, rites of passage and special honors. As Oracle, I have many ceremonial tattoos. Only a circle around our breasts is left bare of markings. Men and boys older than twelve wear loincloths woven by their aunts. Age, clan and family position can be read in the feathers, shells and beads that hang from an embroidered central panel. Other than a red spondylus shell hung from a red string over the pelvis of girls and a jade bead dangling from the bangs of boys, our children under seven *tuns* go naked.

Water Lily's home is quiet, and I pause by the deerskin door for a moment, enjoying a memory. Long before we married, Moon Eagle and his brother mixed tiny bugs—the *cogginele*, which lived in the *nopal* tree—with white plaster to create just the right tint of red earth for the bottom half of the oval walls. It still lifts my heart to see this work of Moon Eagle's hands.

"Jade Skirt, my heart," my husband said to me when I first saw it, "this will be our home, our love nest, and the place where we raise our children. I'm painting it red for our passion, which has no bounds."

He was always such a romantic. I was lucky enough to know what a wonderful husband I had. Moon Eagle was a magnificent man, an attentive lover and a good father. Bitter bile rises in my throat as I remember, yet again, the day he was murdered. The priests dare to call it a "sacrifice," but I call it murder.

I pause in front of Water Lily's door and collect myself. I never know in what condition I will find her or her household. Today, I vow, I will control my rage for the sake of the children.

Just then, my granddaughter, Nine Macaw, tugs open the deerskin curtain and beams at me. She is my sunshine, my rising star and the reason I am still here in these flat, pale lands of Chichen. Were it not for this child and her destiny I would have left after Moon Eagle's death to join my sister, who is ruler and queen of Cuzamil Island. Nine Macaw's remarkable greenish-gold eyes light up when she sees me.

"Grandmother! Greetings of the day." Her wide, expressive face and arched eyebrows make her exceptionally lovely. I can't help grinning back.

Like my mother, Nine Macaw has a willowy, delicate frame and elegant, long fingers. After her coming-of-age ceremony this very month I plan to take

Nine Macaw, now a tender-hearted girl of twelve *tuns*, with me to Cuzamil to begin her training in service to the Goddess Ix Chel. Neither of us will return to Chichen. She will inherit the Rainbow Throne from my sister and rule in Cuzamil.

Nine Macaw has no idea how wonderful her life will be! I touch her smooth cheek in greeting.

"Blessings of Father Kin on you, child." Peering behind the curtain, I sniff the air for broken or spilled beer vessels. I know it's petty, but I can't help myself. I know my daughter too well. But I don't smell anything this morning, so with a lighter step I follow Nine Macaw into the home that was once mine.

"The chocolate is almost ready, Na." Red Earth greets me as she pokes a dry stick at the stubborn fire. She is a good girl, taking over the many tasks of running the home. I pat her on the head fondly. Then I push the curtain aside and visit my old hearth room, so full of memories. I see the lump on the dirt floor, curled up under a cotton quilt. Water Lily snores loudly. A tipped gourd lies next to her listless, outstretched arm.

Disgusting. Does she not care how she shames us all? Red Earth and Nine Macaw look nervously away. Tree Orchid, our orphaned niece, continues to sweep the floor and won't look up from her task. They know how furious I can get with my daughter. They don't want me to make a scene. I take a deep breath and calm myself. Drunks are a rip in the fabric of our lives. We nobles, as advisors to the Seven Lords who rule Chichen, outlawed public drunkenness many *tuns* ago except at public ceremonies. We agreed to tolerate excesses among the elderly and those who had suffered extreme losses, but Water Lily was still young when she started drinking heavily, and no one could say she had suffered more than any other woman. Long before her husband left her to go live with a widow of the Chumux lineage, my daughter was already a heavy drinker. Ix Chel, the Goddess of fertility, blessed her with three healthy children: Red Earth, Nine Macaw and her twin brother, Jaguar Paw. Her husband was not a bad man. Moon Eagle and I doted on her as a girl. Water Lily has no excuse for her drunkenness. I do not excuse her.

I already know from experience that there is no use trying to wake her. I will have to hold my peace until she is fit to hear me. Once more, I will try to talk some sense into her. Only my high positions as Oracle, High Priestess and chief midwife saves my unfortunate daughter from the wrath of the *halach uinic*, our magistrate, who would surely condemn her to a public stoning for this behavior. What will happen to her when I leave here with Nine Macaw and

Tree Orchid? If I hadn't promised our slave, Iguana Wind, his freedom when I leave, I would have him stay here to look after Water Lily. I think again that for her own sake she will have to come with us to the sacred island. At least her gift of fermentation will be of some use during festivals.

I accept a cup of chocolate from Red Earth and sit with the girls and try to distract us all from the disaster in the corner that is their mother. We talk about what we will put in the stew and what is ready to harvest in the garden.

Water Lily, once the delight of my life, was born on an ill-omened day. Trained at Cuzamil to read the calendar days, I knew that the portents of her birth were ominous. I took potions to bring the labor on early to avoid the unhappy birth-day, but fate would not have it. Forty days after her birth, I took my baby girl and went to consult with the High Priest of Chac, who happens to be my baby brother, Blood Gatherer. I found him in the temple. He frowned darkly over his painted bark books.

"This one will have a troubled life," he muttered as thick, blue *copal* smoke billowed around him. "It will be made even more difficult by lack of self-discipline." It seemed a harsh proclamation to make of an infant. I held my precious baby girl tightly and feared for her future.

Blood Gatherer was not wrong about her, though. Water Lily is the only woman in our Chel lineage who has no gift at all for healing. In a noble family famous for our cures and dedication to Ix Chel, Goddess of medicine, my child was a disappointment, although I tried not to show it. She married and learned to make corn beer for our feasts and religious ceremonies. She gave up weaving and now her only talent is brewing beer, which she drinks until she passes out. A terrible disappointment.

I finish my chocolate and put down my gourd, catching Nine Macaw's soft hand in mine.

"Come here, my sun. Put down the broom for now. Help me with my braids. My arms feel stiff in the morning."

"Yes, Na," she smiles at me, so willing and glad to help. She calms my troubled mind, although I see Tree Orchid and Red Earth shoot her disgruntled looks. They will have to do her chores for her. My slave, Iguana Wind, helps with the garden, but since Moon Eagle died and I moved to the temple he spends most of his time assisting in the pilgrims' House of Healing. It isn't fair that Red Earth and Tree Orchid are left with more of the work when I need Nine Macaw to assist me, but this isn't my doing. She is the one who shares my gifts, not Red Earth. I did not ordain things to be that way, but it is my responsibility to train the granddaughter with the gifts. And then how could I not feel a special closeness to her? Grandmothers are allowed to dote, are they not?

I sit in the doorway basking in the warm morning sun. Moon Eagle used to sit here and play with Water Lily while I worked at the hearth. Nine Macaw stands before me tapping her foot and humming. From the armadillo shell where I store things I hand her a turtle-shell comb and the cotton, rainbow-colored ribbons I always wear. I glance down at her delicate feet, long and narrow like mine. She has reached a height beyond my shoulder and can look into my eyes without tilting her head up. Lustrous black hair and square-cut bangs frame her full, round face. She will start her moon cycles any day now.

As the Oracle of Chichen, I am one of two living representatives of the Goddess on earth. Ix Chel speaks directly to her people through me and my sister, Heart of Water. I have been honored to serve the Goddess, but I admit I will be relieved, too, to put down the Oracle's snake-footed scepter of office. The monthly rites I must observe in order to channel my Goddess involve dangerous hallucinogenic plants that are hard on the body. After each ritual, it takes me a little longer to recover. I will go back to Cuzamil and dedicate the rest of my life to Nine Macaw's training, as my own grandmother trained me and my sister.

"What are you humming?" I ask my sweet granddaughter. "It sounds so familiar."

"It's the girl's song for the coming-of-age ceremony for the month of the rabbit, Na," she says, looking a bit shy.

"Ah, yes, I remember it well."

Nine Macaw gathers up my long, thinning gray hair and runs the turtle-shell comb through it. Her hands are deft and confident as a skilled weaver. I love to have my hair combed and I treasure these few peaceful moments with my grandchildren. I chat with Red Earth about the new mantle she is embroidering for her upcoming marriage and I listen to Tree Orchid tell a funny story about her spider monkey, Bobo. Right on cue, a yellow-and-green parrot flaps down noisily and lands on Tree Orchid's arm and cries, "Me! Me! Me!" Kiki adopted Tree Orchid a year ago and now he's part of the family. Bobo enjoys swatting at the bird. We all laugh as the two of them tease each other and I compliment Tree Orchid on her gift with animals. She glows at my praise, but I catch Red Earth casting her a resentful look. I sigh to myself.

"And my dear Red Earth, look how competently you take care of this home and all of us. You will make a wonderful wife. Let us hear more about your marriage plans!" Red Earth eagerly tells me more about her betrothed and their plans for a house.

An Oracle's life has few private, intimate moments. When the Goddess bestows the gift of prophecy, it cannot be neglected. It is going to be the same for Nine Macaw. At her naming ceremony, the calendar priest smiled broadly and declared that this girl's destiny was linked with Cuzamil, Ix Chel and prophecy.

"This precious feather," he declared, "has a most auspicious birth-day. She must be cared for. Guard her well, sister. She will show the gift of prophecy and leadership, but she will come to this during a most unfavorable *katun*." Clearly, he was speaking of this very *katun*.

When the sun rises over the Temple of the Jaguar today, I will have to return to the ceremonial center for the Oracle's rites that prepare me to embody the Great Mother. For the next four days of the full moon, hordes of wisdom-seeking pilgrims will descend on the temple of Ix Chel to consult with her Oracle. It will take me another six days to recover from the herbs that allow me to channel the Goddess.

"This morning, I have some free time," I announce. "I want to go to the forest. Nine Macaw, you will come. You must learn more about *payche*—the skunk root we collected together the other day."

"Yes, Na. That's the gray vine with shiny green leaves and the black root that stinks like a skunk, right?"

"Yes, my jade, that's the one." I am so delighted by her eagerness to learn about the healing plants. Water Lily never showed an interest in learning herbal lore, but Nine Macaw, like me, retains every bit of information she hears. "Tonight, the moon will be full, so the white flower will open sometime today. Without the flower, it can look like any other vine in the jungle. So you must get to know it well."

Her hand pauses in mid-stroke. I feel her tense.

"What about Mother?" she asks tentatively. "She needs help when she wakes up. Today is my turn to clean her after she, uh, vomits."

Shame on Water Lily! It is so unfair to her children.

I straighten my back and exhale. I will not let Water Lily get to me today.

But my poor grandchildren! From inside the house, Red Earth glances at us, then stirs her pots silently. Next to her, Tree Orchid works the grinding stones, but I can feel her listening to us. They are afraid I will start a fight with Water Lily. Nine Macaw returns to the comb and I calm myself down by focusing on the blessings of life.

Water Lily finally wakes and rumbles around in the hearth room coughing and grunting. I catch Tree Orchid's eye.

"Take care of your aunt this morning."

She frowns and is about to protest that it isn't her turn. I raise my hand, palm up, to silence her.

"I'm sorry, child, but I need Nine Macaw to help me gather plants in the forest."

Sighing deeply, the girl makes sure it is loud enough for me to hear, but then she goes to the central well to fetch the water that she will need to clean up Water Lily. Tree Orchid pinches Nine Macaw's arm as she walks by, and Nine Macaw yelps in protest.

"It's not my fault, cousin!"

It's Water Lily's fault, I think to myself grimly, and perhaps my fault as well. I am her mother. But what could I have done differently to prevent this? It is a question I have asked myself time and again, and no answer ever comes to me. Still, I feel the gnawing of guilt, anger and sadness.

Nine Macaw and I take our herb sacks and head out across the courtyard. She can't resist glancing back at Red Earth, who is carrying a bucket of dirty water to the pen out back. Red Earth shoots her younger sister a resentful look. I know it's hard for my eldest granddaughter that her younger sister is the one who is gifted, but Red Earth will soon be a wife and have her own household and children to care for. Her path will be familiar and comfortable. Nine Macaw has much to learn, and much will be asked of her.

"What can you tell me about *payche*?" I ask, taking her hand in mine as we walk.

"The root is black and smells like a skunk. The branches form a cross. You said the cross on a vine is a sign of powerful medicine."

I squeeze her hand. "All correct and well-remembered," I answer.

Leaving the Cocom family courtyard behind, we join the wide, white *sacbe* where bustling, noisy crowds of pilgrims flow like a river in the opposite direction toward the central market. After leaving offerings at Ix Chel's temple, they will make their way to the great Well of Chac, the Rain God, to toss in ceremonial objects of clay and copper. Ground into the road's limestone surface, iridescent ocean shells glitter when touched by the long rays of the sun. Nine Macaw and I walk away from the center of Chichen, passing rolling fields of corn, green fields of pumpkins, orchards of flowering guava trees. The slaves are already hard at work weeding and harvesting. Houses, surrounded by gardens, are painted in the different lineage colors of red, yellow and blue. We pass courtyards buzzing with activity, and elegant, white-stone buildings of noble families who serve as sculptors, artists and builders. Gossamer veils of morning fog drift off the road and into their courtyards.

Nine Macaw lets go of my hand and runs toward a long, palm-thatched house where unmarried boys live. Her twin brother, Jaguar Paw, hears her call and races out to see us. He greets his sister eagerly and then approaches me. He formally holds my hand to his yellow-painted forehead, then touches the earth at my feet. He is becoming a fine young man. I can't help but smile.

"Greetings, Noble Sister and Grandmother. Where are you going?" He has the same green-gold eyes as his twin, and they dance with curiosity and mischief. He looks at our collection bags and answers his own question. "To the forest, today, is it?" He was always quick and impatient. Even now, he shifts his black-painted body from one long foot to the other as if ready to run, and he grins happily at Nine Macaw. I can still remember how he would refuse to nurse unless she was there at the other breast, holding his hand in hers.

Until he moved into the boys' house for his early training last *tun*, they were inseparable. It was hard on Tree Orchid, who always felt left out even though she is their same age. Jaguar Paw dotes on his sister. Even now that he's living with the men, he won't let three days pass without sneaking over to Water Lily's house to be with Nine Macaw.

"You're going to be a famous herbalist, aren't you?" he says to his sister enthusiastically. "They're teaching us to heal wounds, stitch up cuts and carry soldiers off the battlefield. But I want to learn what you know, too. As soon as I finish the training at the boys' house, teach me everything Na teaches you."

Nine Macaw looks up at her brother, already several inches taller than she. "If you teach me what you learn."

"Agreed!"

Just then, one of the military medical officers barks at Jaguar Paw to return to his lesson. The lithe boy flashes us a last smile and dashes back to the courtyard.

We walk on past simple stick-and-thatch homes and work sheds of farmers, laborers and those who serve the nobles. Thinking about the ritual I must prepare for later, I only half-listen to the shouts and calls, the wails of cradled infants and the pounding of stone on stone. But Nine Macaw is thrilled to be in the middle of the jostling crowd and noisy activity, and she twists her head in all directions. Wide-eyed, she watches two peddlers balance baskets of golden plums and rough-skinned avocados on their heads. Plodding his way toward the central market, an emaciated elderly man in a tattered loincloth carries three wooden cages of squealing, nervous spider monkeys. Bent over from the weight of bean sacks tied on tumplines around their foreheads, a clutch of muscled, naked slaves trudges by. A tattooed vendor of amaranth seed-and-honey cakes catches up to us. He and his family live near Water Lily's home. He smiles and reaches for my right hand, pressing it to his forehead in greeting. From his tightly-woven reed basket he takes out a honeyed amaranth cake carved in the likeness of a parrot and hands it to Nine Macaw, who looks surprised and delighted.

"Here, child," he says affectionately, "A small gift for you." He pats my granddaughter on the head. "You were so kind to my youngest son when he was ill." His voice breaks a little. "You brought his food every day; you sat with him, told him stories and helped him pass the long days of sickness in friendship. Our family will always remember your kindness."

Nine Macaw looks shyly pleased and he smiles and then hurries past us. She glances at me and then sniffs the honey cake rapturously. She laughs and spins in a happy circle and then holds his right hand to her forehead and thanks him politely. She nibbles away at the parrot's head and wings and finally gobbles up the last of its tail. She wipes her sticky face with a stickier hand and tugs lightly on my arm.

"I'm still hungry, Na. Can I have something else to eat?" She looks meaningfully at a girl her own age who is strolling by with a basket of candied guavas. I had not thought to bring any cacao seeds with me this morning to buy food.

Along the edge of the *sacbe*, several children have scampered up a *nanci* tree, which is heavy with ripe, yellow fruits. A boy in the tree calls out to Nine Macaw: "Come on up! The *nancis* are ripe and sweet today!"

"Can I, Na? Please!"

I shake my head and pull firmly on her sticky hand. I only have a short time before I have to get back to the temple and start preparing for the ritual.

"Come on, the *nancis* are perfect this morning," the boy says with a friendly grin. "I'll even help her pick."

"Oh, alright," I relent. "But be quick about it."

The morning is getting hot and my attendants will be waiting for me, but I love hearing Nine Macaw's happy laughter as a fruit-smeared hand reaches down to help her climb into the tree. Squeals and laughter ring out from the young fruit pickers. They gently toss fruits down to a naked toddler waiting anxiously on the ground below.

I wait impatiently at the side of the *sacbe*, tapping my right foot. Nine Macaw is still a child, I remind myself, but I can't help remembering how strict my own grandmother was with me when I was Nine Macaw's age. Ah, but times have changed. Children of today are just not as serious and disciplined as we were.

I call to her, "Nine Macaw! Come down."

I have to call her three more times before she comes. Under the hot sun and cloudless blue sky, we continue on our way. That little round face I love so much is happily smeared with the yellow pulp of the *nanci* fruit.

We reach the bent and gnarled tree I had in mind, and from there I lead her off the bustle of the *sacbe*. We scramble down into a dry creek bed and across to the other side. No more than ten paces further we're walking in the shade of a dense jungle. The thick canopy blocks the light, and I pause for a moment to let my eyes adjust. I find the almost-invisible trail and lead my granddaughter into the green, tangled world. The luxuriously earthy aromas of vines, trees and soil are intoxicating to me, more delicious than a pot of stew. I inhale deeply and feel caressed by earth spirits. The trail takes us to a less dense area where soft light cascades through breaks in the canopy, falling in long, broken shafts that illuminate the forest floor amid a chorus of bird caws, hoots, chirps and trills.

I stop to press my forehead against the thick, gray trunk of a sacred *copal* tree. I whisper a prayer of thanksgiving for all the healing this tree and I have done together. I only have to stand near the *copal* tree to feel pleasant currents move through me. Nine Macaw squats down and collects a few of the dried fruit shells. I smile as she closes her eyes and breathes in the heavy, spicy aroma. Being a healer is more than simply knowing which plants to use and how to prepare them. A healer has to use all her senses to know the properties of the plants—their smells, their textures, their shapes and sounds; the energy that flows through their roots, stems, flowers, fruits and leaves.

Several paces away, a troupe of black-faced badgers parade by in single file. The silvery-gray creatures are intent on their own morning tasks and barely take notice of us. Turning once to cast its watery eyes on me, their leader flicks a long tail in the air and continues at the same, unhurried pace. In the distance, the throaty roar of a howler monkey breaks through the trees as Nine Macaw and I walk slowly along the path—master and apprentice, grandmother and child. I approve of the way she moves in silence, yet fully aware of what is happening around her. Children are usually noisy and un-mindful, but here in the forest Nine Macaw has the presence of mind of a much older person.

I motion with my hand to stop and she obeys silently, her eyes flashing with curiosity. We have to stoop down and then crawl under a tangle of thick gray vines.

"Watch out!" I warn, pointing to a thorny bush. Tucking in her arms, Nine Macaw shifts to one side. We make our way slowly through the jungle growth. Suddenly, Nine Macaw can't resist the temptation to pick some tall, red-spiked flowers from a low bush.

"Mother will love these," she says.

I frown. "We can do that on the way back, Nine Macaw."

There is a petty part of me that doesn't believe Water Lily deserves such loyalty from her child. I push those feelings back down, but Nine Macaw picks up my mood anyway.

"You always say that."

We walk on. She is more somber and I wonder if she is thinking about her problematic mother. But soon she is back to her happy self. She spins in a circle, claps her hands and exclaims "Oh, Na, look at this place! It's so beautiful!"

"Yes, my jade, it's beautiful. We're in the bed chamber of the Great Mother."

I lead her under the high canopy of a broad tree. There's a thick vine twining around the trunk. I am so moved to be in the presence of this sacred vine that I kneel down and touch it reverently. I whisper: "*Payche.* I greet you."

Nine Macaw imitates me, kneeling down and pressing her forehead against the thickest part of the vine. I smile at her in approval.

"Listen, child, and learn," I tell her. "We must always say a prayer of faith and thanksgiving to the healing plants. Otherwise, the spirit of the plant will stay in the earth." I can feel the softness of her little cheek against mine. I feel her eager anticipation as she waits for the prayer to begin. "In the name of Ix Chel, I give thanks," I begin, "to the spirit of *payche*. I have faith with all my heart in your great healing power."

I am aware of a subtle shift in my body. There is an ebbing, an upward flow of movement from the earth where the roots of *payche* lie in darkness.

"Do you feel that?" I ask my granddaughter.

She sighs and is silent for a moment, concentrating.

"Yes, Na. It feels like....like a creek running through me. Is that what you feel, too?"

"Yes, I think that is a good way to say it. It's the essence, the spirit of the plant responding to our prayer, our respect." I lean away from the thick gray vine. "Without the herb collector's prayer, we collect leaves, vines and roots, but not the very spiritual essence of the plant. Like us, they are divine beings and need to be acknowledged as such."

I tug at one of the spindly branches. "Look," I say softly. "It is just as I said: here are the newly opened flowers."

It fills me with pleasure to see Nine Macaw's wonder. Her face brightens, her eyes widen with genuine joy. She is charmed by plants, just as I was when I was a child. She is so like me that it makes me ache inside with gratitude to know her. Nine Macaw leans her sun-browned face over my arm and sniffs at a branch where a small bunch of the dangling, cream-colored flowers bloom.

"Oh, they smell delicious!"

"Ah, yes, but only because the moon is full," I remind her. "Right now is the best time to collect the leaves to make spiritual baths for people suffering from fright, grief or even evil magic. When the moon is waning, we collect the roots because then the best of the medicine sinks into the earth where the roots grow. Then they have all the power we need to heal. Do you remember what I told you about how we use the root?"

"Hmm," she answers playfully, pressing an index finger to her chin. "Oh, I know. I know. Don't tell me. Something about when people do harm to each other with the dark arts. Is that right, Na? Did you ever have to use it for that? Does it really work?"

I nod. "Oh, yes. It works. It's a magical plant with its own silent language. It tells you how you can use it if you only look closely, think and let the smell and colors of *payche* communicate."

I watch her lean forward and touch the vine—no, it is more like a caress.

"Close your eyes. Think deeply. Let the plant's spirit communicate with you. Feel the vibrations of the earth."

Smiling, she closes her eyes. We breathe together and she reaches out to hold my hand. I know she can feel it: the waves of movement, the waves of love flowing up to us from the Great Mother.

"You see, my jade, the plants, people and the earth can communicate." She nods, her eyes still closed. "Now just think about the plant and let it speak to you."

After a few moments of silence, I continue: "The dark root that stinks like a skunk; the root grows under the beautiful white flowers, which have a rich aroma only when the moon is full. Lots of evil sorcerers do their wicked work during the full moon."

"Uh huh," Nine Macaw interrupts before I can finish. "I know the rest."

I wait for her explanation, my eyebrows raised. I'm both annoyed and pleased at the interruption of my teaching.

"The root is dark and hidden, like the doers of evil. The flower above it is pure white." She pauses and opens her eyes, searches my face with a question. Then understanding washes over her. "I know! I know! It tells us that light will overcome darkness."

"Ah, you're such a smart little girl," I say, my heart full to bursting. I pat her flushed cheek with my wrinkled hand and thank the Goddess for this sapling who will one day be a mighty tree.

For a few moments I let myself forget about the War God, the drunk daughter and the ritual that awaits me when I return to the temple. For now, I let myself just be a doting grandmother who is grateful to have time with her precious flower of a grandchild.

My mother was named Nine Wind, and she was High Priestess of Cuzamil, where her mother ruled as Queen. I grew up surrounded by those who were jealous of my mother, and of me and my sister. There were always poisonous gossips among the temple acolytes who made my life difficult. When I was close to Nine Macaw's age, I asked my mother with some frustration why she or the Goddess didn't punish them. It was so unfair!

"They hold your life in their hands," said my mother.

I didn't really know what she meant until I became an Oracle. The rites require very precisely measured hallucinogens. A spiteful assistant could easily poison an Oracle, which would very likely be deadly.

When I married Moon Eagle and came to Chichen to be an apprentice Oracle, my mother stayed with me for a full *tun*. She made sure that the trance formula, administered by enema through long-necked gourds, was mixed and prepared correctly.

"Your frogs are too old!" I remember her shouting at the sour-faced assistant and the senior Oracle. The milky drug produced by the glands of older frogs was dangerously hard to control. "And those lotus roots need to be soaked in salt water for a day before you use them!"

The senior Oracle was furious when my mother pushed her aside so she could adjust the mixture to her liking. It undercut the older woman's authority—something no one had done in living memory.

Thinking about my mother puts me in a pensive mood as I leave Nine

Macaw in the Cocom courtyard, where men and women are preparing for the Festival of the Full Moon, Ix Chel's celebration. I hurry to the temple, still thinking about my mother. I am an old woman, but I still miss my mother. I wonder, idly, if Water Lily will ever feel that way about me when I am gone to the Underworld.

My assistant, Turtle Star—tall, thin, and rather unlovely—is waiting at the top of the nine staircases of the temple, hands on hips. She has no doubt spent the morning in the secluded mixing room where the secret formula for the Oracle is prepared. I trust only her to measure the very precise amounts of drained frog glands, dried lotus roots and three types of belladonna flowers—one white and two purple. This recipe is a sacred secret in the Oracle's temple, and many are the acolytes who resent Turtle Star's status as my assistant. She has the kind of personality that can handle the backbiting, and she seems to have had some practice in her own family growing up. At the age of eighteen *tuns*, she was sent to the temple from the far northern province of Tankul by her female relatives. I remember the day she came. Her mother and aunts told us they had given up trying to find a match for her.

"She has overpowered and intimidated every suitor," complained her mother, tugging on the girl's ears. Here, in the Great Mother's temple, Turtle Star's penchant for control and bossiness serves me well. A born leader, she has risen from sweeper of the temple to my personal assistant, and she did it in only a few *tuns*. She is strong willed. I am very fond of her.

I taught Turtle Star myself how the preparation must be made. The white belladonna flower must be collected on the first night of the full moon, and the two purple varieties are gathered at noon on the second day of a full moon. I speak as Oracle of the Goddess for three days of each full moon cycle. Temple maidens who raise the frogs in a fenced yard below my quarters keep their position for a lifetime and never marry because their *chu'lel* is so hot and powerful that it could kill the man who sleeps with them.

"Mother," Turtle Star says, barely hiding her impatience, "it is late and the great hall is already filling with pilgrims. My Lady, we must hurry."

I leave my sandals outside and follow her to the Moon Chamber where, under an open window, I sleep during every full moon. It is important that Ix Chel's moon beams strike the prophet's point, which lies between my eyes.

"We finished our aspersion of the temple and made a beautiful flower bath for you," she reports. The temple has been scrubbed with the white jasmine water. It smells damp and sweet in the stone corridor. Today, hordes of pilgrims pour into Chichen for the great annual Festival of Ix Chel and I feel the heaviness of my mood lift for the first time in weeks. This is a powerful time for the Goddess, and it heartens me to see Her followers flock to Her temple. It's almost as if the War God and the New Order never came to Chichen. This is how it used to be in Chichen before, when people celebrated life.

Women healers, midwives and their apprentices are arriving with offerings of amaranth seeds, honey cakes and baskets of netted butterflies to offer at Ix Chel's enormous round altar. Except for a cup of chocolate this morning, I have fasted today. It will go better for me later if I have an empty stomach. I glance out the window of the Moon Chamber as Turtle Star helps me undress. The pilgrims move in a great long line behind the temple to bathe in the sacred waters of Ix Chel's spring. Dressed in newly-woven, blue-and-white embroidered mantles, women of the first, second and third ages will wait patiently in long lines to have the contents of their medicine pouches blessed by me, the High Priestess. Later, they will dance in great circles around the central square, read poetry and present original songs to Ix Chel, Goddess and Patroness of healers. Tomorrow, they will gather in one another's homes to share healing stories and learn new remedies and prayers from each other, many of which came in dream visions. Our Goddess, primary teacher of women healers, instructs her daughters through dream visions.

I love these full moon days, but for good reason I also dread the ritual to prepare myself to speak for the Goddess. Of course, I feel privileged to embody her essence and to serve her in this way. But the toxic enema mixture has harmful cumulative effects. No matter how careful I am, it will start to affect me in a bad way if I don't retire soon. The previous Oracle became a hopeless addict and died a miserable and painful death before she reached two-times-twenty *tuns*. My mother blamed her assistants' carelessness and vowed that would not happen to me. Turtle Star supervises the preparation, but not everything is under her control. I have to trust in the other acolytes and priestesses who have a hand in preparing the formula, but I know they have jealousies, and I worry. I have seen no evidence of sabotage, but do I trust them completely? No. Only Turtle Star has my full confidence.

I will be physically sick for six or seven days after taking the drugs. Turtle Star will worry over me and bully me gently to rest and eat and gather back my strength. After the days of prophecy and rest, I will then work fourteen days with sick pilgrims, train the young women in midwifery, assist at births and conduct the business affairs of the temple. And, along with other priests and priestesses of the various temples, I will be called to the council chamber to advise the Seven Leaders. It's a busy and full life. I know Chichen women envy my position as High Priestess and Oracle, but they have no idea how much responsibility I have and how little control I have over my own days. When I return to Cuzamil (soon!) I will be glad to pass these tasks on to another. But Turtle Star is someone I will miss. I am closer to her than I am to my own daughter.

Turtle Star hands me a cotton mantle. We stand together in front of the human-sized statue of the Goddess in her guise as Grandmother. It is carved in cedar. I love this image of her with a fierce visage. I know my Goddess can be both gentle and fierce, just like any woman. There is a coiled snake resting on her head. She has claws for feet and holds an upside-down pot of rain water in Her bony hands. In this carving, She is depicted as the Ancient One.

"Mother," I pray fervently. "Today, I will speak for you. Grant me grace and wisdom. Watch over me."

Turtle Star takes my hand. "Come, my Lady," she says sweetly, "to the steam bath." I wrap the thickly woven shawl around my shoulders and follow her obediently to the *nulha*. Apprentices have already prepared the fire and cleansed the entire temple within and without using lustral water made with white jasmine flowers. To rid the stone-lined *nulha* of evil spirits from the watery Underworld, which are known to congregate in damp places, clouds of incense burn in knee-high clay braziers. At the entrance to the *nulha*, a half-moon-shaped stone doorway, three young apprentices of the first age greet me formally and then remove my shawl and mantle. Naked, I sit in the anteroom on a stone bench, my back against the wall, while they sprinkle me generously with the marigold flower water they have prepared. One of them passes an incense burner of spicy *copal* smoke over my head, under my feet and around my body. The others mutter the familiar bath prayer.

"In the name of Ix Chel, Mother of all creation, may Your sacred water bless Jade Skirt, Your servant and mouthpiece. Guide her, protect her and illumine the light of her heart. Make her a brilliant star. Speak to us today through her, Your dedicated servant."

Although I have heard the words countless times, today they move me even more than usual. I add my own prayer: "Mother, I am yours. Use me as You will."

Above the heavy wooden door, a magnificently carved stone lintel of Ix Chel in her three guises as the weaving Maiden, the Mother seated on the crescent moon and the Grandmother pouring water from her clay pot, looks down on me. I reflect that I have been maiden, mother and grandmother, too. I have been blessed.

I let Turtle Star guide me into an inner chamber where, wrapped only in my cotton shawl, I am greeted by three women I have never met before. One is a maiden; one is a mother; and one is near to my age and also a grandmother. They greet me in silence, but warmly, with wide smiles. They are dressed in the traditional blue mantles of temple acolytes, but they are not acolytes. This honor is bestowed on noblewomen or daughters of esteemed warriors and wealthy traders. I look into each of their faces and see only sincerity. They are clearly thrilled to have this opportunity to serve Ix Chel's Oracle and High Priestess, and I am grateful for their faith. The maiden removes my shawl. The mother gently releases my braids and unweaves the rainbow-colored ribbons. The grandmother plucks white jasmine and yellow marigold flowers out of my hair. When she moves to remove my jade necklace I still her hands and shake my head with a smile. She shrugs and then leads me by the hand into the steam room, and we walk on a carpet of yellow and orange marigold petals, sacred to the Goddess. I indulge in their comforting aroma with every step, and the smell of *copal.*

Naked, I lay on a stone bench lined with cotton cloths and I surrender to the spicy heat—flowery and calming. A splash of marigold water sizzles on the hot stones. Perspiration pools under me. My body feels like a rag. The grandmother massages me with skunk root-infused wild coconut oil, one of the sorcerers' potions. It smells of dark, moist earth. Her expert hands leave no part of my body untouched, paying special attention to all orifices. She is tender, devotion oozing from her pores with the sweat. Those who serve me serve the Goddess. I am so grateful for her touch. Very quickly, the skunk root takes effect. I start to float above the clouds of steam. Barely conscious, I feel my body being lifted onto a soft cot. Four women carry me out of the steam room and into another chamber, where one of the assistants places a small clay pipe in my hands. It contains a mixture of a rare purple-leafed tobacco grown only on the Goddess's island and *ix waynay,* the dried purple flowers of a little ground vine, which is also called "sleepyhead." Children love to poke a finger at the tender leaves to watch them close up with the slightest touch.

"Puff, Mother. Inhale deeply," the assistant whispers kindly. Familiar with this routine, I inhale nine times. Floating, weightless, I surrender. Barely aware, I feel Turtle Star slip an embroidered mantle over my head. I tuck my head into a feather pillow and sigh. I am vaguely aware of clinking vessels, grinding stones and then growing whispers of the three noblewomen who prepare the Oracle's enema mixture. Turtle Star rolls me over to one side. I face the white-washed wall. My inner sight is filled with rainbows, dragonflies, spiders and snakes, all totems of Ix Chel. Gently, slowly, the oiled, narrow neck of a dry gourd penetrates my anus. Gushing warmth is followed by cramping pain. I feel the effect almost immediately in the form of flashing lights behind my closed eyelids. Blue, pulsating rings surround me. My chest tightens and I feel a momentary wave of nausea as the enema mixture makes its way into my bloodstream. Then the nausea abates and my heart pounds like a drum. I'm thrown out of my body and I float above the room, watching the assistants scurry about cleaning their utensils. It's like watching Chichen from my morning hillside perch, but here I feel no emotion, no worry, no anticipation. It's as if this whole experience is happening to someone else.

Through a heavy fog appears a shadowy figure. I vaguely recognize it as a male spirit and I'm not afraid when he approaches because I feel neither fear nor pleasure as I float. With a gesture that's both protective and caring, he places a gentle hand on my head. Up close I can see dark green jade hangs from his overstretched ear lobes. Around his corded neck he wears a bright red, crescent-moon-shaped shell pendant. Silently, he stands by my side. Snakes slither around his sandaled feet. I notice these things with detachment. I know that only I can see him, but I also know that he is as real as Turtle Star, who is now pressing her fingers on the pulse in my wrist. Her lips move as she whispers prayers to our Goddess: "Guard her. Protect her. Hold her life in Your hands." Three prayers in the right pulse, three in the left and finally she holds my head tenderly and says the last three prayers. I see pleasing orbs of blue light dancing around her head as she prays.

Then I feel myself tossed and pitched through the air, no longer gently floating, but still detached. I watch the attendants lift the cot on which my body lies. They carry it into the Oracle's audience room. My body is then arranged on a high-backed wooden chair. Turtle Star places my palms on the arms, which are carved snake heads. She secures my wrists and waist to the chair with thick blue bands. Against the high back of the chair, carved in the likeness of a stalking jaguar (its spots are made of inlaid jade), my head lolls to the side. My muscles don't work at the moment, but I notice that I'm no longer floating. I'm back in the body, distracted by currents of movement and hectic, colored patterns that race and charge within me and around me. Bits and pieces of my body dissolve and float as if I'm inside an egg and light is piercing the thin, white shell all around me. My head swirls. My half-closed eyes flicker. Flashing lights and piercing beams blaze across my inner vision.

My heart lurches in fear. Always at this moment of the ritual, a part of me starts to panic at the feeling of dissolution. The fear builds into a terrible pressure until I almost can't bear it, and then I feel Her presence encircle me from behind. With relief and eager abandon, I welcome Ix Chel as She flows into my being. Smoothly, like a waterfall, She fills me. I am floating above once more, and some small part of me watches the expression on my slack face become ecstatic. My closed eyelids flutter rapidly. My limbs spasm and I shake and twitch violently. This is the sign to my attendants that I am ready.

An assistant removes the lid from a large, round basket woven from reeds. Out slither two body-length black snakes. One of them rears its head to stare up at me where I float. The snakes have this ability to see the invisible. I am one with the air, outside my body, yet the black serpent pushes his head back and forth in my direction and flicks its forked tongue at me as if pointing. Then it drops back down and playfully joins the other snake sliding up Turtle Star's arms and torso. When they tighten too much, she winces and pushes a finger into their necks. Obligingly, they loosen their grip. I feel a kinship with them for I, too, have surrendered.

I notice that the protective male spirit is still with me. Outside in the plaza, a drum beats slowly, deliberately, like a dirge. Now I am inside the Goddess's spacious clay image. Three or four others could fit in here with me—it's that big. Turtle Star sprinkles more grains of *copal* mixed with pine resin into a tall clay brazier and they sizzle. Smoke curls into the air. A lithe, diaphanous female body takes shape within the smoke. I breathe her in, smelling the incense and feeling the smoke in my lungs. The gripping tension in my chest relaxes.

The two black snakes slither off of Turtle Star's arms as she removes a leather pouch from a niche in the wall and sprinkles an acrid, blue powder over the coals. The effect is powerful and quick. It shears me from myself and there is no trace of my own consciousness left. The body of Jade Skirt is merely a shell being used by a powerful, swirling spirit. Ix Chel overcomes me in pulsating blue and purple rings. Red beams flash in and out of the purple rings. From outside my body I watch my face go slack again. My limbs have no will of their own. It is wonderful and awful. I feel completely at one with the All.

I watch without emotion, uninvolved. I note that the large reception hall is painted bright blue. It's dark. There are no windows; only one door and no benches or seats. The heavy wooden door creaks open. Dressed in a blue-and-white mantle, a stately noblewoman is the first to enter. Her enormously high white turban towers above a great hooked nose and flattened forehead. I watch, both present and detached. I recognize her as the cousin of one of our women rulers on the Council of Seven. This one is an advisor to her illustrious relative on all matters related to tribute and trade. Slowly, proudly, she paces forward. Jade pendants and anklets clank. The copper bells attached to her sandals jingle, and the smoke-filled, shadowy chamber barely contains her queenly presence. Rivers of *copal* smoke stream out from the mouth, eyes, ears and nostrils of the Goddess's clay image.

A rotund, blue-robed priestess steps out of the shadows and asks the noblewoman, "What is your question?"

The supplicant hesitates. The snakes stream toward Jade Skirt's body where the Goddess sits. One wraps his cold, sleek body tightly around a leg. Suddenly I am aware of the leg that is mine; aware that I don't like the snake to be there. When my heart pounds, he senses the shift and obediently loosens his grip. His companion slithers up the wall of the image. They are agitated. My conscious mind notes that this is not a good sign.

"Tell me, Goddess of the Near and the Far, Consort of Itzámna, Mother of all: will the people suffer this harvest?"

I hear the request, but feel nothing. Both snakes wrap around my arms. Their flesh tightens, squeezing my own. My hands become their heads. My arms are their bodies. My eyes blink. Quickly, my head snaps back. There is a sting of pain. I swirl dizzily, weightless, and a tunnel sucks at me. Like an echo, I hear the answer come from my own lips, but they are no longer my own.

"They would do well to preserve seed as there will be a second planting. The first will dry for lack of rain, but then rain will fall in abundance. They must not lose heart."

The noblewoman leaves the chamber hall. Another stands in her place. More *copal* and dried powders are thrown onto the coals. The two black snakes release me and slither up the walls of the clay image of Ix Chel.

"Speak," commands the priestess to the newcomer. "What is your request?"

Below me stands a heavily tattooed lesser nobleman. Under a light cotton cape that falls above the knees, he wears only a loincloth; blue cotinga feathers make a lofty circle around his topknot of hair. Shell jewelry pierces his lip, ears and nose. As a lesser noble, he can wear no jade.

"My second daughter is unable to bear children," he says with great concern. "Her husband loves her still. What is your advice?"

I sense that his own family wants to abandon the daughter, but he resists. More *copal* and blue powders are thrown on the coal. There is an acrid, bitter taste in my mouth. I am floating. The Goddess speaks through me:

Seek a cure with the midwives of Cuzamil. Her womb is in need of cleansing and strengthening. She must stay there for three moon cycles. Then, if it is to be, she will bear children.

Because this is the Festival of Healers there is a long line of supplicants on this day. I am alternately vaguely and acutely aware of all that transpires. I have no idea for how long I am filled with the Goddess, but eventually I hear someone call my name.

"Lady Jade Skirt!"

It is Turtle Star. Her thin, sharp features stare down at me. She smiles when my eyes flutter open. Our prayers have been answered yet again: I thank Ix Chel for protecting me and delivering me back into my body, which is tired, but whole and unharmed from Her ritual.

"Praise Ix Chel!" I think as I drift back to sleep.

4

I usually don't sleep well for days after the oracular sessions. Disjointed, frightening dreams disturb my rest. I had one such dream last night, in which an aggressive gray-and-yellow snake, one of the most toxic, came right into Water Lily's house. I stood to face it down, but it reared up, defiant, and shot its forked tongue out at me. I chased it with a stick and it slithered away to hide behind a basket, and when I looked for it, it had disappeared.

This dream is not a good sign. It's a warning.

I've had six days of rest in the temple, but today I feel well enough to walk to the Cocom compound to see how Water Lily and the children are getting on. A group of black crows nesting in a nearby tree lets out a long series of high-pitched caws. The sound is grating on my ears—this headache has endured for nearly a week—and I wish they would quiet down. In the Cocom courtyard, my former neighbors greet me respectfully and I greet them back with nods and smiles.

The girls are cooking the morning meal when I arrive. I wave to them and sit on a mat, watching and resting. I'm winded from the walk, still not back to my full strength. Water Lily is lying in a heap on the floor, snoring. Tree Orchid has brought water from the well and now she is sweeping the yard. I smile to see she is carrying a new corn doll wrapped in a shawl around her torso. I delight in the happy chatter she shares with the neighbor's girl. Their brooms, made of dried plant stems, swish over the hard-packed earth..

Nine Macaw and Red Earth are cooking food. The younger girl grinds a ball of wet corn between two dark stones. The scraping sounds of the heavy long stone against another oblong, concave one have been a part of everyday of my life since I was a child. Every forward, rocking motion turns wet, hard corn kernels into soft white paste. Standing by her side, Red Earth scoops little balls of soft corn from the *metate* into her hands. Pat, pat, pat the older girl's practiced hands dance in mid-air turning and flattening the *masa* into round cakes. She dabs on bits of crimson-red chili powder and toasted pumpkin seeds, then folds the little stuffed cakes into dried corn husks to steam the tamales over the fire. Deftly, she drops each cooked tamale into a cloth-draped clay bowl. Red Earth frowns with frustration.

"Na," she complains, "the fire is slow and stubborn this morning." She casts a side-long look at Nine Macaw. "When Nine Macaw should have been collecting dry branches for the fire, she was dancing—again! It's not fair the way she gets to do whatever she wants."

"You know she has to practice, Red Earth," I say gently. "You were allowed time away from chores when you had to learn the dances." But I pat her on the head to let her know I understand her frustration. "I will ask Iguana Wind to come later and stock the woodpile."

They have no father to bring firewood. For the past two *tuns* their father only cuts wood for his new wife and her children. Water Lily could have arranged for their firewood to be delivered. The head-man would have sent one of the slaves attached to the Cocom compound. But that is one of the many domestic chores she neglects in her drunkenness. Again, I decide to hold my counsel. I want my visits here to be welcomed, not dreaded.

Water Lily finally wakes. She reeks of stale beer. Tree Orchid brings her water. The sight of my daughter's red and swollen eyes pierces my heart. She has a narrow face on top of a robust frame, with large breasts covered in purplish tattoos. Not as tall as Red Earth, Water Lily wears a thick, black braid that streams down her back. I see her note the red clay pots of turkey stew and the morning chocolate drink that are barely steaming over the hissing fire. Water Lily glances at me and then away. We avoid talking to each other. It rarely ends well when we do.

Pensive and nostalgic this morning, I sip my chocolate sweetened with honey and miss the simplicity of these daily rituals and the pleasure of running my own household. I miss being a wife. I miss being around young children. The old are so sentimental about the past. When we are actually living in the past, we never know how precious it will seem one day. A *tun* after Moon Eagle died, I left my family hearth to live in the temple. Without Moon Eagle's loving warmth in my bed, sadness became my unwelcome companion. I hoped that the change would be good for me. I hoped that increased temple duties would distract me from my grief and relentless anger at the New Order.

I sigh and then sigh again, deeper and louder. I realize that I have done a great deal of sighing lately. I'm grieving for my husband, and I'm also grieving for the old ways.

Water Lily turns to look disapprovingly at Nine Macaw. The child has stopped grinding corn and, like me, is daydreaming.

"Will you hurry?" Water Lily scolds and snaps her fingers. "Red Earth is right. You're so far away this morning. Pay attention!"

Nine Macaw straightens her shoulders, blinks her eyes and returns her attention to the grinding stone. Red Earth, standing next to her, rolls her big, dark eyes. She taps a corn-crusted palm of one hand against the elbow of the other impatiently, waiting for more ground corn from Nine Macaw's *metate*.

"Sorry, Na," answers Nine Macaw glancing over at me. "The festival is only a few days away. I'm so nervous!" She and her cousin will be dancing the coming-of-age dance in the plaza, which they have been practicing for weeks. "Tree Orchid and I will be in the front," she adds, "and the other dancers depend on us to get it right."

Water Lily moves from behind the hearth to stand squarely in front of her daughter. She pushes her thin face forward, moves some hair out of her eyes and scowls.

"I'm sure the five-times-twenty other girls in that dance aren't dreaming while they prepare breakfast!" she scolds. "Their mothers don't allow it and I won't either." Obediently, Nine Macaw bows her head and attends to her duties.

Tree Orchid comes into the house and stores her broom against the wall. A gifted weaver, she has been at the loom for most of the month of the Deer weaving the simple cotton dresses she and Nine Macaw will wear for the festival. Turtle Star will watch over Nine Macaw and the other noble girls as they embroider rows of red feathers and yellow marigold flowers around the necks and hems of their first ceremonial mantles.

Nine Macaw hums the dance music again and grinds the yellow corn in time to the rhythm. Water Lily pokes Nine Macaw in the ribs.

"You see how she is, Na? Always dreaming! Was I that bad when I was her age?"

"Hah! You were even worse, if you want the truth. Remember how excited you were when you danced for the first time?" We share a smile, and my heart tugs with longing to be close with my daughter. "Leave the child alone. It's natural for her to be excited and distracted right now."

The smile leaves Water Lily's face and she scowls at me, and I regret my words. I've just undermined her authority as the mother. I sigh. Water Lily turns her back to me to check the progress of the dog-and-turkey stew, stirring it with a long-handled wooden spoon to keep it from burning on the bottom. Suddenly, her back stiffens. She swings her head around sniffing the air.

"What is that wretched smell?"

I smell it too. A stench of decay so strong it overwhelms the sweet and spicy smells of food.

"Smells like a flock of buzzards!" exclaims Red Earth, pinching her nose.

My stomach sinks with dread. Heavy, deliberate footsteps crunch down the stone path. Sharp, male voices shout for people to get out of the way. An owl hoots from a branch of the guava tree. An owl hooting in the morning? That is a terrible omen. I reach for my *pi*—my deerskin amulet bag—and grip it in my hand to strengthen my *chu'lel* against whatever is approaching.

I suspect I know the cause of this breath-stealing stench. One of those vile heart-taker priests must be traveling through the Cocom compound. Nothing in the Known World stinks as they do. I pull the deerskin curtain aside to confirm my guess.

"What do those foul priests want with us so early in the morning?"

I try to sound brave for the benefit of my family, but my heart quails as I recall my dream. I call Tree Orchid inside as the neighbors scatter from the courtyard and hide in their homes. It sickens me the way we allow the priests to rule us with fear. I see a few curious heads poke out of windows and doorways to see where the priests are headed.

I know they are coming here. I am not even surprised to see that the heart taker is my younger brother, High Priest of the Rain God, Chac. Blood Gatherer is accompanied by two muscled young men dressed in embroidered white loincloths and painted sandals. They carry him in a reed basket shaped like a half-moon. Wooden support poles perch on their broad, brown shoulders. One walks in front, the other behind the basket. Blue-painted bodies and yellow-stained faces announce the high position of the porters. They are acolytes of the priest. Shells and beads that are sewn into the edges of their loincloths clank tunelessly as they march up to Water Lily's house. Each porter has a high topknot, like a wide-bristled brush, crowned with red parrot feathers that bob and dance in the morning breeze. Red cotton tufts on their deerskin sandals bounce from side to side. Even their costumes suggest blood.

In unison, the two porters halt. Silently, they lower the basket onto the gray stones of our courtyard. Out steps a tall, angular man. I haven't seen my brother in months. His cold, obsidian-black eyes match his black robe. His gaze sweeps the courtyard. Now that it's clear that the priest is not intending to visit them, Cocoms trickle out of their dwellings to stare. Wherever his glance falls, women and children draw back and lower their eyes in obeisance. No woman is allowed to look directly into the High Priest's eyes. Men also look away uncomfortably. Finally, Blood Gatherer gathers up his long robes and strides over to me. Water Lily and the girls are frozen in surprise. I motion to them to move into the back room and they quickly melt into a dark corner of the house.

Before I can even welcome him in, Blood Gatherer pushes past me into my daughter's house. He calls back to his bearers, "You two wait outside."

Up close, he is repulsive and I feel the gorge rise in my throat. Blood-bloated lice crawl in and out of long, greasy strands of black, matted hair. Up and down his reeking robes they creep. A swarm of buzzing flies hovers around his head. If I had already eaten I would be vomiting right now.

Suddenly, I'm remembering a very young Blood Gatherer. His name was 14 Rabbit back then, referring to the calendar day of his birth. I nicknamed him Cricket because of the little chirping sounds he used to make in the cradle when he was excited. Born on the Feast Day of Blood Gatherer, a God of the Underworld, he chose that name when he rose to the office of high priest. He was a chubby little brown-skinned boy with great almond eyes and a sweet, round face. I adored my younger brother; the boy who, until he was six *tuns*, sucked his thumb and cried whenever I let go of his hand.

Like our older sister, Heart of Water, he and I were born on the island of Cuzamil, where our grandmother ruled as Queen and our mother served as High Priestess. My brother and I were inseparable until, at nine *tuns*, I was sent to Na Balam with my sister to train with our aunt. When I returned to Cuzamil at 12 *tuns* to start my training as a priestess-midwife, my blood cycles brought the gift of the Sight. On our island, women gifted with the Sight are held in high esteem and loved and revered. All the attention I received made my brother jealous, and he was also angry because I no longer had time to play with him. Once, in a fit of anger, he accused me of loving Ix Chel more than I loved him. I just laughed and told him he would understand what it was like when he became a priest.

Blood Gatherer was sent away to Chichen to enter the priesthood at age 12. When I saw him many *tuns* later, after I came to Chichen to marry Moon Eagle, he was haughty and proud, barely greeting me before turning away. But for an instant I caught a glimpse of pure hatred in his eyes. What had happened to him that made him so bitter and cruel? There are rumors that the dirty old priests use their male acolytes for sexual pleasure. Had my brother tried to resist? Had they beaten him into submission? Did he somehow blame me?

Blood Gatherer's raspy, asthmatic breathing is the only sound in Water Lily's house. Everyone is cowering, afraid. Am I afraid? A little, I'll admit it. He seems more like a decaying corpse than a man, much less my beloved little brother. In spite of his threatening presence, his wheezing pulls at my heart. Since early childhood he has been asthmatic. Scenes of caring for him when he was a little boy evaporate and I focus on the man who now draws himself up like a mating frog.

"Greetings, Sister."

Beams of morning sunlight reveal swirling, spiral tattoos across his sunken cheeks. His chin bears the outline of a human jaw bone, symbol of the number nine worn only by high priests. My brother's height accentuates his bony, narrow face and small, piercing eyes. He glares down his long, hooked nose at me. Priests of his high rank layer on clay to make their noses longer and wider. Thick ropes of nested hair perch atop his head. In his crusty hands, he holds the arm-length wooden staff of a high priest. Perched at the top is a snake's head, mouth open to show menacing fangs. Blood Gatherer's cold eyes scan the room.

"I bring good news," he thunders as if addressing a festival crowd. "The New Jade Year approaches." He pauses for dramatic effect and then continues in the high, strained voice of an asthmatic. "We plan a great celebration for the Fertility Festival."

Hair on the back of my neck quivers. Everyone knows what the Fertility Festival means since the New Order came. A virgin girl will be chosen from one of the noble lineages and sacrificed to Chac to be his bride. The poor girl will be thrown into the Great Well to die so she can meet her husband in the watery Underworld. I remember when Chac used to be sated with our copper bells, quetzal feathers and a live turkey, a deer or a dog. The rain fell just as well then.

"Yes, Brother, we know this," I manage to answer calmly. But inside, I do not feel at all calm. Heart racing, I gather my inner force, my *chu'lel*, to stand against what I know is coming. The snake in my dream last night—now I understand. He stands before me.

Blood Gatherer's eyes narrow. His lips twist into a grimace. He takes a step forward. He points his staff toward the back room, where he knows the girls are hiding.

"I bestowed this honor on Nine Macaw," he announces. "As a female twin and a noble girl, a virgin of twelve *tuns*, she will make a worthy gift to the Rain God. I congratulate you, Sister, and your family, for earning this honor."

I hear gasps where the children and Water Lily must be clinging to one another in terror. He has just pronounced a death sentence on Nine Macaw. My neck muscles spasm. My head snaps back. I feel lightning quicken in my blood. I prepare to do battle.

"Do not do this," I start to say with all the authority in me as older sister, Oracle and High Priestess of Ix Chel.

"Woman!" wheezes Blood Gatherer, cutting me off. He thrusts his long, tattooed arms wide apart. The gruesome staff halts in mid-air; its menacing fangs hover above us. "This is a great honor for our lineage. Nine Macaw will die a Goddess! We will all see her again in Paradise." He scratches at his skin and continues in his wheezing, rasping breath. "She will be our revered ancestor. She will help us all to cross the great river of the Underworld."

I hear Blood Gatherer's pompous voice as if through water as he continues confidently. "Nine Macaw must be taken to the royal palace. Girls of the Mai lineage will see to all her needs from now on. Jealous spirits of the Underworld will try to steal her soul. She must be guarded."

"No one will take my granddaughter away from me!" I blaze in anger, but he shouts over me.

"Once she is taken to the royal palace, her feet must never touch the earth again! This child is now the earthly embodiment of the maiden Goddess, consort to Chac!" He pushes into the back room and sees Water Lily clasping Nine Macaw. Blood Gatherer bends down and pokes the child in her back with a long, bony finger. "This offering of our precious feather will allow the Rain God and His consort Ix Chel to create our world anew. Stop your crying! This is an honor! You will be a Goddess!" He is shrieking now, and the children and their mother are wailing.

I am beyond furious. How dare he mention the name of Ix Chel in this horrible mission of his?! I grab his loathsome arm to get him away from my children and then I glare at my little brother. Priest or no priest, Blood Gatherer is a coward. How I would like to slap his face, wrest his evil staff away and throw it to the floor, but I hold my hands in check. This is a time for strength to match cruel oppression.

"My granddaughter's life is not a gift to be given to anyone, not even to a God."

I take another step closer to him. Eyes wide, he backs away, stunned. No one ever challenges Blood Gatherer, High Priest of Chac. I press my advantage. "There is a power greater than yours, and I am Her servant on earth."

Blood Gatherer, unaccustomed to defiance, especially from women, opens his mouth to speak, but no words come. He bares rotten teeth embedded with bits of green jade. His wheezing breath comes faster. Nervous hands fidget inside his black robe, stiff and shiny with dried blood. Although I'm nearly two heads shorter than Blood Gatherer, I poke him in the chest with my finger and declare with all the force I can muster from that red-hot ball of fury in my belly:

"I am the Oracle and High Priestess of the Goddess! I am this child's grandmother and temple sponsor! Her destiny is in my hands, not yours. I will not allow this. She will not die in sacrifice!"

Blood Gatherer takes a step back. I press my advantage and take another step toward him.

"You, O Bearer of Death—you know well the prophecy of the calendar priest. Nine Macaw will take our sister's place as Queen. The Rainbow Throne of Cuzamil awaits her." I cross my arms over my chest and glare at him, daring him to contradict our Goddess.

"I am the High Priest of Chac!" His voice cracks a little. "This is not Cuzamil! I rule these affairs in Chichen! You cannot defy me! This child will be a gift to the Rain God so that others may live and eat. You cannot refuse! You will bring disgrace on our lineage. You would insult the Gods? I won't allow it!"

"And, I, Oracle of Chichen and High Priestess of the Great Mother's temple, will not allow you to sacrifice the heir to the Rainbow Throne! Nine Macaw is under Ix Chel's protection, and therefore under my protection!" I punch one fist into the other hand. "Defy me and you will see who rules these affairs, Brother."

"Today is 16 Deer," he says with as much dignity as he can muster, seeing as I have backed him right to the door curtain. "At dawn of 19 Deer, you will make her ready for Chac. The God wills it. I have no more business here."

Grabbing the long hem of his black tunic, he lurches into the sunlit courtyard. His assistants, who have been listening, jump aside and help him into his basket of woven reeds. As he is lifted into the air, his pitiless eyes scorch the assembled crowd. I know he is wondering who heard me challenge the great Blood Gatherer.

"Leave this place!" he barks, and the porters take off at a jog. I watch until he is out of sight, and only then do I feel my knees go weak with the aftereffects of shock.

In Water Lily's house, the dam breaks. The girls crowd around me and hold me tight.

"Na! Na!" wails Water Lily, tears of grief streaking her puffy face. "He can't do it! Don't let him kill my child!" She buries her face in her hands. "I hate him! I hate him, even if he is my uncle and the High Priest!"

I enfold my daughter in a close embrace and soothe her as I did when she was just a girl. It's been so long since we were this close. I have missed her, despite everything she's put me through. When she calms a bit, I see to the others. Red Earth and Tree Orchid are clinging to Nine Macaw and all three are sobbing.

"Be strong, girls," I say to my family with enough force to surprise them from their tears. They turn to look at me. "We are the Cocom-Chel women." I gaze at them with the authority of the Oracle and High Priestess and they respond by wiping their tears and nodding at me. "Fear is an enemy. It weakens us. But we won't give it any power. We who serve the gentle Goddess have our own power. My faith in Her is great, and yours should be too, for She is the Knower and the Preserver."

My mother taught me to trust in the Goddess. But the Goddess herself has taught me, "First, tie up your turkeys; then trust in Me."

I put Tree Orchid, Water Lily and Red Earth to work on practical tasks to distract them from their grief. I send them to collect *copal* and marigold flowers. In the meantime, I rock Nine Macaw in my arms and think. Obviously, it is out of the question that she will be sacrificed. Come what may in this *katun* of uncertainty and change, my brother will not interfere with the future of Cuzamil and Nine Macaw's destiny.

But what is his game? Why did he choose Nine Macaw and not some other maiden? I don't believe for a moment that this has anything to do with my granddaughter being a female twin. When Nine Macaw reaches twenty *tuns*, she will rule the women's island. The security of our Chel women's position at Cuzamil is in everyone's best interest, even Blood Gatherer's. His temple receives enormous profits from tribute and trade with our women. During the last *tun*, the calendar priest clearly showed me that a twenty-year cycle of change and turmoil was ahead for all of the Known World, and the women's island cannot escape the same destiny. We will need a strong leader when my sister, Heart of Water, steps down.

That future leader suddenly faints in my arms. I gently slide Nine Macaw onto the floor and hold her wrist, my fingers finding the lightning in her pulse, which is fat and jumping like a rabbit. That is a sign of terrible fright. I hold my fingers on the pulse and whisper my prayer:

"In the name of Ix Chel, gentle Goddess of the sea, the moon and the weaver's loom. You who see the far and the near; You who are the Knower and the Preserver, take the fright from the body and soul of this child and send it into the sea where the sun sets."

I watch my granddaughter closely while I say the little prayer nine times. *Chu'lel* flows out of me and surrounds her. The pulsing, yellowish-brown haze surrounding my grandchild gradually shifts back to Nine Macaw's usual colors of pink, blue and bright yellow. I lean over her listless body and whisper in her ear.

"Come back, my precious, come back from *mitnal*."

Nine Macaw's eyes flutter open and she shivers. She is still in shock. I cover her with a heavy mantle.

"Be brave, my little feather, be brave. Our ancestors expect us to have courage. We're here; you are not alone. Nothing bad will happen to you, I promise."

Tree Orchid struggles through the doorway with the wooden bucket of sloshing water. She sets it down near the hearth. I lift a hot coal with a broken piece of a clay pot and plop the coal into the bucket to heat the water.

"Tree Orchid, take Nine Macaw outside and give her a bath with marigold flowers. But wait for the water to get hot."

Water Lily hurries back in bearing the *copal* burner. Without being asked, she helps Tree Orchid take Nine Macaw outside. Red Earth feeds sticks into the fire and shoots glances at me. She is about to burst into tears.

"What will we do? What's going to happen?" she whispers.

I place a reassuring hand on her back and then I take a glowing coal from the fire and put it in the brazier. Water Lily brought a tapir-skin bag full of golden grains of *copal* incense. I drop a small handful onto the coal. It sizzles, and then curling smoke rises to fill the room.

"The first thing we will do is cleanse this place of that man's presence," I say with a growl. Red Earth nods, her fear turning to determination. She takes the brazier from my hands and carefully moves through the house, spreading the smoke. I give her a nod of approval, thinking that at least Blood Gatherer's visit has brought my family together in common purpose.

Behind the house, Water Lily and Tree Orchid crush yellow marigold flowers into the bucket of water. With a long-necked gourd, the girl scoops the bath water into the air nine times and it falls like a gossamer curtain, sunbeams glinting off it. Tenderly, she sprinkles and splashes the warm water over Nine Macaw. With a handful of the marigold flowers, Water Lily gently scrubs her daughter's entire body. I watch this ritual feeling an ineffable mix of sadness and joy. Little pink buds of her girlish breasts curl upward like delicate blossoms, a sign that her moon cycles will start soon.

When the bath is finished, Water Lily wraps her child in a length of soft cotton quilting and then rubs her back and neck. Red Earth stands between them to feather *copal* smoke around her sister. I watch with pride as my girls know what to do.

Tree Orchid, Nine Macaw's best friend and constant companion, helps her cousin settle onto the stone bench. Bobo the spider monkey, always in search of affection, scrambles down from a beam to jump between the two cousins. He wraps his hairy arms and legs around Nine Macaw's torso and then lays his furry black head on her chest.

I check Nine Macaw's pulse once more and nod to myself. I smile at her and the others.

"Her soul essence has returned!"

That elicits relieved smiles from everyone. It feels good to be able to do something useful after a shock like the one we've just had.

It feels good to sit in the sun. Red Earth brings a small gourd of the morning stew, which Nine Macaw sips gratefully. No one has eaten yet. An errant lock of hair falls into Nine Macaw's face; tenderly, Tree Orchid settles it behind her ear.

Outside, relatives burn their own *copal* in braziers until the courtyard fills with fragrant, comforting curtains of aromatic smoke. It's as if we're erasing Blood Gatherer's visit. A benevolent breeze floats the *copal* in and around the houses. There is a sense of peace, but I know it's only a momentary lull before the battle begins. There is already a crowd of Cocom gathering in front of Water Lily's house. They mill outside our door like a school of darting fish. They whisper and crane their necks to see in. I know they are burning with curiosity. Whatever happens to one in this family compound affects all. Several children run around to the back of the house and crowd around the stone bench where Nine Macaw is cuddled up with Bobo. Two small boys sit on the ground staring at her.

Then, like a balm, I hear the voice of my brother-in-law, Jaguar Shield. His wooden staff thumps on the stone path, a welcome and familiar sound. My heart gives a little skip of anticipation.

"Leave this to me," he tells the relatives with calm authority. He is a well-respected *nacom*, a veteran physician to warriors. "Return to your fires. We will let you all know what the heart taker wanted." He turns to the two soldiers who accompany him everywhere and tells them to wait outside and let no one enter.

Since Moon Eagle's death, Jaguar Shield has been my champion, advisor and secret lover. Power and quiet authority swirl around him. In small ways he does remind me of my beloved Moon Eagle, but Jaguar Shield is his own man, and I love him for who he is. If our laws allowed it, he would be my husband now. But a widowed sister-in-law may not marry her widowed brother-in-law, so we love in secret.

The curtain parts and Jaguar Shield's long, chiseled face appears in the half-darkness. He's always been as thin as a rope. Moon Eagle used to joke that his brother would disappear if he turned sideways. Every powerful muscle stands out as if carved in stone. Often, he comes to the hospital training center to be the anatomy model for my students.

"Greetings, Noble Sister," he says formally. We're both aware that his guards can hear every word we say.

His voice and that simple greeting gladden my pierced heart. Whatever the problem or threat, my brother-in-law is here for me. He and I are always frank and honest with each other, and I value his respect and his friendship. He touches his hand to his forehead and then to his heart. I do the same and beckon him deeper into the cool shadows of the house. As a veteran warrior-physician and a noble, he wears his cape at calf-length, signifying his military service. Under the cape, wrapped around his taut waist, is a white, embroidered loincloth held in place by a long twisted cloth. Always vain and fashionable, the ends of his loincloth are hemmed with white egret feathers. Jaguar Shield's distinctive aroma of herbal bath oils, tobacco and hearth smoke fills my senses and helps wash away the lingering stench of my brother.

"So tell me," he says. "I'm seething with curiosity. What did that vulture want?"

Jaguar Shield takes my hand and stares into my eyes. His face looks fierce, with the circular-shaped, raised scars that have adorned his dark cheeks ever since I first knew him. Now the scarred circles, once so dashing and handsome, fall into sunken cheeks. A line of ceremonial scars made of small, raised dots outline his chin. Like other men of his generation, the upper part of his ears are now tattered from having been pierced countless times to let blood. Jade ear spools dangle loosely from sagging, overstretched ear lobes. I lead him to the fur-covered stone bench in the back room and invite him to sit. He squeezes my hand reassuringly. No one will bother us in here, so I simply lean my head against his bare chest and take comfort in the sound of his heartbeat for a moment. Finally, I can say the words aloud:

"The buzzard wants Nine Macaw for the Well!"

"*Om bey*! Nine Macaw? This is not right." He frowns and rubs the long, ragged scar on his right thigh, which he always does when he's troubled. A Putun warrior sliced him with an obsidian-studded club and then cruelly twisted it to deepen the wound. Jaguar Shield would have been taken for the Flowery Death if another warrior hadn't clubbed the Putun from behind and dragged Jaguar Shield away to safety.

"What madness is this, to kill children!?" he exclaims, shaking his head in disgust. "These priests and their New Order are a disease to the Known World! What did you say to him?"

"That my granddaughter's life is not his to take; that I am her guardian and temple sponsor; that I will not allow it."

"And he accepted this?"

"Of course not," I say, and despite the gravity of the situation, we share a small smile. He knows me well. I can be quite decisive and obstinate once I decide on a course of action. "Jaguar Shield," I announce, "I have a plan."

"Jade Skirt, of course you do." He smiles fondly at me, and then looks serious, Warrior to Oracle. "What is our plan?"

I hesitate for the barest instant before I say: "I must get Nine Macaw out of Chichen before 19 Deer. We will go to Cuzamil. My sister will give us sanctuary on the island."

Jaguar Shield's face closes. I give him time to absorb the full implications of what I intend. Dipping into the clay pot, I pour two cups of the honey-sweetened chocolate. The fire has gone low from lack of tending. The liquid should be steaming, but I decide it's hot enough. I take the chocolate beater and rub the handle between the palms of my hands to froth the chocolate. Then I hand Jaguar Shield a cup and take one for myself. He stares into his, thinking, while I sip mine and wait patiently.

"You know, Sister, that Ix Chel never fails those of us who love Her," he says finally, reaching over to stroke my cheek lightly. I feel a shiver of desire at this gentleness. "For you, strength is always there. The Goddess will give you clarity and the will to survive what is ahead. Therefore, I know your plan will succeed."

I choke back a sob of gratitude. Like my Moon Eagle, Jaguar Shield gifts me with his respect.

"In three days' time," I say hoarsely, knowing it will mean saying goodbye to him forever. It breaks my heart to think of it. "You know this will mean exile." He will not be allowed to speak with me, visit me, or even speak of me once I am proclaimed to be an exile for defying our priests, who have the support of our rulers. It won't matter that I am Oracle and High Priestess of Ix Chel. To refuse sacrifice is to be a traitor to my husband's lineage. Exile is the punishment, and not just for me and Nine Macaw—for our whole family. I realize then that Nine Macaw's twin brother, Jaguar Paw, and Red Earth, and Water Lily and even Tree Orchid must go, too. This is a disaster. We will all lose our status as nobles. We will lose our home, our fields. The children will lose their futures—Red Earth's marriage, Jaguar Paw's military training, the possibility of a marriage for Tree Orchid. Exile is not an easy sentence, but there is no other way. I will not allow Nine Macaw to be sacrificed for any reason.

Jaguar Shield rubs his scarred leg and sighs. The trenches in his forehead rise up like waves on the sea. A lone turkey feather in his hair knot swings back and forth as he shakes his head mournfully.

"These priests are up to something," he says. "I'm not sure what it is, but something about this doesn't ring true to me. Everyone in Chichen and beyond knows the prophecy of Nine Macaw's birth. Her royal destiny on Cuzamil is as important to the entire Cocom lineage as it is to the Chels. Blood Gatherer stands to profit from his temple's share of trade goods that the Chel queens bring from Cuzamil, so what good is she to him or to any of us at the bottom of the well? If Heart of Water's successor is chosen from another lineage, we will all lose income, prestige, trade and profits."

"I feel this is personal," I say, admitting what is in my heart. "My brother has always been jealous of me and our sister. He was raised in Cuzamil, but then the priests taught him to hate the Goddess. He doesn't say it outright, but I can feel it. Naming Nine Macaw as the sacrifice is his way of spitting on Ix Chel."

"Is his pride so great that he believes he can counter the will of the Goddess?" he asks, incredulous. This is another thing I love about Jaguar Shield. His devotion to Ix Chel is as great my own. "What is written cannot be changed by mere mortals," he continues. "Blood Gatherer would have all of us who honor the Goddess bent over that sacrificial stone or thrown into the well."

I gasp a little. Is that true? Is this more than just a personal vendetta against me? Is Blood Gatherer declaring war on the Great Protector? Is he crazy? A wave of sadness overtakes me and I grip my deerskin *pi*, the amulet bag I always wear around my neck. It holds a tiny wooden image of Ix Chel that my sister, Heart of Water, gave me when I left Cuzamil to marry Moon Eagle.

"Ix Chel will save this child's life," I say with conviction. "Blood Gatherer, the priests and even the Rain God are nothing before Her. Nine Macaw is destined to serve the Goddess and no other. Chac will not have her for a bride."

Jaguar Shield gets up to pace back and forth in long strides. Suddenly, swack! He punches one fist into the palm of his other hand.

"This affects all of our people," he says with a fierce gleam in his eye. "Our Cocom *bacabs*, our leaders, need to know. I will call for a secret lineage meeting. It has to be tonight. I will send two of my oldest grandsons to spread the word to meet in the sacred cave by the *cenote*. Agreed?"

Every passing moment brings more clarity. I feel Ix Chel's presence, and my *chu'lel*, my personal power, rises from within to envelop me in a hot, swirling red cloud. Turning to my brother-in-law, I answer with the wisdom of the Goddess:

"We mustn't be naive, Brother. Blood Gatherer will be watching us."

"Then the timing is propitious!" Jaguar Shield's face brightens. "Tonight, there will be rampant drunkenness at the ballgame." His hand is warm where he grips my arm. Memories of past pleasures shiver through my body. "Blood Gatherer and his acolytes will be busy until dawn killing the losers. But I will leave guards by the cave in case he thinks to send scouts. We will have a password in case he sends spies."

"Let it be Heart of Water," I say. I wish my elder sister was here to deal with Blood Gatherer. No one contradicts Heart of Water, she who speaks with the Goddess's authority—not even our snot-nosed younger brother.

Jaguar Shield gives me a keen look and then says, "I'm proud of you. You didn't let him bully you."

"This is not just about me," I say, voicing my deepest fear. "If the New Order is attacking Ix Chel, then this is not just about Nine Macaw. This is a battle for the hearts and minds of all of Chichen."

"Whatever it takes, you can count on me," he says steadily, winning my heart all over again. "I know that the Goddess favors us, Jade Skirt. She will save the life of Nine Macaw. Her gentle ways will yet win. Praise be to Ix Chel."

I walk him out to the courtyard. Overhead, the dark shadow of an eagle soars over the courtyard and we have a proper and formal parting as everyone in the courtyard casts us surreptitious glances.

"Ix Chel, watch over us," I whisper as he goes to summon his lineage to the secret gathering.

I go back into the house and build up the fire as if I am stoking my own determination. Never has such a strong fire burned in that hearth! I heat up a clay pot of red beans and soon my daughter and the children come inside, drawn by the aroma. It is as my mother used to say: a woman can only cry with one eye. The other must watch the pots, because no matter what the crisis, still there must be food.

The news flies through Chichen faster than Bobo the spider monkey can climb a tree. Already I see the neighbors whispering behind their hands and casting scared, sympathetic and also disapproving looks in our direction. I instruct Water Lily to keep the girls inside today and tell them to make as many tamales as they have corn. They are glad to have some activity to keep their minds away from their fears.

I have to act fast; there is much to do before we can leave. There will be necessities on the great white road to Cuzamil and I must have cacao beans and jade stones for cash. I refuse to leave Chichen as a pauper. So ignoring the stares (some curious, but most hostile), I cross the courtyard and head toward the central plaza, my head held high and my face a mask of indifference. Impulsively, I make a short detour into the great temple of Kukulcan and send up a silent prayer in front of the great stone serpent head. I need the blessing of Kukulcan today, the Serpent God who helps ease communications and creates peaceful exchanges.

I keep my head up as I cross the market square. It's a bit of a shock to see people I've known for decades and people I don't know at all turn their backs to me as I pass. I'm accustomed to honor and respect, and it's hard not to let this rejection get to me. I'm aware that this is only the beginning. Once we set foot on the *sacbe* in defiance of Blood Gatherer, I and my family will become exiles. Scorn, judgment and rejection will follow each of us, maybe for generations. Even so, I am not wrong to defy the priests in this matter, and I straighten my back and hold my head proudly. The voice of my goddess comforts me:

"Be not ashamed. We do this together."

I march along the path that leads behind the great temple to the stone building that houses the Oracle's tribute payments. During my service as mouthpiece of the Goddess, untold numbers of chests and baskets of tribute were collected, including embroidered mantles, cacao beans, precious stones, shells and feathers. My prophecies and the control of the salt and honey trade, which was my dowry, made the Cocom people of Chichen and their leaders wealthy. I feel entitled to take my share today.

A stone façade of coiled snakes and stalking jaguars crowns the entryway to the tribute storage rooms. Under the heads of two gape-mouthed jaguars stand two fierce guards; two others are stationed by the entrance. The two men closest to the door recognize me at once and pull on a thick rope, which opens the enormous stone door. They motion for me to enter and then all four take up position in the doorway, lances pointing outward.

I've passed through this same dark and narrow passageway many times over the years, usually to escort guards laden with treasure for the storehouse. A wise and frugal administrator, I have kept close track of every cacao bean, jade stone, quetzal feather and animal hide paid to the Goddess's coffers. Scrupulous records are kept on fig-bark paper and I personally scrutinize the entries regularly.

But sometimes I just come to visit Smoke Shell, the Holder of the cacao. She's served two previous Oracles and is now nearly four-times-twenty *tuns* of age. Smoke Shell is a trusted noblewoman with family ties to royalty, and she's been a good friend to me over the years. Most people simply call her the Holder. I've often told her that she might retire if she wished, but she refuses to be dislodged because of her age, and I would never force her out. Instead, I put her in charge of only one room of wooden tribute chests, and here she lives quite happily with her few possessions—a stone bed covered with a pile of faded cotton quilts; a wooden image of Ix Chel set in a small niche; a few cotton mantles, bath items, sandals and a few painted cups and bowls. The other coffers of the temple are watched and counted by younger women of her lineage, and they also look after Smoke Shell. The last time I saw her she told me it was a fine life for her and she wouldn't have it any other way.

Wrinkled as a dried fruit and bent at the waist, the frail woman greets me with deference. I place my right hand on my left shoulder and lower my eyes to the ground.

"Esteemed Lady, temple gossip is all about you today," she says in her deep voice seasoned with cracks and quavers of age. "They are saying you will not give your granddaughter to the priests for Chac's Well. Is it true?"

"Yes, it's true, dear Mother."

The cacao keeper shakes her head and sighs. "These are sad times, Jade Skirt. A break like this can never be mended. Are you sure this is the right action to take?"

"I am sure, but it's still going to be hard."

She nods, and gently touches my arm. "I lost a beloved servant to the Gods. She was a precious jade to me. I personally prepared her for the journey to the Underworld and was there when Blood Gatherer threw her into the Well of Sacrifice. I still miss her to this day. But if she didn't go they would have taken my granddaughter instead."

I'm at a loss for words and can only reach out to hold her veined hand.

"Holder, none should have to make such a choice. That is why I defy the priests on this matter. Well I know the consequences of my actions, yet I serve the Goddess and She tells me that no Gods may demand human life as tribute. And Nine Macaw is destined to serve Ix Chel as Her High Priestess. I have no choice; I will do what I must to ensure that she lives."

When I say it that way, it sounds simple and reasonable, but I feel the weight of tradition, obedience and convention bearing down on me. But as a much bigger counterweight, I feel the importance of this act of rebellion, this defiance of a wrong-headed convention. The priests are waging a war against life itself, and I stand on the side of my Goddess, Creator of life!

The Holder pats my cheek with both hands. I treasure her easy affection.

"I fear for you, daughter. You will bring shame on your entire household. Your husband's lineage will no longer know you. Not even your ancestors will know you. Blood Gatherer has the power to erase all your names from clan memory. We are nothing without our ancestors. And, you must leave your husband's ashes here. Alone."

I know all this! I push away a surge of annoyance. Smoke Shell, dear as she is to me, can be annoyingly blunt.

"Nine Macaw must live to rule the women's sanctuary at Cuzamil," I tell her stubbornly. "I have never been more certain of anything in my life. I must save my granddaughter's life to preserve our island for all women of the realm."

"Our women need to have the sanctuary of that island, it's true," the old woman agrees, dropping onto a bench with a sigh. "I would dearly love to return to the Goddess's temple to live out the last of my days there on Her sacred island, but these legs are too old to make the trip. But Jade Skirt, your brother is as proud as you are. You have publicly insulted him already, and if you don't deliver the child for the ceremony, he will retaliate and there will be heavy consequences. You of all people must know this."

"I'm not afraid of Blood Gatherer. I am a priestess of Ix Chel and Her Oracle! He has no greater authority than I do."

"Ah!" Smoke Shells says, her rheumy eyes brightening. "Now there's a thought: daughter, you *are* the Oracle. Could you not make a prophecy that the child must live?"

I shake my head. "Sister, when I took up the scepter of the Oracle's office, I swore never to make up a prophecy for my own sake or for the benefit of any member of my family. It is out of the question." I don't share with her that I've already been tempted by that possibility more than once today.

Smoke Shell looks grumpy. "Don't be so stubborn! Perhaps it really is the will of the Goddess that the child should live, and if you give her a chance She will say that Herself."

"Yes, perhaps, but She will not speak through me again until the next full moon. And Nine Macaw's sacrifice is scheduled for 19 Deer, which is three days from now."

"No doubt Blood Gatherer planned it just so," she says. "It would seem that destiny is on the move," She sighs unhappily. "Lady, enjoy a cup of chocolate with me, then. It will be our last. Once you refuse the priests, we can never speak to you again."

Her words sting, as I know she intended. She wants me to understand what I am about to lose. But then she pats me gently on the back and I feel her love and I know she will still love me even when I am an exile and far away. In truth, the idea of being shunned by the people of Chichen doesn't bother me because I don't plan on living here anymore, but I do feel sad for Water Lily and the children. This is the only home they've ever known. Exile will be an unfathomable loss for them, and there is nothing I can do about that.

Smoke Shell hobbles to a red clay brazier in the corner of the room where she keeps her few personal items. She pours two cups of steaming chocolate brewed with marigold flowers and honey. I take the two painted cups from her unsteady hands and follow my old friend to the center of the room. We sit on wooden stools facing two narrow windows with a view of the white-stone plaza. Rays of warm sunlight make the room cheerful. I want to remember this moment: the music in the plaza—drumbeats and a haunting sound of hollow flutes; the high-pitched voice of the dance instructor calling out the rhythm of the hand drum. I feel nostalgic. Soon I will be gone, never to hear these familiar sounds again. A light breeze scented with *copal* brushes my face like a caress and I breathe deeply of the rich perfume.

The Holder bows her white head over the cup of chocolate and says with pain in her voice, "Never has there been an Oracle as true as you. Never before has the Oracle also been able to conduct the affairs of the midwives. You came here as a stranger to marry Moon Eagle. You were so young, so inexperienced with prophecy, but you have honored your ancestors through diligence. You have integrity, Jade Skirt. I will help you in whatever ways I can."

Her affection gladdens my heart and also crushes me with a feeling of grief. How I will miss her!

"Thank you, Mother. The Temple will need your help. You know my apprentice, Turtle Star Canul Mai. I haven't yet told her that I plan to leave and turn over my duties to her. It would be a great service to me if you would watch over her and guide her as you once guided me so long ago."

"Of course I will. That one has spirit! I like her."

Her approval settles my mind somewhat. My apprentice will be sorely in need of wise advisors, and none is wiser than the Holder. As we finish our chocolate, I am reluctant to say goodbye.

"My life will be less when you are gone," she says quietly, taking our cups. Then she rubs her hands together and gets down to business. "You will need seeds and stones for the journey. Come."

Leaning on a cane, she shuffles over to a red mahogany chest and lifts the intricately carved lid. The chest itself was a tribute payment to the Oracle from a wealthy trader of jaguar pelts from the southern jungles. I commissioned a talented artist to carve reliefs of a long nosed tapir, a jaguar, a peccary and a puma in the richly toned wood. My grandson, little Jaguar Paw, was only seven *tuns* at the time and he was absolutely transfixed by the carver's work, watching him from dawn to dusk. I wonder if that was the seed of his desire to be an artisan carver. From these seemingly insignificant events are life-paths chosen.

The chest holds cacao seeds, shiny and reddish-brown, piled to the top. I hand Smoke Shell my deerskin pouch and she fills it generously. I tie it off with a small strip of cloth. Then she moves to a second chest, this one made of stone. She needs my help sliding aside the heavy lid. It is brimming with sparkling jewels and precious stones. The Holder fills my second pouch with jade beads, yellow topaz and two big handfuls of rare turquoise. I will have more than enough wealth to provide for my family on the journey and in Cuzamil. A momentary pang of conscience strikes me, but Smoke Shell, as if reading my thoughts, winks and tells me, "I will explain it somehow to the royal scribe. And we all know you earned our Temple this wealth."

I hear the wings of a bird fly past the window. From the temple of Kukulcan, a conch shell is blown, announcing the noon hour.

"I remember when the gift of life was a gift of the Gods that didn't have to be repaid," Smoke Shell says. "I remember when the Gods were well-fed on turkeys and dogs. Then the New Order came. Everything is different now."

"Will you send me with your blessings?" I ask, holding out my hands.

"Of course I will, Sister," she says with a warm smile.

She takes my wrist and searches for my pulse. It races against her fingers. She whispers familiar prayers, words that I have said for the benefit of others for two-times-twenty *tuns* of healing service. With each prayer, my body loosens and my shoulders relax. I close my eyes, bow my head and surrender.

After the ninth prayer, I rise and hold the hand of the cacao keeper against my forehead for a moment. We say a silent farewell.

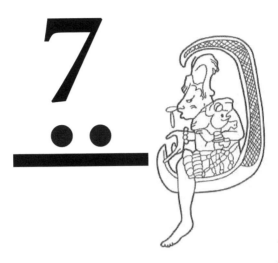

I'm making mental lists of what we'll need for our journey. It will take nine or ten days to reach the sea, so we must have good sandals and warm mantles. Normally, I send my assistants to the market with instructions for what to purchase, but I don't want to involve them in my scandal. I plunge into the chaos of the market alone.

Chichen boasts the greatest and largest market in all of the province of Cupul, and it's the envy of the realm. As I leave the cool temperatures of the temple, the glaring sun feels like an assault. I make my way through throngs of freshly bathed and perfumed men and women who stroll along or hurry through on their urgent errands. Our gleaming white market square is large enough for thousands to spread their wares on mantles or permanent stalls. Tall stone arches painted a brilliant blue line the periphery on three sides. A shaded portico protects the stalls of the wealthier families from the blistering sun. I pass those by. I'm not looking for luxury goods like jade ear flares, precious quartz crystals, quetzal feathers and fine woven cotton mantles, nor do I feel like engaging with the corpulent, well-dressed tradesmen who wear their mantles above their knees, as protocol demands.

I cut through rows of animals for sale—tethered turkeys, barkless dogs and fetid, wild peccaries that strain against *henequen* ropes. Their owners are negotiating trades for skeins of cotton, deerskin sandals and powdered dyes. It's too busy here for anyone to pay attention to me, which suits me fine. I have to dodge a roaming broom maker who shouts bold boasts about how his broom is crafted from the strongest palm leaves cut on just the right phase of the moon. I nod to him approvingly. Everyone knows that palm leaves cut on the wrong phase of the moon will dry and turn to powder quickly. I step aside for a commoner dressed in a ragged, stained loincloth. On his shoulders he balances a tall ladder to which several nervous, black spider monkeys are tied. They squeal, scratch and jump nervously. Known to toss excrement when frightened, market-goers steer a wide circle around the man and his monkeys.

I steel myself as I approach the hairdresser stalls, where noblemen in ankle-length, brightly colored capes and high-feathered headdresses gossip as they puff on reed tobacco pipes and wait their turns. The latest in men's hair fashion calls for high, elaborate hairdos festooned with shells and wooden arches. The hairdressers' shelves are filled with carved wooden likenesses of jaguars, crocodiles, foxes and the hooked beaks of eagles. Famous for their vanity, the noblemen of Chichen carry pyrite mirrors in their shoulder bags and constantly check their hairdos (and spy on the social interchanges going on behind them). Among the idle nobility, gossip is a favorite pastime. Like nervously chattering birds, the men bob and nod at one another, all the while exchanging tidbits of news and scandals. Part of the word "chichen" means "big mouth." As I approach, the whispering starts and they turn their backs. But one glances at me and gives a slight nod of support. My heart lifts a little.

I'm starting to feel exhausted from the sensory overload of the marketplace—all the noise and smells and activity. I wish my slave, Iguana Wind, was with me. He has been gone for a few days now on a gathering expedition with the soldier healers. He learned much from Moon Eagle and the soldiers rely on him now to locate the plants they need for their medicine bags. I don't know if he has heard the news yet about Nine Macaw.

My uneasiness grows steadily as I walk through the dizzyingly colorful textile section. Men with dye-stained hands wave skeins of brightly colored cotton threads at me. Steaming clay pots of stewed deer meat entice me with their spicy aromas. I come upon a man selling white blocks of salt from Cuzamil, which is considered to be the purest and best in the land. I imagine I can smell the sea as I pass his wooden stall. Painted in black and white stripes, three male slaves run with heavy baskets of corn slung from a strap around their foreheads. A strong smell of sweat and dirt follows them.

The marketplace is huge. I've been walking for ten minutes and still have not reached the area where I plan to do my shopping. Granted, I'm taking a lot of detours to avoid the worst gossips. Still, here and there I am seen and backs suddenly turn. I have to pretend it doesn't sting. A woman from the House of Pleasure, cracking her *chicle* gum to announce her trade, flashes me a smile before casting her eyes to the ground. So I do have silent allies.

I find a leather worker. He is selling expensive sandals decorated with multicolored tassels of cotton, red seashells and blue stone beads. The sandals sell for ten cacao seeds a pair. My granddaughters would love them, but what we need are sturdy sandals that will last, so I move on.

I finally reach the far northern end. Under a shady portico sits Nahoch Pop, the corpulent market magistrate. He roosts above the crowd on a stone platform, cross-legged on a cushion under a canopy of palm leaves. He settles all disputes of weight, charges and debts, and collects a percentage from every vendor for the coffers of the rulers. Next to him, a young royal scribe carefully records every decision and transaction in his beaten bark books. Wearing only a loincloth, the young man bends studiously over his labors, occasionally dipping his brushes into clay bowls of colored inks, which he no doubt mixes himself.

I came to the market to shop, but I have another agenda as well. I make a beeline for Nahoch Pop. I'm not fond of the man, but it is here, through him, that I can air my side of the dispute to the people of Chichen. He sees me and imperiously invites me to take a seat.

Nahoch Pop leans forward over his paunch and pushes out his amber-ringed lower lip with disapproval.

"My wife has informed me of everything," he says. "I don't pay attention to gossip, but is it true? Do you refuse to send that green-eyed girl to Chac's Well?"

"It is true. Yes," I say evenly, looking him in the eye so he knows I am not ashamed of what I say.

His anger flares. He slaps his bare thigh and proclaims in a loud voice:

"To refuse the priests is a serious offense, even for the Oracle! You realize none of you can stay in Chichen if you do this." He scowls down at me. "Have you no heart? Don't you care about your family? Is there no blood in your veins?"

People gather around and stare, which was rather his point. He enjoys being the center of attention. The look on the faces in the crowd is one I see often in Chichen: a base greed for gossip.

"Jade Skirt, you are the Oracle of Ix Chel's temple! Very irresponsible of you!" he proclaims loudly.

How dare this oaf scold me! I restrain myself from lashing out at him with strong words. Instead, I say loudly:

"Brother Pop, we all have our duty. I have served Chichen and our leaders for two-times-ten *tuns*. My prophecies have brought wealth and fame to Chichen." A few women and fewer men are nodding at each other. "You all know my duty is to serve the Goddess Ix Chel, and that includes preserving Her women's island sanctuary. Nine Macaw has a sacred destiny to rule Cuzamil. It has been seen since her birth, and her training has already begun. I have a responsibility to my Goddess and to my own lineage, the Chels, to make sure she achieves her destiny."

There are more nods from the people, and Nahoch Pop backs down slightly, aware that he is not talking to just any woman, but to the High Priestess and Oracle of Ix Chel.

"Nevertheless, what a harsh decision," he says shaking his head and wagging his finger at me. "Nothing proceeds well that is not begun well. You were Moon Eagle's wife, but you never accepted the New Order. We all know that about you. Why?"

It is for this that I've come here: a chance to persuade the people of Chichen that human sacrifice is wrong. I answer in a voice loud enough for the gathering crowd to hear.

"Brother Pop, the Goddess teaches that all life is a sacred gift from the Gods. She tells us that we do not have to repay that gift with the very life that She has bestowed on us. The beliefs of the New Order have not swayed me from the truth spoken to me by the Goddess. Priests of the New Order would have us believe that the Gods need our blood, but Ix Chel has told me that the Gods do not."

With a dismissive wave of his hand, he scowls, "Foolish woman. We all want corn and chocolate in our pots, but the Gods must be fed, too. It is not only about Ix Chel."

"But, Brother Pop, long before the New Order taught us to tear out hearts there was chocolate and corn in our pots. You remember. We always fed the Gods well." His scribe gives me a keen look and I think I see a smile, but then it's gone.

Nahoch Pop scowls. His rolls of fat jounce unattractively. "Hmmph. Dogs and turkeys; birds and butterflies, those were acceptable before, but times have changed." With a flick of his hand in mid-air, he dismisses me. "May your ancestors forgive you."

I didn't expect to convert him to my view of the world, but this conversation served its purpose. As I leave, two women of the second age smile at me with the compassion of mothers. I look around hopefully for more allies. Mostly, I am surrounded by angry glares. As I feared, the minds and hearts of Chichen have been lost to the New Order.

I'm suddenly struck with the uncomfortable thought that by saving Nine Macaw from Chac's Well, I'm condemning whomever is chosen to be her replacement to death. Save Nine Macaw's life only to cause another girl's death? I feel a wave of dismay. Goddess, is there no other way? I can't afford to show doubt or fear, especially not here in the central plaza with so many eyes on me. I have to finish making my purchases and get on with this interminable day.

I hurry past the medicine stalls, with their piles of roots, barks and vines. I slow as I pass the stall of an herb seller I know well because he often brings medicines to the temple's healing room. Several people are seated on low stools, waiting patiently for their interview with the herb seller who is also collector, vendor and prescriber. He catches sight of me and turns his face away without greeting. It stings. We've known each other for twenty *tuns*.

Past the medicine vendors are the sandal makers. I purchase strong deerskin sandals for myself, Water Lily and the children. I admire the well-crafted, thick rubber soles and peccary-hide straps. I pay thirty cacao seeds to the sandal maker's child, who stands next to his father. To be sure they're not filled with sand he tests each seed with his teeth. After they hand over the shoes, they both turn their backs to me.

There's no time to weave the heavy travel mantles we will all need, so I trade some of my beads for several ready-made ones from an old friend, Three Cloud. When we were younger, I delivered every one of Three Cloud's five children. She greets me with a friendly smile. One of her strong, young sons hefts the bundles of sandals and mantles onto his shoulders and says he will deliver them to Water Lily's house.

"Are these mantles for a journey?" asks Three Cloud, catching both my hands. "Is it true, you plan to leave us?" I nod and she gives my hands a sympathetic squeeze and then reaches under the wooden counter and hands me a tricolor bag. I admire the red, blue and yellow weave.

"A gift for you," she tells me, brushing away a tear. "May your *sacbes* all be straight and smooth. There will never be another Oracle or a midwife like you, my Lady." She leans in and whispers. "I admire your courage, Jade Skirt. Many of us do!"

Her words hearten me considerably as I head back across the wide plaza and make my way to the Goddess's temple. I find Turtle Star waiting in the corridor outside the Oracle's room. As always, it is blessedly cool and dark in here. Even without much sunlight I can see that my apprentice is flushed and excited.

"Mother!" she cries, touching my hand to her forehead. "I heard terrible gossip this morning. And last night in a dream I saw you and Nine Macaw in the heart of a huge storm."

"Turtle Star," I say taking her by the hand, "let's go inside and I will tell you all."

I feel a pang of guilt as she gives me a trusting look. Turtle Star is barely ready to assume the mantle of Oracle, but I have no better options. Turtle Star, named after the Sky Wanderer under which she was born, is an excellent teacher, a gifted seer and a natural astronomer. I believe she is well-suited for the leadership role about to fall on her shoulders as High Priestess, but is she ready to be the Oracle?

It feels odd to think that in only seven days, I will not be here when throngs of pilgrims pour in to Chichen to throw offerings into the Sacred Well for the celebration marking the end of the *katun*. Most of the visitors will want to confer with the Oracle of Ix Chel and seek healing from our herbalists and healers. It is our temple's busiest time of the entire *tun*. Ix Chel's temple offers herbs, massages and steam baths for those in physical need, and *copal*, prayers and aspersions with water and plants for those in spiritual need. Others, in deep emotional and spiritual pain, sleep in the temple with our snakes to seek a dream vision from the Goddess. In the morning, every dream vision must be interpreted by a priestess of Ix Chel and her healing recommendations carried out.

Turtle Star can handle it, I remind myself.

I lead her to my private apartment at the back of the temple. We sit facing each other on my blue-painted stone sleeping bench and I tell her what happened, and what I intend to do.

"But, Mother, no one can refuse the priests!" She pauses, glances around and asks, "Can they?"

"Actually, they can," I say. "One has the right to refuse, but few are willing to accept the consequences. I and my family will be exiled from Chichen forever. Our names will be stricken from the lineage. Never again will we join in singing and dancing here."

"Exile!" She looks shocked. "No! You are the Oracle! You are the High Priestess! It's madness to think that you could be exiled!"

"Daughter, it is a shock, I know. But you need to accept this swiftly and prepare yourself. I am leaving, and you must take my place here." She turns paler than usual, and I pat her dear cheek with more affection than I've shown my own Water Lily in years. "You are ready," I say reassuringly. "I know you are. My assistants will help you."

"No! I'm not ready. I …I'm not worthy," she cries and wrings her bony hands.

I spend the next minutes countering all her arguments for why she's not ready. Finally, she says what's really in her heart.

"Mother, I want to go with you to Cuzamil! Take me with you."

I'm so touched that she loves me that much!

"My dear girl, that is not possible. Your duty is here. I have arranged for Smoke Shell to be your mentor."

She is not consoled, and I must remind her several times of the importance of her presence and service here for Ix Chel, Herself.

"Remember, she needs you to speak for Her."

Well, Turtle Star has no answer for that. This wasn't going to be an argument she was going to win, and we both knew it.

I lead her by the hand to the dark room where the Oracle's potions are prepared by our priestesses. Sworn to secrecy for life, no one has ever revealed our secret, ancient formulas. As old as the Sky Wanderers, the herbal mixtures that make the shaman's salve and the bitter powders that join our souls with our animal companions are all prepared here. The enema mixture is made in an elaborate ritual using sacred herbs, sacred prayers and *copal.*

Nine women, all of the second age, are charged with this grave responsibility. They're in the mixing room chatting and giggling when we enter. Each touches the earth and then her forehead with her right hand in greeting. Knee-length blue mantles trimmed in white identify their position in the temple. Their long, black braids are wrapped in rainbow-colored ribbons like my own, marking them as acolytes of Ix Chel, She who Manifests in Rainbows. I hold Turtle Star by the arm and tell the women of my plans to leave Chichen. I wait for the shock to pass and then announce:

"As of today, Turtle Star will take my place as Oracle and High Priestess."

Like a sudden rainstorm, dark clouds of jealousy fill the air. My chest tightens as it always does when I sense the mean spirit of envy.

"You must work together for the good of the people," I tell them sternly, looking each one in the eye. "It is your duty to serve the Goddess and those who come to Her temple. Turtle Star must have your full support to take on such a responsibility."

Their faces twist. They want to serve Ix Chel, but their own ambitions are sharp stabs in their hearts. So it was when I first became the Oracle. The previous High Priestess still had many supporters in the temple who were jealous of my position, especially since I was an outsider, from Cuzamil. I had to win their confidence and loyalty through my actions and service to the Goddess. Turtle Star must do the same. I know this, but I fear for her because I love her.

I thank each of the attendants for her service to me and the Goddess and then I motion Turtle Star to attend me—mostly to get her out of there for the moment.

"They will get used to the idea," I tell her with more confidence than I feel. "Did I already say that Smoke Shell will be your mentor? You must go to her later and she will tell you whatever I have forgotten to say."

Teary-eyed, Turtle Star helps me pack my travel gear. What shall I take with me and what must I leave behind forever? Of course I take the medicine bag, my *pi*—a gift from my mother at my coming-of-age ceremony. In it I tuck the small cedar carving of the maiden Ix Chel, which I brought from Cuzamil so long ago. Turtle Star runs to bring a sack of amaranth cakes that I can offer at shrines and caves along the route to Cuzamil.

"Does your sister know you're coming?" she asks with that wonderful practicality I have come to rely on. She sees the look on my face and grins. "I will send one of the boy messengers to Cuzamil to alert Heart of Water. I'll say she can expect you in about ten-plus-four days."

It's depressing going through all my things and knowing I must leave nearly all of it behind. I tuck into my bag a set of snake fangs to puncture the skin of a person possessed by an evil spirit. I leave an extra set of snake fangs for Turtle Star. A small sack of *copal* resin for incense is essential, and a sack of skunk root. A sack of powdered snake-bite remedy, of course, and the Ancestral Stone, which I wrap carefully in an embroidered cotton cloth woven by my grandmother. That one goes into its own three-tasseled sack. I take my Life or Death crystal, a narrow rod of clear quartz that reveals if the person holding it will live or die. Those who will live cause a ray of white light within the center to reach from end to end. If the supplicant will not survive the illness, the crystal ray of light is a mere speck in the center. Many a shaking hand has grasped this crystal over countless generations.

On an impulse, I gather up a handful of rainbow-colored ribbons for my braids. Then I tie my sack and there's no more excuse to prolong my goodbyes. I have a growing sense of foreboding. I need to get back to Water Lily's house and make sure Nine Macaw is safe. Turtle Star walks with me to the entrance. We cross paths with a bevy of maidens and older women dedicated to the gentle Goddess. They circle around me to say their farewells in the way of the Goddess. A ring of maidens, then a circle of mothers and a finally a circle of grandmothers put their right hands on my shoulders and sing a sweet song of farewell. I drink in the medicine of their love and good wishes. It's all I can do to keep a confident smile on my face as I take my leave. I cast a last look at Turtle Star. She looks frightened. I send up a prayer to our Goddess to guide her well.

The hearth room is in shameful disarray. Unwashed dishes piled up on a bench, no fire lit, and not even a coal left to light one. Water Lily, Red Earth, and Tree Orchid are lying on the floor weeping with Nine Macaw in their arms. Clearly, they have been here all morning and afternoon, and I have to swallow my annoyance. Turkeys boldly march in and out of the room, undaunted by the presence of the humans who would normally shoo them out. I clap my hands loudly and scatter the turkeys out the door, and it also gets my family's attention. I pull up a stool and sit myself down in the middle of the room. I see my bundles from the marketplace in the corner of the room. So at least they were delivered safely.

"My hearts," I tell the women and girls, "we must talk. Gather around. There's not much time."

In a rustle of feet and mournful sighs, the little family sits in front of me. Worried, tear-stained faces stare back at me.

"Children, I will not allow Blood Gatherer to take Nine Macaw. In two days' time, we leave for Cuzamil. Already a messenger has been sent to my sister, Heart of Water. She will send a canoe to wait for us when we arrive at the coast. It will be a hard journey on the *sacbe*. Nine, maybe ten-plus-four days. We'll stay with your uncle, my only living son, Spear Thrower who lives with his family in Pole, by the sea."

Nine Macaw reaches out to hold my hand and lays her wet face in my lap. She shakes with relief. Tree Orchid stares woodenly at the floor. Water Lily looks frightened.

"So, then, it's true. Mother! What will become of us?"

"Exile," I say with a sigh. "Exile here in Chichen, but a fresh start for us all in Cuzamil."

"Exile," my daughter whispers, shock on her face. "Never will we join our lineage in dancing and singing again." She reaches for the gourd and I am too overwhelmed with events to try to stop her. She empties the container of strong spirits in six loud gulps.

"What about my wedding?" cries Red Earth. She looks at me with accusing eyes, her fists clenched. My heart weeps for her. She was looking forward to her wedding, to starting her life as a married woman. The timing is terrible luck for Red Earth. Born during the last five unlucky days of the calendar *tun*, Red Earth and her betrothed have very inauspicious birthdays. Both families, theirs and ours, had a brutal time finding mates for our ill-omened offspring. This match might be Red Earth's only chance at a normal woman's life.

Red Earth sobs bitterly. "His family will never accept me after this! Already there's gossip. In the courtyard, they're saying that the boy's family will refuse to let their son marry someone who is unborn and unknown." She shoots me an angry glare. "You would ruin all our lives for the sake of Nine Macaw! She's the only one you care about! There will be no future for any of us after this disgrace. We will all be as dead."

Water Lily sides with her oldest daughter. She folds her arms over her chest and gives me an indignant look. I realize then that she's already drunk. Her words are slurred. "What about this house, where we have lived for so many generations? Are we to just abandon our home? And what will we do in Cuzamil?"

"Do they dance in Cuzamil like we do here?" asks Nine Macaw suddenly, perking up a bit. "And what about Tree Orchid? She is coming, right, Na?"

Tree Orchid clutches my legs and wails, "Don't leave me! Don't leave me behind. Please!"

"Na, Tree Orchid must go with us. I couldn't live anywhere without her," says Nine Macaw reaching for Tree Orchid's hand. "We're feathers on the same bird."

Tree Orchid sobs, tears pouring down her little round face. "I'm an orphan. Without you, I'll be a slave or taken to sacrifice! I have no mother and no father." She's in a panic. "I am no one. Don't... don't leave me. I'm afraid of Blood Gatherer and the other priests....what they do to orphans. I want to be with Nine Macaw."

I swing my head around to speak to everyone at once. "Everyone has to go—Nine Macaw, Tree Orchid, Jaguar Paw, Red Earth and you, daughter. All of us. No one stays behind."

"Mother! No!" Water Lily angrily kicks over a nearly empty pot of beer. "You will ruin our lives and take away our futures!"

"I will save Nine Macaw," I say stonily, daring my daughter to tell me that is wrong. Her eyes slide away in shame, but she kicks the pot and it shatters against the wall.

Footsteps approach and I tense, but it's only Jaguar Paw and two other boy soldiers. All three are painted black from head to toe. Yellow circles ring their eyes, embroidered belts bind plain red loincloths around their waists and thick-soled, deerskin, military-style sandals wrap around their feet. In happier days, Jaguar Paw's belt was woven by Tree Orchid and embroidered by Nine Macaw. It seems such a short time ago that he was a little naked rascal of a boy with a jade bead dangling between his eyes. Now, living with other youths in the boys' house, he is nearly grown, with elegantly crossed eyes. Jaguar Paw puts his right hand to his heart and lowers his eyes in greeting. His voice is full of barely hidden irritation. Nine Macaw's face brightens for a moment when she sees her brother.

"Noble Grandmother, Mother and Sisters. Everyone is talking. They say you are leaving Chichen. They say that we must all go, that we are banished. Is this true?" He moves closer to me and stares into my eyes. Jaguar Paw's raven hair, pulled up in a tight knot at the crown of his head, is fastened with three white egret feathers that bob and swing with every movement of his head. Even through his shiny black face paint, anyone can see that he and Nine Macaw are twins.

"Yes, it's true," I tell him evenly.

"And when were you going to tell me?" He is a head taller than me now, and he waves his right arm in the air, letting me know he is displeased. It's so impertinent, but he deserves to know his future.

"Jaguar Shield and I will make the announcement tonight," I tell him. But I'm glad you are here now to discuss it in private, grandson."

"I just came from guarding the boundaries when I heard that you and Uncle Blood Gatherer quarreled, but everyone is afraid to tell me what happened. Why? What is it?"

I shoot a look at the two black-painted boys and they give nervous bows and slip outside.

"The priests have decreed that Nine Macaw is to be sacrificed to Chac on 19 Deer."

Horror seizes Jaguar Paw and he doubles over and clutches his stomach as if he will be sick. But then he collects himself and glares at me as if I am the priest who has done this thing.

"No! They can't have her!" he screams. Then he's crying. He flings himself onto the floor and holds Nine Macaw tightly.

"Don't worry," Nine Macaw tells him soothingly. "Na won't let them do it."

He looks up at me, a question in his eye. I nod solemnly. He sits up, more dignified.

"Neither will I!" he declares hotly.

"None of us will let Blood Gatherer sacrifice Nine Macaw," I say calmly. "But you know what that means, Jaguar Paw." He looks very young at that moment, and confused. Gently I say the dreaded word: "Exile." I let that sink in. He has to know what consequences will follow from our decisions this day.

"Nine Macaw can't die," he says stubbornly.

"We all agree with that here," I say with a heavy sigh. "That is why we must leave. I will take all of us to Cuzamil. We'll be safe there."

"No!" he says, frowning. "I mean to say, I would battle jaguars to save my sister. But to run is cowardly."

"We will all be forever damned and stricken from clan memory," says Red Earth sullenly. I give her a sympathetic look.

"Children, I know this is hard, but what would you do? See your sister die?" Red Earth's eyes slide away from me. I address Jaguar Paw, who is unconsciously chewing on his thumb as he did when he was upset as a little boy. "Grandson," I say gently, "your uncle Jaguar Shield and I have always believed you would make a better artisan than a soldier. If not a soldier, then you must be an army doctor. You're not suited to either. Once we leave Chichen, there will be no future for you here among the other Cocom nobles. Your uncle Spear Thrower in Pole will apprentice you to a master sculptor. You prefer cutting stone and carving wood over warfare and healing—don't deny it."

"Is this possible?" He looks suddenly young and shy. "Could I become a sculptor? Would it be allowed?"

"It's not the usual way of things for the Cocom, but when I speak to the elders tonight, I believe they will agree."

I don't tell him that it doesn't matter what they say. As an exile, he will be without a clan.

"Look," I say to my family, "we will all have to make sacrifices. Red Earth, I know this loss is the worst for you. Please believe me, I am so sorry. But you're wrong—this is not only about Nine Macaw. Much is at stake here for our Chel lineage and for all women and girls of the realm. My grandmother's Rainbow Throne is to be Nine Macaw's. She must live, not for her sake but for the sake of the Chel people and for the future of Cuzamil."

Red Earth just sniffs and looks away. She feels sorry for herself, but there really is nothing I can do. No one in Chichen will marry a woman whose family is exiled.

"We leave tomorrow, when the evening sun sends rays into the lap of the *chacmool* on the Temple of Kukulcan," I say.

"So, my destiny has been decided!" Red Earth hurls a gourd at the wall and sobs. "We will all live to regret your rebellion against the Gods, Grandmother."

She spits the last word at me and I am about to say something sharp to her when we all hear a great commotion in the courtyard. A moment later, I know why: I smell Blood Gatherer again.

"What now?" I wonder. I feel so weary of fighting, but I brace myself for another showdown.

The turkeys and dogs in the courtyard make a ruckus. Blood Gatherer shouts at them to get out of his way. He sounds furious and petulant at the same time.

"Where is she?" Blood Gatherer bumps into Jaguar Paw at the door. "You! What are you doing here?" he bellows into the boy's blackened face.

"Uncle, I, uh—" Jaguar Paw leans away from the priest's odor and tries not to cringe. The other two boy soldiers have already slunk away. My brother shoves his way past Jaguar Paw into the hearth room. His eyes narrow to slits.

"What do I hear everywhere I turn? I hear that my own sister, whore of the swamps, dares to defy me!"

I keep my voice even and reasonable. "You leave me no choice, Brother."

"How dare you call me that!" he rages. "If you defy me, it will be as if you were never born. No one will know you. You will have no ancestors, no lineage!"

Water Lily and the girls press themselves into a far corner of the room to get as far away from Blood Gatherer as they can. Blood Gatherer enjoys the sight of them cowering, and I watch his right arm cock back to slap me in the face. Suddenly, a hand grabs his fist in mid-air. Jaguar Shield overpowers Blood Gatherer and quick as lightning he twists Blood Gatherer's arm behind his back. My brother struggles, but he can't break the iron grip of the old solider. Then all at once Jaguar Shield releases the priest.

"Get out of here!" Jaguar Shield points at the door with his staff; his other hand firmly settled on the dagger in his belt.

Blood Gatherer's cold eyes narrow. He struggles to breathe.

"My sister has poisoned you, too. You will be damned—you and all your filthy brood!"

I can hear the Cocom gathered outside. They are listening to every word. I pitch my voice as loud as I can and declare:

"Blood Gatherer, you may be Chac's High Priest, but I am the High Priestess of the Goddess and I say you have no power greater than mine. You are not above the Oracle of Ix Chel. She sees the games of power you play. The Goddess sees you, Blood Gatherer. She sees each one of us and She judges what you do here today against Her own priestess and against the heir to the throne of Her island. You want to curse me? Well, younger brother, here is the curse of the Oracle: May your curses turn back on you! May you be damned for what you do to the people of Chichen, turning them away from the life-loving Goddess and teaching them to worship with death!"

I watch his face turn pale with dismay. The curse of the Oracle is nothing to take lightly. I have put all the power of my Goddess into my voice and my bearing. My family needs to understand who I am. They need to understand that saving Nine Macaw is not just a grandmother's whim, but the deliberate act of the High Priestess of Ix Chel. A part of me enjoys Blood Gatherer's discomfort. He has long been jealous and afraid of my power to speak for the Goddess. I have tried not to lord it over him, but now it serves him right.

"You defile your high office!" he sputters. "You spit in the face of the hungry Gods and the New Order. All of us will pay the price of your defiance and your pride! Your duty—everyone's duty—is to feed the Gods. How else do you think They can bring us rains this season?"

"The rains!" I say loudly, aware of my audience outside. "Long before the New Order started tearing out hearts and drowning children, the rains fell. Rains are a gift of the Great Mother as much as they are of Her consort Chac. It is Ix Chel who brings the rain and She has spoken to me. I am Her Oracle! She has said quite clearly that the Gods do not need human sacrifices."

His face fills with a dark menace. Jaguar Shield moves closer to Blood Gatherer, hand still on dagger. He says:

"I am a military man, accustomed to war and unspeakable atrocities. You ask us to bring home prisoners for your sacrifices and I order my men to do as you say, though it pains me to see how you make those honorable and brave men suffer in captivity." His voice rises to a shout. "But drowning a young girl? No! I will not stand by and let this happen. You destroy our way of life. Do you not see that, man?"

I put a restraining hand on Jaguar Shield's shoulder. I'm calmer now. I look into my brother's eyes, daring him silently to look away.

"And tell me why it must be *this* child, Nine Macaw, who dies? Are there no orphans? No captives? No slave girls for you to dispatch? Is her flesh different from theirs? Or do you choose her because you know she has a destiny to fulfill for the Goddess?"

Instantly, Blood Gatherer's eyes shift away from mine. He fiddles with the belt on his crusty robe.

"She was chosen to be the bride of Chac," he says stubbornly. But compared to his earlier self-righteous rage, he seems oddly docile.

"And why is that?" presses Jaguar Shield.

Blood Gatherer raises his head. His eyes dart around the room, as if he's looking for support.

"She's a twin and a noble. And, as an infant, she had that cowlick on the top of her head pointing to heaven."

Om bey! I'm furious.

"What rubbish! This has nothing to do with a silly cowlick."

"It is time for you to go," says Jaguar Shield, leaning in to him, hand still on dagger.

Blood Gatherer's face contorts with frustration. He looks just as he did when he was four *tuns* and didn't get his way.

"May the wrath of all the Gods be upon you!" he curses with a wheeze. "And you!" he points to me, "Cursed product of our mother's womb, may you stand forever at the river and never cross. If you defy me, you will never be safe, you will never rest. I will be at your back wherever you go, to punish you in the name of the Gods!"

He turns and stomps out the door, yanking the deerskin curtain to the ground as he leaves. In the courtyard, Cocom women have been eavesdropping. Their hands covering their mouths. They scatter as Blood Gatherer charges through the crowd. A small child standing next to his mother wails as though demons have grabbed him. Blood Gatherer spits on the ground in front of the house and kicks over a clay pot of water. He hurries out of the compound, the stench of old blood trailing him while the two porters race to catch up, carrying his empty reed palanquin.

I'm shaking. I go back inside and Jaguar Shield follows. Gently, he squeezes my arm.

"A curse," he says, "a threat. Prepare for trouble." I nod. "Jade Skirt," he murmurs so low that only I will hear, "know that you can count on me. I will see you through this storm, whatever it takes. My sons are already angry because I stand with you against the heart takers, but it doesn't matter. What you do is the right thing, and we must do what is right."

"But you will lose everything," I whisper, a lump in my throat.

"Not everything," he whispers back, squeezing my hand. "Not the most precious thing."

When Father Sun begins to dip down to the horizon, I slip out of Water Lily's house and head to Jaguar Shield's home. It's a five-minute walk. I find him napping against the cool wall of his back patio. With every whistling breath, a jade ring in his lower lip dances. I smile at my brother-in-law, my protector and best friend. Even though I was married to his brother and Jaguar Shield had a wife, we have always felt a strong, mutual attraction. Not long after Moon Eagle died, my sister-in-law, Cloud Feather, took a fever and died. There we were, Jaguar Shield and I, both widowed, and our forbidden magnetism intensified. Many nights do I lay awake and wish there was a way around the custom that forbids us from being together.

One night, after a joyous feast of dancing and too much corn beer, the current of our hidden lust carried us away on a flooded river of forbidden desire. He had danced in the circle of men and I in the circle of women. Great, long lines of men and women of the second-age participated in this, which is our most erotic dance. Dancing with snakes, women passed them to the men who worked them into their loincloths until they came slithering out to be grabbed again by the women. This was repeated several times, to the delight of all onlookers. I can still remember how the drum beat like a pulse and the horns blew loudly. Every time the undulating rings of dancers made their way around the central plaza and I passed Jaguar Shield, I felt my heat rise up.

Late that night, on our way home from the revelry, Jaguar Shield simply took my hand and guided me into the shadowy forest. One hand held my wrist.

With the other, he cleared fallen leaves and stones from the ground with his staff. Then he laid his mantle down under a jasmine bush. We didn't need to speak we both knew what we wanted. No law or social custom could keep us apart that balmy night. I lay beside him on the hard ground and let myself feel the strong currents of *chu'lel* pulsing between us. A bright half-moon peeked in and out of flowering branches overhead and a breeze sprinkled us with blossoms. I rejoiced as I felt my beloved slide his rough hands over my skin. The Moon Goddess was with us, and I burned with desire for Jaguar Shield, but he took his time despite his own arousal. He brushed jasmine flowers from my face and his hand lingered on my cheek. My nipples hardened. I tucked my head comfortably in the crook of his arm as if he had been my lover for decades. My hand made its way across his taut chest, appreciating his fine muscles. He lifted my fingers to his lips and held them there. At last, I thought with joy, at last we are together after *tuns* of unquenched desire. How I wanted him! And, yes! Yes, he wanted me.

His hands! *Om bey!* Long, trembling, eager hands. I invited them to explore every part of my body. I quivered and surrendered. He lavished delicate nibbles on my neck. His breath, mixed with tobacco and beer, was hot. He slid a hand over my breast. My back arched. He broke the silence with a whisper, hot breath tickling my ear.

"Since the moment I first saw you, I've wanted you."

Groaning with sexual heat and longing, we found each other in the dark. My jade forest moistened. I lifted my hips, waiting, longing. He pushed his loincloth aside and entered. His member thrust gently at first. Our *chu'lel*, our divine essence, and the invisible, pulsing air around our bodies became a throbbing circle of pink and blue light. We became one writhing body. He paused, then pushed hard and wildly. Again and again, his shaft found its waiting mark in my place of delight. Every muscle of his frame tightened. He held my buttocks with both hands and pulled me closer yet. When his lust was spent, he let out a yell. He heaved one last time and relaxed on top of me. I wanted more. I straddled him until he grew hard again. Now flowers fell on his face and I brushed them off, laughing. He jumped to brush a biting ant off his buttocks. We laughed with joyful abandon. My frame rocked back and forth, up and down. Boldly, I stared into his eyes and groaned until my own desire was quenched. We spent the whole night exploring each other until we were sated, and then I was happily wrapped inside his mantle and we shared the warmth of each other's arms. Forest animals of the sky and the earth crawled, fluttered and crept around us. We felt no fear and neither did they.

Dawn broke. Reluctantly, we released each other. My brother-in-law held my face in his hands and tilted it toward his. With a searching, sad look in his eyes, he held my gaze. We shared perfect understanding of the bitter-sweetness of the moment. Our night together had been perfect; and we knew it could never happen again.

Taking separate paths to our dwellings, he returned to his cold hearth and empty home and I to my duties in the temple of Ix Chel for morning rites. It was either luck or the blessing of the Goddess that the old women who guarded against such illicit sexual unions after festivities had not discovered us in that moonlit forest. I shudder to think of what would have happened. A public beating, shame, and no doubt loss of the high status we both held a as consequence of violating the social taboo against in-laws being lovers.

I watch him sleep now and all the memories of that night rush over me in a pleasant heat. I've thought about that night many, many times over the years. While I miss Moon Eagle, the truth is I never longed for him the way I longed for Jaguar Shield. I still long for Jaguar Shield. I feel my good fortune in having a brother-in-law who is also so unshakably loyal. Here he is, a noble and leader of the Cocom, and he's preparing to go into exile with me. Yet, even in exile we will not be allowed to be together. Only women and children may live on the Island of Women. Once Nine Macaw's training begins, I will rarely be able to see Jaguar Shield; perhaps never again. In this rare moment of privacy, I hungrily memorize every line and whorl of his tattooed face. Does he spend his nights alone, I wonder with stabs of jealousy, or does he call on women from the House of Pleasure? I admit, I've always been selfishly glad that he has never taken another wife.

His house used to be full with his four children and his wife. These days he shares it only with his youngest son, a fat, grumpy daughter-in-law and three small grandchildren. I'm grateful none are home at this moment. I reach over to touch his hand and his barkless, castrated dogs look up from their pen and growl at me. Jaguar Shield leaps up, right hand on his obsidian blade. He blinks and looks around quickly, then settles down when he sees it's just me.

I touch my right hand to my heart and then my forehead. "Brother-in-law," I drop my eyes and laugh. "I was snooping! You caught me."

Sadly, he sighs, shakes his head with an air of resignation and strokes his chin. "Not much to see, is there?" He stands up, arranges his loincloth, tucks an errant feather back into this topknot. He looks around and asks, "No one's here? Where's the fat one?"

"I don't know. The house was empty when I arrived."

He takes my cold hand in his warm one and pulls me into the house. "So, we have a lot to discuss. Come."

Following behind him, I notice that he's walking stiffly. That old battle wound on his thigh is taking its toll. I was there when the army surgeon sewed him up. But these days his right leg seems to drag more. I remind myself to send someone from the pilgrim's House of Healing to massage him with my pine resin salve. I catch myself in mid-thought. Will there even be time to send the salve before we leave?

The front room of his stone house is cluttered, but clean. His carving tools are spread out neatly in the far corner. Cooking pots line the earthen hearth. Long, trimmed reeds lean against beautifully woven reed baskets. He's taken up the hobby of basket weaving and in my opinion he's become one of the finest in Chichen.

Jaguar Shield assumes a military stance and reports as if I were one of his soldiers: "I have arranged everything. We meet tonight at sundown in the Great Mother's cave next to the *cenote*. I expect twenty of our clan to attend."

The purpose of this meeting is to try to sway them to our view of matters, but we both know it will be futile. The New Order has scared and intimidated my husband's clan as much as they have the rest of Chichen. Still, I hope their censure won't be as severe as exile. Perhaps they will spare Water Lily, Red Earth, Tree Orchid and Jaguar Paw. Perhaps only Nine Macaw and I will be exiled.

"Brother, I know you will stand with me, and I have no words to express my gratitude. But please, don't follow me into exile! I can't bear the thought of you being shunned, losing your status. Even to your children you will be unborn and unknown. Let me go on my own. Don't share this fate with me. I hate to think of it!"

"Jade Skirt, I am bound to you," he says, dropping his voice. He looks around to confirm that no Cocom are eavesdropping. Holding my hand in his, he whispers, "I have loved you all these *tuns*. There might be a life for us once we are out of Cupul Province!"

My heart soars even as I feel the weight of responsibility for Jaguar Shield. The truth is, I would follow him into exile were it his granddaughter chosen to go into the well. I don't dash his hopes that we can be together even in exile. To protect women and children from the harsh cruelties of the New Order, my grandmother decreed that men are not allowed to live on the island. Jaguar Shield and I can meet on the coast from time to time, but a life together as man and wife is not possible on Cuzamil.

"Perhaps the Goddess will grant us that luxury one day in the future," I say, fervently wishing it will be so.

"About tonight, we must be ready for rejection," he cautions, bringing my head back to the secret meeting with the Cocom. Would that I could share his calm. I call in my Oracle training to help me control my emotions. It's one of the first things we learn. The moment we let fear, anger, envy or greed take us over, the doors to the invisible world close.

"Blue Monkey will be there," I say, feeling dread in the pit of my stomach. Blue Monkey is a jealous troublemaker with a tongue so evil it's a lethal weapon. Always in her presence I feel the unpleasant tightening in my chest that tells me I am not safe, that someone envies me and means me harm. Blue Monkey loved Moon Eagle and had hopes of becoming his bride. She resented me before I even arrived in Chichen. She hoped to be chosen as Ix Chel's Oracle, but that honor went to me. I know she sees me as an obstacle to all her ambitions, including her dream of seeing her granddaughter, Thirteen Rabbit, rise to a position of power on Cuzamil. I have never done her any harm, but Blue Monkey sees my very existence as a personal affront. I don't deny that she is powerful, but she uses her gifts from the Goddess for her own advantage, which is something a true priestess would never do. During phases of the New Moon I have to be constantly alert to thwart her invisible spears of evil. I know when she is silently working against me because my sleep is disturbed by heart palpitations and dangerous creatures like rats, scorpions and poisonous snakes, which appear suddenly and are intent on harming me. Ix Chel protects me, and I counter Blue Monkey's efforts with *payche* root, prayer and ritual. And while I would never admit it to her because it would give her much satisfaction, Blue Monkey shakes me from my inner balance.

Jaguar Shield gives me a sympathetic look. Everyone knows Blue Monkey's enmity toward me.

"She is the wife of an elder. Everyone had to be invited. Look, don't worry about Blue Monkey. Worrying only helps her cause, not our cause."

"Our cause." Those two, lovely words give me strength.

"There is something I must say, brother. I know the Cocom must be told what happened when Blood Gatherer came to Water Lily's house. But I am not asking their permission to leave. I will never allow Nine Macaw to be sacrificed.

They will call me 'traitor.' They will not stand up to the New Order. This meeting is a formality only. I have no hope of changing their hearts or minds. I have already decided what I must do."

"When have I ever known you to be indecisive?" He stares into my eyes with a love that thrills my sorrowful heart. "Your fate is now my fate. I would have it no other way. But I think you might underestimate my clan. Many are also concerned about the New Order. They might not have the courage to defy the priests, but they will understand why you do what you do. Many love you, and respect you. You have brought us Cocom wealth and honor. I do not think they will all turn their backs on us."

That might be true, I think to myself, if the consequences of my defiance only fell on me. But all the Cocom will be punished for my actions. Even though they are a lineage of high nobles, the whole clan will lose favor with our seven leaders. No longer will they be invited to hold positions within the palace or government. All Cocoms will have to pay higher tribute and receive less than their present share of trade goods, which are distributed by our leaders according to loyalty and favor. I'm truly sorry for that, but material and political gains are not worth Nine Macaw's life. She has a destiny, and on it rests the survival of the women's island sanctuary under Chel rule. I know my sister, Heart of Water, has refused to allow human sacrifice on the island. She will no doubt support us, even though the Chel will face consequences for sheltering us. Trade agreements will be voided and the Chel will lose some economic advantages. I curse Blood Gatherer. My wretched brother knew exactly what he was doing when he chose Nine Macaw for the well, Goddess curse him!

Jaguar Shield and I drink tea together in companionable silence until the last golden rays of the setting sun surrender to the dove-gray evening. Bees, ever industrious, fly by to deliver their pollen before nightfall. Soon, we will be eating the honey of Cuzamil. It is the best in the Known World.

I feel Jaguar Shield's light touch on my arm and realize my thoughts have carried me away again. It seems to happen more often these days.

"It's time," he says. "Father Sun has returned to the Underworld."

Loud, pulsing drums and bellowing gourd horns in the plaza call everyone to the ballgame. Feasting will soon begin. Dancers will be lining up in neat rows, ready for their gyrations. Tonight, for the last time, Nine Macaw and Tree Orchid will dance with them. My heart aches when I remember the desperate, questioning look on Nine Macaw's doe-sad face when she asked me earlier today, "Na, does it hurt to drown?"

Jaguar Shield holds his thigh with one long hand and limps to the hearth to gather up pine sticks to light our way back. In the bed of cold ashes sits a brazen turkey hen. She fluffs her wings and sends gray powder flying. Jaguar Shield clucks at her in annoyance. He chooses three resinous pine sticks and slips them into his shoulder bag. I admire—no, I love—the way he moves with masculine grace and military precision.

At the doorway, he collects his wooden, claw-footed scepter of clan authority. He turns to me, bows, and with a wave of his hand towards the door, says calmly, "*Cox*"—let's go.

Just as we're leaving, we bump into his son, Smoking Frog, and his wife. I can tell immediately by their expressions that they are furious, and probably scared. Neither of them gives us the polite greeting for elders. Instead, Smoking Frog launches into his harangue.

"Father, we heard everything. You shouldn't be seen with this pond scum. It's bad for all of us."

"Step aside, boy," Jaguar Shield says mildly. "I make my own decisions and you are no one to insult Lady Jade Skirt, High Priestess and Oracle of Ix Chel, wife of my brother. She deserves only our respect and loyalty."

"Hah!" Smoking Frog shouts into my face. "Respect! I would just as soon bed a monkey! Let her take her own spawn into exile, but don't go with her. We Cocoms will have a bad enough time as it is, but if you go, too..." He is too overcome to continue. "She's a disgrace to her husband and his clan."

"*Poc*," pleads Jaguar Shield's daughter-in-law, "don't make things worse by being seen with her. Everyone knows she plans to run away. She doesn't care about any of us; she never did."

"Since when," scowls Jaguar Shield at his son, ignoring the woman, "do you conduct my affairs? Now step aside."

They both scowl at me. As I pass Smoking Frog, he sticks out his foot to trip me. I step aside, not even bothering to look at him, and I follow my brother-in-law. This is just the beginning, I think. If I let this runt rattle me, I'll be no good to Jaguar Shield at the gathering. I collect my emotions and tuck them into a small basket in my heart to deal with later.

There is a wide opening in the waist-high wall of the Cocom compound, and there we mount stone steps chipped into a large gray boulder. Generations of feet have worn the center of the steps into shallow bowls. In a few short strides we're on the crowded and noisy *sacbe*, the great white road that runs all the way to the Eastern Sea. As many as twenty people stroll shoulder to shoulder on the solid-surfaced, white-marl thoroughfare. It's no wonder it's packed. Tonight, our seven royal leaders are serving a great feast for all. Nobles and commoners will watch the ballgame that ends in a bloody sacrifice of the entire losing team. Costumed court musicians, troops of dancers, clowns, jugglers and acrobats walk among the crowd as they, too, make their way to the central plaza, where they will be performing for the crowds. Excitement runs high. There will be tobacco pipes and endless cups of sprouted corn beer for everyone. Slaves of the noble families have brewed and stirred their chest-high fermenting pots for days. For a moment I worry about Water Lily. Traditionally, a celebration like this would see her drunk in the first hour. Perhaps after the shock of today's news she will stay sober? Or is that just too much to hope for?

Delightful aromas of *copal* incense, roasted meats and steaming tamales fill the night air. But I'm much too nervous to have any appetite. I stay close to Jaguar Shield. The crowd is making me dizzy. Two sun-burnished men stroll alongside us on the *sacbe*. According to their scarred tattoos they are jade craftsmen. A raised string of round, carved beads decorates each right shoulder. As they approach, I feel their anticipation. The one closest to me, a spare man, has a hungry look in his eye.

"It's been too long since I've been to a good ballgame feast with a sacrifice," he remarks for his companion. "I hear three will go to Paradise tonight: two losers of the ballgame and a northern noble of Labna who was captured in battle."

The other craftsman shrugs his shoulders. "It must be hard to die in sacrifice, but then the reward for the Flowery Death is great. They are the ones who go directly to the Gods, isn't that so?"

I grimace and Jaguar Shield draws me away from the two men and their upsetting conversation. We walk faster and end up in step beside four red-painted, bare-breasted women who laugh and gossip as they walk. The heavy vanilla scent they wear nearly overpowers me and we walk a little faster to get ahead of them. It's a relief to get out of range of their perfume. I take a deep breath and smell hot corn tamales and honey-stewed plums, which are carried in baskets on the heads of men and women in front of us. The group is no doubt hoping to earn an extra cacao bean or two from those who can't bear to wait for the free feast.

On and off the *sacbe*, children of all ages dodge through the crowds, their parents following behind. A group stops and calls to friends to come and pick ripe plums from the trees by the *sacbe*. Generations ago, clan leaders planted the fruit trees along the route for children's pleasure and travelers' sustenance. I have to admit, the Chichen created a beautiful city, laid out with great foresight and maintained with an eye to art and beauty. That is one of the few things I will miss about the place that has been my home for more than half my life.

Jaguar Shield and I are close to the central plaza now. I can hear musicians from the temple of Kukulcan ring out a pounding tune on drums, flutes and horns. Night settles peacefully over Chichen. The Sky Wanderers begin to sparkle and glow in the sky. Above the rolling hillside the golden head of the moon rises. It makes me wish I was inside the temple of Ix Chel, greeting the moon with the other priestesses and not on my way to this clan meeting.

Under the now-waning moon, torch-bearing boy soldiers run along the great thoroughfare lighting the chest-high pine sticks that are driven into the ground lining the *sacbe*. Jaguar Shield nudges me to the side and we leave the *sacbe* through a cut in a low wall. We climb down chiseled steps and pause for a moment to watch the milling crowd below. Priests from the Temple of Fire simultaneously light blazes on the steps of each of the nine temples. The fire illuminates the white-tiled plaza. The gaping, open mouths of the stone masks are now visible against red temple walls. The sound of a conch shell cuts through the din, drawing all eyes to the top of the Temple of Kukulcan, where the white-robed priest gives the signal that the festivities are beginning. An ear-splitting roar of approval fills the air. The great throng flows to a platform in front of the dome-capped Observatory where the leaders of the seven noble families—representatives of the Gods—make a dramatic appearance. They are dressed in all their finery. Each man wears an impressively large jade pendant—no doubt intricately carved—around his neck, and around the waist each wears densely embroidered pelts of jaguar and puma. Not to be outdone, the women are wearing yellow dresses covered with embroidery. Their mantles are gossamer thin, and the quetzal feathers in their headdresses bob in the breeze. Even from this distance, I can see how impressive they appear. Against a backdrop of stars and the full moon, surrounded by blazing torches, the four men and three women pose for the people in front of a doorway made of stone columns.

"That's where you should be standing tonight," comments Jaguar Shield lifting his chin toward the women rulers.

He is so loyal! I smile up at him and say, "One day I will stand with Nine Macaw at Cuzamil in the Goddess's temple. That will be enough for me."

Musicians strike up a loud dirge. A long line of drummers beat out a monotonous rhythm. A red-robed priestess from the House of Pleasure stands in the center of the platform steps and blows the conch shell, signaling silence.

Mesmerized, the crowd hushes. The male leaders kneel like humble supplicants before shallow clay dishes. The music stops; only the steady drumbeat pierces the quiet. I feel the crowd take a deep, collective breath. Although I am not part of this ritual, I feel a tug of my own power by this sacred ritual. I close my eyes and whisper a prayer to my Goddess.

Slowly, deliberately, the four lords push their embroidered loincloths aside. Thousands roar when slowly, each exposes his genitals. Drums throb wildly now. Each of the four lords holds his flaccid penis in one hand. The priests hand them serrated stingray spines. At the top of the foreskin, already shredded from repeated blood offerings, they pierce their members nine times. Sanctified by their life force, drops of royal blood fall onto fig bark paper. Horns blare. There's another roll of the drums. The three women rulers step forward out of the shadows to kneel. The black-robed priests hand them each a stingray spine. Each exposes her tongue and pierces it nine times. Their sacred *chu'lel* falls into vessels lined with fig-bark paper. The crowd gives a collective sigh.

My brother steps forward. My gorge rises at the sight of him. How he must love this. He was always so self-important. I thought it was cute when he was a boy, but now I see how it drives him and corrupts him. He takes the bloodied paper. Then he and eight of his brother priests set fire to them with glowing coals. The flames are golden—a good omen, I think with professional detachment. The crowd murmurs with contentment. The nine priests stand in the smoke and raise their arms to the sky to declare that the Gods have received the offerings. An ear-splitting cheer rises up from the masses. Jaguar Shield and I stay quiet.

The blood-letting ritual is over. The seven leaders enter the great temple and the crowd breaks up to start the feast. As the royal musicians beat out a playful rhythm on their chest-high drums, Jaguar Shield and I make our way down to the plaza. I tap his arm and point toward Ix Chel's temple where a group of excited young dancers wearing round headdresses of marigolds are waiting to dance. Nine Macaw is there, wearing her newly woven blue-and-white dress. Even from this far away I can see her slumped against the wall looking miserable. Except for Tree Orchid, the other girls lean away from her, as if her condition of being Chac's chosen sacrifice is contagious.

It's nearly time for the clan meeting, and Jaguar Shield and I hurry as fast as we can without drawing attention to ourselves. We pass small fires where royal servants fill clay cups with fermented corn beer. People are piling their plates high with steaming turkey-and-dog tamales wrapped in corn husks. We nearly make it across the plaza when someone thrusts plates of food in our hands and then we have to stop to eat the sweetened amaranth-seed tamales and drink a cup of jasmine-scented chocolate. It tastes like sawdust in my mouth. I'm so nervous about the clan meeting. I force myself to smile at the people beside me and then Jaguar Shield pulls us away, saying something polite about how we must look for our family members.

All the talk around us is of the ballgame that will start soon. There will be two players on each team. Losers will be sacrificed. If no player manages to score with a bounce of the rubber ball into the stone ring high overhead, all the players will live to see another day. In that event, my resourceful brother has two war captives ready for sacrifice. The Gods must have their sacrifices—or is it the people who need the blood and the violence? My heart sinks at the thought of all these people cheering at the senseless deaths, believing the Gods delight in this. It is the deepest corruption of our beliefs, but the New Order rules here now.

I try not to think about the sacrifice, but as we jostle our way through the crowd I can't help remembering the first festival I witnessed the heart sacrifice. Atop the temple, the heart-taker plunged his obsidian blade into the prisoner's blue-painted chest. Then he smeared warm blood over the face of the War God's image and stuffed the victim's still-beating heart into the gaping mouth. The poor wretch's mutilated body was tossed down the steps like a discarded corn doll. Priests waited at the bottom and they chopped up the body and distributed arms, legs and feet to the nobles. It's considered a tribute to the sacrifice's nobility and courage to have a noble feast on his sacred remains. The feet are the special prize reserved for the warrior who took him in battle. The sacrifice was a horrifying and gruesome thing to witness, and it left me feeling depressed at the perversion of all the Goddess teaches. My heart grows sick at the thought of it happening again tonight. I can't leave Chichen soon enough!

"Slow down!" Jaguar Shield says, catching my arm, "You're practically running!'"

A few moments later, we're slipping past the Temple of Kukulcan. It's a massive place. Many *tuns* ago, I counted the steps to calm myself as I ascended to my first oracular ceremony in Chichen. Each of the staircases leads to a door that opens to a four-sided square temple at the summit. I knew the architects, engineers and astronomers who built the Temple of the Plumed Serpent. How they labored, planned and counseled for many seasons to devise a structure that twice each *tun*—at equinox and solstice—creates a remarkable play of light and shadow to mark our planting and harvest times. As Father Kin descends into the Underworld, a diamondback snake shadow undulates down the west staircase until it joins the serpent's head at the bottom. It's longer than ten men, a marvel to see. The snake's pointed fangs and long tongue flicker impotently at the crowds.

Behind the Temple of Kukulcan an enormous circle of elder women dance shoulder to shoulder to the thrumming beat of the *tikul*. I love to dance. I wish I was carefree and could join in. They are clad in identical orange-and-yellow mantles. In the firelight, they look like a flock of birds.

Now we pass the Observatory and come upon the Temple of the Eagle Warriors. Soldiers of the Eagle Society link arms and sway in unison around the high platform of the three-storied structure. Jaguar Shield points proudly to my grandson. Jaguar Paw is standing tall and straight as a sapling. He doesn't see us as we quietly slip into the shadows behind the temple. The cave is nearby.

Suddenly, a palace guard steps out from behind a column. He holds up his right hand to stop us and holds up a torch to see our faces.

"Is all well with you?" he asks with all formality and politeness to his *na-com*. He looks at us curiously.

"All is well," Jaguar Shield replies with equal formality. We are close to the cave, but we can't allow the guard to see where we're going. I breathe in deeply and search for the center of Ix Chel's power in me. I find it readily and I use it to spread a pall of confusion over the guard. He looks uncertain for a moment and then turns away from us in a panic. It won't last long, but when it passes he will forget he has seen us. Jaguar Shield and I dart into the grove behind the Temple.

The ability to cast a glamour is a rare gift bestowed by the Goddess. My mother was able to do it, as was my grandmother. We are sorcerers. But we can only cast a glamour when She allows. One day, I will pass on the knowledge to Nine Macaw.

"Well done," whispers Jaguar Shield.

We follow a well-trodden foot path into a grove of red, peeling chacah trees. It's very dark, and we stumble a few times on tree roots, but we don't dare light a torch. We hear the call of a night bird and Jaguar Shield answers with the same call. Then his grandson appears out of the shadows, bows his head and leads us down another path. In a few moments I see a few other men and women of the Cocom lineage silently making their way down the darkened trail to the secret gathering. A strong wind rustles the tree branches. A flock of night birds screeches at us. It might be my nerves, but the omens warn of trouble.

At the mouth of the cave, three young Cocom soldiers painted black look carefully at our faces. Recognizing us, they let us pass into the cave. A few steps later, a young clan member brushes us with branches of the *tzib che* tree while she whispers a prayer to protect us from the evil winds of the *alux*—dwarf-like spirits who guard the Great Mother's caves. Jaguar Shield and I reach into our jaguar-pelt shoulder bags and drop a pinch of *copal* with a few corn seeds into a stone bowl as an offering to the *alux*. The capricious cave spirits will be well-appeased tonight.

I search for my brother-in-law's comforting hand and he gives it a reassuring squeeze as we advance into the cave. He stops to light a stick of pine from a lamp flame. They meet each other with a low sizzle. Down hand-hewn stone steps that have carried generations of people into the womb of the Great Mother, this cave is directly under the Temple of Ix Chel. I should feel reassured by that proximity, but I don't feel anything but dread as we descend. We find our way into the low, fire-lit room and we are greeted quietly by the dozen or so Cocom who have already arrived. I smell coconut oil burning in clay lamps. Their light makes the shadows prance over the dripping walls. In the center of the circle, a hand-carved stone bowl collects the slow drip of water from the roof of the cave. This is the sacred life essence—the *chu'lel*—of the Mother Goddess. Like the others have already done, Jaguar Shield and I dip our right hands in the water and anoint our foreheads with a "U," the sacred symbol of Ix Chel. As the water touches my head, I am suffused with Her presence. Ai, why do I ever worry? Ix Chel is with me always! She reminds me that I am not just a sentimental old woman here to beg for the life of her granddaughter; I am Her High Priestess and Oracle. The Cocom will hear me.

Four of the oldest men take seats in the four directions. In the very center, the fifth direction, and the position of honor, sits Flesh Flower, the oldest female of the clan. She's made herself comfortable on a blue, quilted-cotton mat. Once a famous beauty, she is now a mound of sagging skin over fragile bones. Stringy wisps of white hair parted here and there show her balding scalp. A white mustache sprouts above her wrinkled upper lip. I've known her for many *tuns* and can remember when her face did not look like a dried plum. Her daughter hands her a three-month-old infant, swaddled and asleep, and Flesh Flower holds the child with practiced ease in her lap. I know the story of this child. On a whim, Flesh Flower purchased the orphaned baby boy in the slave market. Flesh Flower's children were scandalized, but now they seem to have accepted it. The daughter hands her a boar's bladder filled with milk from a tamed deer to give the child when he wakes.

Flesh Flower was at one time greatly revered for her dream visions, which blessed the Cocom women with several unique weaving patterns that have been much sought after by the royal household. The old woman spots me now and she smiles warmly and places her hand over her heart in greeting. How wonderful to be greeted by a friendly face amongst the Cocoms. I touch the earth and then put my right hand to my forehead in greeting. As Oracle, I take my honored place in the center, next to Flesh Flower. She squeezes my hand.

Once I'm seated, I look around the circle, making eye contact with the Cocom to try to gauge the mood. Most give me a careful nod of greeting. I am still flush with the confidence of the High Priestess. But when my eyes search the shadows by the back wall to see who is seated there, I lock eyes with my nemesis, Blue Monkey. Her gaze is bitter and spiteful. I nod politely, but she proudly lifts her long chin and turns away from me. She will never forgive me for being wife to Moon Eagle, or for her being passed over by the Red Hand Society—the premiere women's school of healing arts. Although I had nothing to do with that, she blames me. And then, to make matters worse, Blue Monkey actually claims to have been one of *my* teachers! It's a ridiculous lie; we were both girls when she lived on the women's island. But she's an irascible troublemaker who constantly tries to undermine my authority in the temple of the Goddess and the House of Healing.

Oh, I wish we could just get this over with! Being this close to Blue Monkey gives me hives. I force my hands away from my jade necklace. I can't show her how she rattles me.

The Cocom are still trickling in. I steady myself and look for Jaguar Shield, who is seated near a cousin. Just the sight of him calms me. I glance over at Flesh Flower's little infant and take comfort in his contented sleep.

The cave is crowded with almost two dozen perfumed men and women fresh from their evening steam baths. Jaguar Shield, clan leader during this transit of Venus, stands and taps his claw-footed scepter three times on the cave floor. The cavern grows quiet except for the drip, drip, drip of the sacred water.

"Brothers and Sisters, may it be well with you."

Many answer, "And so with you, Brother."

He clears his throat. "You know why we are here. Yesterday, Blood Gatherer came to the house of Water Lily. He has claimed the life of our Nine Macaw to be the bride of Chac."

"That stinker! Who dropped him on his head as a kid?" mutters Flesh Flower. People are chuckling.

Jaguar Shield smiles and continues. "Before our corn is planted, when the serpent crawls down the steps of the pyramid of Kukulcan, he would send Nine Macaw's soul to The Place of No Evil."

"This is an honor for the Cocom?" asks one of the women.

I stand and face a sea of impassive faces. "He would have us believe it's an honor," I say.

"What about the girl's calendar day, and her written destiny? She is to rule Cuzamil! That is a great honor for the Cocom."

"Yes," I say, nodding, "and it is the will of Ix Chel that it be so. Blood Gatherer knows this. Nevertheless, he would give her to Chac."

"This affects everyone in this clan and Chichen, too, for that matter," says one of the men.

"He was there when her calendar destiny was announced," says another from the back of the cave. "Both the Rainbow Throne and the Ancestral Stone are promised to her. What is he up to?"

Out of the dark shadows, Blue Monkey raises a fist and hisses, "What are you complaining about? This is a great honor for one of the Cocom! Nine Macaw will ascend to the Gods!"

I am disheartened, but not surprised, to hear others agree with her. Blue Monkey has her supporters here.

Hand out, palm facing the group, Jaguar Shield silences the muttering. He speaks:

"Brothers and Sisters, I say we can't allow Blood Gatherer to take Nine Macaw. As her family, it's our duty to see that this special child is allowed to fulfill her destiny. To assure her destiny is to guarantee our own."

"Nine Macaw has an exalted destiny," Blue Monkey says agreeably. "She is to be sent to the Gods as a bride while she is young and fresh from their garden of souls. There are other Cocom who can ascend to the Rainbow Throne and serve the Goddess on Cuzamil." She shoots me a look of triumph. She is thinking of course of her own granddaughter.

"I disagree," I say quickly, before anyone else can answer her. "I have seen in dreams and visions that the child's true destiny is to serve the Goddess. She is already showing signs of being a gifted healer. One day she will be a great Oracle and ruler in service to Ix Chel, and this will benefit the Cocom. Nine Macaw has the Sight! Already the Goddess favors her with dream visions even though she has not yet started her moon cycles."

There is interested murmuring. An Oracle from the Cocom lineage will bring great wealth and honor to the clan. An earnest woman's voice rings out from the gray shadows. "That's right! Nine Macaw was born with a caul over her face. They're all gifted with the Sight and live in service to the sick. Everyone knows that," she adds officiously, waving her right hand in the air.

Another voice calls out, "I don't believe it is her fate to die in the Well of Sacrifice. Our ancestors taught that to serve the people is to serve the Gods. She doesn't have to die to please the Rain God."

I take a step toward Jaguar Shield and speak again, feeling all eyes on me. "I have a plan. It's a hard one, but I see no other way."

"Well, tell us. Speak your mind, Jade Skirt," calls out a deep male voice.

"I will leave Chichen with the child. We will go to my Chel people in Cuzamil and Nine Macaw will begin her training at once." My words are followed by a chorus of whispers and gasps. "She should have already gone," I continue, "but she was too sick during the last *tun* with the flux epidemic."

Now I have said it. I am going to defy the priests. Sympathizing with me was one thing; supporting my rebellion is fraught with dangers for each of them, and we all know it. I also know the gossips have already spread the news that I am getting ready to leave, so I can't believe anyone is really that surprised. Still, eyebrows lift; tattooed foreheads furrow.

"You can't just run away!" says an old soldier.

"And what else should she do?" scolds Flesh Flower.

A raven-haired grandmother with thin braids speaks: "Lady, you realize what this means."

"Exile," I say simply. The word sits heavy in the circle. "Nowhere will I or any member of my family join you in singing and dancing, ever again. But Sister, I have no choice. Nine Macaw must live to serve Ix Chel. I am the Oracle. I know this to be the truth. Therefore, whatever the consequence to me and my family, I must face it, because I serve Her."

"This is foolishness!" squawks Blue Monkey. "There are many other qualified girls who can serve Ix Chel and who can be Her Oracle! Why do you think you and you alone are her loyal servant?"

There is a moment of uncomfortable silence. I sigh. I will answer honestly, but it doesn't matter, because Blue Monkey won't want to believe me.

"The Goddess has shown me this: if Nine Macaw does not take the Rainbow Throne, it will be the end of the Chel rulers on the women's island, and the end of our sanctuary. The Rainbow Throne will fall into the hands of another lineage, and in a generation the War God will rule there, too. I am Her Oracle, and Ix Chel has shown me the future without this child. Many people will suffer if Cuzamil turns to the War God. I cannot let it happen."

"And what is the point of this sacrifice to Chac?" Jaguar Shield adds. "Think of what the Goddess's sanctuary, Her temples and healers mean to us Cocoms, and see that this is far more important than one Fertility Festival."

An elder Cocom cousin with spiral tattoos across his chest and an unruly hair knot stands to speak. "Jade Skirt's marriage to our brother Moon Eagle has brought us wealth and prestige. When her sister, Heart of Water, arranged for her dowry to give our clan control of the salt and honey trade, our influence as nobles grew. That alone is reason to save the child's life. If the Chels lose control of Cuzamil, we may lose the trade that has made us wealthy and influential here in Chichen and provinces beyond."

I see heads nodding. No one wants to lose their wealth or status. But then one of Blue Monkey's supporters speaks: "There is another daughter of Water Lily. Red Earth can assume the Rainbow Throne. Then the Cocom are doubly honored by Nine Macaw's sacrifice and Red Earth's position as heir to the Chel lineage."

I try to hide my annoyance. "Red Earth is not blessed with the gifts," I say. "She will not be qualified to serve."

"And again I say there are others who can do the job!" Blue Monkey says with some exasperation.

"But she already explained why it can only be Nine Macaw," says a man.

Blue Monkey sniffs. "Well, if she says so," she says, skepticism and sarcasm in her voice. I am having a hard time breathing.

Jaguar Shield comes to my rescue. "The Oracle does not have to explain herself twice," he says sternly to Blue Monkey.

"But Jade Skirt will ruin us all!" Blue Monkey shouts. "To refuse to send a virgin into Chac's Well is a serious offense now. We will all be accomplices in a state crime! This will not go well for us."

Flesh Flower bends her head to one side, squints up at me and says, "Perhaps there is another solution. You have the right to send an orphan in her place. What about that—what's her name—Tree Orchid? The one whose mother died at birth and then her father committed suicide. Send her to the well in Nine Macaw's place."

I have to fight a wave of nausea. I could never let them take Tree Orchid. "Sister," I say as calmly as I can, "I am opposed to all sacrifice, no matter who it is."

There. I've said it. There's a shocked silence. This is more rebellion than the Cocom expected from Ix Chel's High Priestess. In the beginning I was outspoken about my feelings about the Flowery Death, but as the New Order gained power I kept my views more and more to myself. Blue Monkey doesn't even bother speaking up. She will let me hang myself. I can practically feel her glee.

"Tree Orchid will be indispensable to Nine Macaw when she is High Priestess and Queen," I say, trying to get back to my more persuasive argument. "The Great Mother has shown me that Nine Macaw needs Tree Orchid at her side."

"That's convenient," Blue Monkey mutters loudly.

"And," I continue, ignoring her, "Tree Orchid's own special gift will make her the Bird Oracle of Cuzamil one day. So no, I will not send the orphan into the waters of the Underworld to save Nine Macaw. I will leave Chichen with both girls—with my whole family—and we will go serve the Goddess in Cuzamil."

"But, Sister, if you do this, you can never return," says Flesh Flower, rocking the infant.

I'm surprised when my voice cracks. "I did not plan to return."

Another wave of discontent. Bodies shift, heads turn. Suddenly, the cavern feels too cramped.

"And what happens to the pilgrim's House of Healing? Who will supervise the Dream Temple? What about the Oracle's office right here in Chichen? The school of midwifery? Who will take over your duties if you leave us?" challenges a female voice.

"I understand you are concerned, as you should be," I say, trying to meet each one's gaze. Most look away. "This is a shock for all of us. Let me answer your questions. As to the House of Healing, my assistant, Turtle Star, will take over my duties right away. She has been at my side many *tuns*. I trust her completely. When I was absent or ill, she took my place inside the sacred chambers of the Oracle. My family will come with me and we will start a new life with the

Chel. It will be a loss for each of us, but we are all willing to do what we must to serve the Goddess."

Before I can answer her, another says, "This will be a substantial loss for us in prestige and wealth."

An elder man raises his cane to speak. "I agree that Jade Skirt has brought us wealth and prestige, but if she defies the priests now, all that will be reversed. No longer will we be high nobles with the same favors as before."

Another says, "Right. We stand to lose much more than we would gain from Nine Macaw's future position on the island. Would we sacrifice our wealth and position for the sake of a girl?"

Their bounding waves of greed and fear wash over me. My hands nervously seek out my jade-and-crystal necklace.

"She's not just any girl!" I insist. "She is Ix Chel's chosen one. She alone can save the sacred island. Widows, orphans, barren wives and those who love other women must have a refuge. Our women must be trained as midwives, star watchers, bird oracles and seers and learn the ancient secrets of the old Gods." I watch their faces, trying not to look at Blue Monkey. "She will hold the Ancestral Stone in her hands. As a Cocom-Chel, Nine Macaw's future is your future, too."

"This is not a cowardly decision Jade Skirt makes!" interrupts Jaguar Shield. "The Chel lineage rule of Cuzamil has had threats and challenges to their sovereignty for generations. Yet, even as the New Order gains more power daily, the Chel have maintained the island as the stronghold and home of the Moon Goddess. The Cocom lineage has a responsibility to Ix Chel, who has blessed us with her favors for generations."

There is uncomfortable silence. Greed wars with fear. They resent me for placing this problem at their feet—a problem that has no easy solution.

"Can you assure us that the dowry contracts your sister made with us will be honored?" says one of the old soldiers. "Will we maintain control of the honey and salt trade?"

"How do you know that Nine Macaw will honor that contract when she is grown to womanhood?" asks another with an accusatory tone.

I respond, "I assure you, she will. She is Cocom, granddaughter of Moon Eagle!"

An old herbalist speaks up. "I say that along with the honey and salt, we should demand trading rights for dried fish from the island. We should be compensated somehow. You know we will lose prestige with the leaders and have to pay higher tributes and taxes for this insult."

"This isn't right!" shouts Blue Monkey, standing. "As Moon Eagle's wife, your first duty should be to his clan, not the Chels."

"Blue Monkey, hear me now." I stare into her cold, menacing eyes. "I am High Priestess and Oracle of Ix Chel and my first duty will always be to the Goddess, as should yours be as one of Her priestesses!"

She glares at me but then looks away first. Hah! I know she will rise up against me again, but in this moment I have the upper hand.

A cross-eyed, portly man wrapped in a white mantle leans forward and shakes his fist. Does he remember that I treated the burns on his wife's arms a *tun* past and saved her from terrible scarring?

"Blue Monkey is right. I say Jade Skirt should set her feelings for Nine Macaw and Cuzamil aside. She is a Cocom now and her familial duty should be to her husband's lineage, not the Chels."

The wife of Jaguar Shield's nephew stands and glares at me. When she was a maiden I made her a remedy for a chronic skin condition.

"It's not right! We Cocoms lose our Oracle, our prestige as nobles, a promising young healer, a soldier, and the Ancestral Stone!"

A tall, thin woman of the second-age stands to speak. She has never been friendly. Now she speaks without looking at me:

"There's something else to say. Water Lily has been breaking council law for a long time. She's a drunk and we all know it. Jade Skirt may be Oracle, but her family already brings trouble and dishonor to the Cocom."

The oldest male member of the clan, Seven Lizard, stands up with effort, and asks. "So do you reason it's a good idea to put Water Lily through more shame, more trouble? Does she want to leave Chichen? A shock like this? She may die from drink, and then you will be responsible."

Before I can answer, Flesh Flower raises her hand. "Sister, my heart is sick. We have come to love you as our own. I tell you all there is something hidden here. The heart-takers are up to something. I feel it in my bones."

I take in a long, deep breath. Yes, I think. That is what my bones are telling me, too. Blood Gatherer is up to something.

"Jade Skirt has served us well for what is it? Two-times-twenty *tuns*?" she continues. "We Cocoms and all of Chichen have grown richer on her service and the trade she brought with her marriage contract. I say we let her go freely to meet the destiny she has chosen."

Blue Monkey crosses her arms over her chest, and says, "Never. I will never agree."

"Is there no other way?" asks a younger member of the clan who sits against the wall.

I look over at Jaguar Shield and some of his male *chu'lel* passes into me. I take a deep breath and cast my gaze around the room, catching as many eyes as I can.

"In counsel with Jaguar Shield," I say, "we think this is the best plan. I alone cannot promise you control of the dried fish trade. I must seek counsel with my sister, Heart of Water, but I will make a strong case that you deserve to be compensated for the inconvenience of my exile."

"This is not a selfish, thoughtless act," Flesh Flower says. "Listen, all of you, Jade Skirt cares about our women—about all women of the realm. You should all search your hearts."

Another says, "Blue Monkey is right. There is no greater shame than to run from sacrifice. Many of us here have lost loved ones to the Gods. I am one of those. But we didn't run!"

"Cousins, I can accept your scorn," I say, wanting this meeting to be over. "I can accept exile." I pause and look deeply into their faces. "I cannot accept that Nine Macaw will die in sacrifice. I do not expect your approval. I do not need your consent. When I became an apprentice Oracle, I swore that I would defend the island for the Chels. My sister, Heart of Water, is getting old and longs for rest. Nine Macaw and Tree Orchid are needed."

"I say we can trust Moon Eagle's wife to look after our business interests," says a cousin.

"I say our sister has chosen courageously," says a woman near the back wall. "She has chosen exile and shame for what she believes is a greater purpose. I say the Great Mother wants us to help her, and Ix Chel will look after us when Jade Skirt is gone."

Jaguar Shield speaks: "I agree with you, Sister. That is why I will accompany Jade Skirt and her family to Cuzamil. I believe the Goddess wants us to protect them."

There is a gasp from nearly everyone in the cavern. Between one heartbeat and the next, Jaguar Shield has publicly cast his fate with mine.

"*Om bey!* This gets worse by the moment!" shouts Blue Monkey. Her fiery eyes pierce us both. "I will have no part in this heresy—this shame!" She stands up and forces her way to the exit. "Damn you both! May you stand at the river and never cross! You should suffer for the shame you bring down on the Cocom!" She stomps out, to the shock of all of us. No one has ever walked out of a lineage meeting. But now two men and a woman stand up. They are friends of Blue Monkey. They, too, cast scornful looks at me and Jaguar Shield. Without a word, they stomp out.

Cocoms turn their heads from one to another and whisper. Then, like chattering squirrels fighting over a dry-season stash of *ramon*, they all speak at once. Heads bob and hands dance about. Several others look ready to stand and walk out.

I must get control again. Deep in the center of my abdomen, I search for the Oracle's seat of power. I focus on the Divine Feminine Power within, Her *chu'lel*, and feel it rise up like a fire. I breathe deeply three times, focus my inner strength on Ix Chel, tuck my right hand under my mantle and turn it three times in a circle. My fingers flick at the people around me. When forces spin in an unfavorable direction, it brings a group back to harmony. This is a special magic of the Red Hand Society. I never use the magic hand easily, but never have I needed it this much.

It starts to work. The circle of elders grows quiet. Heads and hands stop moving. Obediently, faces turn in unison to the front of the cavern where I stand. They wait for me to speak.

"Brothers and Sisters, hear me now. It will be for the last time. Please believe that I never meant you or the Cocom to come to harm, but I am sickened by the heart takers." Words I have longed to say for many *tuns* now fly from my lips like an arrow springing from a taut bow. "Sacrifice is murder, not worship! It does not please the Gods to see us defile and dismember each other." Jaguar Shield tries to signal me to stop speaking on this topic, but I don't want to censor myself any more.

"The priests of the New Order are lying to us. Blood runs like a river from our temples. Infants and innocent children are drowned, beheaded. Nobles are cut down in their prime, their wives are abandoned and their children left to grow up fatherless." My voice cracks. "The priests peel off the skin of these poor souls, step inside and parade about for days to celebrate their piety. It is an abomination, a perversion. We keep silent, living in fear that if we speak up these atrocities will be done to us or our loved ones! This does our people no justice. And it disrespects our Gods! Our Gods have never been malnourished. Never before did They demand our lives. This is a way for the priests to gain power, to keep us living in fear. As long as you serve the New Order, you are serving its priests, not our Gods!"

Jaguar Shield steps in front of me. He grips my wrist in his hand. "Please. We are not here to discuss the New Order. That is a subject we should address one day, but not tonight."

"Cousin, Jaguar Shield, you're wrong. This is important and it is a good time to know her mind," says Flesh Flower. "Speak, Sister. Tell us what is in your heart."

Murmurs of agreement bounce off the walls of the cave. Frustrated, Jaguar Shield steps behind me.

Perhaps for the last time I face my husband's lineage. "I was raised on Cuzamil Island, home of the Great Mother. Never once has She asked as tribute for the hearts or severed heads of Her created children. Three generations ago, when my grandmother founded the Rainbow Throne, the Goddess appeared to her in a dream and said very clearly, 'Do not bring me the beating hearts of those I created. I do not require your flesh and blood to live. My sustenance is in the cosmos. I live by starlight. Do not kill each other for Me. There will be rain. There will be drought. There will be peace. There will be war. There will be good *tuns* and evil *tuns*. You cannot control the will of the Gods by offering us the lives We created to love Us.'"

Many heads nod in agreement. Others glower at me. Murmurs of approval and rejection resound through the cavern. At last, Flesh Flower speaks.

"She speaks well. I knew her grandmother, a wise and benevolent leader of women who ruled by her dreams and visions from the Goddess. Soon, I, too, will leave Chichen for Cuzamil to spend the last of my days in peaceful union with other women. I, too, love the Goddess Ix Chel, and frankly, I have never been in favor of sacrificial killing. If our *chu'lel* is in our blood, then it is enough of a gift to the Gods. Throwing children into Chac's Well is something we never did in my day. No one starved then. Why have we allowed this to happen to us?"

Old Seven Lizard stands up again with difficulty and speaks. "Cocoms, these are troubled times." He pauses to rub the few gray hairs on his long, narrow chin. "The priests have told us there is a new way, this New Order. They say that to worship the Gods properly, we must feed Them with our own blood, our beating hearts and our children. In this way will we prosper and defeat our enemies. I believe them. They are the ones who communicate directly with the Gods. Jade Skirt and her grandmother belong to a line of priestesses. Not all of us have dream visions. I, for one, do not and never have. I was taught from early that we must obey the priests, who communicate directly with the Gods. If we do not do as the priests say, the Gods will be angry. We will suffer mass destruction, starvation, drought and floods."

A strong, male voice speaks from the shadows. "As children, we were taught in the School of Firm Hearts and Strong Minds that our greatest honor in this life is to die the Flowery Death. For this we are rewarded by going directly to Paradise. Honestly, I am not sure; but who am I to challenge the priests? They have the sacred books. They have the lamp of knowledge. They read the calendars. They watch the Sky Wanderers. Surely they know more than I."

"It's a lie," I tell him sadly, knowing he will not believe me. "My own husband was the very first war captive to die the Flowery Death of the Putun priests, but he did not go directly to Paradise. In my visions as Oracle I saw him with an entire army of dead warriors. They were suffering, lost and searching for their heads, their arms, legs and feet." There are shocked gasps.

"Moon Eagle, like others who died such horrible deaths, became a lost soul, a wandering spirit. I know these things to be true, for like the priests, I, too, have the lamp of knowledge that is bestowed by Ix Chel to Her priestesses. Each of you must search your own heart. I have searched mine and it tells me that sacrifice is wrong. It is not holy. Ix Chel, the Great Mother, is as powerful as Tezcatlipoca, War God, or the One True God, Hunabku. She and Her consort Itzámna created this world and all the creatures in it. Ix Chel is the Goddess of Love and abhors killing. It is She who makes the rain with Chac. I am Her direct representative on earth. I, too, abhor killing."

"Hmmph," says a Cocom man. "If Ix Chel is as powerful as Tezcatlipoca and if She does not sanction sacrifice, then why has She allowed the War God and the New Order to gain control? Answer that if you can!"

"The truth is, Brother Cocom, *you* have given the New Order this power. You have believed lies told by hypocrites."

"Are you saying our leaders are wrong? They follow the priests."

"The leaders never lose their children to the Gods," Jaguar Shield says. "They keep orphans in the palace and dispatch them regularly for sacrifice."

From the depths of the cave a Cocom asks, "You don't believe that the life of a person, the sacred *chu'lel,* is what the Gods require?"

"I believe that the soul given to us by the Gods is in our blood. It is enough that we all offer our blood to them. The men by piercing their sex, their ears and their tongues. Women offer this vital essence to the Gods when they menstruate. Nine Macaw will grow into a woman whose moon blood will be sufficient offering to the Gods, as it has always been. Like all women she will join her life-power with the soul of the Earth Mother. What sense does it make to destroy her life or to destroy the life essence of any woman? Women are the vessels of life that brought all of us into existence. Without our sacred vessels there is no life and there would be no one to nourish the Gods. To kill a virgin is to kill life. Do you not see that?"

Silence. Blank stares. A few women nod their heads.

Jaguar Shield is at my side. He pounds the scepter three times to get everyone's attention. "Let it be known to all present here and for all generations to come. I do not love sacrifice. I do not believe the priests. I think our leaders have been misled by fear and a lack of faith in our Gods. From this day forward, I, nobleman, soldier and leader of soldiers, stand with Jade Skirt Chel Cocom against the New Order."

I had not expected that! Jaguar Shield's statement causes a great stir in the cavern. Grumbles, shouts, low murmurs, bobbing heads amongst the shadows, wide eyes are everywhere.

A long silence follows Jaguar Shield's proclamation. Then, the military teacher from the boy's longhouse stands up. He speaks authoritatively. Tallest of all the men in the clan, his loud, commanding voice silences everyone:

"Our brother speaks well. So does Jade Skirt. I am no friend of the New Order, but I have learned to live with it. Yet, if I am honest with myself, I, too, am conflicted."

"You are both entitled to an opinion even though it differs from ours," says Seven Lizard. "Our leaders do not persecute those who disagree with the New Order, but we nobles agreed a generation ago that those who refuse sacrifice will be the unknown and the unborn. Think hard on what that really means. That is my advice to both of you. Once made, your decision can never be reversed. There will be no forgiveness."

I am growing frustrated and impatient. A sudden cold tingling in my spine sends a warning that trouble is afoot outside the cave. But I have none of the skunk-smelling root with me. While the Cocom elders argue among themselves, time is running out for me. The feasting and drinking in the plaza above us must be well underway. Where are Water Lily and the children? I touch my jade-bead necklace and sense my daughter's agitation.

"Enough talk," I say when one of the elders finally winds down. "It's time to decide if you sanction our plan or not."

A grumble rises from the group. "Too little time to decide," complains one old woman.

Another says, "I feel like we're being forced into something."

Flesh Flower takes command. "Cocoms! I've eaten a few beans and I see wisdom in this plan. If Nine Macaw does not follow her aunt's rule at Cuzamil, we will surely lose control of the salt and honey trade." Like a good orator, she lets that sink in. "Furthermore, we women need our sanctuary and the Chels have preserved its neutrality and prestige for generations. The priests of the New Order have no respect, no love, for our Goddess. Does it not strike you as strange that they would choose the very child who is to inherit Her throne? Let Jade Skirt take her daughter, the three children, the Ancestral Stone and leave here for the good of all."

A few voice agreement. I'm grateful to Flesh Flower for her words.

It's customary to take time to pray silently before making a clan decision. A timekeeper hits a turtle shell with the palm of his hand. Steady, hollow beats fill the cavern until it is time to decide.

Silently, I bow my head and pray to Ix Chel. She whispers to me: *Whatever happens, whatever the vote, I will protect you. Have no fear.*

I am filled with gratitude. Carried away in my reverie, it takes me a few moments to realize that the drumming has stopped. The cavern is silent. Only the drip, drip, drip of water disturbs the veil of quiet. Then my husband's brother, Jaguar Shield, stands in the center of the cavern.

"Those who support Jade Skirt's plan to take Water Lily, Nine Macaw, Red Earth, Tree Orchid and Jaguar Paw to Cuzamil, move to this side of the cavern." He points with his right hand. "Those opposed, move to the other side." He motions with his left hand.

There is a creaking of bones and a bit of groaning as stiff joints move. Then there is a shuffle of feet as the Cocom elders choose their side. My heart sinks. Only three stand on the right: Flesh Flower, an old soldier and an elderly woman. All the others stand against me.

"I see." I stare at the ground then raise my face. The expressions of my husband's clan show a mix of anxiety, sadness and anger. A few look at me with expressions of genuine disgust.

"I am sorry for you both," announces Moon Eagle's brother-in-law. "Jade Skirt, you are no longer our sister. Jaguar Shield you are no longer our brother. We do not know you."

"You are dog shit," echoes from the back.

"Monkey spit," shouts another.

"I spit on your shadow!" says another.

"You must reconsider!" says the red-painted woman.

"Which route will you take?" asks a *nacom* standing against us. "Surely, you know, you must have some protection these days. I hear there is a brutal gang of thieves operating just north of here."

Jaguar Shield looks directly into the eyes of his fellow soldier. "We will travel through lands of those who will be favorable to our cause. I cannot tell you more than that."

"Stay away from the land of the Tzul and the Xiu, our old enemies," the man advises. "The Xiu would not even give water to a dying Cocom."

The woman who stands with Flesh Flower pats my arm. "Lady, may you meet only straight and flat roads."

"May the Great Mother accompany you all and watch over your every step," says a tearful Flesh Flower. "May there always be chocolate in your pot. May all the eight thousand Gods forgive you. May your ancestors forgive you."

"Wherever you go," says the old man beside Flesh Flower, "whatever happens to you, may your *nopal* flourish." He lays a hand on Jaguar Shield's shoulder.

The others hear these blessings. And then—one by one—they turn their backs on us.

Just like that, we are exiles.

10

Soldiers are waiting to arrest us the moment we step out of the cave. There are four of them wearing mantles from the royal household. They brandish fat wooden clubs and long, sharp spears and they surround me and Jaguar Shield. Everything happens quickly. I feel Jaguar Shield tensing for a fight and before I can lay a restraining hand on his arm Snake Woman emerges from the shadows. She is of the Pech lineage, an old friend who has recently risen to the high office of one of the seven rulers of Chichen. I knew her from our early days at Cuzamil, when we were both young noblewomen in training. She is no friend to me now.

"Jade Skirt Chel Cocom, Jaguar Shield Cocom Tesecum, you are summoned to appear before the council of leaders tomorrow at dawn."

As a young girl, she had the worst complexion and when it cleared up, she was scarred forever. Deep pits dot her otherwise lovely features.

"But, revered Lady, Snake Woman," I protest, "I am about to retire for the evening. Can it wait until the morning?"

She gives me a scornful look. "This is not an invitation, Jade Skirt. It is a command. Be wise. Do not resist."

Blue Monkey! She must have gone immediately to the *halach uinic* to report what happened in the cave. She calls me a traitor, yet she broke one of our most sacred vows to keep secret what happens in a clandestine lineage gathering. The soldiers take a step closer, menacing.

"You dare to treat our High Priestess like a common criminal?" Jaguar Shield comes to my defense. Quick as a snake, a soldier raps him on the head with his club. *Om bey!* Blood gushes from the wound, but it was not a hard enough strike to knock my love unconscious. Thank you, Goddess.

Could this night get any worse? As the soldiers march us to the palace I feel a thickening menace gathering around me, aimed at me. It stinks of sorcery. Or perhaps it is just an ill omen? I wish I had brought *payche* root with me. Just squeezing it in my hand would protect me.

I still have a strong sense that Water Lily needs me. For the second time tonight I breathe in deeply and search for the center of Ix Chel's power in me so I can cast a glamour over these guards. But this time, She does not allow it. Disappointed, I accept that there is a reason for all that is happening to us.

We march in silence into the royal district and past a bevy of guards. We are taken to the back of the main palace, and roughly shoved into a small stone room. I fall on my face and cry out from surprise and the pain of sharp stones scraping the flesh from my head, knee and elbow. Jaguar Shield lands on his arm and gasps. They slam the door and lock us in. The soldiers settle against the wall to chat and gossip about the ballgame and the sacrifice performed by Blood Gatherer earlier.

In the cold darkness, Jaguar Shield reaches for my hand. Above us, a tiny, barred window lets in the night air. One of the Sky Wanderers sparkles in the black sky. I have never been in a prison before, and the smell of human waste is nauseating.

We are silent for a few moments, neither of us prepared for this.

"What do you think this means?" I ask him.

"Hmmph!" he responds, wrapping his arm around my shoulders. His lips graze my forehead. "It's no great mystery. Blue Monkey went directly to the royal palace."

"It's not a crime to refuse sacrifice. Or has that changed, too?" I ask.

My head throbs with pain. My bleeding knee and elbow burn. Jaguar Shield is still bleeding from the head wound. I feel the blood on his face. If our wounds become infected how will we manage the nine-day walk to the sea?

Om bey! Worry about one thing at a time, Jade Skirt! My mother always said I had a great capacity for worry. But who would have ever thought I would be locked up like a common criminal? It's a shock, and I have to admit I feel insulted and hurt to be treated this way. Nobles who are detained are kept in a well-appointed, comfortable room with servants to attend them. Being forced to spend the night in this stinking den is meant to send a message: not even the Oracle and High Priestess of Ix Chel and a noble *nacom* of the Cocom may cross the seven leaders of Chichen.

Jaguar Shield pulls me closer and whispers in my ear. "Don't worry. Others were behind us and saw us being taken. Word will spread quickly and my soldiers will come to help."

But will they? We are exiles now. In spite of his attempt to be comforting, I hear his anxiety and I feel hot waves of tension emanating from him. Fear stalks me like an old enemy. There you are, again. I see you, but you shall not prevail. *Fear leads to weakness. Fear makes you easy to control. Do not open that door!*

I wrench my mind away from fear and focus on the sounds I can hear. There are happy shouts from the distant crowd and the faint tune of someone's music. I think of Nine Macaw and the rest of my family. They are all alone, unprotected.

"Brother," I whisper in the dark, "do you think they have already taken Nine Macaw and the others?"

"Likely," he answers flatly, but he pats my hand. "Stay calm. Morning light will reveal all. For now, we can do nothing."

Nothing. The word shakes me to my bones. If only I had my shaman's pouch with the salve and powders that turn me into Can, the snake, I could walk through this horrible night as a creature of the forest and no human eye would see me. But alas, the pouch is in my apartment in the temple. As if he can sense my frustration, Jaguar Shield squeezes my hand again. I sigh. At this moment there's nothing I can do but take his advice and wait for dawn.

I must have dozed, because next thing I know the door creaks open onto a dull, gray morning. It's another bad omen. We're marched into the palace, where often I have sat as spiritual adviser to the leaders. The council chamber is down a long hallway. Only a wide line of red paint along the mid-section of the wall breaks the stark whiteness. Stern-faced guards block store rooms stacked high with tribute. We pass large chambers filled with precious stones, quetzal feathers, jade ornaments and rare items brought by traders from all over the Known World. A powerful, spicy-sweet aroma of *copal* incense wafts out of a narrow room that's stuffed with the precious resin. Fire-red chilis and sacks of allspice berries fill another room. My eyes burn as we pass.

Guards lead us into an empty chamber and leave us there. I take a moment to mentally scan my body and assess my injuries. My head throbs from last night's brutal fall. After exposure to that filth and vermin, my knee and elbow scrapes are already festering. I'm tired, hungry and badly in need of a drink of water. I conclude that I will recover after a bath, a meal and a good night's sleep. I look Jaguar Shield over and I'm worried about him. He, too, needs a bath, food and rest, but his head wound is deep and needs attention. Blows to the head can become dangerous if left untreated for too long.

Sounds of people starting their day filter into the chamber from outside. I watch a crowd of criminals painted in black-and-white stripes sweep piles of debris out of the central plaza with tall reed brooms. Bent at the waist, children from the School of Firm Hearts and Strong Minds pick up tamale shells, broken clay pipes and cups from last night's revelry. Under *ceiba* trees along the periphery of the plaza, countless drunks sleep. A clutch of women of the third age stand over the men; a cluster of elder women lead other men back to their homes to sleep off their drunkenness. Jaguar Shield dozes against the wall, but I am too anxious. I think waiting is the worst part of life. Age has not made me more patient.

A heavy wooden door swings open. Guards lead us to an inner chamber. Our seven illustrious leaders of Chichen sit on fur-strewn wooden chairs. Their clean, soft hands rest on arms of carved jaguar heads. We stand before them like two dirty wretches. I feel Jaguar Shield's elbow against mine. We wait in silence to hear our fate.

Blue Quetzal glares at us down her long, hooked nose.

"Jade Skirt Chel Cocom and Jaguar Shield Cocom Tesecum, we are highly displeased!" The other leaders pound the stone dais. "Your granddaughter, Nine Macaw, has been honored with sweetness of death by sacrifice." Her raised scepter points at me. "We have been informed that you two plan to run away with the child; that you plan to leave Chichen with the entire family of your daughter, Water Lily."

I speak first. "Lady Blue Quetzal, it is all true."

Her tone is harsh. "Why?" she demands.

I answer evenly, showing no emotion. "Nine Macaw has a special destiny." I raise my head to look at her. "She has the Sight. As an infant only forty days old, a calendar priest proclaimed that her sacred destiny and duty, my Lady, is to rule at Cuzamil Island, the land of my people and the Goddess Ix Chel."

"To go to the Place of No Evil as Chac's bride is as great an honor for your lineage!" counters one of the male leaders, Smoking Mirror. He leans his rotund frame forward and scowls. "Do you mean to refuse to offer your precious feather, a female twin, to the Gods?"

"Yes," I answer calmly. There is a chorus of angry grumbles around the room.

"And when did you intend to inform us of this rash decision?" asks Sun Shield, eldest of the male leaders. He points an accusing a finger at Jaguar Shield. "And you, Jaguar Shield, our much-honored *nacom*, plan to accompany this coward?"

My protector answers simply. "I do. But she is not a coward. She is the Oracle and High Priestess of Ix Chel."

"Why did you not seek our counsel first?" demands Smoking Mirror. "Are we not your leaders?"

Snake Woman wags a scolding finger at me. "You, Jade Skirt, of all people in our realm would do this? You, Moon Eagle's mate, whom we trusted and who has held our confidence now for many harvests—we expected better from you!"

I listen stoically. It is as I expected. They have already made up their minds.

Sky House rubs his forehead and then sighs as if he is deeply disappointed. Although he has lived only a few *tuns* more than I, he speaks to me as if he were a grandfather explaining deep philosophical concepts to a child. I bite back my impatience.

"Jade Skirt, death becomes life; life becomes death. This is the natural way of things. Your Nine Macaw will live again in pure and complete ecstasy with the Gods and the One Eternal Being. She will never know Death. Our Terminated Ones are victorious over Death. She will be immortal. Her one life will nurture many lives. She will have eternal life and be guaranteed a rebirth into infinity. Nine Macaw will live eternally in enraptured oneness with the Divine Creator Couple. Like the hero Gods of the *Popul Vuh* who sacrificed themselves to overcome Death, she will resurrect with the Gods each *tun*. Her *chu'lel* will merge with First Mother and First Father. She will join the source of being itself. Surely, there is no greater destiny than that?"

Before I can reply, Snake Woman cuts in:

"Those who are sent to the watery Underworld become our Divine Protectors, our Revered Ancestors. Their reward for sacrifice is to ascend directly to the Upperworld without crossing the nine dangerous rivers of the Underworld as others mortals must. Surely, you do not doubt that, Lady Jade Skirt."

Sun Shield slaps his hand on his knee. "Even our corn God, Yum Kaax's, sacred body is planted in the earth and must die that we may live! No less is expected from we who are children of the Gods, who were created from Their blood."

"I do not see it your way," I answer slowly and emphatically, making eye contact with all the seven leaders. There is a collective gasp.

"Heresy!" declares Sky House.

"To decapitate," I continue over their angry muttering, "and to tear out human hearts is an abomination of religion. We are of the same generation, so you know that this was not our way. You have been duped by the War God worshippers, the southern Putun, who want our lands, our trade. I believe they have plans to take the island of Cuzamil to further their influence. The New Order's way, throwing children into the Great Well, shows a cold and casual indifference to suffering and pain in the name of religion and sanctity. That is not the Chichen way. It is the Putun way."

The noble rulers of Chichen are offended by what I say. Their countenances grow dark with anger, but I am relieved to finally say what has long been in my heart.

"Why do we have to bargain with the Gods for rain, prosperity and victories? They created all that is, ever was or shall be. Their *chu'lel* is all-powerful, all-pervading, all-knowing. They do not have to drink our blood, eat our bodies and marry our dead virgins to renew life eternally. They love us as parents love their children. They created us to love Them."

"Agreed!" Snake Woman shouts at me. "And in order to love them, we must feed them! Our blood, our hearts and our precious feathers—the children—are the greatest gifts we have to offer them."

"Nonsense!" I hear myself shout back at her. "They created us and all that is at the beginning of the world. They sustain it all with cycles of time, nature, the sun, the rain."

Jaguar Shield steps in front of me. "Jade Skirt and I remember a different time and a different way to love and care for the Gods. You must remember that the New Order came with the Putun traders. Everyone knows it is so; but, no one will say it."

The seven leaders shift uncomfortably on their high benches.

"Theirs is a dry, harsh land," Jaguar Shield continues. "Their soil is barren soil and they see little rain. They have reason to fear the Gods and to mistrust nature. We do not. Here in Chichen, we are blessed with rainfall twice in a *tun*. We have good, deep soil that produces abundant food, and *cenotes* to store water. Ours is a land of abundance. What food we do not grow we can hunt. The Putun have always known scarcity. They must feel they need to get the attention of the Gods by rash acts. I have faith in the cycles of nature and the Divine plan."

Sun Shield responds. "Hmmph! Pretty words, Jaguar Shield. But the world will end, the sun will not rise, the Moon will not ride the Sky Serpent if we do not feed the Gods with life energy."

"You and the priests of the New Order promote a religion of fear," I tell him. "The way of the War God is the way of fear and killing. This is not the way of Ix Chel. She freely gives Her love and protection and nurtures us. There is no need to bargain with Her for what She lovingly bestows. Her way is peace. We are Her people, the crowning glory of our creatrix! Ix Chel tells us not to sacrifice the life She created to feed the Gods. The Gods need no such sacrifices!"

I feel the power of the truth in my words and I stand taller. But then Sky House clears his throat and, casting me a disapproving look, says:

"All children must take responsibility for caring for and feeding their elders. The Gods who are ancient require no less than we would give to our earthly parents."

"Jade Skirt," says Smoking Mirror, "do you not believe that the Otherworld is a dimension more alive, more real than this reality here in the Middle World? Do you not believe that those who die by sacrifice are taken by the Goddess of Death immediately to a place more alive, lovelier and more vital than this one? Only the Terminated Ones can transcend death. They truly conquer what others who simply die cannot. Through their sacrifice they are rewarded with true immortality for themselves and resurrection of the cosmos."

I try to stay calm as I hear this lie of the New Order being delivered by one of Chichen's rulers. "Noble lords and ladies, I am the Oracle of Ix Chel, and I have seen in my dreams and visions that what you say about the Flowery Death is not true." I pause for a moment, seeing the shock on their faces. Chills run up and down my spine. My hands tingle with power and energy as I finally speak the truth to these leaders, who have been led astray by the Putun liars.

"My own Moon Eagle was the first warrior captive to die the Flowery Death. Like other Terminated Ones, he suffered in the Otherworld. I have seen their terrible misery. I hear their screams, their wailing. In sleep, I feel them clawing and struggling to find solid ground. Headless and heartless, they wander to search frantically, eternally for their heads, for their hearts. With no hands, no feet, they continue to search the dark and watery passages of the Underworld for their body parts. I grieve for them, and I will not allow that cruel fate for my granddaughter or yours—not for anyone. I serve the Goddess, She who loves life."

There is stunned silence and finally Sun Shield clears his throat and says, "The child will feel no pain, no discomfort and no fear. She will be well dosed with the formula the priests have prepared. In fact, you may prepare it yourself."

"Never!" I say, disappointed. Clearly, he is not changing his mind. "The act of sacrifice is wrong," I say again, but I know my case is lost.

"Your visions might be affected by your grief at losing your husband," says Snake Woman dismissively. "As Chac's bride, Nine Macaw will be forever in a sacred state of being and have immediate transference into Oneness with the Great Knower and Maker, Hunabku."

Jaguar Shield sees that I've given up arguing. He moves forward to speak.

"Once, the Terminated Ones were only those nobles captured in battles we *nacoms* planned for that purpose. As warriors who carry the very Gods on their backs, their *chu'lel* is the most powerful. Why must we now kill children? What's next—the unborn?"

"*Om bey!*" Sun Shield is offended. "You dare ask such a question?! Kill?! How dare you suggest that! We are not murderers! Children and virgins are fresh, unblemished souls from the Gods' garden. They are fresh blossoms and fruits to be picked for the pleasure and food of the Gods. They do not die, but are given life eternal."

This is the propaganda they have been fed by the priests, and that they feed the people of Chichen. This whole conversation feels so futile. We will not change their hearts or minds here. Smoking Mirror calls for silence with a raised hand.

"We are prepared to forgive all if you will change your mind. We have agreed to accept the orphan, Tree Orchid, in the place of Nine Macaw."

"Very generous and fair," says one of the stern-faced leaders.

I sigh. Tree Orchid again; the poor orphan will always be second to Nine Macaw.

"I cannot allow anyone to be sacrificed in Nine Macaw's place," I answer. "I am opposed to sacrifice. From this day forward, I stand against the New Order." Defiantly, I look directly at each of our leaders so they know I am not ashamed of what I say. "We will leave Chichen. A better life and a kinder way to worship the Gods await us on Cuzamil."

Smoking Mirror pounds the stone floor with his foot and points accusingly at me.

"Coward! Shame!" His great feather headdress bobs and sways above him.

"You rend the very fabric of our society," declares Sky House, crossing his arms in anger

Blue Quetzal glares piously at both of us. "Is your pride so great that you think you can defy the Gods?" she asks imperiously. "Your presence in this council chamber is an abomination."

They are all shouting at us now:

"We don't know you!"

"Traitors!"

"You are the unborn!"

"Get out! Leave us!"

And, finally, what we know must be. Sun Shield stands and waves his snake-foot scepter in the air above our heads and pronounces our fate.

"Now you must leave us; proceed to go. You have received our castigation. Abandon our entrances, our courtyards, your aunts, your uncles, your sisters. Abandon the bones and ashes of your ancestors. May they forgive you. Your names are stricken forever from your lineage!"

I gasp aloud as the enormity of my loss hits me. Will Moon Eagle's soul abandon me, too? How can I live without his spirit? Who will feed his soul on the day to honor the dead? Never again will I sit in counsel with him in the family shrine. Who will visit the little souls of my two dead babies we buried in the corn field? It must be as it is. Scorn, exile, calumny and the loss of everything that makes one a person in this world will not deter me. But it hurts.

"Guards! Remove this filth from our presence at once!" snarls Blue Quetzal. From behind, strong arms grip my elbows. Two soldiers lift me off my feet. Jaguar Shield resists. A chert-studded club slams down on his head. I hear a sickening crack. He falls to the floor moaning. The soldiers drag him outside and dump him on the ground. I am shoved hard onto the ground beside him. I scramble over to Jaguar Shield and see with alarm that his eyes have rolled back in his head. Blood streams down his contorted face from the head wound. Oh, my love! How it hurts to see him lying in the dirt, covered in the filth and dry dust of shame. I deserve this; not him. I feel his pulse at the wrist and sob with relief when I feel the slight flutter of life within him. He lives!

I try to help Jaguar Shield stand, but his dead weight is too heavy for me. It's no use. I simply sit back down in the dirt and lay his head in my lap. With the edge of my mantle, I gently wipe dirt and gravel from his head wounds. I have no idea what to do next. I can ask for help from no one. I can't move him. I can't get him the help he needs. A part of my mind notes the depth of the wound. It's all the way to the bone and bleeds profusely. I tell myself that's good. Wounds that bleed will heal better.

The morning ticks on and we sit like discarded refuse, exposed in our shame in the middle of the royal district where yesterday we were honored nobles and respected advisers. As *nacom*, Jaguar Shield trained and led legions of soldiers into battle. His conquests and my prophecies brought enormous prestige and tribute to the royal and noble families.

Ah, but all that is over. Now we are unborn, unknown, set adrift with no lineage, our identities wiped out. Shocked nobles starting to travel through the city on their morning tasks stop to stare. What must they think of Ix Chel's Oracle and the *nacom* Jaguar Shield groveling in the yellow dust? Gossip flies like feathers in the wind.

I lose track of time. Have we been there five minutes? Hours? I can't tell. I must be in shock. But then Jaguar Shield groans and I come back to the present moment to tend to him. He blinks at the sky and licks his dry lips. How I wish I had water for him.

"Come," I whisper into his ear. "Can you walk? We must get to Water Lily's house." Just thinking about my daughter brings up an intense urgency to make sure she and the children are safe. I try to help Jaguar Shield rise, but he is too weak. I groan with frustration.

Suddenly, a kind hand touches my shoulder. Flesh Flower's grandson stands behind me, looking away. He speaks out of the side of his mouth so I can hear.

"I have come to help!" He is breaking a taboo by speaking to me, so I don't look at him, but I feel a wash of relief. Jaguar Shield and I need an ally right now. The young man slips a dirty slave mantle over my head and does the same for Jaguar Shield. With this meager disguise, we are less noticeable. When no one is watching, the grandson and I prop up the *nacom* and help him walk. We move as quickly as Jaguar Shield can go, which is not fast. The young man leads us on seldom-traveled paths and I almost wish I could sprint ahead to find my family. When we finally arrive at the Cocom compound, Jaguar Shield is shivering from shock. He drags his feet and stumbles along. Women stand in their dark doorways, cooking utensils in hand, staring at us. Some turn their backs. No one touches their hearts as we pass. Little children stare blankly. Men sharpen their tools and sit, heads down, weaving baskets and pretending we don't exist. Close to the well, a bevy of older men chop a shoulder-high pile of *payche* vines to be taken to the House of Healing later. Today, for the first time in twenty *tuns*, I won't be there to receive and store the medicines. The men are scornful in their silence. One by one, they turn their backs to us.

Flesh Flower's grandson carries Jaguar Shield the last steps to Water Lily's courtyard. He sets the *nacom* down gently on a bench and lifts the mantles off our shoulders.

"I am sorry for your troubles," he says in a whisper, and then he's gone.

I am so relieved to be here, yet all I hear is silence. Then a disheveled, terrified Red Earth storms out of the house.

"Na! Na! Where have you been? We needed you!"

One look at us and she stops her rant. "Great Mother! What happened?"

"Help us inside," is all I can say.

Water Lily's hearth room is in chaos. Cooking utensils are scattered across the floor; pieces of shattered dishes are strewn everywhere. An overturned pot of black beans stains the hard-packed dirt floor. I note the footprints in the dark mud—military sandals. I sniff the air. Blood Gatherer!

We lay Jaguar Shield on the deerskin-covered bench. I look for a water gourd, but I can't find one.

"The soldiers marched in," Red Earth is telling me between sobs. "They broke everything! Then they took Nine Macaw and Tree Orchid!" She sobs so hard she doubles over and ends up in a miserable huddle of tears on the floor.

"Red Earth, granddaughter, where were they taken? This is important, my love. Did they say where they were going?"

She clings to my leg and wails miserably. "I tried, Na! I tried to hold on to my sisters! But then one of the men hit me!"

"Was Blood Gatherer here? Where is your mother?"

"Uncle Blood Gatherer took Mother away right after!" she cries. "Na, it was awful!"

A shadow falls into the room. In the doorway stand three men and two women from across the courtyard. They take in all the details of our broken, sad little home but their eyes slide past us now that we are exiles.

"What did you see? What do you know? Where are they?" I ask in rapid succession, not waiting for an answer. They ignore me.

One of the men, Jaguar Shield's cousin and closest friend, silently offers my brother-in-law a gourd of water. The *nacom* drinks and becomes more alert. He turns his head painfully to look around the hearth room.

"Tell us what you know, Brother," I plead to his cousin.

He faces the wall, not me, and says, "They took Nine Macaw and Tree Orchid away. Nine Macaw's wrists and ankles were tied to a pole like an animal! Tree Orchid was dragged by the hair behind her."

"Your daughter," says the cousin's wife, dark eyes flashing in her ruddy face, "They dragged her away." I hear venom in her voice and my heart aches for my poor Water Lily. "I heard them read the charges for unlawful drunkenness." Her wide nose and cheekbones flare with self-righteous satisfaction. "They denounced her in the middle of the courtyard. Everyone in Chichen is talking about the shame you have brought on our lineage."

Jaguar Shield rouses for a moment as if to argue, but then he falls back, unconscious. The cousin shoos the neighbors out and leaves with them.

Nine Macaw and Tree Orchid kidnapped. Water Lily taken into custody. Jaguar Shield unconscious. Rejection and scorn at every turn. *Om bey!* Goddess, help us!

Red Earth is whimpering piteously. "I couldn't save them, Na. I couldn't stop them."

"Poor child," I say, holding her hands in mine. I murmur soothingly, "Of course you couldn't have stopped them. What could anyone have done against the High Priest and his soldiers? I'm just happy you're still here and well."

But, really she isn't very well. Red Earth has never had much emotional strength, and right now she is trembling like a dry leaf.

A task. She needs a task. Work distracts the tortured mind.

"Red Earth!" I say, gripping her shoulders encouragingly. "Pull yourself together for the sake of your sisters and your mother. That is your duty now." I look into her swollen face. "I trust in you and you can trust in me to find Nine Macaw and Tree Orchid. At least we know where to find your mother."

Just then, a corpulent male figure blocks the light in the doorway. It's a magistrate. His official duties include discipline and adherence to rules for ours and three other lineage compounds. Despite a brutal personality, he is respected and regarded as fair. He steps imperiously into the hearth room to survey the bedlam. His head flies back. He frowns, lifts his chin and juts out his ringed lower lip. An oval headdress of green parrot feathers bound to a strip of deer leather, symbol of his office, sits low on his flattened forehead. He is a typical lesser noble: tablets of his office tattooed on chest and arms, crossed eyes, jade-embedded teeth and heavily embroidered loincloth. Like other magistrates, his black-and-yellow cloak falls just below the knees

"What happened to the *nacom*?" he demands in a high-pitched, nervous tone. He struts over to where Jaguar Shield lies and pulls back the damp cloth. The length and depth of the wound surprises him. He draws in a deep breath and bellows at me. "Tell me at once!"

His tone is another blow. No one has spoken to me so disrespectfully since childhood. I stare at the floor and turn my shoulders away from him.

"Soldiers took my granddaughter, Nine Macaw, and the orphan Tree Orchid. Blood Gatherer took my daughter, Water Lily." That was all I could manage in one breath.

"I know all that!" he shouts directly into my face. Cold, black eyes leer down at me from a pinched, pock-marked face. "I didn't ask you that! What happened to the *nacom*?"

"We were detained last night. This morning, one of the palace guards clubbed him." Then what he had said sinks in. I forget myself and turn to look into his face. "If you know that soldiers took the girls away, then you know where they are," I say. I shake a fist at him. "I command you to tell me where they were taken!"

His pointed, jade-embedded teeth flash. He throws back his head and laughs derisively. His jowls wobble. His enormous stomach jiggles. "Command!? You command me?" He takes a step forward, narrows his eyes and glares down at me. "How dare you look at my face! You have no authority. You are the walking and talking dead. I know everything. All of Chichen knows of your cowardly betrayal."

He raises a hand over his head. I back away. "You defy the Gods themselves! They are hungry. It is our duty to feed and sustain Them," he shouts spraying spittle. "Chac must have His bride to bring rain. No rain will fall. We will starve this year. This is what you have on your conscience."

Jaguar Shield's cousin comes back into the house at that moment and intervenes.

"The *nacom* is injured. He needs attention. Let us take him to the healers' temple."

The magistrate sneers. "There is no reason to treat the deceased. He stays here!"

He turns and stalks out, pushing the cousin out with him. A punishing glare of sunlight hits Jaguar Shield's face. He rouses for a moment then falls back unconscious again.

I send Red Earth to my private storage room in the healers' temple to bring wound powders and bitter herbs. I beg her to run as fast as she can, and she pulls herself together and heads off on this most important mission.

I drink water and clear my head, and then I assess the wound and start planning how I will treat it once Red Earth returns. Thank you, Goddess, the chert-studded club missed his eye. He will wake with a wicked headache, but I believe Jaguar Shield will heal. He must!

Waiting is the hardest part. I need something to do. I hold his wrists and whisper the prayers for shock and trauma. Still unconscious, his eyelids flutter and he takes a deep breath. By the time I finish the nine prayers, Red Earth is back, out of breath.

"My dear, you must have sprouted wings!" I say, utterly grateful. She melts with happiness at my approval. "Good work! You are a clever girl."

"I brought your shaman's bag, too. Turtle Star said you would need it."

The bitter herb powder I use first burns the wound. He stirs and grabs my wrist and his eyes fly open. When he sees it is me, he attempts a feeble smile, drops my wrist and whispers. "Are you hurt?"

"No," I answer and continue to work. Typical of my love to ask about me while he is lying here covered in his own blood.

"Find them." He means the girls and my daughter. "Everyone must leave here today," he says hoarsely.

I keep busy boiling herbs and tending to all our wounds. Red Earth cleans the mess off the floor and makes food for us. I praise her cooking, earning another grateful smile.

Food and familiar tasks help me as much as they help her. I'm thinking more clearly now and I wrack my brains trying to figure out where Blood Gatherer is hiding the girls. Finally, as the sun nears the high point, a man I once helped with a private matter slips into our courtyard. He stands by our doorway and whispers the information I need. Nine Macaw and Tree Orchid are hidden in a cave off the road to Canche.

There is no time to lose. Jaguar Shield is right; we have to leave here today. I sit beside him and concentrate on the melding of our vital essences, our *chu'lels*. Think like a soldier, like a strategist, I tell myself. I focus deep within my abdomen. I listen. I wait. Gradually, guidance comes.

"*Seek your* wayeb, *your companion spirit.*"

Of course! Can, the snake, will help me. In a snake's body, I can move about unseen, unknown.

"Red Earth, my dear, you must stay with your uncle. Make him drink this tea. I will be back as soon as I can."

She looks worried. She clearly doesn't want me to leave, but she obediently moves closer to her uncle.

Slipping my three-tasseled shaman's bag over my shoulder, I limp out of the house and head to our family shrine, where many generations of Cocoms are interred. I pass the well. Hard, cold stares pierce me. Cocoms turn their backs. No wonder no one in Chichen has ever refused sacrifice before. The punishment is devastating; but I know I made the right choice.

Perched on a low hill, the circular shrine is rebuilt every twenty *tuns* or so. Under the ground lie layer upon layer of deceased Cocoms, their mouths stuffed with corn for sustenance and a jade bead to pay their way across the wide river of the Underworld. Their souls guide the living. My only relative here is Moon Eagle. I feel inside my shoulder bag for one of his knuckle bones, my talisman. Jaguar Shield's wife's body is here too. My two dead babies, so fresh from the garden of souls, are not here. Custom demanded that they be buried in a corn field.

I duck my head to pass through the oval door. It's empty—people are out working in the middle of the day. Cross-legged, I settle onto a reed mat in front of the low altar. A cedar-carved image of Ix Chel in her guise as grandmother, guardian of the dead, sits alone on the altar surrounded by fresh flowers and honeyed amaranth cakes. I feel so much better being here, in a place of reverence for my Goddess. I give my offering of *copal* grains and murmur a prayer. Niches filled with clay funeral pots dot the walls. A lovely bird's trill just outside the door brings out the tears I have been holding. I remember the sad day I placed Moon Eagle's ashes in a niche just to the left of where I sit now. His painted funeral urn bears the image of a jaguar mask. I loved Moon Eagle's long, slender hands, so when I saw a knuckle bone at the top of the pile of ashes in the Putun priest's hands, I took it. Now I keep it always in my shaman's bag.

Usually, time in the shrine is a leisurely, meditative pleasure for me. I come often to commune silently with the spirit of my husband. Today, there is no leisure. A black spider crawls in front of me. It's a good omen. Nature's great weaver, the spider is a symbol of Ix Chel, She who weaves the universe. Tucked inside my shaman's bag is a jar of red paste that will join my soul with my companion spirit, Can the snake. The magic paste contains frog skins, datura flowers, lotus roots and eighteen other herbs. A dry corn cob stoppers the jar. Another jar holds the bitter powder I must eat to find my *wayeb*. Gratefully, I whisper a short prayer to thank Ix Chel for this sacred transformative power.

Wracked with bruises and cuts, my body complains. No time for that now. I ignore the pain. I leave the Cocom compound for one of the less traveled paths into the woods.

A soft glow of late-morning light blankets the forest. Glimmering dewdrops on low shrubs sparkle like crystals. I hear in the distance the blare of horns from Chichen. A chorus of frogs, birds and crickets soon drowns out the faint music. Here, in the lap of the Great Mother, I feel protected and safe again. My fear drains out of me and down into Her sacred body, the Earth. For a moment, I pause to soak in Her beauty, Her earthy aromas and Her peace, which never succumbs to our travails. Waving palm leaves rustle in a light breeze. Critters scurry over the carpet of rotting leaves. Overhead, a white-spotted owl perches on a low branch, hoots in an eerie, almost-human voice. An augur of death, he startles me. Usually, they hunt only at night.

"*Hay yo,*" I whisper to the fat bird. "You startled me, friend. Good hunting."

He must have been hunting rodents that feed on the bright red *copal* fruits that litter the forest floor. The spicy aroma of *copal*, stronger even than the dry resin, rises up every time I step on one of the rubbery fruit skins. I pick one, crush it and hold it to my nose. It's a little personal ritual that always comforts me. I tuck the skin into my bag then, hurry deeper, deeper into the tangled, green jungle.

At last, I come to a giant *ceiba* tree. I sink down onto the soft earth between two enormous, gray buttresses; like a mother, they embrace my weary body, calm my troubled soul. It has always been this way for me—plants, trees, the earth give me comfort. I feel waves of anxiety for my beloveds, for our impossible situation, yet still I can tap into this deep, unwavering strength. Slowly, I breathe in and out, in and out. I say a prayer to Ixtobay, spirit of the tree, and lay a few grains of *copal* at her base in gratitude.

It is time. I send all the tension in my muscles down through my body and into the earth. I take my quartz-crystal knife and pierce the soft, wet tip of my tongue nine times. My sacred *chu'lel* drips onto the dirt as an offering for the big magic I will work now. As I utter the incantation it feels as though the words are saying themselves on their own. Now my back rests against the sacred tree and in this state of connection to all that is around me I can feel its *chu'lel* surging up and down the enormous, smooth trunk. Its pulse is a powerful current, pushing the life force up to the tips of the spreading branches. Warm sunlight falls in shafts through the air and dapples the ground. Pulsing, pulsing, my heartbeat is in synch now with the great *ceiba*. We are one.

In my woven bag I find the little clay jar of red paste and a second jar of powder. Still leaning against the thrumming tree, I remove my clothing and sit on my mantle. I study the two small clay jars in my hands. They, too, seem to be pulsing in my palm. That is right. This is the way it should be. We are all pulsing with *chu'lel*. I pour a small handful of the dark, bitter powder onto my hand and lick it with my tongue. Searing pain where I pierced it earlier with the knife. Now my heart races. My fingers and toes tingle; throb. My fingers find the other little jar. This red, creamy potion is very rare, a sacred secret. Until Nine Macaw reaches twenty *tuns*, the only ones in Chichen who know the secret prayers and formula to make the shaman's powder and salve are Turtle Star and I. It is highly potent. I prayed over it for six days of the New Moon.

Onto my bare chest and arms I spread the thick paste. Ahh! I love the feeling of all-pervading peace within and without. Now, in a rush, its strange power takes me over. I know what to expect; otherwise, I would be terrified. First I begin to shake; my vision grows narrow; my heart races faster; my hands tremble. I have to focus hard to finish rubbing the paste onto myself, covering my skin. The incantation slithers out of my mouth on its own.

"Beloved Mother, Ix Chel, and Father, Itzámna, You, the Creators, Knowers and Nurturers. Four are the colors of Your sacred directions. Four are the number of *Bacabs* who hold up the Sky in Your name. Four are the levels of Heaven and the Place of No Evil. Nine is the number of the Underworld. Nine is the number of the Middleworld. Nine drops of blood do I offer you, Mother and Father who hold up the Guardians of the Earth. You who are the link to all worlds above and below. Accept my humble offering. I seek your protection and shelter. Nine Benevolent Spirits of the Dark Night, carry my blood offering up through this holy trunk to where Ix Chel and her consort Itzámna rule."

Only Ixtobay, spirit of the great *ceiba* tree, can protect my human soul as I travel in spirit form. I will descend along its trunk into the dark Underworld. This is not a safe or kind place; I feel imminent danger lurking all around me. I can feel the desperate, lost souls, the evil spirits, icy winds and vengeful spirits. They would love to capture a wandering soul. This is no place for the meek or uninitiated. I am wary, but not afraid. I've been here before and I know what to do.

My breath deepens and slows. I continue to whisper the prayer. Fluids in my body join pulsations of the earth and the *ceiba* tree. I drift and become one with the Great All. I feel the moment of transition, although it is very subtle. Suddenly, I am deeper inside the trunk of the tree. It's like I'm a flower petal drifting downstream. I float on the smooth current of green sap. I feel no anxiety or fear. Peaceful souls appear in shapeless white globes that drift up like dust motes toward a warm, pink light. Troubled, angry spirits float down a murky brown river into the Underworld. Bony hands attached to arms of rotting flesh try to pull me into cold, dark waters. I stay my course.

Now "Jade Skirt" is no longer this consciousness. There is just a sensation of floating above a murky river. There is awareness of other shamans seeking their *nagual*, their animal companions.

My *nagual* is Can, the snake. It waits for me in the magical corral where the Gods of the Underworld keep all animal companions. The river leads there, but there are other currents trying to pull me into the shadows, from which I will not return. With effort, I keep myself above the dark river. I call on the Great Can to come to me, to carry my spirit back to the Upperworld. I make my intention clear: I must find Nine Macaw and Tree Orchid.

Now I'm on the ground moving, sliding, slithering. Smooth, sensuous movement propels me, and I have only to think "forward" or "sideways" and my long, serpent form responds. In every scale and fiber I feel the cool, moist earth under my soft belly. Head, body and tail whip back and forth. My Can-senses take in the heady perfume of decaying leaves and dirt. I slip over the forest floor disturbing insects, worms and black, hairy caterpillars. I sense warm and cold spots in the air. Vibrations, pulsing heat waves move right through me. Animals creep around me, crawl over me and fly above me. My vision shatters into a kaleidoscope of colors and forms. I can see behind me and in all directions. I'm overwhelmed and I'm not. I don't resist, but even as Jade Skirt surrenders to the snake, she is still aware in a corner of her/their mind, and that awareness knows this is right and as it should be. All is well.

Can stops, coils, waiting. Something approaches. Not possum. Not monkey. It is a penetrating, musty smell of cat. Jaguar! The enormous black beast paces toward Can. All the nearby creatures are still. Black as the night sky, her powerful muscles flex. She is perfectly formed, infinitely confident. Jaguar moves deliberately toward Can. Yellow-green eyes stare at the leaves where snake is coiled. On paws the size of plates she advances. Flick goes her long black tail. Suddenly, Can uncoils and their eyes lock, Jaguar and Snake. Then Jaguar turns and lopes away; Can follows close behind.

Jaguar leads us to a small clearing with a fresh water pond. Near the trees is a dark, low mouth of a small cave. Dragonflies, those creatures who once rescued Ix Chel from death, dance around the pond, buzzing like a hive of disturbed bees. Jaguar crouches. Snake coils and rears her head. In silence they communicate. What Can feels, Jaguar feels. What Jaguar senses, Can senses. Overhead, Father Sun watches.

From the depths of the cave come faint moans and weeping. A sudden breeze carries the smell of a cooking fire, human urine, saliva and human hair. Jaguar lets out a great, low sound. In a bound of shimmering black, she leaps into the cave, letting loose a roar, and lands on a soldier who is roasting a rabbit over a small fire. The soldier screams as Jaguar's claws rake his flesh and jaws snap his neck.

Can flashes behind her into the cave and finds Nine Macaw and Tree Orchid, bound hand and feet, shrieking in terror. A second soldier brandishes a spear. Can rears up. She hisses. The soldier screams. Snake pulls herself up higher. Flick! Out flashes her forked tongue. The soldier drops his spear and flees screaming into the jungle.

Jaguar turns to the girls. They panic, trying to crawl away. Can moves forward and stops in front of Nine Macaw. Jaguar lies down on his back. He rolls in the dust as if at play, waving paws in the air and clowning around with his tail.

Tree Orchid whimpers in shock. But there is recognition and disbelief on Nine Macaw's face.

"Na?" She leans forward to stare at Can, who curls around her leg and sets a small, green head on her knee. "Oh, Na! You came!"

Their *sisal* bonds are tightly knotted. Can moves to one of the stones around the fire and waits. Nine Macaw scoots to the fire and holds her hands over the hot stone. The *sisal* ropes sizzle, smoke and fall apart. Nine Macaw frees Tree Orchid and the two starving girls devour the roasted rabbit. Can waits while they fill their empty bellies. Respectfully, they offer a few bits to the great cat, who accepts the morsels regally.

Can leads the girls out of the cave and back to the *ceiba* tree. Then Jaguar bounds away into the jungle without a look back.

My snake form dissolves. I'm back inside the great flow of the *ceiba* tree, propelled upward on a strong cold, current. An old woman with one eye, one hand and one foot motions for me to follow. I cannot resist.

I'm tossed back onto the ground under the tree like a discarded rag doll. Human sight returns slowly. Everything is a jumble of shapes and forms. Slowly, my arms and legs become my own again. They ache. The wounds of last night pulse and burn. I stretch out my naked body and rub my cold limbs. I miss the heightened awareness of the snake. This dimension seems dull, overly simple. I stretch out my human tongue and miss the snake's ability to taste the air. I give a prayer of thanksgiving to the spirit of the tree, to the Nine Benevolent Spirits of the Night, to Itzámna and Ix Chel who watch over the souls of those who walk in the bodies of their animal companions. I leave an offering of *copal* and dried tobacco and give thanks to Can the snake, and to the unknown Jaguar, for watching over me and leading me to the girls.

"What should we do now?" Tree Orchid asks Nine Macaw in a voice so forlorn my heart breaks. "Why are we alone again?"

"I don't know," whispers Nine Macaw. "We should get under this bush and wait. Na will surely come for us!"

"What if the other soldier comes back?" Tree Orchid hugs herself miserably. "What should we do?"

Nine Macaw looks just as unhappy, but then she draws herself up and puts an arm around her friend. "Let's pray to the Goddess. Na always says she will help us."

Smiling, I push aside a wide palm leaf and they see me. Their dirt-stained faces light up with relief. They run to me and nearly squeeze the breath out of me. Nine Macaw, who was so brave a moment ago, is now sobbing in my arms and both girls are trying at the same time to tell me what happened.

"And then they tied us up!"

"They wouldn't give us food. They said it would be a waste since we would be sacrificed to Chac soon!"

"And they threw a spear at Kiki, but he was too fast for them!"

I hold them tightly. Still feeling the after-effects of my journey as Can, I can see orange and black-tinted rings of terror seep out of them. Finally, their tears are spent. Nine Macaw's natural curiosity returns.

"Was that snake really you, Na?"

I nod.

"Who was the jaguar, then?" Tree Orchid asks curiously.

That is a good question. Who was Jaguar? Can has encountered her on other forays with her *nagual*, but never was she so much needed as this day.

"I don't know," I answer truthfully. "Perhaps someday I will find out."

"How did you do it?" Nine Macaw asks shyly.

I smile at her. "You will find out yourself one day soon, my precious flower. But I must find something to eat or I will not have the strength to walk home, and I think you must also be very hungry, no?"

Tree Orchid has been whistling her special tune for Kiki and Bobo. They usually know where she is and come to her quickly, but they are nowhere to be found. She looks worried, but Nine Macaw grabs her hand and pulls her to a nearby tree laden with the gray-green, knobby fruits of wild *anona*. The two girls climb the low trunk and shake ripe fruit down to me. I bite into one. It is perfectly ripe, the soft, pink flesh sweet and creamy. For a moment, we forget our troubles and fill our grateful bellies. The girls even have a contest to see who can spit out the shiny black seeds the furthest.

"Why do they hate us?" Nine Macaw asks, slumping down to lean against me. Tree Orchid snuggles under my other arm.

"Why did they break everything in the house?" Tree Orchid asks miserably. "They scared Bobo!"

"Precious feathers, they are scared. They are angry because I will not send Nine Macaw or you, Tree Orchid, to the Well of Sacrifice. Our leaders have declared us Exiles."

Their eyes widen. They glance at each other and back at me.

"No one has refused to send a loved one or slave to sacrifice before," I explain. "People are afraid that Chac will punish them. They think the priests should punish us. People hate what they fear." They stare at the ground and nod, understanding.

"It's my fault," Nine Macaw whispers.

"No!" I shake her firmly by the shoulder. "No! You have done nothing wrong. Your uncle, Blood Gatherer, chose you on purpose because he knows you are chosen by the Goddess. He uses you to make war on Ix Chel. It is wrong, what he has done. But children, any sacrifice is wrong. I truly believe that. It is why I would not let them have Tree Orchid either."

The little girl pales, and I pull her into a reassuring hug. "Ix Chel teaches us to cherish life. The heart takers are wrong. The blood priests are wrong. The New Order is wrong. That is why we must leave Chichen."

"Where is Mother? Where are Red Earth and Jaguar Paw?" Nine Macaw asks worriedly. I'm glad she is thinking of them. I am, too.

"We will be together," I say reassuringly, although I am not sure how. I look around to orient myself. Father Sun in the West. That means Chichen is to my right. To the left is the trail that leads to the *sacbe*. There we can start our journey to the sea. Which way to go? Back to Chichen? That's out of the question. Nine Macaw will be captured again. But will we be safe on the *sacbe*? And I didn't bring supplies for the journey. We need shoes, mantles, cash and food.

It's a two-day walk to Na Balam on the *sacbe*, but once we get there we should be safe. Since my grandmother's reign at Cuzamil, the great white road between Na Balam and Cuzamil has been a zone of peace. Anyone may travel unmolested to the Sacred Island. My grandmother built inns for travelers, supplying all the food and workers, and my sister has honored the treaty and kept up the inns. But Na Balam is a two or three day walk from Chichen.

Just as I begin to whisper a short prayer to Ix Chel for guidance, we hear footsteps approaching. The girls cling to me like vines, and I can feel them tremble. I tune in to the energy around us and I know from the way my skin feels that there is no danger. Still, we wait, breathing silently. Out of the underbrush saunters Jaguar Paw. A mask of shiny black paint covers half his face from upper lip to forehead. Stark white rings of paint around his eyes make him look frightful.

"Na!" he says out of breath. "Sister! Tree Orchid! At last! Na, I've been tracking you since early this morning. You disappeared." He wears only a loincloth. Around his upper arm is a ring of red parrot feathers. In his right hand, he grips a long, wooden spear.

"Grandson, we are so glad to see you!"

The girls embrace him and Jaguar Paw pats them on the back and smiles at all of us.

"Jaguar Shield sent me to find you."

"Is he alright? Is he up? How is his wound?"

Tall for twelve *tuns*, the boy assumes a manly, take-charge air. He shifts the woven bag on his shoulder and says, "Uncle said to tell you not to return. I am to take you to a place to hide until he comes." His face darkens. "Blood Gatherer, all the priests and the Council of Leaders are furious. Blood Gatherer denounced us all this morning in public. He has sworn revenge. Every one of us is cast out. Exiled!"

I am about to comment, but he holds up his right hand to signal silence. He's right. "No more talking, Na. Follow me. Be quiet. Spies are everywhere."

So, now our lives are in the hands of a child soldier. Faith. Faith.

Jaguar Paw leads us deeper into a pathless, darkening jungle. I must say, I'm impressed. He gallantly holds flesh-ripping, thorny branches to one side so we women can pass unscathed. He ducks under thick palms and holds back the broad leaves for us, particularly solicitous of Nine Macaw's safety. Under our feet, the earth is littered with jungle plant life in all stages of birth, growth and death. Silently, with the tip of his spear, my grandson points to thorny tree trunks we should avoid and the gnarled roots on the overgrown trail that might trip us, and he even prevents us from walking into a nest of biting ants. In stately, measured steps he guides us skillfully through the jungle. Despite our dire circumstances, I really enjoy seeing this side of my grandson. He reminds me of Moon Eagle and Jaguar Shield. He has their same gentle, protective instinct and sculpted muscles ready to respond.

A flock of bright red, yellow and green-feathered parrots fly low and squawk at us. Howler monkeys, so close overhead that we can see their hairy, round faces, bellow as they race through the branches above. A cool wind blows gently through the greenery. After a while, Jaguar Paw is careless and walks too fast for us to keep up with his long strides. Left behind, I'm unsure of where to go through the thick, unbroken foliage. Tree Orchid taps my shoulder. With a finger to her lips, she motions for us to stop. Eyes closed, head cocked she listens. Her head moves lightly from side to side.

"The birds know," she whispers. In a moment she points to a narrow, almost invisible animal trail. We follow it, trusting. Jaguar Paw is right there, walking ahead of us. I throw a little stone at his head. Ready to attack with his spear, he turns. I motion to him and he comes obediently.

"You must wait for us. Look behind you and be sure that we are with you. Be considerate. We're not soldiers." I scold, putting my fist under his chin so he'll know I am serious.

"Sorry, Na. Don't tell my uncle, please."

I nod to let him know I won't. He walks only slightly in front of us from then on. I'm thinking about Tree Orchid and her gift with birds. She is a special one, too. I give her a look of approval and she beams at me before looking away shyly.

We stop suddenly in a small clearing where deer have made a lair of dry straw. Jaguar Paw grabs Tree Orchid's arm just as she is about to jump into the inviting straw. With his spear, he stirs the straw. Out of the dry brush crawl legions of fat, blood-filled deer ticks. We back away quickly. Jaguar Paw leads us along the edge of the clearing to a rough log. Gratefully, we plop down on it, but then red, biting ants gnaw at our feet and legs. Nine Macaw yelps, and then so do I as a stinging caterpillar falls from above. Soon, we're a blanket of welts, bites and ticks. Then, my most dreaded enemy of the jungle crawls out of the rotting log to torture me: the hairy worm! I'm usually extremely wary of hairy worms, carefully looking for them under leaves, but now one finds my hand. Cloaked in black, toxic hairs, its finger-sized soft body stings like a hundred thorns. My hand is on fire! I leap up and the loathsome creature falls to the ground. With the tip of his lance, Jaguar Paw spears it handily. Giggling, he pokes it at Nine Macaw. She jumps. I catch her just in time to cover her mouth or she would have let out a scream.

"Bury that cursed thing!" I order. The boy laughs, but he obeys.

Now we must wait. Darkness falls. In the silence, I contemplate our plight. What happened to Red Earth? Has Water Lily been stoned in public? Who will care for her wounds? Tree Orchid and Nine Macaw are barefoot, their thin mantles torn and dirty. Food doesn't worry me much as I know we could forage and hunt for days and survive. But how will we manage without the sturdy travel sandals or the mantles I purchased before the sky fell in on us? Where will we sleep? How is Jaguar Shield's wound? I even find time to worry about Turtle Star. Are the other priestesses taking care of her, or plotting against her? I moan and put my head in my hands. What a mess.

Ix Chel's wisdom comes to me. I tell myself, "Jade Skirt, stop worrying. Stop it! All will be revealed in its own time. Whatever has happened cannot be changed, and whatever is to happen is already written."

By now, Father Kin has sunk into the West to ride the black jaguar into the Underworld. Alone, on the opposite side of the clearing, hidden in the brush Jaguar Paw watches. He responds to every subtle shift and change of jungle sounds. I am tucked down in the brush as well, dozing with the girls tucked under my arms, when a bird squawks. There is an unmistakable crackle of dry leaves and now a steady thump of footsteps. Jaguar Paw looks at me. Finger to his mouth, he shakes his head. It's only a troop of furry brown badgers on their way to whatever badgers do at this time of day—hunting for food, no doubt. Heads and tails up, they prance officiously behind their leader, an old male. Battle scars and mangy fur mark him as a seasoned commander. Just behind them saunters a fat, pink-eared gibnut, which looks like a mix of its squirrel and rat relatives. Smoothly, silently sniffing at the ground, he ambles along the trail behind the badgers. Jaguar Paw raises his spear to shoulder level. He hesitates a moment, and then his weapon whizzes to meet its mark; the brown, hairy chest of the gibnut impaled neatly. It's almost a shame to see the soft fur soaked with crimson blood. Jaguar Paw crawls out and grabs the tip end of his spear to pull in his prey.

Proudly removing the bloody spear, he lays the food at my feet. I whisper a prayer of gratitude to the little animal whose sacrifice will sustain us. Hands on its warm, still body, I guide its soul to leave in peace and thanksgiving. It's bad luck to kill an animal for food without giving thanks and guiding its soul to Paradise. A thoughtless, disrespectful hunter could be haunted and even killed by forest animals for neglecting the death rite. Jaguar Paw wipes his spear with a leaf and then ties the gibnut's legs with a vine.

In the underbrush we crouch. We wait. We wait. Heads in my lap, the girls sleep, but I am too worried to doze. I wish Red Earth was with us. I worry about her. And Water Lily—how will she survive without her drink? I grasp my jade bead necklace and I can feel my daughter's frustration and fear.

At last, we hear the steady rhythm of human feet on the forest floor. Jaguar Paw stiffens, ready to pounce, but I can tell there is no danger.

"Hold back, hold back, my son," I whisper.

Our household slave, Iguana Wind, followed by two soldiers and Jaguar Shield come into the clearing. My heart soars to see these allies and my beloved. All of the men, except for Jaguar Shield, carry a basket of supplies strung from their foreheads by leather straps. Iguana Wind reaches us first. He has nearly served his full ten *tuns* and earned his freedom. I feel a wash of gratitude. He's loyal, intelligent and strong. We will need him. Jaguar Shield manages to cross the clearing and then, exhausted, he collapses in my arms. The soldiers quickly attend to him and I reluctantly give him up to their care. I see the head wound is healing well, but he has a fever and perspires profusely.

The soldier give us no greeting or eye contact. The older one addresses himself to the tree behind me: "The *nacom* is still not well, but he insisted on seeing you safely to the sea." I feel his scorn. "He is my commander. I have no love for you or for what you have done, but out of respect for my leader, I will stay with your family until we reach the Eastern Sea."

The younger soldier also addresses the tree instead of me:

"I, too, offer my service. I owe a great deal to the *nacom*. When my father was captured in battle, the *nacom* rescued him with no fear for his own life. I was born after that, so were it not for him, I would not be. He is my commander and the best military instructor ever known in Chichen." He lays down his basket and continues in a derisive tone. "I am here for him. I, too, do not approve of what you have done to your husband's lineage and these unfortunate children."

Only a few days ago, these soldiers could not have spoken to me, High Priestess and Oracle, with such disrespect. They would have been severely punished for insubordination. But now I accept their disrespect. I cast my eyes to the ground.

But where is Red Earth? She would not have stayed behind alone.

"Where is my granddaughter, Red Earth? What happened to my daughter, Water Lily?"

The soldiers will not speak to me. They busy themselves helping Jaguar Shield. Iguana Wind steps forward and grasps my arm. Short and stout with a long lower lip, his enormous hooked nose falls over his jaw line. We treat our slaves as members of our family. Iguana Wind called my husband, "father" and Moon Eagle called him "son." Now his kind face looks grief-stricken and I am overwhelmed with despair. It's bad news.

"Tell me, Son. Tell me at once!"

Nine Macaw pulls on my torn mantle anxiously. Tree Orchid covers her face, waiting. Jaguar Paw stands near his sister protectively.

"Red Earth has taken a different path," the slave tells us gently. "She chose to be taken to Paradise by the Goddess Ix Tab."

I scream, fall against Iguana Wind and bury my head in his broad chest. I sob like a child. It can't be! Tree Orchid and Nine Macaw are wailing. Jaguar Paw jams his spear into the earth again and again in anger.

"I am sorry, Sister," says Jaguar Shield, struggling to sit up. "I am so sorry. It was I who found Red Earth. A nephew told me what he saw: after you left to find the girls, she ran to the house of her betrothed and they turned their backs on her. The boy hid inside the house. No one would speak to her. So she ran back home." He is silent for a moment. Nine Macaw, Tree Orchid and I are rocking back and forth together, shaking with our weeping. "It was too much for her," my brother-in-law continues. "I found her hanging by a rope from the rafters."

Red Earth's limp, cold body swinging from a rope—it can't be!

Jaguar Shield lays a comforting hand on my head. "We must forgive her and bless her soul, which is free now. Be comforted, dear ones. She is in the Paradise of suicides with Ix Tab."

We cry until we are out of tears. There have been so many shocks in the past few days—it feels as if we've simply lurched from bad news to worse news and now to the worst possible news. My poor, dear Red Earth. Unfortunate child. She chose suicide and a guaranteed place in Paradise rather than exile and shame. Was it cowardice or valor? Perhaps she made the right choice for her. But, oh, oh, my precious feather is gone! She died alone, rejected and heartbroken, and so young. We all had so much hope for the happiness she and her betrothed might wring out of their ill-fated lives. Who will care for her body now that we are all outcasts?

A wave of guilt crashes over me. Red Earth always believed I loved Nine Macaw more than I loved her. It wasn't true; I loved them both, but I loved them differently. I didn't feel as close to Red Earth because she didn't have the gifts of the Chel line, and those parts of me are so central to who I am and how I live. I could never share that with my eldest grandchild. In Nine Macaw I found a child who does share it, understands it, is nourished by it the way I am. But in choosing to save Nine Macaw from sacrifice, I ended up losing Red Earth. Poor Water Lily! How must she have taken the news? I weep, heartbroken, and I can't even pray to Ix Chel to help us. It is too late for Red Earth.

And what of Water Lily? When I can find my voice, I ask the soldiers, but they turn from me, uncomfortable. Jaguar Shield is dozing, but I shake him awake. I must know. Where is Water Lily? Does he know what happened?

"I did not see her," my brother-in-law tells me, sorrow in his voice. "I had no news of her. The last I heard, she was taken by the magistrate. Have faith, Lady," he says to me kindly. "Ix Chel will not abandon us."

His presence is a comfort, but his words—well-intentioned—feel empty. I know it was not the Goddess's fault that Red Earth left us; each of us makes our own choices. But a childish part of me wonders what good it is to be a Goddess if you can't save one young girl from such despair that she would take her own life! I know this isn't fair, but I think it anyway.

All night, I worry and grieve and blame myself, and finally I fall into an exhausted sleep. My dreams are haunted by Red Earth's restless spirit. I try to say goodbye, to give her my blessing, but she is too far away to hear me and I spend the hours thrashing around, trying to reach her.

When I wake, I feel heavy and exhausted. The cold, thin light of dawn is starting to break and the jungle is waking up. The monkeys are screeching and birds are singing greetings to the morning. The girls are still asleep on the ground next to me, wrapped around each other for warmth and comfort. Their tear-stained faces are smudged with dirt and insect bites. Jaguar Shield snores peacefully. I would love to go to him, but a guard rests beside him and I don't want a confrontation. I don't see Jaguar Paw or the second guard, but Iguana Wind is awake. I feel comforted by the silhouette of his familiar bulk. He has been with us since he was captured in a bitter battle with the Putun. Moon Eagle offered him slavery for ten years to save his life from the sacrificial stone. Iguana Wind came from a lineage of lesser nobles, but he was well-educated. Like others born on the day of 5 Monkey, he is an excellent storyteller and the children love him. He was always grateful to Moon Eagle for sparing his life, and he has been a loyal and capable addition to our household. His understanding, sad smile now says more than any words I need. Here is one who will never hate me, even though I am an exile. In this recent storm of turmoil, his loyalty touches me.

I would love nothing more than to lie on this ground and never get up again, but the children will wake soon and they will need me to be strong. We have many, many miles to walk until we are safely on the road to Cuzamil. The thought of the journey without Red Earth and Water Lily fills me with despair. More tears leak from my eyes.

Iguana Wind is at my side, helping me rise. He leads me over to the pile of baskets the men brought last night. I was so distraught over the news of Red Earth that I didn't pay attention, but now I sift through the baskets and for once there is some good news. Jaguar Shield brought all my market bags. There are sandals, mantles and a change of clothes for each of us. With relief I see he remembered my ceremonial bag of sacred items. The sack of cacao beans and precious stones is neatly tucked away at the bottom of the smallest basket. Wrapped in my grandmother's embroidered cloth, wonder of wonders, is the Ancestral Stone! How did Jaguar Shield manage this? There are cooking utensils, two clay pots and my medicine pouch. Strung like beads on a twist of hemp rope are balls of ground pumpkin seeds and dried blue corn. These will sustain us all for the next few days. To make a thick, nourishing drink, we have only to drop the balls into water. Despite my grief, my morale does lift a bit. There are eight people traveling in our party, and I calculate that we have just the right amount to feed each of us three times a day for three days. By that time we should have reached the province of Ekab, where we can walk the *sacbe* and stay at the inns provided for travelers.

I repack the baskets and wake the girls. They cling to me, all the fears of the past few days making them act like much younger children in need of comfort.

I help them walk behind Iguana Wind to a clearing not far away where there is a fresh-water *cenote* and a cave. Iguana Wind explains that we will rest here and give Jaguar Shield a chance to heal. I want to be moving, to know we're out of reach of Blood Gatherer, but I see the wisdom in this plan. The children need to rest and heal. I haven't even had time to tend to the rope burns on their wrists and ankles where their captors bound them.

The girls are too shocked and exhausted to do more than curl up together against a wall of the cave and watch me rub salve on their raw skin. I cuddle them both and they cling to me as if I will disappear if they let go. Red Earth's absence is a raw wound. I can't even let myself think about Water Lily. Where is she? Does she know what happened? How will she ever find us?

The two soldiers have carried their *nacom* into the cave. Jaguar Shield is very weak, barely conscious. I would go to him, but the soldiers are caring for him now and I don't want to challenge their authority. Also, I sense—in that way that the Goddess has granted me—that he will heal from his wounds. I look for my grandson and spot him at the edge of the clearing collecting dry wood. He stays off by himself so he will not show emotions to the other men. It is lonely to be a man. I'm worried about him. His sister is dead; his mother is missing. But as a man, his mourning must be silent, stoic.

After consulting with the soldiers, Iguana Wind gets to work making a small fire in the cave so the soldiers can make Jaguar Shield's medicinal tea. Iguana Wind is an expert spark-maker. He sits cross-legged and twirls his wooden fire stick in an indentation in a small gray stone. The rubbing creates sparks. In the palm of his hand he holds a handful of dry grass. The sparks catch the tinder, which smolders and then bursts into flame. He keeps the fire small and practically smokeless so that it won't give away our location to any soldiers my brother might have sent to search for us.

By the water's edge, Jaguar Paw neatly skins and guts the gibnut, then spears it through with a green stick. He digs two forked stakes in the ground on either side of the fire to hold the skewer so the meat will roast evenly. Tears stream down his face as he methodically turns the gibnut to cook the flesh evenly. This simple task seems to steady him. The smell of cooking meat makes my stomach growl, but also fills me with revulsion. It smells like death.

We spend the day sitting silently, lost in our own thoughts. The girls doze against my shoulders. One of the soldiers fills a leather sack with water. It's fashioned from a deer's stomach. The water gurgles with every step he takes across the cave. He washes a handful of roots in one of the clay pots and then mashes the roots with his hands until the water turns a murky brown color. He crouches beside Jaguar Shield and gently washes his head wound. I watch, but don't comment. It looks like he's doing a good job. Most of the soldiers learn healing during their training. Some are more gifted than others.

"Girls," I say after a time, gently rousing them. "Find the other clay pot and heat water for our *atole*."

Dear hearts, they wipe their eyes and stand up at once to rummage through the baskets. They fill a clay pot with water from the *cenote*. To make a hearth, they set three large stones on the ground. Jaguar Paw helps them balance the round pot over the stones and soon the water is steaming over the low fire. I drop eight dried corn balls into the water, stir, and add pumpkin seed meal.

"Keep that fire low," grumbles the older soldier.

Stirring the gruel—such a simple task—is comforting. The familiar is always comforting. Homeless we may be, exiles, hunted, but I can stare into the pot and nearly float away as if hypnotized.

While the *atole* is cooking, Iguana Wind offers to show Tree Orchid how to use the fire starter. The younger soldier goes to patrol the area and make sure our trails are well-hidden while the older soldier brews tea for Jaguar Shield, who is still lying down. Jaguar Paw still tends the meat, but when the others are out of earshot he tells his sister, "Mother will be with us soon. Don't worry."

Nine Macaw hops up and gives him a hug and he allows it, then gently pushes her away. She falls into my arms, weeping again.

"Na," she whispers, "did Red Earth kill herself because of me?"

"No! Her death was not your fault, child."

"But if I had agreed to go to the Well of Sacrifice she would still be alive!"

"But then we would be weeping for you," I tell her gently. "Listen, Red Earth made a decision in a moment of great despair. I wish so many things had been different. If I had taken her with me; if Water Lily had been home; if Blood Gatherer had never come to our home—there are so many things that we can regret, but what happened is already written. We must do the best we can even though we don't know what the outcome will be."

"But—"

"Nine Macaw, hear me: you must never regret that you are alive. Never! We will miss Red Earth, but you did not kill her."

I feel her absorbing my words, allowing for the possibility that it's not her fault. "What about Mother, Na? Is she—do you think she's also—"

I pass my right hand over the jade beads we share and feel that, yes, she is alive, but frightened and alone. Relieved, I tell Nine Macaw, "Water Lily is alright. I can feel her."

Just then, we hear a noisy flap of wings. A bundle of green and yellow feathers arrows down from the sky toward us. Tree Orchid lets out a shriek.

"Kiki!" She flings her hand up and her devoted parrot lands neatly. Nine Macaw leaps up and lets out an amazed shout of delight and Jaguar Paw is grinning. The bird is just the medicine they need right now. They fuss over him, tell him what a brave and clever bird he is, feed him pumpkin seeds and stroke his feathers. I'm not surprised the parrot has tracked Tree Orchid down. The girl has a special relationship with birds, and the Goddess knows we need comfort right now. The little fellow squawks happily on Tree Orchid's shoulder. The young girl beams and Nine Macaw looks on admiringly. The bird's arrival is one less heartache for Tree Orchid and Nine Macaw; one thing they have not lost, in the midst of so much loss.

"Don't cry! Don't cry!" shrieks the bird in that eerie way parrots have of speaking in our tongue.

The noise brings the younger soldier back to the camp to investigate. He orders us to make less noise.

"Bowls," I call to Nine Macaw in a soft voice. She digs eight gourd bowls out of the pile. As I fill the bowls one by one I see more tears streaming down her face. Tree Orchid is right beside her, sad little face streaked with tears, too. "We must be strong, now," is all I can think to say.

We sit in a circle around the embers of the cook fire sipping the warm *atole*, lost in our own thoughts. Jaguar Paw uses his obsidian knife to cut the sizzling gibnut into eight pieces. I take for myself and Jaguar Shield, and I bring him his food—ignoring the disapproving guard. He's propped up against the wall of the cave. I sit beside him and we eat together.

"We knew this would be hard," he says softly, for my ears only. "I never expected Red Earth to hang herself, though." He takes a long, slow sip of his *atole*, leans back and closes his eyes. "Who can judge?"

Comforted by each other's presence, we savor the tender, moist meat of the gibnut. Here, next to him, I feel at home in the world. I feel his masculine strength and tender, protective love. As always, being near him is a balm to my soul. I know he would fight demons to protect us.

Our meal finished, Iguana Wind pokes at the embers and hums a favorite song of the court poets. The other men join in quietly and soon our sad little camp is blanketed in a soothing melody like a baby's lullaby. The sun is starting to descend to the horizon. I'm surprised that a whole day has passed. It's rare for me to do so little in a day, but grief takes so much energy, as does worry. Was it only yesterday that I rescued the girls? And the night before that Jaguar Shield and I spent as captives! It seems like all these events took place weeks ago.

Thanks to Jaguar Shield, we have everything we need to survive as fugitives in the unforgiving jungle. I spread out two of our mantles and motion to the girls to come and lie beside me. I cover us with a third mantle. We snuggle against one another more for comfort than for warmth. Their muscles feel stiff; their *chu'lel* thrashed and crushed by the events of this sad day. Beneath me, the Earth Lords send a soothing wave. I feel the flowing stream of love rise up to caress me. I sigh deeply.

Through the camp wafts a cool evening breeze. All is quiet, including Kiki, who has settled on a low tree branch covered in red fruits. He picks and pecks as he eats, cocking his little golden head from side to side listening for what we can't hear. Parrots make excellent sentries. I know he will squawk out a warning if anything or anyone dangerous approaches.

We're comfortable, but I sense that no one is especially sleepy. We've slept plenty already today. There is a lot of restless movement. Suddenly, Iguana Wind announces, "I say this is a good time for a story." He clears his throat.

Yes. Yes. Thank you. A story. Perfect.

A flash of happy anticipation flushes color into the sallow faces of the children. Jaguar Paw moves to the other side of the dying fire to sit next to Nine Macaw. She sighs and plops her head on his lap.

"Well," begins Iguana Wind. All eyes are on him. The soldiers settle back and each lights a tobacco pipe; Jaguar Shield is alert, listening.

"Children," begins our storyteller, "listen to my words and hear the ways of those who came before you and of the old ones. We tell these tales that you may know the past to better prepare for the future." He gives a dramatic pause, and then continues:

"This is a tale of the Great Mother, Ix Chel, She who is the Heart of Water; She who is in white stones; She whose home is in caves and She who is the Mother of all animate and inanimate beings of the Known World."

I exhale and feel Her presence. I expand my awareness and send Her my gratitude.

"When Ix Chel was a young woman, She was too independent and headstrong to be controlled by any God, either in heaven or in hell. Her father,

Hunabku, the greatest of all the Gods, tried to keep the Goddess home so he could teach her to be obedient." Nine Macaw and Tree Orchid smile a little at the idea of Ix Chel being treated like any disobedient daughter.

"But one day while He was out, She eloped with the Sun God! Well, as you can imagine, that made Her father furious. So He hurled a bolt of lightning, and in anger He killed His own daughter."

The children look surprised. The Goddess was killed? They squirm, wanting to hear what happens next. Iguana Wind looks unconcerned as he stirs the embers. He waits an extra minute to build suspense and then continues:

"Swarms of dragonflies came to Ix Chel where She lay. For thirteen days they sang and buzzed their wings over Her. It was then that She finally revived. She returned to the home of Her husband, the Sun God. Now, in time, the Sun God became angry because She would not obey. He began to beat Her and to mistreat Her." I notice Jaguar Paw scowls at this news. He has been taught this is not proper behavior for a husband.

"So the Goddess ran away with the God of the Morning Star. She hid from Her cruel husband and angry father. But after a short time, the Morning Star God became weary of Her refusal to obey Him. He tried to lock Ix Chel up."

Tree Orchid shakes her head at Nine Macaw. They both know it won't work. Again, Iguana Wind pauses to poke at the embers before he continues.

"Once again, the Goddess escaped. This time, Ix Chel ran away with the God of the Vultures. But the Sun God heard of it, and He came up with a plan to retrieve His wife from the land of the vultures. He killed a deer and climbed inside the skin, pretending to be dead. When the vultures came to eat the deer, the Sun God grabbed one of them by the wing and forced her to take him to the house of the King Vulture. There was a terrible fight between the Sun God and the Vulture King. The Sun God was victorious and took Ix Chel away."

Iguana Wind leaned back and sighed, warning us that there was more to the story and it would not be good.

"Soon, the Goddess grew tired of Her husband's jealousy. It was just like before. They quarreled constantly, which caused the heavens to thunder and bolts of lightning to strike the earth. The Sun God was so frustrated with His disobedient wife that He took away Her brilliant rainbow colors and left Her with only the pale light of the moon. But Ix Chel had a pet rabbit who managed to escape from the furious Sun God. It hid in the moon—you can see it when the moon is full."

"But what happened to Ix Chel? She wanders the nights, making Herself invisible whenever Her cruel husband shows His fiery head. But from each of these Gods—the Sun, the Morning Star and the King Vulture—our Mother birthed children who are now walking on this earth and have established all of the lineages of our people. Ix Chel is the rainbow that lights up the days of rain. She shows Her love for us when She rises to light the darkness. During the dark days of the moon, She is resting from her travels. You can see Her sitting in the moon, holding Her rabbit while they watch over the Earth. She takes care of women and children, guides our healers and takes our bodies into Hers when we die."

He offers this last thought gently, and we all think of Red Earth being taken into Ix Chel, and we are comforted. I bless Iguana Wind and his gentle heart for this healing tale. It's an old, familiar story told many times around hearth and camp fires, but tonight, under the light of the rising moon, we all feel the Goddess watching over us.

That night, I dream of a rising moon that shimmers over a sparkling path on a dark sea. As if they had wings, graceful forms of dolphins at play rise up into the air. The sea beckons me. I feel that I could walk over the moonlit ocean. At the end of the shining path is Cuzamil. Countless canoes manned by muscled men carry women and children to the island. In a royal, palm-covered canoe sits Nine Macaw, Tree Orchid and I. On the shore, Heart of Water waits for us. When our eyes meet, her face contorts into a mean scowl. She points at me to signal that I should return to the mainland. In a fright, I awaken. Great Mother, what is the meaning of this evil dream?

After that there is no more sleep for me. The hard, stony ground has no comfortable spot. What does it mean? Heart of Water would never look at me with such scorn. She would not send us away. So what does this dream signify? I worry over it like a sore tooth until I'm exhausted. Whatever it is, I tell myself, it will be revealed. For now, my sack of troubles is full enough.

Another dawn breaks over the jungle. Iguana Wind and Jaguar Paw start the morning fire. One of the soldiers brings more water so the girls can prepare our corn-and-pumpkin-seed gruel. Silently, solemnly, we drink our breakfast while the rising sun soaks up the damp night air. It's strange for men and women to eat together, but here in the bush the usual social customs don't apply. The men efficiently clear the camp, hide all traces of our fire and remove all signs of our presence.

Jaguar Shield is brighter and stronger this morning. His stamina amazes me. Only a few days ago, I thought he might not survive, but today, he is back in charge, nearly as strong as ever. With seasoned authority and erect posture he peers intently into every face. All eyes are on him.

"We will stay off the *sacbe* until we reach Na Balam, a two-day march." His voice sounds hoarse, but strong and confident. "There, Jade Skirt's own lineage, the Chels will welcome us. Iguana Wind is from Tulumha by the sea. Are you sure you can remember these back trails?" he asks my slave.

Iguana Wind smiles with pleasure. "Like my own mother's face, my lord. Freedom, my wife and family await me. Be assured, I can and will lead us to the great road at Na Balam and beyond if necessary."

"Good. Beyond Na Balam, I doubt anyone would have heard of what happened in Chichen; at least not yet." Again, Jaguar Shield searches each face as if taking our measure. His gaze lingers on the two soldiers. "We are all sworn to secrecy on this journey. Now that we are all officially exiled, Red Earth in Paradise with Ix Tab and Water Lily punished, the Council of Leaders will not bother to send their soldiers after us. But Blood Gatherer is another matter." He pauses a long moment. "He is powerful, and wrathful. That is always a dangerous combination. Therefore, we stay hidden until Na Balam."

"May the Goddess protect us," I say. The two soldiers turn their faces away. They won't acknowledge my presence. I must be humble in their presence. We need them, and feigned humility is a small price to pay.

"We must be quiet," Jaguar Shield tells us as we get ready to depart. "Speak only when necessary and always in a low voice." To the three children he says, "Today is our most dangerous day. If we are followed, it will be today. I expect you to obey. No laughing or loud talking. Understood?"

They answer as one, "Yes, Uncle."

He frowns at Kiki and says, "And you keep that parrot quiet!" Tree Orchid nods solemnly and motions to Kiki to take to the skies for a while.

Iguana Wind leads the way; one of the soldiers follows behind him, weapons ready. Jaguar Shield and Jaguar Paw are in the middle. The other soldier walks behind me and the girls. The men's cocked heads and darting eyes take in everything at once. They remind me of Kiki, actually. We halt only when Jaguar Shield stops to catch his breath. His head wound shows dried blood through the cloth. When we pass a young *naba* tree, I pick some leaves that I'll use to wash his wound later.

We trudge along in uncomfortable silence on difficult trails that are overgrown, riddled with thorns and infested with ants, but we make our way as silently as we can. Nine Macaw and Tree Orchid are continually distracted by a rainbow of berries and flowers that clutter the ground. I keep herding them back on the trail, and this requires my constant attention. It's my duty to be sure they behave, yet I, too, wish to stop and pick berries and flowers. The girls put flowers in their hair and Tree Orchid collects dry seeds to make a bracelet, all the while trying not to stumble.

Nine Macaw is entranced by all the plants. "Can we eat this one, Na?" she whispers, pointing to a low bush with serrated leaves. "Is this one good for medicine? What's this one's name?"

Her love of plant lore usually delights me, but today it's hard to be patient with her constant questions. I reach out to catch Nine Macaw only a moment before she trips on a tree root.

"Girls!" I scold in a whisper. "Pay attention! Be careful where you step and what you touch. The jungle here is full of poisonwood."

Chastised, they tuck their arms to their chests and walk obediently in the middle of the narrow trail. Any casual contact with the dreaded black, oozing sap of the poisonwood tree causes a blistering rash that can only be cured with the red, shaggy bark of the *chacah* tree, which looks just like the skin infection it cures. Fortunately, wherever poisonwood trees grow, *chacah* trees are always nearby.

Mercifully, there are few mosquitoes this morning. After a while, the girls walk like old people, heads down and backs bent. Suddenly, the lead soldier lifts his right hand to signal a stop. He motions for everyone to hide. What's this? I grab my charges by the shoulders and pull them down behind a fallen tree trunk. Without a sound, the men melt into the bushes. In a moment, there is no trace of them except a quivering in the air. The girls tremble against me as we wait. I hear a rustling, the cracking of twigs. I freeze, listening. An invisible weight squeezes my chest. My heartbeat pounds in my ears. A snort. An offensive odor. That foul stench makes the blood in my veins go cold. Could it be? Has Blood Gatherer found us? I hold my breath with fear. Tree Orchid and Nine Macaw are rigid as wood.

Through lacy fern leaves I wait to see our pursuers, and then I spot them and laugh with relief. It's just a herd of collared peccaries. Of course—that's what I've been smelling. The leader, an old male, stops a short distance away and sniffs the air. His hooves tear up the earth. Behind him, a string of adolescents and babies sniff the ground, searching for food. We stay down, because wild boars are dangerous, unpredictable animals. A sudden noise can provoke a charge, and their tusks are deadly. Tree Orchid whimpers. I put a hand over her mouth. From an overhead branch, Kiki flies to her. He squawks. Every boar's head turns toward the sound of Kiki's flight. Like a moving stream of water, tension ripples. Whizz! An arrow flies into the herd, which turns and stampedes away into the dense brush. The smallest of the herd lies bleeding from the arrow in its chest. The older soldier stands over it to remove the arrow.

"Aha!" he says softly, but triumphantly, "meat! May the Gods be praised."

His eyes meet mine and he nods curtly. I kneel on the damp earth beside the beast and look into its dull, dead eyes.

"Nine Macaw," I whisper, "come and say the prayer this time."

She lays her small hands on the peccary and says solemnly, "Thank you for your life, which will sustain us today. We commend your soul to the Lords of the Day. May they see you safely to Paradise."

In one quick movement, the soldier moves forward, turns the pig over and slits its throat. Its crimson life force flows back into the earth. Jaguar Paw covers the blood with dirt and leaves. He ties the animal's feet with a piece of vine and slings it over his shoulder.

"Hurry now," whispers Jaguar Shield. "We must keep moving. We're still too close to Chichen."

For the rest of the morning, white limestone ridges and low caves dot the flat, rocky terrain. Jaguar Shield allows us one quick stop to rest and fill our gourds with cool water. An iridescent, blue and black mot-mot bird flies down to a low branch to visit Tree Orchid. Usually shy and hidden, his long tail is twice the length of his body and splits at the end into two half-feathers. Even the soldiers are enchanted.

"It's because of you, Tree Orchid," whispers Nine Macaw. "The birds always follow you."

Smiling, Tree Orchid feeds Kiki a green seed pod from the ground. "I know what they're feeling," she admits in a low voice. "They speak to me. It's always been that way."

Ix Chel's island home is famous for women who have the ability to read the future weather patterns in the flight of the swifts. The flock returns to our towers to roost every *tun* at the same time. Tree Orchid will be cherished in Cuzamil. I feel glad for her. And then, with a sudden jolt of grief, I am crying silently Red Earth, who will not be with us in our new life.

We continue our trek through the jungle. The trail grows wider and easier as the day passes, and Jaguar Shield lets us pause briefly under a *k'nep* tree, which is covered in fluffy pink flowers and draped with sweet orange fruits. The girls and I want to stay longer and collect fruit, but Jaguar Shield is anxious to move on.

Lips pinched, hands splayed out wide he says, "I hate traveling with women! But, alright, go ahead only be quick and quiet about it, will you. This is not a family outing."

Lithe as a monkey, Jaguar Paw scales the tree and shakes it until the gifts of the Great Mother rain down over our heads. The children and I gather the juicy fruits. They stuff as many into their mouths as they do their sacks. It's quick work and Jaguar Shield gets us moving again in a few minutes.

I remember other, happier days collecting *k'nep* fruits when my own children were small. This is the first time Water Lily and I have been so far apart. When I hold the jade necklace, I see contorted faces jeering and cursing at her, and hands flinging stones. Water Lily is hurt, but she survives. Poor thing—no matter what her past faults, she needs my support now. I send her beams of love through the jade. I hope she can feel it on some level.

As the sun passes the midpoint of the sky, we are walking through a dense canopy when suddenly Kiki squawks loudly, "Don't cry! Don't cry!"

The men immediately raise their weapons and I grab the girls and press them down so I can cover them with my body. We hear a high-pitched screech and a small, dark shape falls from one of the trees.

"Bobo! It's Bobo!" cried Tree Orchid, unmindful of our need for silence. "He found us!"

The spider monkey jumps into Nine Macaw's arms and cackles. His little mouth opens into a toothy grin.

"Quiet!" Jaguar Shield orders, furious. "Do you think there is no danger here? Do you know what will happen if we are found?"

The girls pale and Tree Orchid looks at the ground, ashamed. We walk again in silence, and I can feel Jaguar Shield's frustration and annoyance. But the girls recover and soon they are smiling and nudging each other, silently pointing to flowers and rocks and Bobo and Kiki. Even Jaguar Paw comes over and pets the monkey fondly on the head.

We run low on water by late afternoon. This month of the Deer, hottest of all, is the last before the rains start. Heat waves dance in the air. Even under the protective shade of the jungle we're getting burned by the sun. I wish I had thought to bring a special skin salve to block it. In spite of the dry weather, the air is oppressively damp. A maddening, ear-splitting screech of cicadas grows louder and louder until I feel the need to cover my ears. But it's no use, like *maguey* needles, the high-pitched sound of their rubbing wings gives me a throbbing headache. It's odd. They're usually loudest just before the rains fall, but the sky looks clear.

We stop at a narrow, shaded *cenote* to eat and rest. Jaguar Shield whispers that we will continue walking until we can no longer see our feet. We must get farther away from Chichen. Although we've walked all day, it's been on rough back trails that wind in a roundabout route, so we're still too close to Chichen and too far from Na Balam. Jaguar Shield is irritable. I wonder if his wound is bothering him. His curtness is affecting the rest of us. Jaguar Paw crouches on the ground and carves a piece of mahogany wood he picked up on the trail. He's scowling and won't meet my eyes. He won't even acknowledge the girls when they come over to him, curious to see what he's carving.

I understand. All that he once knew is gone. His mother is missing, his sister is dead. The future is uncertain. He's just a boy with a heart that is heavy with grief and he doesn't know how to express it.

"C'ox!" Jaguar Shield orders, and we're walking again. It feels like we've been walking and walking for hours. Ordinarily, I love walking in the jungle, but it's been a hot day and even as the sun starts to descend I'm sweating and uncomfortable.

Jaguar Shield stumbles a few times. The younger soldier catches his arm, and the *nacom* shakes him off, irritated that he needs help. My brother-in-law is clearly not feeling well, but I would never insult him by suggesting it in front of the others. I worry as he pushes himself on. I even get a little mad at him. Why are men so stubborn? There are plenty of adequate places to stop and make camp. But Jaguar Shield drives us forward and risks his health.

Finally, he calls a halt. I have to admit he's chosen a perfect place to rest. This *cenote* is a long and wide cave filled with water and covered by a high outcropping of limestone. There is clean water as blue as the sky reflecting rippling patterns of light onto the chalky overhang. I sigh with relief. It's so nice to be in a cool place. Broad leaf palms and wide branches of *ramon* trees give shade. Footprints of animals speckle the sandy shore.

As the soldiers set down the baskets, they sink into the shade. Jaguar Paw gathers himself to dive into the water. The older soldier grabs him by the arm and spins him around forcefully.

"Have you learned nothing?" He glares into Jaguar Paw's stunned face.

"What?"

"Cool down, first, boy, or your body will go into spasm from the shock!"

Jaguar Paw shrugs and walks away, stung by this public rebuke. Iguana Wind motions him to come over and then distracts him by making a game of guessing each paw and claw print. I half-listen as they discuss whether this print is a male or female jaguar; whether that one is a fawn or a tapir.

While one soldier paces around the clearing, eyes alert, soon the other four men wade into the water. My grandson, still a boney boy, has barely a promise of a male member. Hands folded, he hunches over to cover his loins. Jaguar Shield's physique, erect and muscular, has not a hint of fat. How serenely, regally he walks and then gracefully dives into the cool, blue waters. Except for the deep, dark battle wound on his thigh, he is perfectly etched. When he moves, every muscle bulges, flexes. His nakedness stirs me. Iguana Wind and the younger soldier undo their topknots and set the feathers down. Like thick black curtains, their hair cascades down their backs. Mesmerized, I admire their taut buttocks. They slide into the blue water; droplets glistening on their sleek, brown bodies. Up from a shallow dive, they shake their heads. Water flies in all directions making a brilliant ring of wet light in the still air.

I'm practically drooling! I need to stop this. I take the girls by the hand to hunt for food at the side of the *cenote. Ramon* trees prefer to grow by water and here we find several whose fruits generously litter the ground. In a short time, we fill our sacks. Sweet and juicy on the outside, the starchy seeds within can be boiled with our dried corn tonight or roasted in a bed of coals. Jaguar Paw steps out to signal that the men have finished bathing. Iguana Wind slings his rough slave's hammock between two trees to rest. On the shady ground, the others find a spot to lay their mantles.

Undressed, the girls and I wade into the cool, waist-high water of the *cenote*. Soft, white sand soothes our tired feet. Around our legs tiny red-tailed fish dart and nibble. The girls try to catch them, to no avail.

The water is cleansing for the body, and also for the spirit.

"Girls," I say quietly, "this water runs in an underground channel right to the well of Chichen. Let's ask Ix Chel, who lives in all water, to carry our love and prayers on Her flowing current to Water Lily. Then, we will ask that this water, Her sacred body, wash away our sadness."

I can feel the men watching our circle of women. I sense Jaguar Shield and Jaguar Paw wish to join us in the ritual, but it would not be proper.

"Put your hands in the water," I instruct. "Think of your mother surrounded by a soft blue light. See her smiling. See her with us on Cuzamil Island."

Tree Orchid whispers, "Come back to us, Mother, come back to us."

Silent, Nine Macaw has gone to a deep place within herself. I wait patiently, knowing what she is experiencing.

"Na," she says softly, "I feel her sadness. She's all alone. She misses us." Her eyes fly open and I see tears gathering. "I miss her. I want my mother. I want our old house back. I want my sister."

"I know, my little feather," I say. "All will be well. I have faith that Ix Chel, guardian of women and children, will help your mother and Red Earth. Pray with me."

They both wipe their tears and then nod to me that they are ready.

"Mother Goddess," I begin, "You know our needs. I place my faith in You to watch over us, to guide us and to protect our dear Water Lily until she is with us again."

Golden eyes rimmed with tears, Nine Macaw wraps her skinny arms around my waist. Behind her cuddles Tree Orchid until we are three layers of love and grief. One hand on each forehead, I whisper more prayers. They tremble. Tears flow. Like an old blanket, a dark gray sheet of grief and fear falls away from us. Absorbed into the body of the Great Mother, it dissolves in the *cenote*.

"Thanks be to the spirit of water, Ix Chel's earthly body." I use a gourd to scoop water up and pour Her divine essence over us until we are cleansed.

We're all much calmer after the bathing and prayers. The girls go off quietly to pick flowers and I close my eyes and touch the jade necklace. I feel my daughter's spirit and I know that she lives. Through the beads, I see an image of Water Lily with us on Cuzamil, and I sag with relief.

As the sun moves west, Iguana Wind delivers a clay pot of fresh water. Into the pot I drop and stir dried corn balls and some pumpkin seed meal. Tree Orchid measures out the shares then carries a gourd bowl to each person. Nine Macaw passes around another bowl of *ramon* and *k'nep* fruits. Although, it feels safe and protected here, still we eat in silence as a precaution. Bobo and Kiki, always close overhead, feed themselves from wild fruits and pods of the jungle.

When the meal is over, Jaguar Shield stands tall and straight in the middle of the camp site directing each of us in our assigned duties. Iguana Wind and Jaguar Paw and the soldiers patrol the area and erase our tracks. Jaguar Shield sends them off with a nod, and the three turkey feathers in his topknot bounce with every move of his graying head. To avoid attracting attention in case we meet anyone on our journey he has chosen to wear a plain, commoner's mantle. Made of rough *maguey* fibers, the mantle is tied in a large knot over his left shoulder. I find him alluring in it.

My husband's brother instructs the girls to gather, wash and put away all the cooking materials. He supervises them while they wash the *ramon* nuts and store them away for another meal. Conditioned to be thorough, he stands over them while they scrape and scrub every bit of food off the gourds with sand and place them in a shaft of sunlight to dry. They work hard, but they enjoy his attention. In his own way he is letting them know that they are safe and he is there to protect us and watch over us. Ah, there is no other man like him! After he sees us safely to Cuzamil, I hope he will stay in the coastal town of Pole where we can meet often. That is a pleasant fantasy to contemplate.

The girls finish their chores and settle down to play a favorite children's game that uses nine stones each. Into the air they throw one stone, and before it lands they have to pick up one, then two, three and so on until they can grab all nine pebbles before the thrown stone lands. My heart gladdens to see them carefree. Children respond quickly to ritual baths and prayers. I can see that the rippling, heavy air of grief and trauma that has been with them since I found them in the cave is much diminished.

While the others are busy, I squeeze the balsam leaves into a pot of water. I catch Jaguar Shield's eye.

"Let's have a look at your wound,"

Obediently, he sits down in front of me so I can remove the stained dressing from his scalp. I'm pleased to see the area is still an open wound, but not infected.

"It's healing well enough," I murmur, concentrating, "but it needs a good cleaning and a fresh cloth."

"Whatever you say!" He gives me a private smile and his hand squeezes my ankle. Desire glows in his eyes before he looks away as if disinterested.

"Put your head on my lap and lean back," I instruct. I clean the wound thoroughly with the balsam leaf water and then I press around it. There—a tiny piece of chert from the royal guard's club is still embedded in his flesh. He winces when I touch it.

"This has to come out," I say. Luckily, it has started to move toward the surface, but it's still in there fairly deep.

"Iguana Wind!" I call. My slave has just returned to camp with an armful of wood. He hurries over. "I need a pair of pincers."

"Yes, Mother." He's been by my side and Moon Eagle's for many *tuns* and from us both he has learned much about healing—even serving as my assistant in the pilgrims' House of Healing. He jogs into the jungle and returns moments later with a handful of black *zubin* thorns. He shakes off the small ants and then fashions the thumb-sized thorns into a pair of pincers using a thin strip of vine to bind them at the end. I always marvel that his large hands can create such delicate work. I give him a smile of approval and he grins.

With such a fine tool it takes me only a moment with a steady hand to remove the chert. I drop the tiny piece of stone into Jaguar Shield's palm so he can see the culprit.

"This wound needs to be closed up," I murmur to Iguana Wind. "Bring me a good amount of the fat, red warrior ants so I can choose several of the strongest. And be sure to collect them off of trees and not from the ground." I don't need to tell him this, of course, but I say it for the benefit of the soldiers, who are eavesdropping. The ants from the tree will have cleaner legs and be less likely to spread infection. "And bring a strip of the soft *zubin* bark."

Iguana Wind takes Jaguar Paw along to search for the biting warrior ants. I glance over at the soldiers and wish they would give me some privacy with Jaguar Shield. I want to tell him my vision of Water Lily being with us in Cuzamil and of my disturbing dream of a scowling Heart of Water. Perhaps he can help formulate a plan to get Water Lily safely out of Chichen. But I don't trust the soldiers. They seem to grow more hostile toward me every hour. I understand it. They are afraid of me, the honored Oracle and High Priestess who chose exile. And they blame me for Jaguar Shield's exile, and probably, too, they resent me for my courage to defy the priests. It's complicated, and complicated is uncomfortable for most people. I have seen enough of human nature—including my own—to know that when people feel conflicted they find it easiest to retreat to anger and hatred. As if he can read my thoughts, the older soldier glares at me and then turns his back with exaggerated disdain.

"Those pesky ants are everywhere," I say mildly as I busy myself cleaning Jaguar Shield's wound once again. "They should return soon." The edges of his skin are red and raw, but I don't see any more slivers of chert or debris that need to be removed.

"Even pesky ants can serve a good purpose," comments Jaguar Shield, still leaning comfortably against my legs. I am enjoying the physical contact and I can tell he is, too. When the guards aren't looking, he strokes my leg, and I have to bite my lip to keep from smiling.

Jaguar Paw and Iguana Wind walk quickly out of the trees. The boy carries a gourd covered loosely with a piece of tree bark. The excited red ants are trying to push the bark off and scamper out. He's wisely holding the gourd on a wide palm leaf, and Iguana Wind reminds him to keep it away from his body. A bite from one of those ants is extremely painful. I'm glad to see Iguana Wind also brought a nice, long strip of the *zubin* bark.

Jaguar Paw sets the gourd on the ground and the seething mass of ants struggle to escape. The strongest are already on the top, and they're the ones I want. I use the thorn pincers to pluck out a fat, thrashing ant.

Nine Macaw is suddenly at my side. "Please, may I watch, Na? I've never seen this done before."

As usual, I'm delighted by her passionate interest in medicine. She will make a fine healer one day soon. I give her a nod and she scoots down and out of the way. Tree Orchid, who has been building a little family courtyard with stones, doesn't want to be left out. She wiggles in beside Nine Macaw. Jaguar

Paw importantly holds the bark lid on the gourd so our ants won't escape and bite the girls.

"Now hold still," I caution Jaguar Shield. Transfixed, everyone—even the soldiers—watch as I carefully position the ant over the middle of the wound and let it dig its barbed front legs into either side of the swollen flesh. Those legs clamp down so deeply that they can stitch a wound closed. Jaguar Shield winces, but he holds steady. Quickly, I pinch off the ant's back legs and body. Eight ants later, the wound is nicely closed. Iguana Wind pounds the strip of soft, fibrous *zubin* bark against a rock and hands it to me so I can dress the wound. It needs to stay clean and dry while the skin grows back.

"Well done," remarks my patient. Still a bit wobbly, he stands up to show us that he is fine. He tilts his head up and checks the angle of the sun through the palm trees.

"We will stay here until Father Sun has finished His western journey. Tomorrow will be much more arduous than today, so I suggest you all get some rest."

His words bring us back to our predicament. The almost festive feeling we were sharing a moment ago is replaced by grim reality. Red Earth. Water Lily. Blood Gatherer. Exile.

I wake suddenly. Something is wrong. It's Nine Macaw—she's moaning and tossing as if someone is chasing her. I shake her lightly to wake her from her bad dream and she curls into a ball, clasping her knees to her chest.

"What is it, my feather?"

She groans. "My stomach, Na. It hurts!"

"Let me have a look." When she turns I see that her mantle is stained red between her legs. The blessing of her first moon has come! I show her.

"My first moon?"

"Yes, my heart, it is." I stroke her cheek. "Today, you are a woman and a vessel of life. We'd better wash your mantle and find some moss."

If we were at home in Chichen, this would be an event to celebrate, an important rite of passage for Nine Macaw. We would go to the temple of Ix Chel and make offerings and prayers. Ordinarily, a grandmother washes a girl's first stained mantle in a special tub always set aside for that purpose. The water and blood are poured out into the family's corn field as a blessing. Here, we have no ceremonial wash tub and our family corn field is only a memory. I will just have to do the best I can to make it a special occasion for her.

I wake Tree Orchid quietly and I whisper to her what has happened. "Let us give thanks that Nine Macaw has started her moon cycles. Come with us now and we will celebrate!"

Tree Orchid hops up, excited, and she tenderly hugs Nine Macaw and kisses her forehead. I'm so grateful for Tree Orchid, who came into our lives under such sad circumstances. She has been a blessing to all of us. She has a kind and loving nature. It's no wonder the birds and animals love her so.

"As soon as we get to Cuzamil, you both will have your coming of age ceremonies and I promise you it will be a great celebration," I say. Both girls grin, but then Nine Macaw's smile fades.

"I wish Red Earth was here. She said she had a special gift for me when I started the moon cycles." Her lips curled into a sad bow, "I miss her. And I miss my mother."

"I wish we were still in Chichen," Tree Orchid says sadly, "and everything was the same and everyone was alive and together in the same place."

I have to say, "If we had not left Chichen, Nine Macaw would be with the Mai girls in the royal palace getting ready to be the dead bride of Chac."

As soon as the words are out of my mouth, I regret them. I know it sounds callous, as if I don't think Red Earth's life meant as much as her sister's. I hurry on. "Come, now, we have a few things to do to mark this great occasion!"

The girls follow me away from the campsite and the eyes and ears of the men. Kiki flies down silently to perch on Tree Orchid's shoulder. Bobo follows overhead, swinging from tree to tree. I lead the girls to a slender *ceiba* tree and I take my granddaughter's hand.

"Nine Macaw, stand over the earth and let some of your divine woman's essence flow onto the ground. Tree Orchid, you and I will sing the first moon cycle song together." The little orphan beams with pride. Together, we sing the song that all girls learn from their grandmothers:

A woman is a river, ebbing and flowing.
A woman is a river, ebbing and flowing.
A woman is a tide, ebbing and growing.
A woman is a tide, ebbing and growing.

Nine Macaw stands under the sacred *ceiba* tree until a few tiny drops of her maiden's blood fall to the earth.

"Now, your *chu'lel*, your sacred essence, is one with the *ceiba* tree, the earth and the Great Mother. This tree and the Goddess will always know you. You are now one with Ix Chel and the tree that is Her earthly abode." Both girls are filled with wonder and excitement. "She will protect and guard your womb, your sacred vessel of life."

We sing the maiden's song one more time and I wrap my arms around both girls and hold them. I remember Red Earth's first moon, and Water Lily's, and my own. I miss my granddaughter. I will always miss Red Earth.

"We had better get back," I say with a deep sigh. "We're not safe away from the camp."

Longing in her eyes, Tree Orchid asks, "Will I start the moon cycles soon, Na?"

"Of course you will, dear heart. Ix Chel will attend to you just as She did Nine Macaw. Then we will all be women and sacred vessels of life together." The girl gives me a hopeful smile and I touch her cheek. "We had better get that moss," I say.

Tree Orchid bounds ahead. "I saw some hanging on a branch just off the trail. She expertly scales the tree and collects handfuls of soft, green moss. I tear the hem off my dress and fashion a simple loincloth for Nine Macaw who ties it around her waist and secures the moss. She scowls. "It scratches, Na."

"You look like a boy," Tree Orchid giggles.

"Never mind that; it's the best we can do. Stop giggling, Tree Orchid." I pat Nine Macaw on the back, "Tomorrow night, in Na Balam, we'll get some proper cotton and moon cycle garments for you."

Back at the camp, the two girls—no, the girl and young woman—settle down again to rest on Tree Orchid's mantle. Arms wrapped around each other, they whisper-sing the song they learned for their coming-of-age ceremony, which they were never able to perform. Iguana Wind hears them and comes over.

"Is all well, Mother?" he whispers, deep concern in his eyes. How lucky, too, we've been to have him with us. He has served with dignity and grace. Soon it will be time to release him from his servitude.

"Yes, Son, all is well."

I must have fallen asleep. The next thing I know Jaguar Shield's hand is on my shoulder.

"Come, Jade Skirt. We must leave now."

The men have already gathered up everything and the baskets are strapped to their heads. The girls and I gather our things and get in line. The sun is beginning to rise. For a while Jaguar Shield walks alongside me. Head bent toward me, he asks quietly, "What happened last night?"

I tell him and his eyebrows shoot up.

"What timing for her."

We share a look. On the night before Blood Gatherer would have sacrificed her, Nine Macaw was blessed by the Goddess with her first moon. There are no coincidences.

"We did not go far enough yesterday," he admits. "We will not reach Na Balam today. We will be there tomorrow, Goddess willing."

"Maybe Blood Gatherer will leave us alone," I say.

He scowls. "I wouldn't relax about him yet," he warns. "He is devious and clever, so we have to keep alert at all times."

Neither of us say it, but we're both thinking that today is 19 Deer, the most inauspicious day for travelers.

"I don't feel that we're being followed, do you?"

"No, I don't. But, I'm a soldier. I can't put faith in a feeling." He pauses, exhales a long breath. "I trust intuition, but let's not be too trusting. Your brother's desire for revenge is relentless."

We trudge through the jungle, through the tangled, sweltering vines and thorns and tree roots. My love's muscular frame, fluid and rhythmic, moves like a dancer. Turkey feathers in his topknot sway with every well-placed step. Ahead of me, Nine Macaw walks as if she has an uncomfortable wad between her legs, which of course she does. But happily, the moss does its job and there are no stains on her mantle.

I stay alert and worry about my brother and the soldiers he has no doubt sent to hunt us down. So when I hear a great stomping I feel a rush of fear. I'm sure it's the men. Before we can hide, a female tapir and her young crash through the brush at a run. Her wrinkled hide, stout frame and short legs strike me as lovely. The tawny baby, speckled and dotted along his spine, stumbles along beside her.

Nine Macaw sighs, "Oh, look how cute the baby is, Na."

Tree Orchid peeks, "Can we keep it?" she whispers.

I laugh, give Tree Orchid a hug and whisper in her ear, "It's just a baby. It belongs with its mother." The animals veer off into the underbrush. All is quiet again. Our party of exiles and soldier-escorts march on.

It's a long, tedious day of looking over my shoulder at every rustle and noise. I simply can't relax, but by late afternoon I realize that the tickling sensation at the back of my neck of being watched has gone away. Are we out of danger? Perhaps I can actually enjoy the mystery and beauty of this jungle journey. If circumstances were different, I would be truly loving this adventure on the back trails. It's thrilling to be right up close to the creatures and to sleep under the stars. I ask my intuition whether it's safe to let my guard down.

For now, comes Her answer.

It seems to be cooling off, and I realize there are clouds covering the sun. At first it's pleasantly dappled and then the sky grows dark and menacing. Is the rainy season beginning now, too? I can't believe Chac is angry that we did not send Nine Macaw into his well, but a part of me shivers with fear. This looks like it's going to be a violent storm, and here we are out in the open.

A crack of thunder makes the girls squeal. Kiki and Bobo arrow down from the trees and jump into their arms. Bobo changes his mind and leaps back into the tree, then down onto Jaguar Paw's shoulder. The boy takes the spider monkey in his arms and I think he is as glad as Bobo for the comfort. The cicadas stop their incessant screech as if they, too, are waiting to see what Chac will send. The men whisper to one another uneasily. A few drops of light rain fall, but somehow the storm holds off.

For the rest of the day, we move along the trail like seasoned travelers. Not a whimper or a whine from the children. We are all focused on getting to Na Balam quickly. Even the parrot and monkey are subdued. We're so worried about a storm that we're not thinking about other dangers. Suddenly, we hear voices, echoes of drums and the high tune of flutes.

Iguana Wind, still leading the party, stops abruptly. Up goes his hand. All eyes are on him. As though his ears could stretch into the noises, he tilts and lifts his head. Waiting, breathing, we stand in absolute silence. Jaguar Shield consults with Iguana Wind in a low whisper and then motions to Jaguar Paw, who lays down the dead boar he's been carrying and slips away without a sound to scout ahead. When he returns just as silently a few minutes later, he whispers in the *nacom*'s ear. Jaguar Shield makes his way back to us.

"No reason to be frightened," he says softly. "We're just very close to the great *sacbe* that leads to Na Balam." To the girls he says, "If we can hear them, they can hear us. We must be absolutely quiet. We can't attract any attention." He turns back to face me and adds, "We stay here until this group passes."

"Of course. That is best. I'll be sure to keep the children quiet," I whisper.

"Na," whispers Nine Macaw, "I'm hungry."

Tree Orchid nods, "Me, too. And, I'm tired. How much longer before we stop for the night?"

"Soon," Jaguar Shield hisses. "Now everyone be quiet until I say we can talk again!"

Drums, flutes, horns and voices. It must be a parade on the *sacbe*. That means nobles or royalty on the move, which means soldiers, guards, priests with weapons. A procession of costumed musicians followed by troops of dancers was once a friendly, familiar sight. Now it brings waves of fear. How quickly our lives have changed.

It grows quiet after a while and Jaguar Shield gives the signal to start moving again. Until nightfall, we move along the trail in utter silence. I can tell the girls are miserable, scared again and exhausted. There's nothing I can do about it.

Ix Chel can't be seen tonight. The storm clouds cover Her face. Thunder booms and lightning makes us jump. I can hear animals dart and dash through the jungle, taking shelter. Ants of all types are on the move. Armies of leaf-cutter ants, harbingers of rain, balance bits of chewed leaves on their pincers. Over their red, segmented bodies, the leaf parts wobble and dance. Other ants walk up and down trees to return to their thorny homes. What will we do tonight if it rains? How will we manage? I put my trust in Iguana Wind and Jaguar Shield to take care of our needs. The Rain God, Chac, lets out a brutal bellow that makes me and the girls jump in a fright. The men laugh.

At least no one is lingering on the *sacbe* in this weather. It's perfectly quiet. Our trail, which I can barely make out in this darkness, winds past a large cave. Jaguar Shield leads us into it and I'm relieved to see it's dry.

"Girls, "I order, "quickly! Gather firewood."

They moan and complain that they're tired, but they run out and do as they're told. I explore the cave to make sure there are no animals lurking, and in the back I find some of the softest moss I have ever before seen, lovely and smooth and take it to where the girls are gathering wood. I help my granddaughter change her moss and show her how to bury the stained moss in a shallow hole under a rock.

"How do you feel," I ask her.

She sighs, looks at the ground and says, "Tired, Na, and hungry."

"Me, too," mutters Tree Orchid. "I wish we were at home making chocolate."

"Soon." I answer. "Be patient. The hardest part of our journey is almost over. Be brave."

Nine Macaw shrugs. "Yes, Na." Her tone lets me know that she doesn't really believe this journey will ever end.

Suddenly, we hear a scream of pain. I race to the cave and see Iguana Wind lying on the ground. He's holding his leg and whimpering in agony.

"Snake!" he gasps. "It's in the cave. Careful! Everyone, be careful!"

"Quick, quick," I command Jaguar Paw. "Get my medicine pouch. It's in that basket. Hurry!"

I inspect the leg. Redness and swelling already on his right ankle. I can see the double puncture wounds. It was a deadly snake. I feel cold inside. Not Iguana Wind! Dear Goddess, please help him!

Jaguar Shield is at my side. Without delay, he ties a tight band around the leg under the knee and cuts into the bite with an obsidian blade. "There," he says in hushed tones, "The rest is up to you."

19 Deer. It's the most unlucky day of the *tun* to travel. I've been on edge all day and now here it is, the danger I dreaded. A deadly snake! I shake my head to clear away distractions. I'm ready. At my side, Jaguar Paw holds my medicine pouch.

"Nine Macaw!" I command. "Find the snakebite leaves. *Makulan.* The female—not the male."

I sprinkle my snakebite powder onto the bleeding cut. And now it starts to rain. Without discussion, Jaguar Shield and the soldiers lift Iguana Wind and carry him into the cave. The soldiers look anxiously at the ground for the snake, while all my focus is on the patient. I was trained on Cuzamil by the best female snake doctor in the realm. I have treated countless snake bites. Attended to immediately with the right remedies, most snake bites—even from the most deadly vipers—are not fatal. The venom will make Iguana Wind sick, no doubt, but it will not kill him. That is what I tell myself as I dig through my medicine bag.

"Jaguar Paw, run and get me root and bark of the *zubin* tree. Each piece has to be the length of Iguana Wind's arm. Take this piece of string and measure his arm. Be quick!"

The girls are back with the leaves. "Good work," I tell them. My patient is quickly slipping into shock. I chew a handful of the peppery *makulan* leaves into a poultice. I apply the wet mash directly over the snake bite.

"Get water boiling," I command. The younger soldier is on the chore, clumsy with anxiety. Where is Jaguar Paw with the *zubin* root? I need it now!

He comes running back, hands full of root and bark. I grab it from him and force a piece of root into Iguana Wind's hand.

"Son, chew this! Do it now!" He thrashes back and forth on the ground, deaf to my pleas. I can hear my mentor's nasal voice in my head:

"*Zubin* bark breaks down the venom and draws it out. Chewing on the root is a powerful sedative. A frightened person's heart pounds harder, which rushes the blood and venom more quickly through the body."

I jam the root into his mouth and he stops resisting me and starts to chew and swallow the juice. Good. Good. I beat the *zubin* bark with a stone until it's wet with sap. I tie it snug over the wound to keep the poultice of dry powder and mashed leaves in place. My snakebite powder, made of nine barks and roots, is the oldest formula in the healer's temple. But it's only part of the full treatment needed to save this precious life. We wait. He chews and grows quieter and more relaxed. Good. The leg oozes pure blood, then green slime. That, too, is good, but not good enough. Finally I start to see yellow fluid and then brown. The color is back in Iguana Wind's face, but he has fainted.

The soldiers have made a blazing fire deep inside the dark cave and everyone huddles in the light of it, aware that the snake is still in the cave with us. Outside, roaring thunder and flashing lightning continue to herald the beginning of a storm. A powerful wind blows dry-season dust right into the cave, making our eyes gritty. I'm so focused on saving Iguana Wind that when I hear footsteps behind me, coming from the dark back of the cave, I'm more annoyed than alarmed. They come: clunk, stomp, clunk, stomp. I look up to see who is disturbing us and I'm momentarily confused. It's a child dressed in rags and animal skins. No—it's a dwarf!

With a lumbering gait he shuffles from side to side on stunted, bowed legs. In his right hand, he holds aloft a dead snake on the end of a forked stick. We're all so shocked that no one says a word. At first glance, his pitted complexion makes him look hard. His bulging eyes seem too large for his face. A jaguar-skin tunic covers his body. Knee-high boots fashioned from tapir skins still bear the hooves, which stick out in front like a wart on a nose. Warts! The creature's nose is covered in brown, bulbous warts. He is easily the ugliest human being I have ever seen. I lean over Iguana Wind protectively. Wide-eyed, Tree Orchid and Nine Macaw cling to Jaguar Shield's legs.

The soldiers get over their shock and lift their spears, ready to attack. The dwarf is unarmed. He smells of damp earth and smoke. He gently lays the snake on the ground and holds his right hand over his heart to signal peace. Up close, his eyes startle me with their tenderness and sadness. I can see immediately that there is no guile in him; only pain and an inner sweetness. I trust him. So when he bows his head in respect and then bends down to inspect Iguana Wind's leg, I move aside so he can see. He peers at the wound, pokes the swollen leg. His ugly head sways from side to side. Is he mute? No. In a deep, husky voice, the dwarf speaks. I don't recognize his language. Jaguar Shield moves forward. Haltingly, he speaks in the same unintelligible words. The dwarf's face lights up. A genuine smile softens his frightful face. Several times, he nods at Jaguar Shield's questions. They embrace as friends. What's this? Jaguar Shield holds our intruder at arm's length. His head barely reaches to Jaguar Shield's waist, but, with warmth and affection, they pat each other on the back. The dwarf pats Jaguar Shield's buttocks. The children snicker.

"Who is this?" I ask Jaguar Shield.

"This is Sting Ray. I thought he was dead," he answers, one hand on the dwarf's shoulder. "I haven't seen him for many, many *tuns*. We fought side by side in many battles, but not as allies—as enemies! When I knew him he was the assistant to a Putun *nacom*. Sting Ray comes from the far south."

On the ground next to the fire, Sting Ray pulls his black, shoulder length hair away from his face, sniffs the steeping pot of *makulan* leaves, smiles and nods at me in approval. In a kind and warm tone of voice, he speaks to Jaguar Shield, again nodding toward me and smiling.

"He says you are well-trained. He says he could not have done better himself."

Sting Ray speaks again. He takes Iguana Wind's right wrist in his gnarly, hairy hand and waits for the pulse, then frowns. Again, he feels the pulse. His lumpy hand presses mine tenderly. Those deep, pained eyes look into mine meaningfully. He's telling me something important, but I don't understand until he lays the long, black and yellow snake at my feet. Ah, yes! Prepared correctly, its roasted meat is both food and good medicine. This snake is one of the most dangerous. We call it the three-step devil because it usually kills a person by the time he has taken three steps.

I slit open the snake's belly and we all sigh with relief at the sight of a partially digested rabbit. Since the snake devoured the rabbit so recently, it could not have made enough venom to kill a man. Jaguar Paw follows my instruction and chops off the head and tail and buries them in a corner. Intestines and organs removed, the snake's hollow body is chopped into pieces and spit over the fire. Jaguar Paw also skins and spits the little boar over the fire. Sizzle. Soon, snake and boar fat drip into the fire.

From the depths of the cave, Sting Ray walks back and forth bringing food and sleeping furs. The girls are delighted with the soft deer hides and jaguar pelts, which are positively luxurious after nights of sleeping on our mantles on the hard ground. He draws a handful of *makulan* leaves from his rough shoulder bag, which is cleverly fashioned from the shell of an armadillo. He motions for Jaguar Paw to store them away for another bath to cleanse the snakebite wound. He digs around in his bag again and brings out handfuls of dried fruits and seeds for the children.

I'm so worried about Iguana Wind. He is still unconscious. Sting Ray crouches down and dips an old piece of cotton cloth into the hot *makulan* tea, then waves it in the air to cool. Gently, he lays it on Iguana Wind's forehead. Smiling broadly, he mimes a person sleeping.

A delicious, comforting aroma of roasting meat fills the cave. The children are fascinated by Sting Ray. When he smiles, his face changes from horrid to tender. He waves Nine Macaw and Tree Orchid over. Palms down, he extends both his hands toward them. They stare. Three times more he shows he has nothing in his hands until the last time there appears a brown nut. They squeal in delight. The dwarf laughs with them. They beg for more. Sting Ray's dreadful face lights up.

Sting Ray keeps the children distracted with more tricks. It's another thing to be grateful for. Dear Goddess, thank you for sending a friend just when we needed him.

I wash Iguana Wind's ankle with the tea and apply a new poultice of *zubin* bark. Foul fluids still drain from the fang bites. I sprinkle on more of the precious anti-venom powder. He wakes up and moans, but with each passing moment he looks a little better. When his eyes open and he tries to smile at me, I exhale with relief. I know now that he will survive. It might be days until he's recovered, but I believe he will live. I give him a drink of water and order him to chew more *zubin* bark. Then he slips into a peaceful sleep, chest rising and falling rhythmically. This reassures me even more. Patients about to die from snake bites exhibit rapid and shallow breathing.

I turn to the others. "I can't be sure," I announce. "It's too soon. But our friend will probably live." A crash of thunder follows my words, as if the sky itself is agreeing.

"Wonderful! Now let's eat," says Jaguar Shield. "We need our strength. Tomorrow, if we move from here, we will have to carry Iguana Wind on a stretcher."

Sting Ray heats up fat cakes made of *ramon* nuts. He handily draws them out of the coals with a stick and offers one to each of us. We all moan with pleasure. The nuts are ground with wild allspice berries, and they taste lovely. The roasted boar is pulled apart limb by limb, the largest portion going to Jaguar Shield, the soldiers and myself. The rest is shared among the children and the dwarf. After, he makes us a pot of bush tea. Through Jaguar Shield, he explains that it will ease our tired, sore muscles.

After we eat, the rains finally come. The pattering sound is welcome music and after a long dry season the smell of rain is intoxicating to me. Or perhaps it's simply the relief at having survived another day and my relief that dear Iguana Wind will live.

The soldiers are whispering to each other, concern on their faces. I know what the problem is. Nine Macaw's death was supposed to have appeased Chac and coaxed him to bring the rains, but here is Nine Macaw, very much alive and licking grease from her fingers, and here are the rains, earlier than usual. No doubt the priests will find some way to explain this. Probably they sacrificed another hapless virgin and now they are congratulating themselves on their indispensable service to the rulers and the people. But in the meantime, these soldiers are wondering why Chac is not punishing us by keeping away the rains.

Blood Gatherer will be worrying about these kinds of doubts among the people. For this reason as much as his own vindictive nature, he will search for us and try to eliminate us. With Ix Chel's blessing we've made it this far. But Blood Gatherer, like me, is a sorcerer. He may not be following us himself, but he will surely do his utmost to bring danger, hazards and bad luck to us. He has divining stones and it is rumored the blood priests know secret, ancient prayers to the Evil Forces.

I throw a few grains of *copal* onto the coals and immediately feel calmer. That familiar spiritual presence flows gently around the cave like a blessing. I will not be afraid. Ix Chel is with me always. Her protection is more than a match for Blood Gatherer's evil.

Around the fire, Nine Macaw and Tree Orchid are playing with their stones. Jaguar Paw whittles on his carving, which is slowly becoming the sleek form of a stalking jaguar. Already the cat's four limbs are done and the boy is etching in their magnificent muscles. At his feet grows a small pile of aromatic wood shavings. He feels my gaze and glances up. We share a smile.

The soldiers move the sleeping Iguana Wind to a pile of soft furs. I tend to the wound again, changing the dressing, which gives me a chance to inspect the blood and green matter draining out of it. If he is to live, a thick, black gel—the very pocket of poison—must flow.

Jaguar Shield moves to my side of the fire. Our elbows touch. I want to lay my head in his lap and feel his strong hands caress me. I want his manly frame against mine. How sweet that would be. He calls the three children to us and tells them to bring their mantles.

"It's been a hard day for all of us, but right now we are safe, dry and have full bellies. There is much to be grateful for," he says. The crow's feet around his eyes deepen and he breaks out into a wide smile. "I say this is a good time for some riddles."

Jaguar Paw pretends disinterest. Close enough to hear, he cocks his dark head toward Jaguar Shield. Our riddles, a famous pastime for young and old alike, are in ready supply for moments just like this one. He begins in a low, slow voice:

"Tell me, guess if you can, what is it that drags its intestine as it ambles along the foothills of the mountain?"

The two girls frown and search each other's faces. "Say it again; say it again!" they beg.

Jaguar Shield repeats the riddle. "Think. Think. You know what it is," he laughs.

Jaguar Paw turns suddenly and shouts, "A needle! The thread is the intestine and the hills are the cloth."

"Right! Very good. You are a clever boy," answers Jaguar Shield with an approving nod.

"Another! Another!" shout the girls. I remind them to quiet down.

Leaning back on his elbow, Jaguar Shield searches the roof of the cave, thinking. "Tell me, guess if you can, what is it that is seized in a black forest and dies on a white stone slab?" The soldiers lay back resting their heads on their doubled arms and chuckle. Everyone loves riddles. But no one knows the answer to this one.

Jaguar Shield shakes his head and says, "Alright, if you can't guess it I'll tell you. It's a louse that you pull from your hair and smash on a white stone."

The children groan and complain that it was a stupid riddle.

"Hah!" says Jaguar Shield leaning forward. "Not as stupid as you, then." His knotted, bony hands fly up to his face. As if in great thought, he rubs his chin. Anxious for the next riddle, everyone leans forward.

"What is a mountainside that has a spring of water in it?"

I'm about to guess, but hold my tongue. More laughter from the soldiers. One of them pokes at the fire and throws on another log; dancing sparks fly into the air. Asleep on one of his furs, the dwarf snores rhythmically. One of the soldiers pokes him in the ribs. He grunts and turns over.

"A cave!" calls out Tree Orchid.

"No!" exclaims Nine Macaw. "It's a temple next to a *cenote*."

Jaguar Shield laughs. "Our nose, you sillies."

"Ugh!" say both the girls at once.

"I knew that!" announces Jaguar Paw in a voice that is not in the least convincing.

"Another. Tell us another," beg the girls.

He smiles so warmly at them that I want to hug him. "Alright, just one more. You're not doing very well. I thought you were much more clever than this," he teases. "What are they that go pushing along wrinkled faces?"

"Pushing along wrinkled faces?" repeats Tree Orchid who searches my face for the answer. I smile at Jaguar Shield.

Nine Macaw taps her chin with a finger and stares upward. Tree Orchid sits holding her knees, staring deeply into the fire as if she could find the answer there. Something dawns on her. Her face brightens and she says jumping up, "Knees! Knees!"

"Right! Very good, you got one, you clever girl," I say. Nine Macaw's jaw tightens. Her face tenses.

"No fair!" she cries. "She already knew that one. No fair!"

Jaguar Shield grins at them both. "Seems fair enough to me. I asked the riddle and she answered it."

"Na!" whines Nine Macaw. "She's always doing that. She thinks she's so smart. I didn't even get a chance to give an answer."

Tree Orchid stays wisely quiet. Thunder roars in the distance. A strong wind blows in a spray of rain.

"No fussing, now, or we will have to stop the riddles," I scold.

"Nine Macaw, here's one you should know," Jaguar Shield says smiling at her over the yellow light of the fire. "Tell me. Guess it if you can. What is it that we enter in three places and leave by only one?" Chewing on a piece of dry reed, he sits back again on his elbow. He smiles and waits. And he waits. And he waits.

"A shirt! A shirt!" calls out Jaguar Paw, almost jumping into the fire.

"Right you are. I thought you were still off somewhere in your head," says Jaguar Shield.

"I didn't guess any at all!" complains Nine Macaw again. "I don't like riddles. They make me feel stupid. Tell us a story."

"Yes! A story," chimes in Tree Orchid, "Tell us a story now, please!"

Jaguar Shield sighs. He winks at me. It's clear that he intends for me to take over. "Alright," I say, "but only if you go to sleep after just one story. Agreed?"

"Yes, yes," they answer in unison. Jaguar Paw, suddenly interested, moves closer to Nine Macaw.

Iguana Wind stirs. His eyes open wide.

"Water. Water," he mutters, his voice high and strained. Wonderful! He will live to see the light of the next day. Beaming at him with relief, I hold a gourd to his lips. He drinks all of it and falls back on the furs.

Through the flickering flames, three little eager faces stare back at me. In the past few days they have experienced shock, fear, violence, shame, suicide, loss and the very recent trauma of Iguana Wind's snake bite. A story is just what they need now. Our stories tell children who we are. Stories tell our history. Stories of wonder and adventure teach them about pride and courage. I think of what I will tell them as I change the herb-soaked cloth on Iguana Wind's forehead and put another bunch of dry sticks on the fire. Then I begin:

"One day the Lord of the Woods called together all the animals that could run and said to them: 'Come here, my children, I wish to explain something to you.'

"When all were in His presence, he led them to a savannah and said to them, 'I have assembled you to tell you that I wish to see which one of you is capable of winning a race to the big *ceiba* tree on the side of the road. The winner will receive a prize. I have had a bench placed there for the one who arrives first to sit on.'

"The big fox spoke first: 'My Lord, how can you think it possible that any one of us can win a race against Big Deer? You surely know that he is much faster than any of us. He runs like a whirlwind! We will all be left behind in the dust. We haven't sufficient power in our legs to outrun him.'

"The rabbit added his opinion. 'What Big Fox says is true.'

" 'Yes, yes' all the creatures cried in a noisy chorus to the Lord of the Woods. Even the serpents who run like lightning across the skies agreed. 'It's true; none of us could possibly win a race against Big Deer.'

"But a young green-and-brown lizard slipped down from the branches of the *k'nep* tree to the feet of the Lord of the Woods and said to him, 'Lord, what is the prize you offer?'

" 'If you win,' he replied, 'I shall put a feather headdress on your head, so that everybody will know that you have won a race with the deer.'

"All the other animals laughed when they saw the poor little lizard talking to the Lord of the Woods. 'What does he think?' they asked. 'He must be insane, that little fool of a lizard.'

"He heard what they said and turned on them, shouting, 'Shut up, you devils! You're afraid of the Big Deer, but I'm not. I'll show you all what stuff

I'm made of. I'm little, yes; that's how you see me. Nevertheless, we shall see if I cannot make myself worthy of a feather headdress.'

" 'Look at him. Look at him,' all the other animals mocked.

" 'Yes, look at him!' exclaimed the Lord of the Woods. 'You all shut up! Come, Big Deer, stand here; and you next to him, little lizard.'

"The lizard obeyed, saying, 'Only one thing I ask.'

" 'Speak!' said the Lord of the Woods.

" 'What I wish is simply this: that you make everyone shut his and her eyes when we start off.'

"The Lord of the Woods agreed, 'Very well, little lizard,' and addressing the others, he said, 'When I count to three, all of you close your eyes. Those who do not obey shall be punished. Have you all heard?' They had.

"Then he began the countdown: 'One, two, three,' and the race began.

"When the other animals opened their eyes, all they saw was a cloud of dust on the road. Not even the Lord of the Woods was there. He had left by air so he could arrive at the tree first to see who won.

"When Big Deer had run some distance, he thought, 'Why am I hurrying so ? The poor little lizard surely must be buried in the dust I stirred up with my hooves at the start. Poor little thing!'

"When Big Deer arrived at the *k'nep* tree, trotting contentedly, the Lord of the Woods received him smiling. Deer looked at the bench and made a quick movement as if to sit down on it. But before he touched it, the voice of the lizard caused him to jump: 'Look out, or you will crush me, Big Deer. Go away, for I got here before you did.'

"Big Deer was speechless. How did the little lizard do it? He must have a devil in his body!

"By this time the other animals arrived and when they learned that the lizard had defeated Big Deer, they were amazed.

"The Lord of the Woods approached the little lizard and said to him, 'Very good! You are an intelligent little fellow. Here's your prize.' And he handed him a feather headdress.

"Only the Lord of the Woods knew that the little lizard was able to seat himself first on the bench because he had arrived on the tail of the Deer!

"And that's how the lizard got the fancy red crest that adorns his head and back."

The children sighed with contentment. Head in my lap, Tree Orchid says, "I can run fast, too. If I was in a race even with a deer, I would win."

Jaguar Shield stands up, stretches and announces it's time to sleep. I can't remember the last time someone told me when I had to go to sleep! I tuck the girls in and check on Iguana Wind. His chest rises and falls rhythmically, yet his body still has not released the black pocket of poison. There will be no rest for me until I see that flow and know for certain he will be all right. While the others sleep, I listen to the pounding rain and wait. I finger my jade beads and try to feel where Water Lily is. I sense she is alive, but I can't see her or feel her state of mind.

When Iguana Wind wakes a second time and asks for water, I lift the dressing over his wound and, in the light of the embers, see the much-awaited black, gelatinous mass. The swelling is considerably less and best of all, a thin, pink stream of watery blood flows down his ankle.

"You will live, dear one," I tell him. "Rest now. All is well."

It's a new day, and 20 Deer takes the burden off the back of 19 Deer. I'm glad to see the last day of this unfavorable month and the first day of the month we call Enclosure because it's a hopeful time when we prepare the fields for planting. The morning air is noisy with *chachalacas,* the early morning birds, who call noisily from treetops. A mother deer and her young, spotted fawn cross in front of the cave opening. Silently, I watch. The doe's eyes widen and her head snaps back when she spots me. In unison, mother and young disappear into the dense jungle.

Last night's fire has gone out. I slept deeply, peacefully and it seems so has everyone else. No one else is up yet. I check on Iguana Wind. His color is good and his pulse and breathing are normal. I check the wound and see that it's nice and pink; healing beautifully. He rouses.

"You're better," I tell him.

Through parched lips he answers. "Gods be praised. How long have we been here?"

"Only since yesterday. The snake bit you at dusk. You came through it re-markably well."

"Did you see it, Mother? What was it?"

A shadow moves behind me. Sting Ray, in his rough animal skins, peers over my shoulder.

Instinctively, Iguana Wind draws away from the dwarf. "Who is this?" he asks suspiciously.

The dwarf's child-like face expresses his eagerness to be of service. I speak softly. "His name is Sting Ray. He killed the snake. It was a Three-Step Devil, but we found its belly full."

Iguana Wind falls back, hand over his eyes. "Gods be praised. I shall see my family yet." Smiling faintly, he looks at Sting Ray and tries to raise a hand. "I'm grateful to you, friend,"

"He doesn't speak our language, Son. Jaguar Shield knows him from their military days. He's a Putun from Xicalango."

Iguana Wind's face darkens. "And you trust him? A Putun?"

I smile up at Sting Ray. "So far, son, he has shown us no reason not to trust him."

Sting Ray grins and rubs his belly, looking questioningly at Iguana Wind. "Do you think you could eat something?" I translate.

He laughs and tries to sit up. "Actually, I'm famished! What do we have to eat?"

I sign to Sting Ray that I will start the fire and prepare some warm corn and pumpkin gruel. Into the depths of the cave he disappears, on a mission he can't explain. Before we leave, I must get him to show me the rest of this strange dwelling.

The rest of our party begins to stir and we take up our morning chores. The girls sprinkle water on the dirt floor and sweep out the debris from last night's meal. Jaguar Paw and the younger soldier bring fresh water. The older soldier gets the fire going again and adds wood. Then he props up the skewered snake meat to roast again. Jaguar Shield comes over to see how Iguana Wind is doing. When his arm brushes mine, the *nacom* lingers a moment, leaning into me. Currents of excitement course through my jade forest. What a silly love-sick woman I am!

With the fire burning merrily, I heat a pot of water and I dig into the baskets for the string of dried corn balls and the sack of roasted pumpkin seed meal. Just then Sting Ray returns with his short arms brimming with bounty: dried fruits and more *ramon* cakes to roast over the fire. Waves of pleasure and mutual caring fill the cave. We've survived our first days as exiles; Iguana Wind survived the snake bite, we found a friend and shelter, and, thus far, we are not being followed.

After Iguana Wind takes a few sips of his gruel he falls back against the furs. The rest of us eat roasted snake meat and the corn-and-pumpkin-seed gruel until the pot is empty. The girls clean up the bowls while the men check all our baskets and carrying straps. With some of last night's herbal brew, I wash Iguana Wind's wound and make a new dressing of the *zubin* bark. Then Jaguar Shield's wound must be cleaned with the same tea. Nine Macaw and the soldiers look with interest at how the ant stitches have neatly closed the wound.

What we need now is a way to carry Iguana Wind. Jaguar Paw learns from the soldiers how to build a sturdy cot of palm leaves and green tree limbs. This litter can be carried or dragged. When they finish and all the gear is loaded, Jaguar Shield calls everyone into the fire circle. We are silent for a moment, listening to howler monkeys, birds, frogs and the flutter of wings.

"Today, sometime before Father Kin descends into the Underworld, we will arrive at Na Balam," he announces.

One of the soldiers looks over at Iguana Wind. "What about him? He's sure to slow us down."

"Yes, yes, I know," answers Jaguar Shield. "It will be awkward. Everyone will have to help, even the children."

"You should leave me here," protests Iguana Wind. "In a few days' time, I can make it to Na Balam on my own."

I shake my head. "Not possible," I say. "You still have the slave tattoos. Unless I am with you to declare your freedom, you could be captured, tortured or sold again—you might even be sent to sacrifice. No, son, you stay with us."

"She's right," nods Jaguar Shield. "You've earned your freedom," he says with a hand on my slave's shoulder. "We intend to see that it is granted you with no setbacks. Your wife and children have waited many *tuns*. They may not even know you're still alive. We all stay together."

Iguana Wind only stares at the ground and nods. He turns his head away. Only I see the lone tear fall from his eye. Often in the last ten *tuns* I have empathized with this captured warrior, whose honor to the military code kept him bound to the agreement to be our slave. What must it be like to be another man's slave; to know that you may never see your loved ones again? He doesn't even know if they are alive or if his wife, thinking he's dead, has taken another husband. What fate awaits him at the end of our journey?

"Son, I will bathe you in the sacred waters of Pole. I will dress you in ceremonial feathers. I will be there with you when you are returned to your family."

He smiles faintly. "That reunion is all I want for what is left of this life."

"You deserve this," I tell him. "I will make sure that you are free and back with your own people before I leave for Cuzamil." His eyes fill with tears of gratitude. I know we will miss each other, but there is no substitute for freedom, and he had a whole life before he became Moon Eagle's prisoner and then slave. I hope it is still there, waiting for him.

Boom! Sting Ray pounds a wooden stick on a deer hide drum to get our attention. Common to most adults throughout the Known World, rudimentary sign language is our universal language, so we understand the jagged signs of his stubby hands. He motions that he knows the back trails well and will accompany us until we reach the *sacbe* to Na Balam. Already, he has filled a basket with fruits and nuts and signs that he will carry it to our destination. Touching his heart, Jaguar Shield accepts his offer of help.

The younger of the two soldiers steps into the growing light at the edge of the cave. Taut muscles glisten in the morning light. "It's a short walk to Na Balam now. With Sting Ray's help, we should arrive before nightfall. *Nacom*, can we hear Sting Ray's story? How did he come to live in this cave?"

Jaguar Shield speaks to Sting Ray. Silent, the dwarf keeps his head down for a long while. Then, he nods. But before he speaks, he hands a dried plum to each of the girls and another to Jaguar Paw. Not to be left out, Bobo stands in front of Sting Ray and flips his body upside down. The dwarf rewards him with a handful of fruits. He has more gifts for the children. Sometime in the early morning hours Sting Ray made each of the girls a little doll woven from palm with curious tufts of hair from green moss. Their tiny mantles are cut from bits of brown inner bark of palm trees. Nine Macaw and Tree Orchid are charmed by their new dolls and thank him prettily. For Jaguar Paw, he cut a hollow reed, filled it with a foamy tree sap and now demonstrates how to blow into the reed. Little iridescent bubbles seep out the end of the tube and drift into the air of the dark cave. The children are enchanted.

"Come, let us sit and listen," says Jaguar Shield. He takes a seat close to the dwarf and begins braiding rope from strips of green palm fronds. For an anchor, he twists the palm leaves then loops them around his big toe. After everyone has found a place around the low fire, Sting Ray begins, with Jaguar Shield translating.

"After twenty *tuns* of service as assistant to a *nacom* of high noble blood, I was to be allowed to retire. My military duties included preparing the *nacom*'s war costumes, securing the finest feathers and jade for his headdress and hiring the best weavers to make his cloaks. I personally made his deerskin sandals and shields. Ever since he was a boy soldier, I'd carried his weapons and dressed him for battle. Together, we captured four enemy soldiers, which made him a hero and raised him to the high office of *nacom*. We lived in Xicalango, far to the southwest at that distant sea. I first met Jaguar Shield on the battlefield at the Place of Seven Hills. In fact, I once saved my *nacom* from his expertise with the obsidian-studded war club." At this news, the soldiers laugh and salute Jaguar Shield, who accepts their accolades with a smile.

"After our last battle with the Puuc, I was to be released from duty, afforded many high honors and given a lifetime share of booty and tribute from our past victories. I had a wife of small stature just like me. I adored her. We were like two doves together. In service to the queen mother, she was attached to the royal household of the Chontal lineage. Our only child, a daughter, died when she was six *tuns*, in an epidemic of bloody flux that took many young children that year. We were never blessed with another child. The queen mother was very old and shortly after I was released from duty she died. Everyone in her household was to be sacrificed and buried with her so they could serve her in the afterlife. I begged and bargained for my wife's life, but the queen's son insisted that his mother could not possibly be expected to cross the great river of the Underworld without the servant who had been at her side for so many *tuns*. 'Who will prepare her food? Who will care for her?' he asked me. I planned to storm the royal household to free my wife, but it was an impossible dream. Only days later, there was a great state funeral and seven-plus-ten of the royal household were beheaded and thrown into the queen mother's grave. My wife—my heartbeat—was one of them."

There is silence. All eyes are on Sting Ray. His head lowered with grief, he continues his tale. "I tried to start a new life, but I never had a peaceful heart again. I had no wife, no child and no love for the new leader-prince, who was a coward in battle. I hated him. I thought only of revenge. In my crazed head, beheading him and killing his wife seemed like fitting justice. My anger and despair grew to such a pitch that I felt I should end my own life and find my wife in Paradise with Ix Tab. I went mad and roamed the countryside like a lone wolf. All day, I drank corn beer and every night I fell into my bed unconscious.

"After three *tuns*, I came around and tried to start a new life as a toy maker, something I had always loved to do. I made paper dolls for magic ceremonies, bubble reeds, clay utensils and all the little miniature objects boys and girls use in their first ceremony at three months old. I made lances and shields for the baby boys and little looms and spindles for the girls. Yet, my heart ached. Every time I saw the prince, my anger raged. One night in the men's house, I drank myself into a stupor during a festival at Xicalango. I got into a fight over a trifling matter and killed a man. He made fun of my size—my warts too—

then said he wanted to see the size of my male member. We fought. Most men underestimate me. I smashed in his head with a heavy rock until he stopped breathing. I ran from the men's house and passed out on the way home.

"Sometime in the dark, moonless night, I felt a thief pulling at my robe and my loincloth. I reached for my knife and stabbed him. He fell over on top of me. I passed out again. In the morning his lifeless body and clotted blood covered me like a heavy boulder. I heaved the dead body off to one side. I saw his face and cried; it was my friend. He must have wanted to pick me up to carry me home. He was no thief. Horrified and filled with self-hatred, I staggered away. I was once a peaceful man; now I had killed two men in one night. I was an outlaw. Murderers are punished with disembowelment while still alive! I ran like a madman along back trails for many months. I rested for a while outside of Chichen. I thought of settling there, but feared I might be recognized as an enemy soldier. I wandered about these jungle paths, full of self-pity and hatred for all men. One day while contemplating suicide, I stumbled upon this cave. In time, I found comfort and solace in solitude and knew I could never return to my people. I've been here ever since, nursing my sadness and the little contentment I may deserve in this lonely peace."

We are silent for a few moments, absorbing this man's sad story. Jaguar Shield sighs and lays a hand on the small man's shoulder. He says something in the dwarf's language. He doesn't have to translate for me to know that he is telling Sting Ray we sorrow for him.

"Would Sting Ray show us his dwelling?" I ask. I'm curious to see how he lives in this place.

After some consultation, Jaguar Shield tells me, "No one has ever been in his dwelling before. He's honored. We can go, but Jaguar Paw, you stay here with Iguana Wind." The boy swallows his protest and nods obediently.

Sting Ray leads us back into the cave for twenty steps. The tunnel is shoulder-high. The dwarf and the children move easily, but the rest have to crouch to get through. Then he leads us around a sharp corner and we're standing in a domed room with a wide, arched exit to the outside, which lets in light. It's a trickle of light, though, because the cave mouth is hidden by thick vines and bushes. I take a deep breath and enjoy the delightful aroma of dried fruits and wood smoke. Against the far wall, a low sleeping bench made from sticks and vines is covered with expertly cured deer skins and the pelts of jungle cats. We have to duck to avoid hitting our heads against baskets of stored food hung from overhead. Rough-hewn clay pots rest neatly inside niches carved into the soft limestone walls. Although it's bare of niceties, this cave home looks comfortable, functional and very tidy.

Nine Macaw and Tree Orchid exclaim over a miniature table and chair made of tree branches lashed together with vines. Nine Macaw giggles and sits down daintily, and Tree Orchid pretends to serve her food in the single wooden dish, bowl and solitary wooden spoon. I feel suddenly sad. I walk to the fire pit and in my chest I feel Sting Ray's intense loneliness. I have a vision of him sitting by this hearth crying. I move away, but it's not better by his sleeping bench. I am rocked backward by images from his nightmares. I have to turn away from the others and collect myself, put up shields against feeling so intensely. Jaguar Shield is busy inspecting the dwarf's obsidian-pointed lance and chert-studded club. He and his soldiers admire its unique craft.

Sting Ray hefts a basket almost as tall as himself, and he effortlessly ties it to a leather strip around his forehead and smiles, indicating that he's ready to go. Jaguar Shield hustles us back to our part of the cave, anxious to get moving. But a sour-faced Jaguar Paw waits with Iguana Wind, and he gives his uncle a pleading look. Jaguar Shield is annoyed, but he relents. "Go look, but be quick!" Sting Ray sets down his basket to lead my grandson back to see his home.

While we wait, we erase evidence of our presence. The soldiers then lift their baskets and also take up two end poles of Iguana Wind's makeshift cot.

I place a ball of *copal* at the entrance to the cave as an offering to the *alux*, little nature spirits who inhabit these jungle caves. I would have preferred a few more days recuperating here and enjoying Sting Ray's hospitality, but we have to reach Na Balam. Nevertheless, I think we all feel refreshed by Sting Ray's kindness. On the trail, he walks between Jaguar Shield and Iguana Wind. He uses sign language to ask Iguana Wind if he is thirsty. He offers him food, and occasionally peeks at his leg. After his initial reaction to being near a Putun, Iguana Wind has become just as charmed by the dwarf as the rest of us.

After the rains, the jungle floor is a muddy, slippery mess of fallen leaves, fruits and dry pods. Every step is an effort in the mud, and the children laugh at first about the sucking sounds when we pull our feet out, but after a short time we're all exhausted from the effort of walking in it. The aroma of wet earth and rain-freshened air is delightful. Creatures of the jungle seem to agree as they fly, flit and dash around us. Bobo and Kiki are nowhere to be seen, but we can hear them both above us.

In spite of the burdens on their backs and the weight of Iguana Wind's cot, the two soldiers entertain the children by calling their attention to different paw prints of wild animals on the trail. I'm gratified to see how much friendlier they have become. They choose to forget the young ones are exiles, although they remain aloof from me. I realize in the days we've been together they haven't told me their names! I will have to get used to this kind of treatment. As long as my family is safe, I can bear it.

Now that we are close to Na Balam, Jaguar Shield allows more conversation. He slows down to walk beside me.

"We will have to be the vigilant ones," he grumbles. The soldiers are distracted by Iguana Wind and the children are chattering like squirrels. "Let's not relax our guard yet."

"Of course. Whatever you say." Then in a low voice I ask him the question that's been on my mind for days. "What will you do when we reach the Great Water?"

His handsome, strong profile stares ahead for a few moments, and then he sighs deeply and at me. "We cannot hide or deny that we are in-laws anywhere we go, but I expect—I hope—you will have more freedom once you are settled in Cuzamil. Then, I could see you more often."

"So, you would plan to stay at Pole?" I ask, trying to keep hope out of my voice. I don't want to influence his decision.

"You and Nine Macaw will need a champion at Pole. Iguana Wind and I will have your back and be your eyes and ears on the mainland." He stops me with a hand on my arm. His breath falls like a delicate flower on my upturned face. "Jade Skirt, there is no life without you and no other woman for me. Where you are, that is where I wish to be," he whispers.

Oh, my heart. I wish I could stop right then and there to caress him, to look forever into his fiercely tender eyes. Strong currents of *chu'lel* flow between us. The waves make my knees weak.

He whispers, "You're the only one I could love."

Tears well up in my eyes. He squeezes my hand, then in long, manly strides, returns to his position at the front of our line.

Except for sinking and sucking in and out of the relentless mud, the rest of the morning is uneventful. Iguana Wind even sleeps for a while in spite of the rough terrain that makes his journey bumpy. Sting Ray halts the march so he can quickly cut some vines to tie around Iguana Wind in order to keep him from sliding off the litter. Jaguar Paw watches everything the little man does with fascination, following him around like a puppy.

"No stopping to collect fruits or *ramon* nuts today," Jaguar Shield scolds the girls as he wipes perspiration from his face. "By evening we will be in Na Balam. Jade Skirt's family will provide for us then."

I hope this is true, but news of our exile must certainly have traveled to Na Balam by now. Traders who ply the *sacbe* from settlement to settlement are notorious gossips, and news that the Oracle and High Priestess is exiled is too juicy a tidbit not to pass along. I honestly don't know how my Chel lineage will take this news of my defiance of the priests. I will have to prepare myself for the possibility that they might treat us like the walking dead. Was that the reason behind my dream of Heart of Water's scornful face and cruel eyes? Would she also reject us, even though everything I did was to serve the Goddess? The very idea sends a chill down my spine. My whole world is upside down, unsettled. I have to remind myself that not every dream is a prophecy.

Tree Orchid sidles up to me and says, "Na, it won't rain today. I know because the birds are so calm. Kiki has a certain smell about him just before it rains."

"You're such a smart girl," I say, touching her flushed cheek. "When we reach Cuzamil the temple assistants will be thrilled to know you can already read the birds."

"Why is it important, Na?" she asks curiously.

Stepping around a large stone, I answer. "Because, my jade, the island of women is famous for its Oracles. There is even a Bird Oracle."

"Really?" She is fascinated by this idea. "What does the Bird Oracle do?"

"Well, you've heard of the *cuzam* birds? They're swifts that return to the island every *tun* at the same time. From the birds' flight patterns we can tell the weather for the coming *tun*. Moon Rabbit is the oldest Bird Oracle. She guides all the plantings of the realm using the bird signs. Most importantly, she warns us about storms and hurricanes well in advance."

"I want to be the Bird Oracle!" exclaims Tree Orchid, clapping her hands together.

Striding next to her cousin, Nine Macaw calls out, "Me too!"

"Quiet them down, will you?" scolds Jaguar Shield.

When the sun is overhead, we stop for rest and food at a small fresh-water *cenote*. It's cool and inviting, but immediately, we're plagued by swarms of hungry mosquitoes. Swatting at the little invaders, the girls cry and complain.

"Na, why aren't they biting you?" Nine Macaw asks. "They're all over me!"

"Mosquitoes won't bother you if you know how to control your *chu'lel*."

"Teach us!" says Tree Orchid. "Please, Na! How do we do it?"

"*Chu'lel* streaming from good feelings has a smell," I say. "You need to create good feelings inside yourself and create that smell."

"That sounds hard," Tree Orchid says, disappointed.

"Controlling it from the inside is hard," I agree, "but you can learn to do it. You can learn to control the whole situation by the smell you make, by the *chu'lel* you create."

"Dancing gives us good feelings! Come on!" Nine Macaw exclaims. She grabs Tree Orchid's hands and they spin around. I focus my thoughts on making love to Jaguar Shield. Little by little, the mosquitoes drift away and leave us in peace.

Everyone gets busy with chores—collecting water, unloading the food and utensils. Everything is too wet from yesterday's rains so there will be no fire, but we content ourselves with a soaked, uncooked gruel supplemented by Sting Ray's dried plums. Jaguar Shield points to a place in the sky and declares that we will rest until the sun has reached that position. I take Nine Macaw a few steps away to change her moss and then we spread our mantles and rest in the shade. Sting Ray attends to Iguana Wind. I stretch out next to the girls envying their ability to drop off to sleep so easily. Earlier talk of the Oracle at Cuzamil makes me think of dear Turtle Star. How does she fare in her new role as Ix Chel's Oracle of Chichen? Will she be able to handle the joys and horrors of the most honored position for a woman, other than queen, in the Known World?

Under broad, green palm leaves I wake with a start. Jaguar Shield is shaking my shoulder. "Time to go," he says softly. "Get the children ready."

Arms wrapped around each other, the girls are fast asleep. Tree Orchid's wilted headdress falls over their faces. They are so peaceful and innocent. At this moment, Nine Macaw reminds me of her mother. What has become of Water Lily? I must have faith that I will see her again. Like broken transplanted branches, we will survive to sprout and grow again in new earth. Life breaks everyone sometimes, but we Chels like to say we only grow stronger at our broken places. I touch Nine Macaw's shoulder. Eyes blinking against the sun, she smiles up at me.

"Na," she whispers. "I saw Red Earth. She's happy in Paradise with Ix Tab."

"You saw her just now?"

Tree Orchid's eyes open. "Cousin, I saw our sister. She's happy now," proclaims Nine Macaw.

"Did she say anything about me?" pleads Tree Orchid.

"She didn't speak. I only saw her. She was smiling. I knew she was happy. She didn't have to tell me," says Nine Macaw. I believe her. My dream visions also began when I started my moon cycles. It is a deep comfort to know that Red Earth is happy now.

While the men plan the next few hours on the trail, Iguana Wind sits up on his cot to join the conference. How grateful I am to all of them, even the soldiers, who despise me. Jaguar Paw, on the edge of the men's circle, looks strange now that his skin is completely bare of black paint and his eyes are no longer ringed with yellow. Once we reach Pole, Jaguar Shield and my son, Spear Thrower, will make arrangements for Jaguar Paw's future. A master carver need only see the magnificent jaguar the boy carved in the last few days to appreciate his great potential. I vow to see him placed with a worthy teacher, a true master.

The younger soldier looks at the sky, now clear and blue. "It will be no later than sunset, I'm sure," he says shielding his eyes, "if we make good time."

"When we reach Na Balam," says Jaguar Shield to the two soldiers, "you will be my guests, then you are free to return to Chichen. Your debt to me as your *nacom* will have been paid."

They nod, and one is about to speak when suddenly we hear a dull, buzzing sound coming up from the earth. A mound of earth erupts in a small hill and a swarm of termites fly out.

"Flood flies!" I cry. They zoom toward us on papery brown wings like a writhing snake pouring out of the dirt. Rubbing their tiny, translucent wings, they fill the air with a frightening whine. Legion after legion, they come. The mound of dirt roils. Surrounded, termites fly into, over and all around us; they land on our gear, inside the open baskets, in our eyes, our mouths, ears and nostrils. Wherever they land, their translucent wings drop off. It's a nuisance, but they aren't dangerous like fire ants or spiders. Still, there are so many! They're searching in their blind way for logs of rotting wood. It's impossible to escape the rushing hordes. The men drop their burdens and slap futilely at the little demons. Jaguar Paw chokes on one, falls to the ground and covers his head. The girls run to me, try to scream, and choke. I open my mouth to tell them to keep their mouths closed and I choke. I cover my head but I can feel them crawling in my ears, my eyes. *Om bey!* That wretched humming sound!

"Run," shouts Jaguar Shield. "Run!"

We make an attempt to gather our supplies, but every single item is crawling with termites.

"Get out of here!" he shouts again. "Drop everything!"

All four men grab a handle of Iguana Wind's cot and run with him. In spite of our situation, the look on his face is comical and, I have to laugh as he bounces over the jungle trail holding on to the sides of his cot, now blanketed in seething termites. *Crunch. Crunch.* Papery wings fly up from the ground with every step.

I'm worried about leaving all our belongings, but Jaguar Shield grips my arm and pulls me along. We jump and swing away from the attackers as we run. My chest aches. I gasp for air but only suck in another mouthful of flood flies. The loathsome creatures are relentless. Every gasp of breath sucks handfuls into my lungs, and now I understand the true danger. I feel my lungs burning. I can't see—they are in my eyes! Shouts ahead. I hear a splash and then Jaguar Shield pulls me in after him and we're all dunking ourselves over and over in the murky, salty water until the termites are drowned.

The girls are frightened, hysterical. The soldiers double over with laughter, which may well be shock. Jaguar Paw, stunned into silence, can only stare at our ridiculous scene. Jaguar Shield splashes over to me. He pulls dead termites and wings out of my hair. Everyone does the same for the person closest. Sting Ray, over his head in the water, struggles to stay afloat and hangs on to Iguana Wind's litter.

"It doesn't last very long," advises Jaguar Shield. He ducks into the pool again. "As soon as they settle down, we can go back for the rest of the gear and food. Nothing to do but wait."

"It's salty!" gasps Jaguar Paw. "The water is salty. How can it be? Are we dreaming?"

I explain how salt water pools are often found inland where the ever-sinking limestone touches a deep sea water table that suddenly rises up to the surface.

The situation is ridiculous and soon we're all laughing uncontrollably, even Sting Ray. Nine Macaw splashes Tree Orchid. Tree Orchid splashes water on Jaguar Paw. The soldiers splash each other and soon we're frolicking like water sprites. With my Oracle eye I see bolts of pinkish-red *chu'lel* release into the air above the pool.

Sting Ray makes eye contact and rubs his round belly. I nod. Termites are good to eat. I remind Jaguar Shield that the little pests could be gathered up in mounds to roast and grind with chili.

"Hmmm," he responds. "Maybe not today, though."

In all the excitement I forgot about Kiki and Bobo. Where are the little cowards?

"Have you seen, Kiki?" I ask Tree Orchid. She sits with Sting Ray, half in the water, on the edge of the pool building a little house with stones and bits of palm leaves. To make a wall around her little house, the dwarf lines up little round stones. Contentment beams from her. Children. So fresh from the Garden of Souls, nearer to the gates of paradise, contentment and playfulness is their natural state.

"He's eating his fill of termites," she says. "Over there." She points with her lips to a low branch further inside the jungle. There sits the yellow and green bird sucking in his little brown treats.

"And Bobo?" I ask Nine Macaw. She points to the tree canopy above us. Lucky for him he can climb high enough to get away from the onslaught. Staring down at us and laughing, he clings to a high branch. Never for a moment does he take his sharp, dark eyes off Nine Macaw and Tree Orchid.

It's getting late and the termites continue to swarm. Sting Ray disappears and comes back bearing our baskets. It takes him a few trips to get them all. We spend time cleaning out as many of the termites and wings as we can.

"We must get back on the trail," says Jaguar Shield when we finish. "Jaguar Paw scouted ahead and it's clear of nests."

Even though we have to trudge in wet clothes and sloshing sandals, we are relieved to get going. It only takes us two hours more when at last we step onto the great *sacbe*. We were so close to Na Balam and I didn't even know it.

Sting Ray puts down his basket and speaks with Jaguar Shield. "He leaves us here. He will go no further." Sting Ray turns to me, hand over his heart and bends down to touch the earth at my feet. One hand over my heart and the other on his shoulder, I beseech the Goddess to bless his return, his days and his journey through life.

The children run to him. "Don't go!" they shout together. "Na," pleads Tree Orchid, "can't he come with us?"

I smile. "Of course he is welcome, but I doubt he wants to. Ask him."

Jaguar Shield translates the children's request. Eye to eye with the two girls, Sting Ray smiles broadly. He mutters something unintelligible. "He said he has no desire for change. He's happy where he is."

I move closer to Jaguar Shield. "Tell him" I say "that I would be happy to see him again at any time. Tell him I admire him very much and am grateful for his help." Jaguar Shield interprets.

Arms wide open, Sting Ray bids us farewell and then turns on his makeshift tapir boots. Like a shadow he disappears into the thick jungle.

We turn our faces to Na Balam.

15

What a bedraggled troupe we are as we approach the city. A pale Iguana Wind props himself up on his cot with one arm. Stained with dark, dried blood, his leg dressing is about to fall off. Jaguar Shield's head band is stained with red and yellow. Kiki, rapidly bobbing his head up and down, sits on Tree Orchid's wrist obviously uncomfortable and ready to take flight at any moment. Nine Macaw holds a nervous, scratching Bobo firmly by the hand. Jaguar Paw no longer wears any paint. He looks like a scrawny boy with nervous eyes. People are giving us looks, but no one recognizes us. I have to stop myself from looking over my shoulder to see if Blood Gatherer's soldiers are waiting to spring out and grab us. I tell myself not to be foolish. Na Balam is a safe place for us. I can see the concentric walls looming in the distance. We'll be there soon.

This city was named for the black jaguar and it was built as a double-walled fortress by the industrious Puuc people. The concentric walls are very effective at warding off invasions and surprise attacks from aggressive southern Putun. Unlike Chichen, Na Balam has only a single ruler, and he is wildly unpopular. For one thing, he married a Putun foreigner, and he is said to be greedy for tribute and cruel to his subjects. In fact, he claimed so much land for this royal *sacbe* that three-times-twenty people could stand shoulder to shoulder across the smoothly paved road. At the moment I can't curse him for that, because it's a pleasure to walk on such an easy, light-filled surface after so many days in the rough jungle.

From both sides of the road stretch rolling hills of avocado trees, plum orchards and pineapple fields. Corn and bean plots nestle between small home-steads dotted with white-washed thatch houses. The verdant fields and thatch houses make me homesick for Chichen. How I long for the warmth of a famil-iar hearth, a home with my daughter and the normalcy of daily chores. I envy the women in their lineage courtyards.

What a mood I'm in! Those women have baskets of their own problems. I'm being foolish. Every life has clouds. Nobody escapes tragedy or trouble.

Speaking of clouds, the one that was covering the sun drifts away and we're nearly blinded by the white glare reflected off the great white road. Ever gallant, Jaguar Shield cuts and trims wide palm leaves for us to hold over our heads. When he hands me mine, he brushes my hand suggestively. The soldiers have to stop and rearrange Iguana Wind's litter so we move over to the side of the *sacbe*. Jaguar Shield is gazing at the city walls when suddenly we hear a roar. Jaguar Shield leaps in front of me and stands protectively with his arms out. The girls are confused and cling to my mantle.

"Boy! Get back here," he yells to Jaguar Paw, who has been walking ahead of us. He scampers back and joins his sisters. The soldiers drag the litter off the *sacbe* just as the ground thunders and a crowd stampedes out of the city. It's chaos! Some are clutching bundled feathers, mantles, babies, clay pots. It seems whatever was in their hands they just held onto and ran! One old man is trying to drag a big sack of yams. I'm afraid he will be trampled by the frantic mob. Jaguar Shield grabs his sack and helps him move off the *sacbe*.

"What is happening here? Why are you running away?"

"Wherever you come from, go back. Na Balam is doomed!" He abandons his sack and takes off running.

"You!" Jaguar Shield yells, trying to get a commoner to stop. "Tell me what is happening!" The man keeps running, but a crazed commoner dressed in dirty rags shouts: "The end is near! The end is near! We are doomed!"

Hot waves of panic and rage grip my center. I nearly double over from the emotional onslaught. I block the energy as best I can, but it makes me feel weak and nauseous. Jaguar Shield is frustrated that he doesn't know what the danger is.

"Stay here with the children," he tells me. "Wait for us on the side of the *sacbe*. I'll go ahead and see what madness has taken over Na Balam."

"Brother," I plead above the din. "Reconsider. If we are separated and you are detained, how would we find you?"

Iguana Wind raises his hand. "With respect, *nacom*, it will be easier to protect them than to lose them."

The spiral tattoos on my beloved's cheeks widen as he puffs out an exasperated breath. But he considers what we're saying. Another thing I admire about Jaguar Shield: he is fair, and that makes him wise.

"You're a bad soldier, Jade Skirt," he grumbles, sitting down beside me to let me know he won't leave.

"That's because I'm not a soldier at all. I'm a grandmother looking after her brood; nothing more."

Jaguar Shield grunts his annoyance but he motions to the guards to move us all back even further from the *sacbe*. We stay low and wait as the hordes trickle down to a few last stragglers. At last, the *sacbe* is empty. My brother-in-law motions for us to follow and we head into the city.

Na Balam usually has well-guarded gates in each of the four directions. The western gate is wide open. As we approach it, a clutch of commoners bearing trade goods run past and shoot us guilty looks. They are probably looters. There is one guard at the gate. He looks stunned, but he remembers his job and holds up his hand to stop us.

"What's your business here?" One side of his hardened face, grotesquely twisted upward by a mean battle scar, causes him to smirk and squint perpetually. Ceremonial scars and tattoos completely cover his broad chest and arms.

I hold each girl by the hand, step forward and announce confidently. "I am Chel. I seek my lineage members. These are my grandchildren and the men who accompany me." The solider glares at the men, but then a conch blares and he looks panicked. He abruptly turns and runs out the gate.

We enter Na Balam and find that the city is in chaos. In the narrow space called a Killing Alley that was built to trap invaders, a swarm of people clutching over-stuffed sacks are running frantically in every direction. Jaguar Shield herds us all together and we slide along with our backs to the wall. It's smart – this way no one can run into us from behind. When we get to a sizable niche in the wall he orders the men to put down the litter and guard us all. Without discussion, he disappears into the tumultuous throng. As I watch his back, I feel dread. Will I ever see him again? The girls hide their faces against me. Nearly strangling me with his powerful, hairy arms, Bobo jumps on my back. Kiki has already flown away. I don't blame him. I wish we all could take to the trees.

It seems like forever, but it's not that long when I see Jaguar Shield returning. He's coughing, and I can see the cause. A thick cloud of acrid, black smoke rises up behind him. Na Balam is burning.

"It's a revolt," he pants. "Not sure what it's all about. It's dangerous here, but it's dangerous everywhere. The target seems to be the royal district and…the coffers. You have family here, Jade Skirt. We must decide now. Look for them or leave?"

Goddess, what should we do? Before I can feel Her answer, two black-painted soldiers and a young nobleman in a torn feather cape run toward us, lances forward. I brace for trouble. I lock eyes with the nobleman, and his head draws back in surprise.

"*Om bey!*" he shouts at me. "It's the Lady Jade Skirt, right? Is that you?"

I hesitate, but clearly his long, angular face and greenish-brown eyes can only be Chel.

"I am. Who asks?" I respond, still confused.

The nobleman stops, but the other two continue running. "I am White Dog Muluc Chel," he says gasping for breath. "Your cousin is my grandfather. Come with me, quickly. Everyone follow me! No questions right now."

An ugly, unsettled feeling washes over me, but I'm not sure where it's coming from. I look to Jaguar Shield and he nods toward my kin.

"Let's go," he says.

"Hurry!" urges White Dog. "Bad place to linger." We pick up our baskets, lift Iguana Wind's cot then trot after the young nobleman. Between the two walls, he leads us to another gate. It, too, is flung open and unguarded. A raging clamor greets us. Harsh sounds—stones tumbling, shouts of rage, screams of agony. Somewhere nearby, boulders crash to the ground. I feel the comforting, protective touch of Jaguar Shield's arm on mine; his face is a taut mask of disbelief. Clinging to me, the girls turn pale. Every muscle in their little bodies tenses. I hold so tightly to their hands that they nearly turn blue.

I ask my cousin's kin, "What happened here?"

"Too much to explain right now," he shouts. "You chose the worst possible day to visit us, Lady!" Protectively, his hand darts out to hold me back. A wave of fleeing nobles races past high, feather headdresses bobbing over the melee. On their heels, an angry, stone-throwing crowd shouts obscenities. We follow dumbly behind this man who claims to be my kin. Goddess, grant it be true. Our guide pushes us down a narrow lane, turns a corner and disappears. I know where we are. These are streets and lanes of my childhood, but with the smoke and crowds, I can't get my bearings.

The two soldiers are panting from exertion at carrying the litter. Iguana Wind grunts.

"Enough," says my slave, and swings his legs to the ground. "Thank you, but I will walk from here." He wobbles to his feet, then staggers from the weight of his body on his wounded ankle. The soldiers drop the cot and support him. I turn to see where my grandson is and I find Jaguar Paw at the back of our column tripping over himself to gather precious quetzal feathers that have fallen. Just then, a looter dressed in a coarse tunic of *henequen* fibers scurries past bearing a bundle of feathers. As he passes I'm assaulted by waves of greed and envy.

From behind, a strong, heavy hand grips my shoulder. "This way, cousin. Quick! Follow me." Another familiar face. Familiar but unknown. A disheveled young nobleman, feathers askew and body paint fading. He looks like my sister, my son and even a bit like Nine Macaw. On high alert, his eyes flit in all directions.

"Who are you?" demands Jaguar Shield.

"I am Chel. We are expecting you." His eyes scan our group. "All of you. Come!"

Expected? Jaguar Shield and I exchange concerned looks. This seems like a worse and worse idea, but we have no choice at this point but to follow. We force our way into the rushing throng, trying to stay together. We follow our self-appointed guide through smoke-filled alleys and narrow lanes littered with debris. Behind the homes and closed shops of feather workers, shoemakers and potters, mothers pull children and elders out of harm's way. *Clack. Clack.* Shutters slam shut. Between two streets of red-painted stone houses, we turn into a narrow alley of the nobles section of Na Balam.

My Chel lineage compound is close by. I haven't seen our Chel family members since Water Lily and I brought Nine Macaw and Jaguar Paw home from Cuzamil as newborns. The houses here are closed up, but I see signs of people hiding inside. The few Chel faces I spot peeking out of windows and doorways look terrified and furious. I feel waves of anger from everyone we pass. A few stop and glare at us, but most are in a hurry to get somewhere. What has happened to Na Balam?

The young man points to a wooden entryway at the end of a narrow, shadowy lane and with great relief I recognize my aunt's house. My sister and I lived here as girls. Without a word, he pushes the door open. Inside the dark house is a crouched, gray-haired figure. My aunt, World Bridge!

Her voice cracks. "What is happening out there? Who do you bring to me?"

"Mother," answers the young man, "these are your kin." All eight of us crowd inside her hearth room. The old maven holds out her boney right hand to the young man. With her other she clutches a cane carved in the likeness of a serpent. Like all Chel women, she wears her white hair in braids wrapped in rainbow colored ribbons to honor Ix Chel. Pendulous, wrinkled breasts hang in the middle of old-fashioned, animal-head tattoos that cross her abdomen. Under one breast, a benevolent tapir's head fills me with nostalgia for those days when I was young and laid my head against my aunt for comfort and stories. She's shrunk dramatically since I last saw her. Only twelve *tuns* have passed, but she has aged much more than a count of *tuns*. She sniffs the air, thumps the dirt floor with her cane and commands, "Speak! Who are you? I am nearly blind."

I bend down to touch the hard-packed earth at her feet. "Aunt, dear Mother," I start. "It is I, Jade Skirt, returned to seek your shelter."

Her dear face brightens. A nearly toothless mouth opens into a wide, warm smile. I fall into her embrace and lay my cheek against her head. I am a child again, and the sweetness of this reunion sends me into a flash flood of tears. She pats my back reassuringly and I recover quickly. This is no time to fall apart. The others are watching, waiting to see what we should do next. Although it's calm in here, just outside on the street rancorous voices are shouting and clay pots are smashed. Our young guide slips silently outside and our soldiers follow to guard the door.

World Bridge, my mother's youngest sister, was my first mentor long before my mother took over my training at Cuzamil. At only nine *tuns*, I was sent with Heart of Water to train with our aunt. I returned to Cuzamil when I was twelve *tuns*. In this very house I had my first moon ceremony. My mother, the High Priestess of Cuzamil, seldom had time to visit, but World Bridge was a wonderful aunt. She has four children of her own, and back then she was a very gay, comical woman with a ready laugh. She loved to entertain us with antics, stories and paper dolls. Her husband, Earth Star, was the opposite. He was the enforcer of sumptuary laws in the noble district. He was the *halach uinic* who punished commoners for wearing their cloaks too long, or headdresses too high, or colors reserved for nobles and royalty.

My aunt waves a hand at two stone benches pushed against the limestone-brushed wall and invites the others to sit. Iguana Wind sinks down gratefully. I introduce Jaguar Shield, my slave and the children, and they put their right hands over their hearts in greeting.

"Aunt, please tell us what is going on here in Na Balam?"

She grunts. "Hmmph! You mean you don't know?"

"We travelled on the back roads for days. We have heard nothing," answers Jaguar Shield.

World Bridge stares at him. Although nearly blind, she has the Chel gifts and I know she can read my bond of attraction to Jaguar Shield in our *chu'lels*. She gives me a sharp, knowing glance and I blush. Then she shakes her head, points at me and scowls. "You started this!"

"What? What did I start? I have only just arrived. Tell me, what happened?"

Her crooked finger points at me. "All the world knows what you did." She pauses, rubs her nose then points at Nine Macaw. "Is this the child?"

"This is my granddaughter, Nine Macaw." I answer pulling her closer to me. "Future ruler of Cuzamil," I add stubbornly.

"You refused to send her to Chac. You ran. So your brother came here looking for you."

My heart leaps. "Blood Gatherer is here?" Everyone draws in closer.

"We are living in a time of madness!" she declares. In a much softer tone she says, "But please forgive my manners. Everything is upside down, and myself, too." She reaches up and feels around for one of her baskets. She tosses a handful of dried plums to the children, but her vision is not good and most of them are scooped up by Bobo, who scampers away into a corner with his prizes.

World Bridge spread her arms wide. "Come children, let me bless you."

Cautiously, Nine Macaw, Tree Orchid and Jaguar Paw gather around her. They lower their eyes, place a hand over their hearts and bow in front of their great aunt. Too tall for her to reach, Jaguar Paw kneels before her on one knee. Gently, she places a hand on their heads and whispers a short prayer. "May you live peacefully, calmly in the lap, in the bosom, in the embrace of Our Mother, Our Father the Sun, Lord and Lady of the Earth. May they watch over you, precious greenstone, precious turquoise, oh child of noble lineage."

When she finishes the prayer for each child, she stares at Tree Orchid and asked. "Whose child is this? I see no Chel in her."

Anxious for the news, I struggle to be calm. World Bridge was always this way. She takes life at her own pace.

"Aunt, Tree Orchid has no mother and no father. She is of my husband's lineage and has lived with us since her mother went to Paradise with Ix Tab and her father followed."

The noise outside is getting closer. I want to shake my aunt and get her to tell us what is happening out there. She senses my tension and motions for us all to sit again. I find a stool for her and one for me. The girls sit at my feet, clinging to my legs like tender vines. Nine Macaw is sucking her thumb again.

"Your brother, that Blood Gatherer!" she starts. "How could such a sweet boy turn into such a wretch? He was playful, cried easily. One day on Cuzamil Island when he was only four *tuns* old he told me his plan was to marry you, Jade Skirt. I warned your mother. Even then, I saw a troubled, jealous nature in him."

I remember she is an incurable talker, so I interrupt her. "Please, Aunt, what's going on here in Na Balam?"

Her face tenses. "Well, give me time. Young people are so impatient these days." She waves her right hand in the air. "Fast, fast. You want everything so fast. Why is that? Can't you wait?"

I lower my eyes. "Yes, of course," I say. "Forgive me. It's just that we're surprised to see so much turmoil here in Na Balam. We wonder why there are so many fires and people fleeing the city. How is it that the young man who brought us here knew to expect us?"

Turning on her low stool to face everyone, she begins at last. "It was only yesterday that your brother came here looking for you. When he couldn't find you, he told the foreign princess that he must have a virgin girl of a noble lineage to sacrifice at Chichen. My husband was furious. He and the other magistrates told Blood Gatherer that he has no authority in Na Balam. He has no right to demand a child of ours for sacrifice. In spite of our Putun royal princess, the people here—we nobles—have never supported the New Order. Well I remember, Jade Skirt, how your husband, Moon Eagle, was the first war captive to die in sacrifice." She shakes her head, pounds the ground with her cane. "The priests of the New Order say that the only way to preserve the world is to feed the Gods our own flesh, our own blood. They say they speak with and for the Gods during their blood-letting rituals, but we Chels revere the gentle Goddess. She does not ask for the blood sacrifice of Her children."

"I agree, Aunt. You understand why I would not let him have Nine Macaw for Chac's Well." Nine Macaw tightens her grip on my arm.

World Bridge coughs impressively. I am about to get up and pound her on the back when she stops and continues the tale. "Of course I understand! I helped raise you, didn't I? Ix Chel does not approve of these sacrifices. We were taught by our ancestors to offer butterflies, fruits of our labors, the blood of our ears and noses and the blood of our women's wombs. That is sufficient!"

How my heart lifts at this easy affirmation of what I believe. I have felt so lonely in Chichen. Here, my people understand things the way I do.

"Blood Gatherer warned the magistrates that there would be no rain unless we gave a girl to Chac. Hah! It rained that very afternoon and every day since. We Chel of Na Balam know there is no reason to kill our own people to feed the Gods." She peers in the direction of Jaguar Shield's face, then leans forward and pokes his chest with her cane. "Why, my husband's penis was so sliced up he could hardly use it, and we were still young!" The children giggle. Jaguar Shield grins and Iguana Wind laughs out loud.

"Rain always fell," continues World Bridge. "Yes, there were times when we could have used more rain, but we always knew the Gods loved us. We honored them by caring for the earth, the trees, our crops and the waters. Our temples were built in the likeness of the sacred mountains they created. They visited us in dreams. We grew our food. We fed our children and slaves. We honored the creatures of the forest with ceremonies." She sighs for a moment, lost in her memories. "When our men hunted, deer willingly laid down their lives. No one starved, not ever. If we ran out of corn, we ate *ramon* nuts and yams. We were happy. Once for each *tun* ending, we might sacrifice a turkey or dog from the yard, and that was sufficient for the Gods."

There's sudden shouting outside the door and the sound of scuffling. Before Jaguar Shield can investigate, it stops and there is silence. He calls out to the soldiers and they call back that all is well.

World Bridge continues. "We have always struggled with the priests of Chichen." She shakes her head violently. "It was the Putun. They brought the ravenous War God, Tezcatlipoca. I blame them. And then our leader married a Putun princess, daughter of a foreign interloper. She's from Potonchan, in the far southwest, where sacrifice of war captives, slaves and criminals is common. When my husband and the other magistrates refused to give Blood Gatherer a virgin to sacrifice, he went to her, and whatever he told her, she ordered a maiden to be sacrificed to Chac to be sure that the rains continue." She points her cane to a clay jar supported by a tripod branch in the corner. "Water. Get me a cup of water." Jaguar Paw fills a clay cup with water and brings it to her. She gulps it down, wipes her mouth with the back of her hand and continues.

"The princess is a forceful, domineering woman," she says scornfully. "She commands her husband. This morning the princess ordered palace guards to bring every noble maiden of twelve *tuns* to the central plaza. No doubt, your brother thought he would flush you out of hiding," she says to Nine Macaw, who trembles and hides her face in her hands. "It's a good thing you had not arrived yet!" I think about our leisurely morning spent listening to Sting Ray's story, and the flood ants—all those things that delayed our arrival. I see now that Her hand was guiding us.

"Families of the young maidens wailed and cried," my aunt continues. "Girls and mothers fainted. Fathers were outraged. But every young girl was dragged from her home. But it was noticed that the two daughters of the princess stayed in their rooms, and then tempers raged even more. Blood Gatherer marched up and down the line of virgins and finally he pointed at one of our own kin—a Chel. Her mother screamed and then fainted. A lance flew through the air. It struck the priest who was right beside your brother. Went right through his chest, my husband said. He died right there. My husband said he never did see a man die so fast from a lance wound."

She's talking faster now. "The people's anger flared like a bonfire. They rushed at the priests. Soldiers beat the crowd back with their clubs and shields. Someone yelled, "We are Chel! We are Chel! No sacrifice! Hide the virgins!' Someone else shouted, 'Kill the filthy priests!' The soldiers tried to defend the priests, but then someone yelled, 'Don't let these Chichen priests kill your children!' That turned the fight. The soldiers went after the priests and leaders because many of the virgins were their own daughters and relatives, you see. My son said it was a shock to the leaders when the soldiers suddenly formed a barrier of shields around the girls. Fathers and mothers grabbed their girls and ran for it. Two children from one family were trampled to death. Such a shame! And the stinking priests ran to hide in the royal residence, where the princess sheltered them. Fathers, soldiers, nobles, craftsmen, commoners and slaves joined forces to storm the palace. No one likes these leaders. They are greedy and vengeful. So the people had enough. I hear they set fire to the tapestries in the princess's apartment, ripped apart the banners, threw the clay images of the War God down the stone steps and managed to kill another of the heart takers."

We are all stunned. Violent defiance against the leader and priests, and on top of that murder of two priests!? And two children trampled to death? A whole city is burning to the ground because I defied the priests. What madness have I set in motion? Yet, I trust Ix Chel completely. She must have Her reasons. I have faith in the Goddess, but my heart goes out to the mother of the two dead children and the families of the maidens. An image of my own dead Red Earth opens the raw wound in my heart. So much fear, hatred and confusion—

is this only the beginning? Where will this take Na Balam, and their province? What does this mean for us?

The door flies open and in storms an enormously obese man, who pushes past our guards. He is a magistrate, as round as he is tall. Crimson blood flows from his shell-ringed nose and tattooed temple. Torn and blood-stained, his elaborately embroidered puma loincloth is attached to him by mere threads. Jade and shell jewelry hang from his corpulent body. Earrings, necklace and pendant, anklets and bracelets jingle and clank with every thudding step. He frowns at me.

"Are you Jade Skirt Chel Cocom?" Etched teeth, inlaid with pale green jade glimmer as he speaks. Narrow, keen, observant eyes survey the room, taking in everyone, everything

My heart hammers. I open my dry mouth to answer. Jaguar Shield moves in beside me.

"Who asks?" he questions, staring right into the intruder's stone-cold eyes.

"And who are you?" challenges the newcomer.

This is not Jaguar Shield's battle to fight. "I am Jade Skirt Chel Cocom. Who asks?"

Om bey! He smiles! With great effort his hand, stretching over his enormous belly, goes to the earth and then to his forehead, the most respectful, honored greeting it is possible to give another.

"I am Great Skull Pech Tzib, the magistrate here, assistant to the palace. You can see we are in a tragic state." Twisting his enormous neck to peer behind me at the two little girls, he asks, "Which one did he want to take?"

Protectively, Jaguar Shield takes charge. "We don't know you. We're only travelers on our way to the sea." He calls for his soldiers. They confer quietly and then take up positions inside the door, weapons raised.

In the meantime, the magistrate is looking around for a stool. Jaguar Paw offers his own and Great Skull smiles at him in a friendly way. There is nothing threatening about the man now. Is it a ruse? He flings his shimmering, white, duck-feather cape over his shoulders. "To be truthful," he admits, "I should be out there fighting to protect the royal family and their palace." His chubby hand slaps a puffy red knee and his voice rises to a high, nervous pitch. I see red rings of energy swirl around him—anxiety, anger, fear. "They brought foreigners here! Our Putun princess and her husband are greedy, cruel leaders. You're a Chel. You know we at Na Balam cherish our women and girls. Their fertile wombs ensure that our lineage continues. *That* is what the Gods want of us." He sighs heavily, shakes his great head and laments, "Then the priests brought this destruction on our heads, too. Brother fights against brother. This is not the way of our lineage."

I feel wary of Great Skull. Is he being honest? From across the room, Jaguar Shield's eyes meet mine. He, too, seems uncertain about our visitor. "Lady Jade Skirt," Great Skull continues, "we magistrates, the *halach uinicob*, support your decision. I have the authority to tell you that you are safe here. Only, I strongly advise that you stay here until the people's anger against the priests has been spent. No one is safe on the streets of Na Balam right now."

A weight lifts from my shoulders. The magistrates support me! I am almost giddy with relief. "What happened to the black-robed priest known as Blood Gatherer?" I ask. "He is my brother and the priest I defied."

"Hmmm," he answers. "Yes, news travels fast. We knew of your refusal before you arrived. Like leaf cutter ants, traders carry news all over these lands."

Jaguar Shield asks our visitor harshly: "Where are the priests of Chichen? Where is the one called Blood Gatherer?"

Before he can answer the sounds of battle outside are almost deafening. More stones tumbling, shouts, screams, the crackle and boom of fire. Someone or something thuds against the door. There is swearing. When it quiets down a moment later, the magistrate smirks.

"Blood Gatherer and the other cowards are inside the royal palace hiding like frightened children. I won't fight against my own people and my own relatives for those foreigners. Three of my granddaughters were in that line of virgins. Like the soldiers, I have joined with the rebel crowds." He struggles to get his enormous body off the stool. "My advice is to wait here a day or two. I can post soldiers outside to guard you. It's better if Blood Gatherer doesn't know you arrived." He bows lightly to World Bridge, cracks open the door and looks furtively up and down the street, then slips into the running crowds. Jaguar Paw watches him leave through the window and then shutters it closed.

Jaguar Shield paces restlessly. "The man's a fool to tell us to stay here. If he knew to find us here, so will Blood Gatherer. Maybe that is his plan."

Iguana Wind adds, "I say we leave now, *nacom*, and quickly. The town is still in turmoil. We can slip away while the priests are hiding in the royal palace." The men circle around him to confer in hushed, serious tones. The soldiers are shaking their heads. "You men go and check that the path outside is clear," says Jaguar Shield.

"Na" whispers Nine Macaw, pulling on my arm. "I have to change." Oh, yes, of course. How could I forget?

"Aunt," I say to World Bridge. "My granddaughter has begun her moon cycles. We need a change of garments for her."

Smiling broadly, World Bridge claps her hands together. "Did this happen on the back trails?"

Nine Macaw drops her eyes shyly and nods.

Tree Orchid announces, "I'll be next, Aunt."

World Bridge laughs and reaches for their hands. "My dears," she starts. "Know that this is a blessing from the Goddess, Our Mother. Know that this is something only women can do. It gives us power. The power to Create! There is no greater love or power on Earth than to be the vessel of Ix Chel, Mother of all Creation." She motions for them to sit in front of her on the packed dirt floor. When seated, she places a hand on each of their heads and continues softly, "May the Goddess Ix Chel look favorably on both of these maidens. May She bring you long life, loving husbands, fruitful wombs, milk to grow strong mothers and strong warriors. May your *sacbes* be smooth and straight. May your *nopales* flourish."

Without warning, tears stream down my face. Those were the same words she said to me when my courses started.

World Bridge leads us into the second room at the back of the house. In a niche are the menstrual cloths neatly folded away in an embroidered cloth bag. Someone used red-dyed rabbit fur to embroider the image of Ix Chel on it. She is sitting in a crescent moon holding a rabbit. Since it is common for grandmothers to gift the first menstrual cloths, most elders keep some in their homes. Nine Macaw looks at the soft cotton cloth, sighs with relief then tugs at her mantle. "Please, Na, can I change right now?"

"Of course you can," answers World Bridge. She smiles warmly and holds Nine Macaw by both shoulders. "You are a Chel. The flow of this blood will bring you second sight. Like so many women before you, dreams and visions will help you to see beyond the veil. With this blood you will create our lineage. Always remember that women, bearers of the lineage, are favored by Ix Chel. Her essence, Her *chu'lel* is in your womb. It is from your womb that you bleed. Your womb is Her womb." The girls nod at her, but fiddle with their mantles restlessly. It's a strange time for such lessons, but World Bridge continues. "Your blood holds the memory of who we are. Through our wombs, women are one with the Great Earth Mother. Your blood is Her body. Only through you can She create Her children, our world."

Then my aunt looks at me. "Remember, Daughter, the time of month when she started her courses will be her power days forevermore."

I smile. "Of course, Aunt. I would never forget that. It was 18 Deer." It bothers me that my aunt, not I, gave the maidens their first instructions.

Tree Orchid is weeping silently. World Bridge notices and asks, "What is this? Why do you cry, little feather?"

It is hard for her to speak through her tears, but finally she says, "I have no mother and father so how can I be the vessel of the Goddess? I have no lineage!"

I search for a comforting answer. The truth is that Tree Orchid could only marry another orphan. Without a mother and a father, neither one will ever have a true lineage connection. Even if born within a marriage, their children will be without lineage. Those with no lineage are social pariahs. Most orphans become slaves or are kept to bargain exchanges for daughters or sons chosen for sacrifice. As Chel, our lineage comes through the women, but Tree Orchid is of Moon Eagle's Cocom lineage.

"You must tell her," advises World Bridge. "She should know what lies ahead."

I caress Tree Orchid's trembling head. "Precious jade, you are and always will be ours. We love you and will care for you as one of our own. But it's true that as an orphan you have no lineage to transfer to your children. But every woman's womb—orphan or not—is the vessel of the Goddess. Your womb is Her sacred vessel of Creation."

Nine Macaw takes her cousin's hand and wraps her other arm around my waist. "Don't cry, cousin. Our babies will grow up together on Cuzamil just like Na and her sister, Heart of Water did."

Tree Orchid wipes her eyes, but she is not consoled. "Where's Kiki? Maybe he got burned up or smashed in the street," she cries. "I want my bird! Where's Kiki!"

Bobo hears her distress and finds us in the back room. He climbs onto her shoulder and she hugs him tightly.

Footsteps. A shadow falls between the back patio and the hearth room. I strain to see who or what it is. World Bridge's aged husband, Earth Star, must have been sitting on the back bench this whole time, perhaps asleep in spite of the world-changing events around him. The lean old man tugs on the few stray hairs on his chin and greets me.

"Welcome home, Jade Skirt," he says with a raised hand. I put a hand to my heart and touch the earth in front of him. "Now, which one is the orphan?" he asks, peering at the two girls. I take Tree Orchid by the hand to stand in front of my uncle. He reaches for her hand and says, "I heard. Come here, child. Let me look at you."

Pulling away from him, Tree Orchid hugs me tighter and won't budge. I sit next to Earth Star with her. Gently, he places his long-fingered, tattooed hand on her head. He closes his eyes. Tree Orchid's eyes dart toward me, but respectfully she keeps her head still. While he contemplates, World Bridge quietly attends to Nine Macaw with a basin of water and a clean, dry cloth. Earth Star's eyes do not open. His breathing deepens. I remember how he used to do this to many children when we were growing up. Finally, he nods and then opens his eyes. I watch his powerful profile. His long, wide nose bears a turquoise ring on the right side. A lifetime habit, he tugs at his gray topknot. Gently, he squeezes Tree Orchid's hand, peers into her face.

"What feels like a curse now will be a blessing to you," he says with a kind smile. "I've eaten a few beans, so I know. This is your destiny, child. No one can struggle against what the day Gods have ordained." With one hand, he lifts her chin to peer into her eyes. "They have their own plans for us. Everything that has happened to you—everything that will happen to you—was written before you were born."

Tree Orchid weeps again, face in her hands. "This family," continues Earth Star, "holds you in their hearts. Don't fret. The Goddess has a plan for you." Earth Star waits a moment, then turns to ask me. "What is her calendar day?"

I search my memory. "She is Nine Wind—Thirteen Motion."

His eyebrows shoot up. His head draws back. "An orphan with such a destiny! She sees beyond the veil and has a kinship with the winged creatures. Cuzamil will welcome her. Her true destiny lies there with your kin."

"But, but," stammers Tree Orchid, "if I ever have a baby will it be an orphan too?"

Before anyone can answer there's a loud crash, shouts and a struggle in the front room. I'm just getting to my feet when four soldiers storm into the room and point their lances at us. One of them wields a war club in his right hand. In the fading light, I see the shimmer of a long obsidian blade. Behind them stands a member of the royal family dripping with feathers, jade and the rare yellow metal from the Putun highlands we call "blood of the sun." A wooden headdress carved in the likeness of an eagle with talons poised for prey, soars and rocks menacingly over his head. Arrogant, cold eyes set deep within a scarred and tattooed face. I see swirls of fury seeping out of him. His eyes sweep the room and he scowls.

"Who is the maiden Nine Macaw?" he demands stepping toward the little girls. Reflexively, I pull them both behind me.

Jaguar Shield moves out of the shadows, his blade in hand. "Who are you? By what right do you enter this house?"

The intruder's eyes narrow. He stares at Jaguar Shield, curling his lips in disgust. "How dare you question me!" The soldiers move in closer, weapons ready. Lance in hand, Iguana Wind steps in behind Jaguar Shield. He braces himself against the wall to hide his injury.

"Prince," Earth Star says politely, "these are travelers I have welcomed into my home."

Forward swaggers the prince, his jewelry clinking with every step. He glares at me, pointing a finger. "Is this the pond scum who defied the priests of Chichen?" he snarls.

Goddess, send us help! Nearby, several black crows caw. From the rooftop, an owl hoots and my heart pounds with fear.

Ready for battle, Jaguar Shield takes a formidable military stance in front of me and the girls, his lance pointed at the soldiers. In a flash, one of the young soldiers lunges forward and pounces on Jaguar Shield with a ferocious howl. Jaguar Shield throws up his lance to defend but a second soldier steps in and before I can see what happens I'm grabbed from behind and hoisted into the air. I struggle and twist around as they bind my hands and feet. Where is Jaguar Shield? Is he hurt? I catch a glimpse of Iguana Wind held by the neck as he stabs at the soldier with his obsidian knife. Then I'm carried out, Tree Orchid and Nine Macaw behind me kicking and screaming. The arrogant Prince slaps them both hard across the face, first one then the other, which makes them shriek and sob all the harder. Earth Star is suddenly beside us. He makes a valiant grab for Tree Orchid, but he is no more trouble to the soldiers than a mosquito. The club lands on his head and my uncle falls to the floor, unconscious. That is the last I see before we are tossed like limp dolls into a reed basket. It reeks of blood and decaying flesh. Blood Gatherer. I can smell his stench. It makes me gag.

"Courage," I say to the girls as we all struggle to free our hands. We're a tangle of limbs. "Courage," I say again. I feel something wet on my mantle. Blood! Whose is it? Hands still tied, I check myself, then Nine Macaw, then Tree Orchid. It's her. There's a long, deep gash across her calf. The tendon above her ankle hangs white and impotent. It has been severed. This could cripple her if we don't attend to it quickly. When I touch the wound she screams and faints against me.

The basket is lifted. We're thrown against each other and Nine Macaw is sobbing, frantic. Through the weave of the basket I can see fire, smoke and crowds running to and fro. The soldiers are running on the *sacbe*. I see flashes through the weave—soldiers battling each other, women and children running and screaming. I hear a baby wail in the smoky air. In front of the soldiers, an elder falls. She is kicked to the side, where she is left to bleed in a ditch. Is this, then, the end of the world?

Anxiety from worrying about everyone is far worse than any physical discomfort I feel. What happened to Jaguar Shield and Iguana Wind? Where are Jaguar Paw and the other two soldiers? Where are they taking us?

Now we're being carried up stairs. Lots of stairs. It must be a temple or a royal residence. These are the only places in Na Balam with flights of stairs. Echo of sandals against stone; the stench of blood takers. I looked through the weave. We're in the royal palace surrounded by nobles, royalty, priests and magistrates. Everyone looks haughty and furious. The basket thuds to the ground. I take a deep breath and connect with Ix Chel as two rough hands grip my arm and toss me onto the cold stone floor. The smoke-choked palace is in ruins. We must be in the prince's sumptuous private chamber. A high mural of a dancing procession of musicians dressed in animal costumes covers three walls. Outside, as if to rival the blazing sunset, rebellious fires of Na Balam light up the early evening sky. Like two wet, slithering fish Nine Macaw and Tree Orchid are dumped out of the basket. Slipping in Tree Orchid's blood. Nine Macaw scrambles over to me across the tiled floor. Tree Orchid is unconscious. Her injured ankle bleeds profusely. First things first. I face my captors.

I hear Ix Chel's voice: *Look fear in the face. Don't give in. Fear makes you easy to control.*

A dark hand points a finger at me. "You!" he shouts. "You started all of this mayhem. There is blood on your hands!" My accuser is an older male member of the royal household. His dress, speech, feathers and facial scars are Putun.

"Who dares to take me prisoner in my own homeland? What is my crime? Who answers here?"

Jaws drop open; eyes widen in surprise. "We are the highest authority of Na Balam," answers one of the high nobles, headdress askew.

I stare into the hardened face of one who could be the leader. "Who is we?" I demand.

"We are Xiu. We rule here."

I hurl my words at him with contempt. "I am Chel! High Priestess and Oracle of the Goddess Ix Chel, our highest authority. I am Her mouthpiece. She speaks through me now! What you do to me and to mine you do to Her!"

One of the black-robed priests laughs spitefully in my face. "Hah! Once you were the Oracle of Ix Chel. Once you had authority. Now you are nothing. You are not even born."

"She's a dangerous woman," says a nasal voice I know too well. "This wretch threatens the power, the order of the state." From behind an array of wooden and feather headdresses, Blood Gatherer steps forward to face me. Did he always have that mad gleam in his eyes? I can see him now; so clearly can I see the decay and filth of this man who brings death.

"This scourge, this swamp witch and her brood cannot live. Kill her!" he shouts, spittle flying, breath rasping. "Kill the exiles! I, too, am Chel, and I say she acts alone."

"The Goddess will not stand for it!" I yell as the soldiers advance toward us. And as if Ix Chel herself agrees, a flying fury blows into the room from an open window. It's Kiki! Ominously, he screeches "Not stand! Not stand!" So surprised are all the priests and nobles that everyone freezes in place for a moment. Then Kiki is a lethal arrow flying into the face of the Putun noble. His sharp beak pecks at the lord's eye. The man screams, slaps at the brave parrot. Three others lurch forward to grab the bird, who grabs the lord's headdress and yanks it off his head. It's too late for the eye. He will have to get used to looking sideways at things from now on, I think with satisfaction.

Tree Orchid is awake. "Kiki!" she screams. "Come! Come!" He coasts gently over to Tree Orchid's shoulder. But then the prince makes a grab for the bird and Kiki goes mad. He dives right into that arrogant prince's face and pecks at his eyes. The noble screams and falls to his knees. From all directions, soldiers leap in to defend him, but Kiki flies out the open window. The prince is wailing pitifully. I use the moment to my advantage.

"Lords, we are Chel, returned to our lineage homeland. I expect to be welcomed. I expect shelter and protection! I have done no wrong here."

Blood Gatherer's blood-encrusted hands move like the talons of a starving hawk. He wants to shred me with his bare hands, but he is too weak. I see him now, yes. He is weak in every way but hatred. The Goddess shows me the rotted soul of this one. His *chu'lel* is a black sickness that poisons everything around him. All my focus is on this destroyer. Blood Gatherer advances. I stand guard in front of the girls. He points a greedy finger at Nine Macaw. Nine Macaw stares back defiantly. She doesn't cower, cry or shrink away. Her *chu'lel* is strong and bright. Both girls borrow courage from the little bird. They sit up straight, ready for what comes. I'm bursting with pride.

"That!" he murmurs, pointing his finger at Nine Macaw. "That is the maiden. I want her." He swings around waving his hand at the palace guards. "Take her!"

"You want her?" I say, my mocking tone keeping the guards in place. "This isn't about Chac at all, is it, Brother? This is about your plans to take the Rainbow Throne of Cuzamil for yourself! That is your plan, and it has been all along! Admit it—Chac doesn't need a virgin maiden to grant us the rains we need. Chac has always loved His people, and we have always served Him well without human sacrifice!"

"Blasphemer!" he starts to say, trembling with rage.

I fill my voice with Her voice and point my finger at him. "You defile Creation itself! You blaspheme against the Goddess!"

Bang! The great doors fly open. Into the royal chamber storms a flood of angry citizens. The nobles and their guards are unprepared and they are quickly taken by the hostile mob. I feel weak with relief.

"Nine Macaw!" I call out, frantic. "Where are you?"

"Na!" I hear with relief.

Suddenly, arms encircle me, the tender arms of my beloved. "We were delayed," he murmurs in my ear, "but I see you handled things well."

As soon as my hands are untied I embrace him, not caring who sees. Jaguar Paw and the two soldiers are untying the girls. They form a protective circle around us. The older soldier scoops up our wounded Tree Orchid. Jaguar Paw protects his sister as we make our way through the middle of the violent crowd and out the door.

"Wait!" I say. I need to know what's happened to Blood Gatherer. I look back and see him bound to the jaguar throne beside the blinded prince. Like frightened rats, the other royals and nobles have somehow scattered away into doorways and stairwells. Those who were not so fast are being kicked and thrashed by the mob.

"Hurry!" urges Jaguar Shield. "No time to lose. We have the advantage."

"This way! Follow me!" shouts a Chel soldier. I recognize my cousin, Sky House! As children, we were playmates. He quickly places a hand over his heart in greeting, then we're following him to a narrow stairway hidden away behind chamber rooms. Downstairs, through a perfectly round door, we find ourselves stumbling through a war. The din of rebellion is nearly deafening. Fires light up the night with an eerie glow. Torch-bearing men run in all directions. We make our way through the streets of chaos.

"Down with the New Order," people scream. "Kill the Putun! Kill the filthy priests!" Their angry cries ring out from street to street, house to house, rooftop to rooftop. "We are Chel! We are Chel! Our land; our rule!"

Sky House leads us back to the narrow lane where World Bridge and Earth Star are waiting. My dear aunt stands alone in the middle of the room holding my Ancestral Stone. Abruptly, she turns to face me, her eyes wide and mouth open in shock.

"Save the child! Save Nine Macaw! She must live, Jade Skirt. It is absolutely vital that she live to inherit the Rainbow Throne! I saw it all in the stone!"

"Yes, Mother," I say, my voice husky with emotion. "Nine Macaw must rule in Cuzamil. I have seen it, too." We grasp each other's hands in perfect understanding. What a relief it is that someone else knows just exactly how high the stakes are. The child's destiny will affect the future of all women for generations to come.

Iguana Wind is assembling medicines to clean Tree Orchid's wound, sending Nine Macaw and Jaguar Paw to fetch what he needs. Jaguar Shield is conferring with Earth Star, who says he recovered from the blow to his head with only a bad headache. Bobo has adopted my uncle and rides on the old man's shoulder chirping protectively.

Sky House raises his right hand for attention. "You should know what happened before you arrived. I must unload this burden."

"Tell us what you know," says Jaguar Shield. "Be quick, man! We need to leave!"

"I was guarding the prince when I heard the priests and the rulers talking about you—all of you. Everyone knows the foreigners have taken control of our royal household. But I heard the Putun filth promise Blood Gatherer they would give him an army to march on Cuzamil once he kills the heir, Nine Macaw. They promised him the Rainbow Throne and scepter if he agrees to destroy the Mother's temple and builds a temple to the War God in its place. Blood Gatherer doesn't care about rain for the people, or food for the Gods. He cares only for the riches of Cuzamil and his own power."

I feel physically sick. My own brother is the cause of all this suffering. What happened to him? A person with no lineage allegiance is like a bird without wings, a fish without fins, a tool without a handle. My grandmother, my mother and my sister have always paid outrageously high tributes to Chichen's priests and rulers. These men grew wealthier and wealthier, and greedier and greedier!

He hates us. How did I not see it before? There can be no peace, no security in our world as long as Blood Gatherer lives. If he is out to destroy us, then I must destroy him first.

I blink. For a moment I lost contact with the room. Now Jaguar Shield takes my hand.

"Sister, we must go now! The rebellion could turn in the prince's favor at any moment, and we can't risk staying here. They will come for the child again."

How I wish I had seen my brother lying dead on the tiled floor of the prince's apartment! I know that wishing for another's death turns one's *chu'lel* sour and nasty, but I can't help it.

"*Nacom.*" The soldiers hold out a sack of dried fruit to me and Jaguar Shield. I realize I'm starving and I hungrily eat a handful. The older one offers me a second handful. I'm surprised by his courtesy, but I keep my head down as I chew. I am grateful to these two men. They have proven many times over the past few days that they are honorable and that they would give their lives to protect us. But they have made it clear what they think of me.

I'm wrong. The older one clears his throat loudly so that I look up. Then he bows respectfully.

"Lady, I am Cloud Deer," he says, right hand to his heart.

"Lady, I am Eagle Rain," says the younger one, right hand to his heart.

Surprised, my heart fills with gladness. I return the gesture warmly.

"We have learned much during these last few days," the older one continues. "And we do not believe you are the walking dead. We see you, Lady Jade Skirt. We see your family. We are honored."

Tears spring from my eyes as Cloud Deer and Eagle Rain repeat the same greeting with Jaguar Paw, Nine Macaw and Tree Orchid. They look amazed. Jaguar Paw is grinning so wide he resembles Bobo. Jaguar Shield watches his men with satisfaction, and then turns to me and gives me a nod.

It will take many days to reach Cuzamil, but now we know who our true enemies are, and who our friends are. I feel Her presence enfold me like a warm embrace.

"Goddess," I pray, "Lady, Mother, watch over us and guide us safely to your island."

Glossary

of Mayan Terms, Maya Gods, Goddesses and Places

* All Mayan words are in Yucatec Mayan

Alux – Supernatural beings akin to elves and fairies. They serve as guardians of the forest plants and caves and are known to be mischievous. Offerings are made to them before entering caves or before clearing fields to plant.

Anona – *Annona squamosa*, a shrubby tree that bears a sweet fruit called a sugar-apple

Atole – Liquid made from ground corn and water, to which may be added ground pumpkin seeds, beans and chocolate, and typically sweetened with sugar or honey.

Bacabs – Four sons of Itzámna and Ix Chel. The four gods who hold up the corners of the sky, each associated with a color: red for the south (Hosanek); white for the north (Cantzicnal); black for the west (Saccimi); and yellow for the east (Hobnil).

Bal-che – *Lonchocarpus yucatanensis*, a tree bark fermented with honey to make an alcoholic drink.

Can – Snake

Ceiba – *Ceiba pentadora*, Silk Cotton Tree, Yax che (first, sacred, greenish-blue tree), Kapok. Sacred tree of creation and center of the Maya cosmos.

Cenote – originally *dzonot*, circular sink holes perennially filled with water formed by the collapse of underground caves.

Chac – Rain god of the Maya

Chacah – *Bursera simaruba*, a tree with many medicinal uses including relief from irritation caused by the black resin of the Chechen tree, which burns the skin.

Chachalacas – *Ortalis vetula*, a common brown-colored bird first to call in the morning hours; makes a loud, squawking sound.

Chacmool – Reclining male stone statue facing outward and holding a bowl thought to be a receptacle for human hearts, discovered beneath a temple in present-day Chichen Itzá.

Chel – "Rainbow"; one of the ancient lineages of rulers of Yucatán until the time of the Spanish Conquest.

Chichen – "Mouth of the well"

Chicle – *Manilkara zapota*, "Chewing" or "Move your mouth"; a jungle tree that exudes a milky latex that can be made into chewing gum when cooked.

Chu'lel – Inherent sacred life force present in all things and called forth during Maya rituals and ceremonies. Chu'lel is thought to be especially strong in virgin water, rain, copal tree resin, wind, blood, plants, mountains, sun and sky.

Cocom – One of the ancient lineages of rulers of Yucatán up until the time of the Spanish Conquest.

Cogginele – *Dactylopius coccus*, also known as cochineal, an insect that lives on the pads of the nopal cactus

Copal – Resin extracted from the copal (*Protium copal*) tree; used as incense during rituals, prayers and ceremonies.

C'ox – "Let's go!"

Cuzam – Swift or swallow

Cuzamil – "Place of the Swallows," island sanctuary of followers of Ix Chel, the Maya goddess of medicine, the moon, fertility and weaving. Contemporary name is Cozumel.

Gibnut – *Agouti paca*, a nocturnal rodent of the forest about the size of a rabbit, much prized as food by Maya hunters.

Halach uinic (*pl. halach uinicob*) – Head man, local magistrate, principal man of a village

Hay yo – "Greetings"

Henequen – *Agave fourcroydes*, a strong, hard fiber derived from the leaves is used to make twine and rope.

Hunabku – "The Only God" or "The One God," believed by the ancient Maya to be the Creator of all the other gods and goddesses.

Itzámna – Lizard House (Itzám na) or House of Spraying Divining Stones (Itz am na). Male creator god and consort to Ix Chel, the female Creatrix.

Ix Chel – "Lady Rainbow," Creatrix, Maya goddess of medicine, the moon, weaving, fertility and consort to Itzámna; the Sun god; the Vulture god; the Morning Star; and the Rain god, Chac.

Ix Tab – Goddess of suicide

Ixtobay – Mythical female creature of the Underworld who lives in the Ceiba tree.

Ix Waynay – *Mimosa pudica*, Lady of Sleep, Goddess of Sleep, Sleepy Head, Sensitive Plant, or *Dormilon* (Spanish). A ground-runner plant with purple flowers and leaves that close up, as if asleep, when touched. Used to induce sleep and relaxation.

Katun – A period of twenty years or 7,200 days in the Maya calendrical system.

K'nep – *Talisia oliviformis*, a rainforest tree that bears delicious fruit encased in a juicy outer coating rich in Vitamin C.

Kukulcan – Serpent god or "feathered serpent"; eases communication and creates peaceful exchanges among humans.

Makulan – Species of the medicinal *Piperaceae* family, also known as Piper, Button Wood, or *Cordonsillo* (Spanish).

Maguey – *Agave Americana*, Century plant; a fibrous species native to Mexico used to make fermented beverages. Fibers used to make sacks, ropes and clothing for slaves.

Masa – Dough

Metate – Grinding stone

Mitnal – Ninth and lowest level of the Maya underworld, eternally cold and dark; a place where those who did bad things in life are sent after death.

Na Balam – House of the Jaguar

Naba – *Balsamina peruviana*, the medicinal balsam tree of the Maya, used to treat kidney and bladder conditions; fresh leaves used to wash new wounds.

Nacom – Military captain or leader

Nagual – Animal companion spirit of shamans

Nanci – *Brysonima crassifolia,* a small, yellow, wild fruit favored by children and often fermented into wine.

Nopal (Nopales) – *Opuntia cochenillifera,* an edible and medicinal cactus with large, thorny pads and red fruits.

Nulha – Steam bath

Om Bey – "Wow! Oh, dear! You don't say!"

Payche – *Chiococca alba,* or Skunk Root, or *Zorillo* (Spanish), a medicinal forest vine with skunk-smelling roots; considered a shaman's ritual herb.

Pi – Bag usually made from deerskin that holds an amulet or sacred items belonging to a healer or shaman.

Poc – Father-in-law

Popul Vuh – Creation story of the Maya

Ramon – *Brosimum alicastrum,* or breadnut, also known as *Cha Cox* (Mayan). A tall tree that bears oval, green fruits with a juicy coating. Fruits are similar in flavor to apricots. Inner seed is starchy and nutritious.

Sacbe – Raised roads built by the ancient Maya; also known as the "white way" because they were coated with limestone stucco; used as primary thoroughfares within cities and in some areas between cities.

Sisal – *Agave sisalana,* a species of Agave native to southern Mexico, produces strong, white fiber used for making rope and bags.

Sky Serpent – Ecliptic in the sky on which all the constellations and planets move

Sky Wanderers – Stars, planets and constellations

Tezcatlipoca – War god of Central Mexico

The Place of No Evil – Heaven

Tikul – Two-toned wooden drum played with a rubber-tipped stick

Tun – 360 days, or a Maya year

Tzib che – *Crotalaria cajanifolia*, a tree sacred to the Maya; used for ceremonial and ritual brushing.

Wayeb – The last five days of a 360-day calendar, considered to be unlucky

Yum Kaax – Maya Corn God; also thought to be god of wild plants and animals.

Zubin – *Acacia cornijera*, a thorny, narrow-trunked tree inhabited by biting ants; bark and roots used as a first-aid remedy for snakebite.

About the Author

Dr. Rosita Arvigo DN, a native of Chicago, is a naprapathic physician, herbalist, international lecturer and author. She has lived in remote areas of Mexico and Belize for more than forty years. There, she studied with many traditional healers including Don Elijio Panti, the renowned Maya shaman of Belize, and midwife/herbalist Hortence Robinson. Both of her teachers were recipients of the coveted National Living Treasure Award.

Rosita and her husband, Dr. Greg Shropshire, founded Ix Chel Tropical Research Centre in Belize. The organization is dedicated to the preservation and study of medicinal plants of the rainforest. They founded the Belize Association of Traditional Healers; Bush Medicine Camp for children; The Rainforest Medicine Trail; and Rainforest Remedies, an herbal concentrate company. In 1987, they founded the Belize Ethnobotany project with Dr. Michael Balick of the New York Botanical Garden.

Rosita is the founder of The Arvigo Institute, which trains practitioners in the Arvigo Techniques of Maya Abdominal Therapy and Maya Spiritual Healing. Now retired from clinical practice, Rosita focuses on teaching and writing.

She divides her time between Belize, Mexico and Chicago. *The Oracle of Ix Chel* is her first novel.

The author's nonfiction books include:

Sastun: My Apprenticeship With a Maya Healer with Nadine Epstein (Harper One, 1994)

Rainforest Remedies: 100 Healing Herbs of Belize with Dr. Michael Balick (Lotus Light Enterprises, 1994)

Remedios de la Selva: Cien Plantas Medicinales de Belice with Dr. Michael Balick (Lotus Light Enterprises, 2013)

Rainforest Home Remedies: The Maya Way to Heal Your Body and Replenish Your Soul with Nadine Epstein (Harper One, 2001)

Plantas Medicinales en el Norte de Guanajuato; Medicinal Plants used in Northern Guanajuato (Arvigo Institute, 2013)

Food of the Gods: Vegetarian Cooking in Belize (Cubola Press, 2010)

Spiritual Bathing: Traditions from Around the World with Nadine Epstein (Celestial Arts Press, 2003)

Messages from the Gods: The Useful Plants of Belize with Dr. Michael Balick (Oxford University Press, 2015)